BODMIN, 1349

AN EPIC NOVEL OF CHRISTIANS AND JEWS
IN THE PLAGUE YEARS

Roberta Kalechofsky

Micah

Kalechofsky, Roberta.
  Bodmin, 1349.

1. Great Britain--History--Edward 111, 1327-1377--
Fiction. I. Title.
PS3561.A4165B6   1988   813'.54   87-28339
ISBN 0-916288-24-2

Book Design and Production:
Robert and Roberta Kalechofsky

Illustrations: Dover Pictorial Archive Series: Beardsley's Le Morte Darthur, 1972; Devils, Demons, Death and Damnation, by Ernst and Johanna Lehner, 1971; Pictorial Archive of Decorative Frames & Labels, ed. by Carol Belanger Grafton, 1982.

The writing of this book was made possible through the generous support of the National Endowment for the Arts with a Literary Fellowship in Creative Writing for Roberta Kalechofsky.

TABLE OF CONTENTS

BOOK ONE: SALVATION HISTORY

BOOK TWO: SALVATION HISTORY

For Kal, whose perseverance saw this through

In 1349, European man perceived that his problem, like ours, was survival, not salvation. We have still to work out that religious insight.

In our time the fate of man and the fate of life are one, and we would be less than wise to ignore the survivor's voice....To new prisoners on their first night in Sachsenhausen, a survivor spoke these words:

I have not told you of our experiences to harrow you, but to strengthen you....Now you may decide if you are justified in despairing.

The Survivor, by Terrence Des Pres

BOOK ONE

SALVATION ROAD

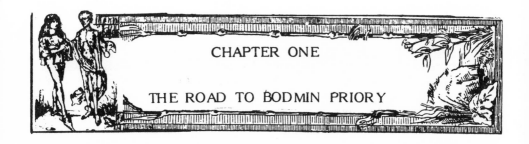

Will Langland, a good man in search of peace in the
year 1348, came from York to the priory of Bodmin in
the early spring of that year, six months before the
plague came to England, although the news of it had
already reached the shores, carried in the throats of
birds that crossed the waters from Europe, and each
man dealt with the rumor as best he could.

Will walked the road to Bodmin in the county of
Exeter and thought in the manner of his times: "A man
can choke on his thoughts if he be by himself too
long." The loneliness of travelling alone was harder to
bear than he had bargained for, and his feet were sore,
the scenery now soothing, now bleak, depending which
way his thoughts blew, back to his wife who had run
away, or forward to peace at Bodmin. Will walked
doggedly, putting the distance between himself and his
wife, she to Europe and he to the priory, he a man
who loved living itself, a glass of ale and a lass upon
the knee, the hum of a river in his ear and the look,
oh! the look of a beauty as his hot eye caught hers.
He, this Will of the world, went to make inquiry about
matters of faith.

In his way was a fork in the road: two roads as
plain as his two hands, two feet, two eyes and two
ears, and never a sign to tell him which road to take.
He sat down against a rock to deliberate and cut
himself a piece of cheese and bread to help the

matter, and the dew and dream of the scene fell upon him. He laid himself down in the wilderness of this world and dreamed a dream of fair earth, of wife and home and hearth: pasture, farmland, and hill all about him, his boyhood's beloved countryside, with cows and sheep and rounded hills. And on the flat of the land the windmill and around the bend beside the bank the watermill, and all around in the further distance God's spire and the air adrift with bells and the earth beneath, God's great gift to man He loves, laid clean with arable strips and humps of growing edibles, and a crouching man or woman to gather them, pare them, peel them, and bring them to table, and one early lass to carry an apronful to her babe or man to give him a taste of goodness to come: warm milk smelling of the cow's grass, Betsy beloved of poor farmers, patient in the pasture, standing ready to hand, her great moo God's voice to a starving man, and Will's wife so dear on their wedding day kicking her shoe up a tree.

"Fetch it, fetch it. Aha! I'll give you my body if you fetch it, aha!"

Oh! love, I climbed into the tree and set my eye upon a blossom for your hair and fell into your arms afaint with love and heat. Oh! love, you kicked your shoes off and danced upon the river and all about you the guests laughed and the cows mooed and the sheep baaed. And you called through all the sacred voices, "Will. Love. Now." Such was Will's great love. To walk barefoot in her grass, to drink from God's good running stream and let his eye go blind with looking at the hot sun upon it, God's great rivers flowing with milk and honey and oil and wine and in each Will dipped his love and she rose three times on their wedding night raining love and the guests and the bells laughed all night and all day and the smell of the hay on the next hot day made him dizzy with more desire and he bellowed like a bull as he drove his plough through field and furrow and bed, and the steam came smoking with green flies from the cowpile behind the shed.

- 4 -

And this was Will's great love. He caught her behind a hill and under a tree and in back of Betsy and before the bells stopped ringing the thing was done in the heat of the day and all the folk passed into church in the evening in the village, and the stars cooled him not a bit. This was his great love for three years, three months, three weeks, and three days, a lass and grass and a roaring river and hay in the hot sun. Oh! love. Where has she gone, Will? Gone to doom, he thought unkindly, damning her as he bit his cheese and chewed his hard bread. Ah! Will! Oh! Will! She was your great springtime heat. You clutched her to your bosom when she was warm to hand and wrapped your long legs about her and three times called upon your ram's horn and now the altar lies in shambles and weeping flowers. She to Europe and you to Bodmin. Plainly the road has become twain. He, with Christ's help, to heaven, for he cared not for this world anymore, a world of rude rumors and ruder fates, grey mists and grimy clouds. He for heaven where all voices sing the same and that was good enough for him. He for the eternal choir and she for the constant cackle. "Whore! Greatest deceiver of them all, deceiver of all good Christian men. Whore of Babylon!" Let her be in Europe! He to Bodmin, and he rose up and set out upon the road.

The birds cawed and flew in circles. Will brushed his crumbs to them with a curse. "Get yours," he thought. "Who cares what for what?"

The birds dove and dipped for the crumbs, while Will chose his road and kicked the pebbles in the dust. The grass turned brown before his eyes. "Now what?" he thought, and blinked unhappily, and woke from his good dream. No doubt about it. The earth had turned upside down, the cows lay in the field with blackened tongues, the sheep on the hillside staggered and stiffened and fell one by one. The lambs bleated, all ribs and shrunken heads and weeping seared eyes. Five thousand sheep in one field lay rotting, their coats all black with vermin, and before Will could hide his face a thousand, thousand men, a thousand, thousand, thousand men came over the hill, with black and furry tongues, and cried out to him in the language of famine, "Europe is coming, Will, and you will not escape, run as you can." And the vultures hovered and circled but wisely came not to earth, for the dead lay rotting in the sun and rotting in the hay and rotting in the furrows with the vegetables, and mothers turned to slime before their children's eyes and fell before the dead could close their eyes upon their children or their children upon each other; and in every town and in every village the dead lay in higher and higher heaps, brothers in the arms of sisters, the mother dead in her labor and the half born babe dead of the plague, and young gentlemen in knight's armor dead upon their horses, and the shepherd dead upon his hill and the sheep dead all about him, and the young husband dead upon the altar and the weeping bride gone home to die and to bury her parents who buried her brother who buried his wife who buried her sister who buried her husband who buried his father who buried his son who buried his mistress who buried her child from plague and shame; and the tavernkeeper and the fiddler, the yeoman and the farmer, dead, dead, dead in the fields, dead in the roads, dead in the byways, and none to ring the bell of mourning and none to bury them, no, not priest or friend, for all who could have fled and only the gravediggers can prosper for never have there been such prices for burial without benefit of prayer; and fires lit the length of Europe to burn the dead and clean the air, and men with garlic who bathed in vinegar with charcoal on their bodies; but nothing helped and the whole earth stank for never had the earth known such smells and sights, such putrid winds and deaths. Will saw it all and shook with rumor and vision and called out to his great foreboding: "Oh, God, what have we done this time? Thy great punishments are beyond all

reckoning and all thy great good earth and all the air
above it and all thy animals created with love and
genius stiffen here with fright, their ears flick this
way and that to get away from thy wind and they
stand, even as I do, trusting to Providence and scared,
hopeful in thy judgments and terrified." Will's tongue
dried even as he prayed and he tasted Europe upon it
and regretted that his wife was there and prayed that
God would cancel his harsh thoughts about her, but
God knows he knew not what to do with her or about
her.

Will tasted Europe upon his tongue and looked about
the countryside now restored to former good, Betsy,
brilliant Betsy in her generous charity and all the good
fattling sheep, sheep and lamb, the young and the old,
and thanksgiving broke out in him in a sweating prayer:
"Oh, God, look Thou upon these handsome sheep and
cows, look Thou upon these folk in field, Thou who
saved a gourd, look Thou now before Thy great death
cometh."

Will tasted Europe upon his tongue and like all men
stalked by a bad rumor, disavowed all his past mean
thoughts to man or beast, even to his wife, prayed to
be remembered for his good deeds and not for his bad
thoughts, reminded God that a man's temper is wind,
and his heart is better than his mouth, and prayed that
God keep far from England this death that no man
could see. Having done what he could to stave off
disaster, he took a drink from his pouch and hastened
through Barnstaple to Bodmin, to arrive there before
ghosts or doom or evil spirits or loneliness or the
plague catch him unawares.

He crossed the bridge over the Tamar River into
Cornwall and took stock of himself again. "You have
but a little way to go now, Will, that is to Bodmin,
but a great distance to heaven for your mind shifts
about like bog. All your thoughts are muddied and
confused. Did not Adam deprive you of Paradise
because of love of Eve and would you repeat that

sorry fate for love of your wife?" He saw he must strengthen himself against his thoughts of her and, as is the custom of everyone resisting temptation, he magnified his temptress, and was seized with desperation as if the world's fate lay with him, as he knew it did with every good man who wished to be a good Christian man. He spat into the river, gesture of defiance at Adam's weak member, and crossed the bridge into Cornwall.

And there put up in Launceston for the night where the talk at the inn was of Edward's doings and bad bishops, the pope in Avignon, the wars in Spain, the Jews, the Moors, the sheep, the evil French, the plague, the war, the trade in tin, and worse than all the rest, the price in barley and wool, and clay pits wherein a man may sink feet first to eternity, so what need had an honest sinner of hell?

"Ha! Will! your hot eye is upon me," the innkeeper's daughter crowed.

"Much good it does my eye," Will said.

"Where are you bound for?"

"I be bound for Bodmin Priory."

"To be a monk?" she winked at him.

"Aye, to do the Lord's work."

Claryce chuckled in her throat. "The Lord's work," she sang out. "God help all men to love the Lord's work as I do." And she caught his hot eye on her wet lip and whispered to him, "You have a hot look, Will. Wilt bed with me awhile?" No sooner did she whisper this to him than to his surprise his member stood bolt upright and he winked back at her, "I be not at Bodmin yet."

"You have a good day's journey, I warrant," she said.

"More's pity if I make me not a good monk tomorrow, I'll be a good man tonight."

But in the morning he felt differently about it. His tongue felt green and dissolute and thoughts of hell attacked him. He looked at Claryce curled up in the bed and blamed her and Adam for his fall. "You betrayed me," he said.

"So say all men," she mumbled.

"Nay," Will said, more to himself as a continuation of the thoughts that were pressing on him, "Adam satisfied no lust when he was betrayed by Eve. It was not his member but his heart that drew him."

"You is ready to be a monk," Claryce yawned. "You was more honest last night."

Will condemned her as a whore and left Launceston in a somber mood. It was a mystery how attractive and proper his desire seemed at night, and how rude it appeared in the morning. He blamed his wife for causing this delusion. "Had you not tricked me like the whoring devil you be, I would not have been tempted by the whore," he said. He took the road through the Moors, which added loneliness to his sense of shame.

If ever there was a landscape to give a man respect for the devil it was Twelve Men's Moor which Will crossed in the grey light of the dawn. Not only grim and craggy with twists in the high rocks and the high tors that looked over one like shapes the eye had never seen before, there was not a sign for a man to go by to know where he was heading. Not a bird's sound broke the air nor a lizard brought movement to a brush. Nothing liked the Moors. Will was unlearned, but he was a speculative man, and all manner of thoughts blew through him, and he decided that an empty space that has no social friendliness of any kind in it, or inhabitant to assure a man of the force of life, is an evil thing. And a lonely man in that empty space, though he call upon God, it is fear that answers him.

Will got hungry, but would not stop to eat. He got tired, but would not stop to rest. Such psalms and prayers as he remembered fluttered through his brain. "What has man to fear if the Lord be with him," he said, and tried to blow the spirit of Christ upon the

Moors. But this spirit, familiar in his village church, familiar in the folk who greeted him there, was not familiar here at all. Christ seemed not to know the Moors. He seemed to like a human scene as well as any man, for it was easier to think of God where mankind was or had been. Will looked upon this naked nature and felt a jolting disbelief, a thing different from whether one believed precisely this or that, but whether one believed in anything at all, in God or man or in the world.

The place was like hell to Will, though he had fancied hell to be a crowded place, full up, so to speak, with a lot of whimpering and crying people and a lot of crawling things with wings and teeth and claws and such, so that a man was always covering his head or privy parts and was in constant motion to protect himself against swirling objects. But here hell was silence and a lot of empty space, more like what he had been told Eternity would be like. "Nay, it can not be," he said, wondering of what use such an eternity would be and fearing he was losing his wits. He thought of his good dog, Rug, and a dumb thing it was that he hadn't taken the animal with him for company. "There be no lizards in these rocks but all manner of creeping things be in my head. Nay, Will," he chided himself, "you will not fall to doubting on your way to Bodmin to become a monk," and he took stern hold of himself and paused. "Let up," he said out loud, "and best pray now while your wits are still in place," and he clumped to his knees and made the sign of the cross. "Lord, Lord, help this sinner on these Moors. you must know where I am, for you made this place. And I pray you, Lord, not so much for understanding why you made this place, but for courage to pass through here and to keep my wits to serve you. I will say now with the psalmist that you alone must be my shepherd here, for I see none other, and though you take me through this valley for reasons unbeknownest to me, I will not fear the passage, seeing how you took it into your mind to make it." Then God's spirit blew through the Moors for Will, and he triumphed over primordial matter.

He came at last to Dozmare Lake lying in a flattened hollow between the hills. For all its boast that it was here that Bedivere threw King Arthur's sword, Dozmare Lake was a clammy, gloomy water lying under a clammy, gloomy sky. The naked eye, innocent of its legends, saw nothing in it but gloom and the effort one must make to cross it or walk around it or sink beneath the boggy shore.

"Heart, man," Will said to himself, "it is but a little way more," and though he knew he was bound for heaven it was thoughts of a bowl of soup and a log upon the fire that set his feet to walking fast and drew up the heat of Claryce's flesh.

"Nay, not so soon again," he said. "This time I am forewarned and forearmed. Aye," he sighed, "and alone too. Well, that must be God's sign that I am heavenbound, for God knows if flesh were here I would sin again."

And so by nightfall, what with saying one thing to himself and then another, he had crossed treacherous Twelve Men's Moor and Bodmin Moor, the craggy spine of Cornwall. He crossed brook and bog and marsh, and climbed cliff and tor and found by evening an old pilgrim's resting place in a wild wastrell laying by the side of a wasted road, deserted of mankind but himself and, God give him cheer for a blasted day spent in cold misery, another fellow traveller sitting upon the wall of the place.

"Good day," Will said, "what be this place and who be yourself?"

The fellow traveller was a stringy looking fellow, scabby but cheerful, flee bitten but dogged with a sprightly eye for argument and adventure. "I'm called Walt of Landsend," he said, "this place be Capella de Temple, built for pilgrims who be bound for Jerusalem."

"I be bound for Bodmin," Will said.

"I for London," Walt said. "Where hail you from?"

"Settle."

"Where be that?"

"Settle on the River Ribble, hard by Kirkly Lounsdale."

Walt shrugged his shoulders.

"Has heard of Harrowgate?" Will asked.

"Nay."

"Has heard of the River Lune?"

"Nay."

"There be where Settle is, upon the River Ribble not far from the River Lune against Harrowgate. A long journey from where I stand now. I be upon the road three weeks, all the way through Wilts and Somerset and Devon, and all the time walking but for a single day when a wagon gave me a ride with two oxen."

"Mankind is not good these dayes," Walt said, dispassionately. "It is a bad time for God and man."

"Mean you the plague?" Will asked.

"Plague and popes," Walt said.

That was a cue to Will that Walt was a political man. He shrugged his shoulders and said, "What is that to an Englishman?" and looked at Walt more keenly. "What manner of man are you?"

Walt laughed. "I'll tell you for you have an honest face, but it is atwixt you and me that I be a priest."

"For sure?" Will asked, surprised, for the man had an unpriestly look about him.

"For sure and true," Walt said, but he drew his fingers under his throat to indicate the ax.

"Art a criminal man?" Will asked, uneasily.

"Aye, a criminal priest, as all good priests are."

Will was not dense. He was aware of the loneliness of the spot and the cutting temper of the man. "Good day to you, Walt," he said.

"Make you for Bodmin Priory?" Walt called after him, but Will felt he had shared enough information with a stranger. Walt called after him again, "Monks and priests are sworn enemies, for the monks eat the fat of the earth while the priests starve with the sheep. Good day to you yourself, monkman. Keep your vest laces untied for your spreading belly."

Will kept his ears shut, for it was never good to hear seditious talk. The man was intemperate and careless of the distrust he spread, sure clues of a desperate nature. Will had enough to do with the weariness of the journey without being bitten by a rabid stranger. He shrugged the words away and crossed Cornwall, King Arthur's land, as rumor had it, and in that year under the guidance of good John de Grandisson, the seventeenth bishop of Exeter.

It is said that Cornwall was first populated by a Celtic people, ruddy and foreign looking to the English. Places abound in legends of cutthroats and saints, bloody wars and miracles. The site of Bodmin Priory, it is said, was first chosen by a hermit named Goron who, in 348, had founded a single cell where the grand monastery now stands. Here he had lived his life, as saints used to do, surrounded by the moors and sky, living on berries and lizards and the Gospels which he sang night and day, so that the stones were worn smooth with his songs. Goron yielded his site for the future of the commonwealth of Bodmin saints, to St. Petrock, who is accorded to be the true founder and patron saint of Bodmin Priory, and whose bones are kept beneath its floors.

Will was not aware of any of this. He had never heard of Goron or St. Petrock, nor did the past as a number mean anything to him. The past to him was the year of the Great Storm or the year his brother Davey got the smallpox. All Will saw about him was a grey countryside, a desolate land that was hard on the eyes, where sky and earth were the same color as slate, a country of broken rocks and forsaken battlements, settled by Celtic missionaries and early Romans, so that no one could now tell what part was nature and what part humans had left behind, whether the rocks were placed by Roman, churchmen, or God. And here in the heart of it all sprawled Twelve Men's Moor and icy estuaries and behind every rock the sound of unkind water wearing the earth away and cutting brooks from quagmires.

"Well, Will," he said to himself, "you like not the scenery after a day's travail. But here is landsend and spirit's beginning. Stick that into your mind and let it root there."

The demesne of Bodmin Priory began at the bottom of Twelve Men's Moor and stretched to the Cornish Heights and to Truro on the coast. Its village lay at the southwest end of the moor, on the main Landsend Road which some say once was a transpeninsular route between the two estuaries, the Fowey and the Camel. The village had sixty-eight families, cotters, villeins and serfs, a freeman called Leboren, a miller, a reeve, a blacksmith, and a priest called Clooke the clerk, and three leper houses, St. George, St. Anthony, and St. Laurence. But the salt from the sea ten miles away was on everybody's tongue.

Will came at last to the gate of the priory in the ringing him to lay the monastery stones, and where his bones now lay in an ivory box beneath their floors. "Safe," Will said to himself, "or safe enough." The ringing of the bells in the coming night echoed this thought, and Will knew he had taken the right road, away from the world, away from his wife who had deceived him. For how can a man settle the score with his soul unless he take a great step out into the wilderness of his being?

Here was the great gate of peace and behind him the night where no man would cross the moors after dark. Here was peace and order, Matins, Prime, Tierce, Sexte, None, Vespers, Compline, three and six and nine and noon, three and six and nine and noon. Here was silence and prayer, here was learning and God. Here was the voice of a brother soul, not the quarrelsome voice of a difficult woman. "Through all eternity she will stand outside the gate, Matins, Prime, Tierce, Sexte, None and Vespers, and will cry. Ha! Ha! While I will sing all day in heaven with pater, ave, and creed." There was nothing left for him to do but to knock upon the door.

"True, true," the bell tolled, "now is this monastery your Eden. Guard yourself against the works of woman. Here is order, Will. Here is the mastery and mystery of order. The soul is nought without order, it is nought but fluid and efflorescence. It has no shape but what order gives it. This is the secret of monk's stones. Order is man and time and building, each brick and bush and chore and prayer in place. Here is harmony between man and time and building, in the great transept of the church, as in the transept of the soul. Seekest peace? Fasten thy anchor in order. Seekest joy? Lay hold of praise to God. Here thou leavest earth's cares to the earthly, thy ancient passions and heat to the fire-eaters. Shalt stoke no more that fire that crackled at sight of thy wife. Three years, three months, three weeks and three days is enough for any man to burn. Now slake your thirst in Christ's waters. Your choice is clear: thy soul or thy wife, heaven or earth, the eternal choir or the cackle in the grass.

Six bells tolled in Will's head: peace, peace to thee, Brother Will, peace to thy distraught member. It is but a small part of thy being and no part of the eternal soul, for in heaven it is useless. Put it aside as thou hast put aside thy wife. Hast heard of an angel fornicating? Cut thyself off from thy wife and from temptation to return. Cut it off, Will. In heaven it is useless and would but frighten the angels.

So the bells tolled, saying first one thing and then another. The tunes bellowed about in Will's head and gave such thoughts that knocked about, fear of going in and fear of staying out, that to still the matter once and for all he raised the clangor on the gate and banged it with all his might, lest standing there he lose heart at the sight of heaven.

"Hold your peace," the gatekeeper grumbled. "I am not deaf, and Christ knows there be nought in this doorway but bells and knocks. What manner of man is it knocks so hard at twilight?"

"I be Will Langland from York," he shouted above the bells.

"The devil care where ye be from, you be a hard knocker. Have you got your seal on you?"

Will took out his pass with his bishop's seal on it and the gatekeeper, though he could not read, looked it over carefully under his torch. "That be a good seal to seal you in a lifetime," he said, and opened the gate for Will, and before him lay the priory of Bodmin like an anchor in the ocean of worldliness, great, green acres of landed peace that swept across more acres to the cluster of buildings huddled in the stillness of holy stones, cloister and tower and transept.

No sooner did Will take a step towards them than he heard a ssshhhing in the grass.

"I say ye hid it in your pants, Brother Sneak."

"You may search me, Brother Catseyes, come and search me with your gaming hands."

"Wouldst have me touch a filthy body? Give me the dice and not another word."

"Now, Brother Catseyes, wouldst accuse a monk. of gaming?"

"What's this? Will said, and the bells stopped tolling.

Brother Ralph stepped out from behind a tree. "Who be you?"

"Will Langland, to begin service tomorrow. If this be Bodmin, what be this talk?"

Brother Ralph laughed, untroubled. "All God's children quarrel. We be but God's children. Came you a long way?"

"From York, all the way by foot but for half a day on a wagon with an ox."

"That be long enough. Came you to take up the monk's life?"

"Aye, and put down the burden of this other one."

"Aha," Brother Ralph laughed. "We are all fishes in God's net. Now is it cast this way and now that way." And he looked Will over and winked to Brother Walter who winked back and shrugged his shoulders and shook his head and flicked his ears.

"Now, what be this game?" Will said to himself.

Though Will did not speak, Brother Ralph divined his question. "Brother Walter will not break his vow of silence to a stranger."

"Aha," Will said, "methinks his head wags more than his tongue would."

Brother Ralph, as Will was soon to learn, took such comments placidly and was rarely offended. In like manner, he asked, "What news of the plague?" as if it were all one to him what the world said, he having heard enough of it by now.

"Pray it comes not to England," Will said.

"That be for certain it will not. Here be no Jews to let it in. Praised be Edward."

Brother Walter's amen hung in the air, but Will preferred not to address himself to this remark. Instead, he said parenthetically, "I saw in a tavern I stayed in in Launceston, The Sign of The Red Whale, it was called, a hard writing upon the wall where I had occasion to go, having drunken more wine than is usual, what with the innkeeper and his wenches singing,

> White wine, red wine,
> Gascon and Spanish
> Wash down your meat
> With the finest Rhenish

and I did my best to accommodate all men of good

will in that tavern, not thinking of my bladder nor my pocketbook until it was too late for either and I jumped to the wall not a drop too soon."

"Now what was this writing?" Brother Ralph said.

"What writing?"

"This writing upon the wall, Brother Long, that you just spoke of where you hurried to the wall not a drop too soon."

"Aye, not soon enough as matters turned out and my leather hose got one good soaking. But so beclouded was my head I could barely read this sign being but a newly reading man thinking his way through the wine. Well, to be brief, it said when you see the sun awry and two monksheads in heaven, one that talks much and one that shakes his head as if he had the palsy and when a maiden has her magical powers about her then the plague and the famine shall judge the world and Davy the ditcher shall die of hunger unless God in his mercy grant us at once a truce with his judgment."

"What made you of this sign?"

Will laughed ruefully. "See you mercy, brothers, Christ's or man's. I tell you plainly I had more of Claryce the whore who watched me through a hole in the wall and called out, have you not a drop left, Will?"

"Now, now, none of that here," Bother Ralph said. "That be not monk's talk fit for monk's ears."

Will felt himself properly chastized, for had he not shaken the dust of the world from his shoes. "You be right," he said generously, "I forgot my pledge."

Brother Ralph was equally generous, detecting Will's honesty. "It be best to leave such thoughts outside the gate. What were you, Will, in York?"

"A laboring man, a shepherd when there were sheep, with a little learning, and a married one."

Brother Walter cast his eyes toward heaven. "That be a laboring man twice over," Brother Ralph said. "And you left your wife for the sake of Jesus Christ?"

"She left me and I left her and I left her once and she left me for good then. First we quarrelled and then I left her, and when I returned she left me and so then I left her. Now we are apart. What were you in the world?"

"I was a babe," Brother Ralph said. "I came here at age six without mother or father, only a mean uncle. Some man took me on his horse and said I best be cared for by the brothers. How be it to live beyond the gate, Brother?"

Will scratched his head.

"I mean be it good or bad?"

"It be a bit of both," Will said.

"Can you get into heavean if you live out there?"

"If you be a good Christian," Will said, and then laughed slyly. "I tell you something to warm your tempers a bit. Some say out there all good men get into heaven except the monks and Jews and Saracens. Have you never heard that saying?"

"Na, I never did. But I tell you what. I tell you that them that says it be jealous for our clean souls that we keep so white for Christ's sake."

"Aye," Will said, "an' they be jealous for the Jews?"

"They be right there," Brother Ralph said, "for no man without baptism can go to heaven. Where think you the Jews go when they die?"

"I know not," Will said, "nor will thinking upon it one way or the other or altogether tell me, for I have thought and thought and do not know."

"We best return," Brother Ralph said, seeing Will's impatience. "You might as well begin at once to rehearse the rules. Keep your eyes upon the ground and your tongue in your mouth. If you have chosen to serve God you must begin by mastering yourself, first tongue and eyes and lastly cock and I fear that since you was a married man you best begin at once no more to think upon your former life, for evil is first thought upon and then is remembered and then is done. Better it would have been had Adam covered his mouth that knew the apple and wherein sin entered than covered his loin which knew not of the apple. Keep your mouth shut and your eyes cast down and you will make a good monk. Think upon Adam's sin that lusted for the apple and for his wife. It is that way with sin, all cut from the same cloth, desire and lust."

Homely Will was overcome by such a speech. Though he knew he had a soul, never yet had the ambulation from the body to the spirit taken such a circuitous route and never had apple led him to temptation for woman.

Brothers Ralph and Walter brought him to the guest house where he was to stay for three days, according to the rules, before he could petition the brethren to be admitted among them.

Bodmin was a modest priory and its guest house was a modest stony square room which had a single cot and a blanket, a cruet of oil, some scented hay upon the floor and a crucifix upon the wall. A large monastery, such as Glastonbury or Cluny, could accommodate a king and his retinue. But not Bodmin, which had seen better days and worse days and was, in this year when Will arrived, on a middling course of prosperity. It housed only eleven brothers, but held a title from William's time to the land and the villages about, the woodlands, pasturelands, five thousand sheep and more. It leased the mill on the nearby river and collected fees from the grindingstone. Though Bodmin was modest, it clung to an income of sorts on the edge of debts. The Norman tower was antiquated and looked primitive in an age of stone lacery, but the tower boasted six bells and the priory a fashionable lady chapel.

No one came to greet Will that night, not even the guest-master, Brother Benedict, who left the problem of novices to Brother Bernard whenever he could. Brothers Ralph and Walter walked silently along, having said all that was fit to say for the day, and only the swish of their boots and linen capes made a sound as they moved. They showed Will to his room and bid him goodnight. Will thanked them, and hoped to put the bidding to good use, for he was tired with his three weeks' walk, and tired with thinking, and tired with the talk of plague wherever he stopped, and tired most of all with the tiredness that comes to a man who changes his way of life and must find new habits and new ways of thinking.

But when he sank upon his cot, sleep, for which he would have paid a pence, did not come, for all that this was the first time that he had a room and a cot to himself, and scented hay upon the floor. In his worldly life Will had been a great sleeper, first on the bosom of his mother, then penned and pinned between his mother and father like a skiff between two waves that heaved all night and thrashed and spewed out dreams, while his brother Davey lay crosswise at the bottom of the bed, hanging on to Will's toe like an anchor lest a legjerk from his father send him sprawling on top of Rug, the sheepdog who lay on the floor. Will not once had had a bed for himself until this night, and his loneliness was keen without his wife or Rug, who filled her bedspot with smell and snore in her absence.

This room had nothing in it but a light, a crucifix and a cot, and he missed the smells and snores and farts that once had lullabied him all night long. At Matins and at Lauds he heard the bell that woke the brothers for their nightly prayers, and heard or thought he heard their slippered footfall and their distant voices. He woke at Prime feeling not at all like a man who had come in search of peace.

And later at breakfast, as he sat apart from the others in the refectory, in a caracel that was kept for novices, he discovered that the morning meal was only a quarter pound of bread and a third of a pint of beer, eaten while Brother Benedict read from the Book of Martyrs. Will ate hopefully, but with little pleasure, no different from the others whose acquaintance he was soon to make: Brother Stephen from Ireland and Brother Thomas from Scotland, Brother Harald from York, Brothers Claude and Bernard from France, Brother Benedict from Rome and Brother Anthony from south of there; Brother John from hereabouts, Brothers Ralph and Walter also from hereabouts, and Brother Namlis from nowhere. These were now Will's family to take the place of his brother Davey and his sheepdog, Rug, and other members of his natural family. Here was his holy family: Brother Stephen, scabby and saintly, who had made his way in a corked wicker basket that bobbed from Bantry Bay to Barnstaple across St. George's Channel, and arrived with a bleached, bald head and a single tooth in his mouth, faithful, fearless, fierce and feared. Like other Irish saints before him, he did not hold with Roman rules, cut his tonsure as he pleased and kept a private dating of Easter. He preached that the Irish were a lost tribe, that the prophet Jeremiah had made his way to Ireland via Egypt and was known to the saintly community everywhere in Ireland as the prophet Ollam Fola. He himself had seen tombstones in Bantry Bay with legends of: "Aaron de Hibernia, Jusaeus, etc., dead with wife and child, Sept. 12, 1189," and who had put such tombstones there, he would like to know and how had this Aaron come to Ireland.

Prior Godfrey advised Will in a private chat that morning "that there is nought to any of this," but that Brother Stephen held these notions "to vex the English with antiquity as well as with other sundry and peculiar matters."

Brother Stephen had not removed his hairshirt in thirty years. He ate but a single piece of bread a day which he chewed with his single tooth, and felt no ill effects. His body had adapted totally. His flesh was worn away to nerves and vessels, strings and things that clung with suckers to his inmost will. Like most other men, Will admired and was awed by him, and believed the world was saved by such, content as he was himself to lapse from practice now and then.

Then there was Brother Thomas, an easier sort of man, who had come with the Scots in 1333. He had been a soldier, and loved to jab and stick, playfully. When the Scots receded, they left Brother Thomas behind who took up the staff to Jerusalem, with begging bowl and two mild eyes that won the hearts of women, who passed him along as far as Byzantium when hard luck overtook him. He acquired the French disease and palsy and a little paunchy belly. He shook and twitched and itched his way back to Dover and came to rest at Bodmin Priory. His eyes were now weepy blue and he prayed constantly to St. Mathurin, even throughout the night, to the consternation of the others who shared the dormitory with him.

Brother Bernard was an altogether different man, with a reputation for great learning though he was slow of speech. His birthplace was in Provence, a descendant of the Albigensis who had been done away with in the Great Crusade. A few offspring had survived and passed the trauma of their history down through the generations. Bernard was now a faithful Christian, with no leaning towards heresy or extinction. He was scholastic, honest, ponderous, and very melancholy, digesting tomes of arguments, pros and contras Arians, Monophysites, gnostics, Marcionites, and other sundry histories of heresies and wars and strategems against them.

He was the the master-of-novices as well as the cantor or precentor, and had charge of regulating the right hand side of the choir. But chiefly he was the librarian and archivist in charge of records, lists, necrology and charters, and faithfully kept the ledgers and records of the daily life of Bodmin, as well the habits of the birds thereabout. He was tall and thin and kind and looked down upon the world from a height of melancholy memory and melancholy learning.

But though Brother Bernard had great learning he

could not impart it. He had not an inkling of how to go about ordinary conversation. Talk passed through him ponderously as grass through a cow's stomach, chewed twice over. Will had to learn his Latin on his own and he stumbled through the chants and prayers from one mnemonic device to the next.

Bernard's countryman from the north of France, Brother Claude, was again a different sort. A perfect warrior, he had fought triumphantly against Saracens and other infidels in Spain and Egypt and the Holy Land, and wherever else they could be found. He had seen Jerusalem and the Holy Sepulchre, travelled with his squire, dined in castles, and had picked up along the way a little Latin, a little Arabic, and much refinement in the art of love. He was in Rome in 1300 when Pope Boniface had appeared before all the world wearing the imperial insignia and carrying the two swords of spiritual and temporal power while heralds ran before him and proclaimed, "I am Caesar! I am the Emperor!" Brother Claude had seen what there was to see of Christendom in that century, its crusades, its great jubilee, its auto-da-fes and pilgrimages, and was soon to see the plague.

Misfortune overtook him in the form of age, when his hand could no longer bear the weight of his sword nor his body that of his armor. He fell from his horse one day near a chapel on the River Seine, while baroque images of hell sucked at his brain, drawing off the moisture from his mouth. His loyal squire hacked his suit of armor from him and exposed the grey skin to sun and air. "S'done," Sir Claude said.

"Not so, m'lord," his squire murmured.

Sir Claude pressed his eyes shut. The sun, the sight of past processions, of jousts, the brotherhood of shout and smell, of sweat and danger, the knighthood of ten thousand men with plumes and banners bearing down upon the infidel, the castles, the fruits, the dainties, the sweat, the venison, the beribboned ladies with bared bodices and veils across their faces, the nights beneath stars and furskins.

"S'done," he said and lay inert upon the ground.

"Steady, m'lord," his squire said.

"Nay, I will have it back," Sir Claude wept. "It is the sweetest life on earth."

"Perhaps on earth," his squire said and led him to a chapel near at hand where his master discovered the afterworld of knighthood. The year was 1336. A poster on the wall announced that the Doctrine of Benedictus Deus had been proclaimed, which clarified the state of hell, revealing that punishment took place immediately after death. Brother Claude perceived he had not a moment to waste. He denounced war, he denounced lust, he denounced himself. He presumed he was a changed man and sought his peace at Bodmin, "a grisly cheerless place which is punishment enough and will reduce my stay in hell," he thought. His arms aged appropriately, his legs aged as well so that he tottered when he walked, but his loins refused to age, and he soon became famous for his lusts. He worshipped Mary and feared hell and by his sixtieth year was dark and grizzled and corpulent in paunch and jowl. He prayed day and night to St. Caesarius and was a dangerous mysogynist, though no one could restrain him if a woman crossed his path. Twice Priory Godfrey had sealed the laundry maid's lips with coins. Brother Claude was given services to perform that kept him within the cathedral walls. He had to regulate the singing on the left side of the choir and prod the sleepy monks awake during the Night Office. Better it would have been had he remained a boon companion and died upon his horse, for he carried his wars within himself and became dyspeptic to everything that lived.

Brother Claude and Brother Harald, it seemed to Will, were peculiar kinds of men, without a good word for human flesh. Brother Harald was quick to recommend odd remedies for spiritual incontinences: that Brother Thomas' tongue be taken out, that Brother Claude's clapper be removed, "else it will ring all up and down the countryside before the plague takes him."

It amused Brother Harald to say such things, for he did not wish to be at Bodmin where his father had put him. Brother Harald was one of those who believed he deserved better, deserved at least to be an abbot, for he had a genius for administration, while Prior Godfrey had none. Hence, his talents and his soul were wasted, one by bad luck and the other by an unrelenting hypochondria.

His father had married a daughter to Baron Roundsleigh's nephew, one son he kept at home with him, but four others he had put away in monasteries to shift as they could with the circumstances. One was the famous Abbot Roland, a second was a nullity and was sent to be a monk at Skye; the third was a monastic disgrace, hot as a dog in heat; and the fourth was Brother Harald, sent to Bodmin to keep an eye on the manor there, while the first and eldest son sat in York and ate venison and had his fill of women, and never Christ seemed to care. The brother that was the famous abbot chose to be in France, "for advancement's sake," Brother Harald said through bloodless lips, "now that the pope is in Avignon." Still, he practised monkhood perfectly, kept all his vows, never lost his place in the Psalter or sang a false note.

But Brother Harald's talents were not altogether wasted at Bodmin Priory. Since he knew the value of movables as well as land, he was given the care of altar cloths and candlesticks, the hangings, ornaments and corporals. He looked after the lighting: four cressets in the cloister in the wintertime, and four in the church, in the nave, at the choir-gates, at the top of the steps to the sanctuary, and in the treasury. Such tasks pleased him, for while he required little food and little sleep and no sex, and was lean and hypochondriacal, he liked to be in charge of things like gold and linen and souls and minds, and best of all to go about through the priory grange on a horse, for he had been bred to the medieval respect for land and all forms of institutional power in pope and king and baron and bishop; and most of all he had the medieval covetousness for landpower, and so served Bodmin Priory very well. He performed the services of gathering rent and overseeing the overseers punctiliously, and next to Brother Ralph who was born an eunuch, was the only one Prior Godfrey could trust to go outside the monastery walls to collect the tithes and taxes, for which tasks he was well suited, being an exacting man without nerves.

Of the lowborn, Walter, Ralph, and Namlis, was nothing much to say except that Brother Namlis had a hump and no tongue. Between them and Brother Thomas they divided the work of the kitchen and the lavatory: the cellarer's chores were Brother Ralph's, who did the catering and the marketing. The cook was a hired servant who kept an apprentice, who was his son. Brother Walter was the kitchener, whose duty it was to clean and count the household goods, plate, linen, napkins, baskets, barrels and anything else that moved from the kitchen to the refectory. It also fell to him to keep the fish fresh with damp cloths and to keep charge of the beer allotments.

Brother Namlis was the chamberlain. He had charge of old clothes, and kept the supply for the poor, as well as tallies and lists for the laundry. He was chosen for this latter because the duty involved social intercourse with the laundress, a paid servant from the village. Brother Namlis was no eunuch, but Prior Godfrey believed his hump would help him keep his vow of chastity. Brother Namlis was fond of women and women were fond of Brother Namlis, but in an appropriate way, which left him free to do his duties. He kept the supplies of catskins and lambskins ready for the winter, of pigs' fat to weatherproof the boots, he was in charge of baths and shaving and the communal feet-washing every Saturday. He also kept the heating-room or calefactory ready throughout the winter months so that the brethren could take refuge there from the cold. He did the tailoring, for which he had great talent and often could be seen sitting at a carrel in the cloister with crossed legs, his hump hanging on his back, sewing a brother's hood while the others studied Latin or read. Brother Namlis sometimes went with Brother Ralph to market to purchase cloth and needles, which he loved to do, to push and jostle and make his way in the market crowd, and gape and snort and smell, for in all the world there is nothing like a trade for entertainment.

Brother Thomas saw to the lavatory and Brother Stephen, as refectorian, set the table and kept the hay and rushes on the floor clean and smelling sweetly. And finally, of Brothers Benedict and Anthony, the first was from a Roman family with pride of lineage and land. He was the guest-master because he was considered knowledgeable in men and manners, being very patrician in his carriage. But his Christianity had in it some Marcionite matter, which the Church had labored to purge, to no avail. Underground, here and there, in written and in oral tradition, the Marcionite heresy which looked upon God the Father with a jaundiced eye, expressed itself towards Jews and women and the Creator of matter with greater vehemence than was usual, even for the Medieval world. Brother Benedict had renounced his wife, his land, his castles, the Hebrew Scriptures and meat, and in their place embraced the law of chastity. Unlike Brother Claude, Brother Benedict altered the function of his appetites and his nature, but not of his temperament.

He was large of girth, the picture of the type of monk regarded as a glutton, lecher, viper and dicer, but he was in fact as ascetic as Brother Stephen. Inside his large body were tissues and organs which had become dehydrated with fasting. His liver was comatose and did not do its proper job of cleansing the

bile. The fecal matter was often green. Brother
Benedict rightly suspected cancer, but Prior Godfrey
was certain the trouble was extremes of abstinence.
He disapproved of such extraordinary measures. He
even loathed them on patriotic grounds, regarding them
as "continental," "Spanish," or "Italian." Brother
Benedict ignored Prior Godfrey's order to be sensible or
consider another monastery. Believing there was a
connection between corruption in the world and his own
corrupt nature, redemption of the world became for
him a matter of moral willpower. He fasted on behalf
of Avignon and simony, on behalf of luxurious cardinals,
on behalf of the Pope for having a mistress, on behalf
of his wife whom he no longer saw, on behalf of his
children, two of whom had gone to Jerusalem and
married Saracens. But he never transcended his self
denial and acquired peace. Within his corpulent and
dignified frame, he was remorseless, somber, and
agitated. More than anyone else at Bodmin, he
conveyed the authority of the embattled spirit, the
metamorphosis of sinner turned saint, and the idea of
personality as an historic form.

Virginity was the distinguishing mark of Christian
salvation. Aquinas had declared it to be the state
closest to that of the angels. Its reputation seemed
firmly fixed, if not its practice. Consequently, woman
was despised as the stumbling block into heaven, and
lusted after. But it did not follow from this that men,
even when they practised chastity, necessarily hated
women and regarded them as inferior. There were
other options, and the monks showed as much variety
of attitude in their observance of chastity as they did
in the practice of their other vows. Some, like
Brother Stephen, were vigorously chaste, but regarded
men and women as equally depraved; Brother Anthony
was chaste, but regarded woman as salvageable;
Brothers Walter and Thomas never thought about
women and resorted to private acts; Brother Ralph was
never troubled and never thought about the matter;

Brother Namlis was always troubled and would have sinned gladly if given the chance; Brother Claude denounced woman and was unchaste as often as he could be; Brother Benedict had ceased communication and would not even read about female saints, or appear in the queen's presence if summoned there, and Prior Godfrey condemned all unpragmatic attitudes which hampered his administration and for this reason could not abide either Brother Anthony or Brother Benedict.

Brother Anthony came from a little further south in Italy than did Brother Benedict. They were rivals in spiritual matters as well as in class. Brother Benedict spoke French and Latin, but Brother Anthony had made the pilgrimage to Jerusalem on his knees and afterwards had lived on locusts in the desert. He carried splinters between his nails and was purged of earth and matter. Morning, noon, and night he said the psalms with his eyes upon the ground.

It might be thought that he and Brother Stephen were of one cloth, but saints can differ quite a bit. Brother Stephen had been known to laugh and had an edge of humor to him, though he was quick to tell a man his failings. Brother Anthony communicated with no one. Fenced in as he was with prayer as he ploughed and fished and drank his bowl of soup and said the Gospels four times a day and had known no other speech for forty years. He was appointed as the infirmarian, since he knew herbal secrets, and had the care of the cemetery, which was a charge of some scope, housing as it did six centuries of saintly lives sleeping beneath rose bushes and mint patches, some in crypts with Celtic crosses. A stone angel of Gabriel's demeanor stood guard over the hallowed ground, blowing a silent horn and calling the faithful to the resurrection.

No one ever discovered what had brought Brother Anthony to Bodmin Priory, since he was originally a hermit, having lived most of his life on a blob of sand in north Africa. It could not have been a longing for

social intercourse, for he never broke his vow of
silence, even when the brethren had permission to.
But perhaps it is a mistake to believe that the hermit
found peace in his lonely hermitage. We should not
overlook in the hermit-saints' literature the repetition
of never-ceasing battle with temptation that beset
them. No doubt Brother Anthony found this unique
torment in his loneliness, a perpetual bedazzlement and
betrayal of the senses, beastly hallucinations which he
transcended only occasionally. The cries of the
damned were very real. Aquinas regarded them as the
chief reward of the saved, those who would be
fortunate enough to sit in heaven and listen eternally
to the cries of the tortured. The energies of medieval
man were mobilized by these terrors of the afterworld
and of Christ's judgment, and in this world by a
rapacious hunger for land and earthly power. His
breathtaking colorfulness and adventurism and profound
cruelty are of a piece. No other people combined
piety with greed for gold and land with such historic
force. Thus, the Middle Ages have become famous for
being both spiritual and earthy. But here on earth,
Brother Anthony heard the cries of the tormented
inside his head day and night. He found succor from
these voices at Bodmin, not among the living, whose
grimacing silences and tawdry gossip he could hardly
bare, but among the dead to whom he sang the Gospels
all day long.

Brother John was the last and youngest member of
Bodmin. He was fifteen, and still a novice, but
distinguished because he was Bishop Roundsleigh's
firstborn and, in opposition to his father, had conceived
an appetite for the holy life. He was yellow haired
and milky skinned, and Bishop Roundsleigh had a
French wife picked for him, and planned for him to
inherit his lands which lay in the north of England,
near York, as well as in the southeast near Barnstaple,
as well as in the south of France in the Provence. But
Brother John chose instead a cubicle and a caracel,

and not at Cluny but at Bodmin. Prior Godfrey regarded him as the most valuable object in the Priory, next to St. Petrock's bones, but Bishop Roundsleigh swore up and down the countryside that he would have his revenge for this.

Such were they about the table in the refectory that morning, each seated according to his station and rank, eleven brethren in black capes and hoods, all bound for the same port with tonsures cut in the same manner (except for Brother Stephen), all pressed into the same duties day and night, spring and winter, all praying with one voice, all eating the same food, all sleeping in one place and at one time, all rising together to pray, to work, to read, to sing, to eat, to weed and plant, and plant and weed, all attending to their wants at the same hour and in the same way, all recognizing the same God, all copying the same Bible (except Brother Benedict), all obeying the same bells, all living in the same calendrical climate that made of each season and each hour a ritual, each ear attuned to the same great toll, each man's hopes bound for the same heaven and in fear of the same hell, each living in the same eternity, grasping the same time and the same spirit with one mind, tilling God's earth for the same purpose.

Yet it was not long before Will could distinguish which man smelled of Europe and which man smelled of English soil, which came of landed people and which of the landless, and which man he felt at ease with. Though each man's soul was known to God alone, it was not long before Will felt their individual weight and not long, despite their vows of silence and the grace of only half an hour a day in which to hear the human tongue in idle conversation, before Will knew what each man's life had been before he came to Bodmin. For the great gossip of the world, like the salt of the sea and the climate of Cornwall, could not be kept out.

The distinctions of personality pervaded the monastery. Traits there were that transcended the order or were irrelevant to it, and traits which could not be absorbed by it, and traits which sometimes, but rarely, were transformed by it. This life suited some very well and others not at all. Some adjusted, while others developed kinks and fell into terrible depressions or developed unseemly habits: ticks and twitches, palpitations, nail-biting, eye-rolling, murmuring, deafness, or were given to bedwetting and became childish and ludicrous, banal and senile, weepy and melancholy, remote and transcendant, or morbidly irritable. The religious spirit is not democratic. Some have more of it than others. It is not like the right to vote: available to everyone. As St. Bernard noted, "The sun does not warm all those on whom it shines: many of those who are taught what they must do by Wisdom are not equally inspired to do it." Here was the best of institutions created for the noblest of reasons: to save the world; yet the human traits of well being and sourness, the capacity to love and enjoy, the tendencies to hate and revile, the temptations to insurrection and rebelliousness, lapses into boredom and remoteness, in short the human range of humankind is recorded to have remained the same during these formidable and strenuous soul-saving centuries.

As with any institution or vocation, some are better suited for it than others. The status and availability of a dominant institution will attract the unsuitable as well as the suitable. The chronicles kept by the monks indicate a sociology in spiritual matters, social drifts and norms and appetites, modes of pettiness and viciousness irrespective of salvation. It was not unheard of for a monk to arise from an ardent prayer to the Virgin Mary and forcefully seduce the closest female peasant. Medieval literature abounds with such anecdotes and with the populace's fiery resentment of monkish venery and greed.

For some, such as Will, preoccupied with "holy," "sacred," "chosen," and "redemption," the monastery was a welcome place. But other monks suffered unendurable tedium, called the "monk's disease," or accidie, diagnosed as melancholy or "vicious impiousness" and suffered it in the face of Christ.

On that first morning Will did not know what the others thought of the poor breakfast fare, but he remembered the lard and eggs that lay on his breakfast table in York, and a terrible regret settled on him as he thought: "It is not enough," and immediately felt each eye say back to him, "It is." He dared not raise his eyes while all ate standing while Brother Benedict read to them from the Book of Martyrs and the glorious tale circled above them. Will looked covertly at the eleven brothers in cassocks and capes who appeared to be steady souls, not at all troubled by their meager breakfast.

The reading was finished with a murmuring amen and amen and a ringing bell, and as soon as the bell was finished and all filed out to say Mass, up comes the thought to Will again, "It is not enough," and behind him, next to his left ear, though the brother moved not a lip, Will heard him say, "It is," and next to his right ear as distinctly as the bell tolled, though that brother too moved never a lip, he heard another one say, "Bad thoughts make a great noise." The first was Brother Stephen who had a way of saying much with few words or none at all, and the second was Brother Harald whom even Prior Godfrey respected for his cleverness and wished him somewhere else.

"Come, Will," Prior Godfrey said to him, and invited him to his private room where, to Will's happiness, he offered him another quarter pound of bread and another third of a pint of beer and said, "Now, Will, we mean not to have you spend your first day weeping for what you left behind." Will sensed that his appetite had been revealed, but he assured Prior Godfrey that he was full to the level of his adam's apple. Prior Godfrey winked at him and said he doubted not but that such a long log as Will would find more room inside himself, and pushed the bread and beer forward. Will thought it would be churlish to quarrel on his first day, and thanked Prior Godfrey and ate gratefully, but feeling awkward. The room was severely silent except for his chewing, or so it seemed to him, until Prior Godfrey cleared his throat, said "ahem" and "well," and took St. George, his falcon, from his perch where he sat in front of the bay window and put him on his wrist like a jewel and walked about with him and said again, "ahem," or "well," and finally, "Now, Will, what shall I tell you of your new life. You must know somewhat of it already or you would have gone elsewhere." Here there was an embarrassing pause, and Will felt that Prior Godfrey wished him to give an explanation, a confirmation of his calling towards the canons, but Will had made up his mind to be as quiet as he could be for as long as he could, though he could not say why he had laid this command upon himself. But Will often laid commands upon himself and they would take hold of him as keenly as a superior's command: he would no more question the one than the other. So he kept still and looked respectful and inspired as he felt it befit a man who wished to begin a monk's life. Moreover, he did not know if Prior Godfrey could settle his peculiar problem and he decided, between craft and faith, to practice craft. Once the great cow was out of the barn she could give milk to any man, but while Will kept his hand upon the latch and his tongue in his mouth he was the master of his fate.

So when Prior Godfrey said to him, "You were a married man," Will said, "Yes," and said no more, but sat on his chair and ate his bread and gazed wonderfully at St. George, who tinkled the little bells attached to his leg, engraved with the name of Bodmin Priory on them, his black eyes wise with the knowledge of his descent from Osiris and Isis, his speckled chest filled with pride of lineage, and that his master, Prior Godfrey, had accomplished the art of carrying him properly, at the fashionable height and distance from the waist.

"You therefore give up more than some," Prior Godfrey said, forcing his attention back to Will, "and I know full well it will not be easy for you to become a monk, for even when you swear and war against the flesh the flesh will remember your wife by itself. Thou hast a hard battle, Will, and I must ask if you are prepared to do such battle day and night, to still the burning that be in the heart and elsewhere."

He paused at his lectern, where he kept his accounting book and business notes concerning Bodmin Priory, and waited there for Will's reply. Will knew he should give an account of himself, but only said, "I cannot say. I have been away more than three weeks and my heart has been so heavy, nought more can I feel but grief and loss and confusion."

"How long have you been a married man?"

"Three years, three months, three weeks, and three days."

"And your wife left you for another?"

Will shifted in his chair. He would not have this particular construction put upon his marriage, yet he could not find another that suited him. "We left each other somewhat," he said thriftily. "First, she left me, but only in a manner of speaking, but in such a way you might say by her manner of speaking that I must leave her and when I returned she left me and so I left her. I cannot say how all this leaving began because I loved her right well but she wouldn't forgive me for a knock I gave her on her head and wept and left me."

Well, what was in it, Prior Godfrey thought, but a little of this and a little of that, as in most matters. He advised Will to pray to St. Caesarius and picked up a crumb from Will's plate and offered it to St. George.

"Now, Will," he said, "you shall be neither here nor there if this be the matter. If you have still a longing for your wife you may put your soul in danger. You must think upon what the good doctor Aquinas said, that virginity alone can make men equal with the angels and it is already late for you. You cannot any longer be as the angels and in eternity you will be leaven though you may still save your mortal soul. Think upon it, Will, whether you came here for peace or for faith."

"I came for both," Will said pugnaciously. "I have wrestled with Christ because of my wife and I have wrestled with my wife because of Christ and now I must choose a road and walk upon it. I have been a laboring man with a little learning and I mean to become a learned man and to labor now to know God's will for this world. I have been walking three weeks and sometimes the scene looks this way and sometimes the scene looks that way with every green thing turned black and I know that here you have great books that will tell me how I should look upon these things and I came not for peace or faith alone, but for help, for peace and faith and help are one to me."

What another would have made of this speech cannot be known, but Prior Godfrey, as the administrator of an establishment, never addressed himself to imponderables. He dipped his quill with dye and wrote a note in his accounting book. "Canst speak a bit of Latin?" he asked.

"I speak nought but the English tongue."

'Your letter said you had a bit of learning."

"Only in matters natural, not in matters of many languages. I can read my native tongue and have preached somewhat here and there to my fellowman."

Prior Godfrey looked up from his accounting book and said sternly, "Here we pray and sing in Latin and do God's work, for you know right well that prayer will redeem the world, prayer will redeem the lusty men outside these walls. It is a great thing to dwell in brotherhood in one house, but it is a hard thing. 'You must know your place, hold your tongue, keep your eyes down and your stomach from talking when it is hungry, to pray when it is cold, study when you be tired, stay awake when you be sleepy, eat little and pray much, keep your tongue still and your thoughts clean. Here you know we do only God's work. Here we all row together like Noah's helpers. We be an ark upon the waters and our mariner Christ who oftentimes has sailed the sea calls us to tell us of where the perils be, the perils within and the perils without, perils of ourselves, perils of enemies, perils of the high sea and perils of ports where drunken sailors be among them that wash their deeds in wine. Christ guides us through many bitter storms, for we be

the sailors upon a ship called Holy Church and if you be
here you must row with us and take your orders like a
sailor in danger of death upon the high sea. With
poverty you must renounce the world, with obedience to
your superior you must renounce your worldly pride, with
silence you must renounce frivolity and with chastity you
must renounce the flesh and all these vows you must
keep. We be not like the Jews who be children of the
flesh but we be children of the spirit, circumcized as St.
Paul has said in the spirit and not in the flesh as was
the Hebrew. Therefore it be for you that separation of
husband and wife be your sign and your price of eternal
life. It must be this way for love of wife leads man into
privacy and love of finery and soon he buys a house to
dwell in with his wife and so he takes himself a wife and
forsakes his soul, as the old god said to Adam you shall
cling to your wife and forsake the others, which was a
law given to the Jews. But it is not fit for Christian man
to do so. He must follow Christ's words when Christ said
to leave your brother and your wife and your children
too, leave all, even your cat and follow after him, who is
the son of God. You cannot have it both ways, Will, you
must choose Heaven or earth, Christ's way or the old
Adam."

The length of the speech amazed Will, containing as it
did a few words on the virtue of silence. He was
furthermore perturbed by it because, like any other man,
Will preferred a bit of this world and a bit of the other
and to avoid, if he could, a hard choice. Prior Godfrey,
on the other hand, felt he had set the record straight,
showed Will the road he must travel and if matters did
not work out well Will had only himself to blame.

"Do not say I will begin tomorrow to do God's work,
or that God will forgive me if I think once more upon
her. For if you think once you be as good as married
again. First you think, then you want. There is no
doubt but that the way back to the world is through the
woman, for what led Samson astray and what Adam and
what caused David to sin and led Solomon to idolatry so
that God must divide the Jew's kingdom, and what be the

bride of Israel but the whore of Babylon. If you wish to go to Heaven you must stamp out thinking upon your wife, and if the devil sends her to you in your thoughts make the cross and call upon the name of holy Mary. Remember Will, if you choose the monk's life, the holy spirit will be your Eve."

A bird perched upon the window sill with a worm in its mouth. And as often happened with Will, who was a great lover of the world, whenever bird or animal looked him in the eye, he looked back at it. "So it is," he thought, regarding the bird, "Christ said the great Father will feed us as he feeds the birds in Heaven, but it seemes to me we be as the birds on earth. And who can tell why God made the earth this way and not another and why He gave to man a worm that he must carry upon his soul."

Will did not say any of this to Prior Godfrey, who liked his own speech well enough. Will never said such things to any man, for such thoughts were barely in his head before they blew away. They went by like a shadow, without enough substance for language. All of Will's life, as he planted and seeded, he thought such thoughts, for the earth gave a man different sights from those he had when he looked up to heaven. Shepherding and planting, Will would think, "This earth that God created with love and genius must be substantial to the heart. This flesh that will be made clean through and through in the Resurrection, why is it not holy here on earth?"

A man, he discovered, could read good things in the stars and hear a heavenly music, but the tune of the earth kept changing. It could not be heard this way or that. It was full of chase and hunt and dark beguilements, buzzing gnats that ate your brains out and a green hillside of white flowers, fields of rock and bog and marsh to befuddle your wits. Will was a torn man, half in love with the world for all the good things in it and the rest of him filled with hatred for its malice and its diseases. And the shadow of his hatred would come upon him from nowhere, and was so ever since he could remember and had nothing to do with what any man had taught him or preacher had preached, but came with the wind and went that way. So he could not tell Prior Godfrey about it, for it was in and out of his brain before he knew it.

"Now is heaven sufficient, Bodmin thy Eden," Prior Godfrey said. "Here poverty is blessed, here are sinners converted, here the fallen are raised, the stricken succored, the poor are fed and here is silence worshipped, for language is but corruption. Of the making of books there is no end and of whys and why nots even the infidel ask. One idea spawns but another, even as rabbits do. Knowledge is quicksand. The more a man struggles to know the further he sinks. Here is nought but faith, Will. Christ did not say a man must study to be saved. Such did the pagans, yet we know they burn right well. Plato and Aristotle, they be not in heaven, for they had not the word of Christ that he is raised from the dead. They worshipped reason which is nought but a bird which flies away. The mind is like this bird, it is transitory and all that it knows is shadow. Plato proved all this and said himself that the soul alone is eternal. The mind is a net. Many waters flow in and out of it, but the soul is a good container made by a goodly potter which holds all the right morsels. If you choose to stay and put on the habit, Jesus Christ will be your portion, your knowledge, and your world."

"I came not to seek advice," Will said impatiently, "for I made my mind up before I set my foot out the door of my house, and while a man has more thoughts in his head than he cares for, I have chosen my road and mean to walk on it. I be not learned, but I be not ignorant."

"Well, then, Will, I will show you all the grounds so that you may see how fair your new home will be. Hard though it may be to be a monk the cloister is the fairest world upon this earth. When the flood fails and the fishes lack fresh water they gasp and die with drought upon the land. Likewise is a monk who delights in living outside the cloister. He be like a fish outside of water, for here is our life in common. Here is all property sanctified by the church. She owns everything as God owns everything, and the church, as you know, is the trustee for Jesus Christ as Noah was God's servant and the master of his ship, so is Christ the master of our cloister which is likewise an ark which swims upon the worldly flood.

He then led Will out to see the grounds, carrying St. George on his wrist with impunity, letting him take flight when he wished to, for not the peasants of the land nor even the eagles of the sky would dare to trouble him.

Bodmin was as spacious and fair as Prior Godfrey said it was. There were grounds for gardening and shepherding, a pond stocked with carp and pike, a sweet smelling herbiary, vineyards and granaries, a woodshed with wood piled high enough for three winters, an infirmary and a cemetery. Behind the refectory was the kitchen with a bake-house, a hay-house, a brewing house, a stockfish house, a pudding house, a house for keeping beer, a collumbarium where Prior Godfrey kept his pigeons and doves, a pantry, and a boulting house where the corn was sieved.

There were thirteen servants on the grounds: Adam, the larderer who had charge of the live animals and who milked the cows and made the butter and slaughtered the fowl and ground the spices and was in charge of the keys to the pantry and the hay-house and the stock-house and, as general husbandman, ran all day between the animal-keep and the kitchen in his leather apron; and Mathew the bell-ringer who was a short, thick man with bowed legs and rounded shoulders and thickened arms; and Peter the gardener who was long and lean with a tired face, whose third wife had died in the birth of his fifth son; and the cook who was a giant of a man who daily worked three cauldrons of boiling soup, and his son who worked the spit in the fireplace and whose eyes were blind from its smoke; and Michael, Michael the gate-keeper whom Will had met the night before; the carriers, Rufus and Luke who removed the refuse and brought the fuel; and the breviator who went about like a letter-carrier from monastery to monastery, and from monastery to village and read the scrolls of news and the names of the recently deceased.

Of the women servants, there were two pudding-wives who came on the occasions of guests or holidays, to bake or make special soups and sauces, the elderly Moll with grey hair on her chin and her dim-witted granddaughter who had one eye; the two launderesses, Beth whom the smallpox had robbed of skin and Rose who limped pitifully and snivelled when she spoke. They came on Monday and Thursday to collect the washing from Brother Namlis, and whatever could be given to the poor.

It took three hours for Prior Godfrey to take Will about and show him all there was at Bodmin and to relate to him how each thing had come to be and was attended to with ritual and with love; how Brother Bernard drew up the mortuary role when a brother died and how he gave it to the breviator who carried the death notice to the other monasteries and religious houses in England, and how this breviator was received with honor and was entitled to the mattress of the deceased. Prior Godfrey told Will of the cunning names by which place or person had come to be known at Bodmin, how the cemetery was called God's Acre, how it was Brother Anthony's responsibility to keep the sacred plot free from wandering animals and weeds and marauders who were known to dig up the graves even of monks in search of treasure; how Brother Harald had to see to the reliquaries and the shrines, the altars and the sconces and the cloths and to look after the supply of wax which sometimes was as much as thirty pounds a year; how Brother Claude was called the watchman because it was his duty to prod the sleepy monks who nodded at Matins. He told him how Brother Namlis made grease for their boots and stored lambskins and catskins for the cold weather, how Brother Stephen cleaned the refectory and purchased five loads of straw three times a year to carpet the refectory floor with, how he scattered bay leaves in the necessarium: how every domestic duty had its wise servant, for however a man may hope for heaven he must still keep his earthly home in order. He told Will he must bathe four times a year and let his blood four times a year, in April, September, October and February; and was most particular about these last orders.

They circled Bodmin twice, until Prior Godfrey came to the end of the history and the gossip, for Bodmin Priory, like all great institutions, had its own history and had undergone vicissitude and permutations. "There hath been monks, then nuns, then secular priests, then monks again, and last we come, the canons regular in this, St. Petrocke's Church." The priory had been a Benedictine monastery at one time, and the religious orders that had come and gone reflected the adjustment each age had made to crisis and to inspiration. Bodmin was now an Augustinian monastery, "and not Cistercian, Benedictine, French or what," Prior Godfrey said, for he had no taste for "religious aliens."

"Henry I loved the canon and now we have two hundred and eight houses in this land, and we feed the poor and care for them, keep hospital and hear confessions, and here monks do not eat meat."

Bodmin was only a small priory at lands end in Cornwall, but Prior Godfrey knew that it was as good a link as any in the medieval chain of rex et sacerdos and the trinity of clergy, king and usurer which has vanished with its labyrinthine economy, leaving behind its monumental stones and the memory of the usurer.

Bodmin was small, as monasteries were considered in that day, for there were far greater establishments, such as Cluny and Glastonbury which undertook not only the salvation of souls, but the world's business by way of finance and industry, art, culture, and administration. At Cluny and other such monasteries, four hundred monks could find joy, as well as popes and kings with retinues of servants, scholars, artists and usurers, tax collectors, lawyers, and soldiers. The abbot of such an establishment was as important as the governor of a modern state. In such a monastery, lay servants and serfs tilled the earth and performed the mundane tasks of delivery and trade and carting out the refuse, to protect the monks from contact with a soiled world; to provide them with the leisure to pray and copy, compose and read. In this form, the monastery was the dominant institution in Europe for a thousand years, in which time some 40,000 monasteries had acquired institutional power, some spiritual gain, and then oblivion.

A paradox inheres in the history of salvation, for the monastery was created to offer man an alternative to the world. But where it established itself, common civilization flourished: industry, art, finance, and administration, and even the business of salvation acquired a history.

The monastic movement can be traced to pre-Christian times, to the Essenes and the Jewish Theraputae in Egypt, and before that possibly to Eastern religions. Its early Christian beginnings, however, are inauspicious: a counterculture movement of desert hermits on Egyptian soil who retreated from the Roman world, men like Brother Anthony, hermits of the lonely cell whose only defense against evil was retreat and abstinence. Spiritual longing led them away from civilization at first, as it later inadvertently led them back. They froze in caves of Cappadocia and burned on African sands and dined on wine and wafers and apocalyptic visions until the earth and its inhabitants became shadows. Their skins became the color of chestnuts and as wrinkled as an elephant's. Their beards grew everywhere and their skins fell detached from their bony structures. They became scabs and ribs and acquired lice and warts, training themselves to sit still for forty days and forty nights until their knees could not unbend, and they ceased to move; or like Simon Stylites stood continually upon a column sixty feet in the air and unhinged their knees only to pray; or like the Irish saints, they stood in icy water up to their necks and sang the psalms for hours. Legends of prodigious feasts attend these saints in search of God. They chained themselves to rocks, they lived in wattled huts, in holes, in cages, in baskets. The birthpangs of Christianity were terrible. Its saints willingly confronted the hazards of solitude and nature with a naked spirit. But none ever reported that the world is saved.

A follower of St. Francis, Brother Salimbene, records the imitatio dei of a fellow monk: he had himself circumcized "to be very like the Lord and lay down by a woman's side and there did drink her milk." Energies drawn from the primal therapy of a religious day! But what of salvation! Saint! tell me, what of salvation.

Early ecclesiastics suspected the monastic movement in spite of such influential proponents as Basil, Chrysostom, Jerome and Augustine. But by the fifth century, the movement had the support of the papacy. In 410, Honoratus established a monastery in southern Gaul and between 413-416, John Cassian established the monasteries of St. Victor and St. May, which housed over five thousand monks and nuns. Still further civil order was required for bands of roaming monks who plagued the countryside with all kinds of fervors.

There seems to be a millennial rhythm to European history. In 529 C.E. the schools of the Athenian philosophers closed after a continuous existence of a thousand years, and the Roman emperor Justinian formulated his Code; St. Benedict of patrician Roman lineage, hailed as "a very Roman of the Romans," emerged from a cave in a gorge in the wild Abruzzi, where Nero once had had a palace, and there gave his famous Rule at Monte Cassino which tamed the desert ascetae and brought stability to their flaming fervor. Guiding this tradition of the desert monks, with their desperate requirements of solitude and asceticism, he brought their ardor within the grasp of all men's potential, and established the monastic tradition which saved Europe from the Goth for the benefit of future generations. He gave the desert saint a home behind the walls of civilization, where he mastered many arts and industries and grew very wealthy and very necessary. Looking back, we see that all forms of social life, however desperate the hour and the spiritual need, are drawn towards civilization.

St. Benedict and his sister, Scholastica were buried with the gratitude of loving followers in a grave where once had stood the altar of Apollo. Literature cannot embellish this historic fact. Thus, and tritely, the new order buried the old order and even the Romans were glad to see it go, and now worked in the monastic fields in the lowly garb of monks.

The Church became very rich and popes sat on gilded thrones, but such as Brother Anthony still clung to rocks and sat in the deserts, and now prayed for the salvation of the Church. Reform movements came and went, and Boniface Vlll ignored them all, and in the year of the first jubilee he had himself addressed as "Caesar" and "Emperor."

By the end of the next millennium there were many kinds of monasteries: Benedictine, Cluniac, Cistercian, Carthusian, canons regular of the order of St. Augustine, Premonstratensian canons, Gilbertine canons, Knights Hospitaller, Knights Templar, Dominican Friars, Franciscan Friars, Friars of Our Lady, Friars of the Holy Trinity, Crutched, or Crossed Friars, Bethlemite Friars, Pied Friars or Frates de Pica; Friars of the Sack, Trinitarians, Bonshommes, and many others. Monasteries bred monasteries as clusters and colonies. Great establishments, such as Cluny, gave birth to daughter and sister establishments which fell under complex administrations. In Charlemagne's time, the entire town of Tours, composed of 20,000 people, was monastic, its numbers swollen by political prisoners, opponents of Charlemagne, and by others pressed into monkhood by their lords, or recruited into monkhood like soldiers, and bought like slaves, "condemned to monkhood," as some complained. Sad to say that so much of the grandeur of an era, of its art and learning, rests upon simple criminal impulse and plainest vainglory.

Still, the flock gathers where there is wealth and social safety. Vagabonds and orphans, civil servants seeking sinecures, prelates seeking power, discarded soldiers and multitudes of boys sought salvation in the monastery. It functioned as an orphanage, as an old age home, as a place of retirement, as a resting place for pilgrims, as a barracks for armies, so intimate was this religious institution with the social needs of its day.

Orders arose in response to the Crusades, in response to the growth of cities, in response to reforms, in response to political pressures, in response to financial needs, or for the production of wine or wool, and monasteries arose even in sheer spite, in response to other orders. Monasteries were established on the basis of trade or philosophies. Monasteries arose which followed the Roman sentiment of regarding manual labor as degrading, and monasteries arose which honored manual labor. Monasteries arose which stressed contemplation and scholasticism, others which developed esthetic ambitions and became skilled in the production of stained glass windows, illuminated texts, and chanting. Many abbots shared with the imperial rulers a passion for building on a colossal scale and bled the peasant with taxes for these glories. As much as any Puritan in Milton's day, St. Bernard retched at this extravagance of the combined force of art, religion and imperial design. He reminded his fellow monks that their concern should be for souls and not for stones. But souls vanish and stone remains, and what remains on earth counts for its history. Still other orders arose, like the Cistercians led by St. Bernard, which denounced art as a distraction from the spiritual life. And finally monasteries arose which denounced the monastic habit of separation from the world, the cycle came full swing and there was no one prevailing philosophy of how the monastery would accomplish the work of salvation.

As Prior Godfrey showed Will the grounds of Bodmin Priory on this afternoon, and related to him its history of wars and skirmishes with the local gentry, disruptions and eruptions, its great visitors and processions, and showed him the new scriptorium with its great new Latin Bible, the garden where his best roses blew in the sea wind, and the treasury buried beneath the spot where they stood, where the notes of debts and credits of the priory, its jewels and relics and precious objects lay buried, nothing of the dismal future occurred to him. He had every reason to believe, as he took Will about, that his was an eternal order, but his is a vanished order we address ourselves to and bid come forth from the winding sheet of history. Prior Godfrey's bald and slightly oily forehead looked serene, and his round, Nordic, uninteresting, mild and plain blue eyes looked trusting in the order which he knew and loved. He could not even see six months' time ahead when Brother Claude's lascivious ravings would come to an end and Brother Harald's hypochondria would be mocked by reality. Of the brethren, only two would survive and of the paid servants only Moll, the pudding-wife. The bell-ringer would be found dead in the Norman tower with a black tongue sticking out of his mouth, and Michael the gate-keeper would be found dying of thirst outside the priory wall.

The midday bell rang. Prior Godfrey had been tried in his competence and felt relieved to go and rest. "I will not detain you any longer," he said to Will, "but I will advise you to eat a good meal. It makes the body better able to let the soul labor for God's sake. But I would you go first to the necessarium, for a monk must keep himself clean. We be not like some that let in the lice to eat of their bread and their bodies. Heaven must be clean," Prior Godfrey said with an emphasis that suggested hostility for hidden enemies and ideas which eluded Will. "If Christ let in dirty monks, they would not keep it clean, and it is not dirty, for none have said so of heaven, but that the streets are of marble and the saints wear spotless robes."

Prior Godfrey's insistence upon these matters, to the exclusion of other matters, confounded even Bishop Grandisson. When he made his visitation, Prior Godfrey showed him first the necessarium. "Your books, Prior Godfrey," Bishop Grandisson would say, "not your lavatory. I would see your accountings, not your toilets."

At night, in bed, Brother Harald would silently rehearse this scene with delirious disapprobation. On the other side of him, where they slept, Brothers Benedict and Claude communicated their disdain for the English with a secret telepathic device which the other brothers were privy to. Brothers Ralph and Walter dreamed of dice and

Brother Thomas tossed and yelled, "I dareye, I dareye," and woke in the morning, wrinkled and unfit.

Bishop Grandisson was God's wise, good, and courageous administrator for four decades in the see of Exeter, and a word must be said for him. He was a good man in a bad time: 1328-1369. Englishborn in Herefordshire in 1298, he was French educated, as was any educated man of his day, and rose to be chaplain to Pope John XXll in Avignon, and was consecrated there in the Church of the Friars at age 36, before he set out for England to assume his duties, the previous Bishop Stapeldon having been murdered. The see was in shambles when he crossed the channel at Christmastime and arrived in Dover on the 3rd of February, 1328, and at his diocese on the 9th of June to lament the case of a monk who had married, and of one who had not merely married but had sent food from his table to "one Joan, the wife of Henry Cosyn, his partner in sin," and to excoriate the practice of child-marriage among the Brotherhood of Brothelyngham, and to avert an attempt upon his own life on the 13th of October in the year, 1343, and to censure an invasion of the Scots, the first of several that took place in that dark century.

But it was on October 24, 1329, when he first visited the Priory of Bodmin, that Bishop Grandisson understood the scope of his duties. Rot was in the fields. Negligence was everywhere. Ink blots like bats adorned the scripts and the margins of holy texts were ornamented with unspeakable ditties:

Adam had a wife named Eve,
She hid her apple where she pleased;
He put his serpent between her knees,
So God He cast them from Paradis

Neither had the straw been changed from the refectory floor in more than a year and an odor was discernible everywhere. There was no lard in the larder or tallow in

the storeroom or fish in the pond. Evidence of gambling
and gaming and dicing was everywhere. The bishop
issued an ordinance for the reformation of these abuses.
He dismissed the then prior and had a new one put in his
place. Things at once improved, and then slid to a side
and changed the shape of their corruption. The larder
was stocked and the hay removed, but neglect and
mismanagement continued in other ways, undreamed of by
the bishop. The lavater was cleaned, the monks were
shaved, the linen kept in order, but bible scripts remained
untouched, the fields unharvested and the poor scrounged
the countryside for food. Ten years before Will arrived,
the priory walls, the great gate and sundry other buildings
had been battered by the storms of 1338 and were in
desperate condition. Bodmin was forced to do unholy
things to raise money for repairs, because things did not
repair themselves even when set aside for spiritual use.
Storms, like plagues, are careless with the sacred, and
Prior Godfrey put up St. Petrock's bones as collateral for
a loan.

But worse was yet to come. The year before Will
arrived, the almoner was removed for an unspeakable
offense, the numbers of paid servants increased in an
alarming way, were reduced, and increased again. Bishop
Grandisson sent Prior Godfrey away and appointed an
interim administrator to patch things up: books and
records and discipline. When Will arrived at Bodmin,
from the point of view of history, things were not as
good as they could be, but hardly as bad as they had
been. Things had improved from deterioration to stasis.
Prior Godfrey had been returned and was at pains to
know what Bishop Grandisson now wished reformed.
Bishop Grandisson was a nuisance! Prior Godfrey sent
papal letters to Avignon, but Bishop Grandisson came of
an established family and had a manor at Cyst in Exeter
and a residence at Chudleigh. In fact, Bishop Grandisson
could have settled for land and power and bribes and
promises and peace. Instead, he settled for such as Prior
Godfrey. He undertook the reformation of the monasteries
in his diocese, and the thankless job of lecturing to the

heads of powerful families who neglected their lands and their duties, and bled the people with taxes on their crops; who went abroad to raise money from the usurers, to return to England to wage war to win more land to neglect; whose sons were priors and abbots and had the care of souls and monasteries and neglected churchlands to travel abroad and consult with kings and other heads of other powerful families.

It was one thing if Walt of Landsend scratched his scabby cheeks and protested that the times were bad. It was another thing if Bishop Grandisson, born to wealth and rank, undertook the tedious job of checking books and records, stock and larder, and listening to every complaint and asservation from monks' lechery and claims of miracle births to accusations of spite and wrath and greed and gluttony.

Oh, Bishop Grandisson! You could have hunted and wenched and slept under three layers of fur. You could have sported a falcon on your wrist, but did not. In every age and place there is a man who plugs up the hole in the dikes of sin with nothing but soul and effort and keeps the times from going utterly to rot.

So Will was to learn that when things went wrong, he was to bring his petition to Bishop Grandisson, though Prior Godfrey considered himself unfortunate in having been appointed such a bad-tempered bishop, precise in his figures and so fussy about trivial matters, altogether unbecoming in a bishop, whose complaints should be set on higher things than book-keeping matters. There was neither lechery nor usury, to speak of, at Bodmin Priory, and certainly no uncleanliness. The evidence that Bishop Grandisson brought him of an unfortunate thought here or there scribbled in the scriptorium was unbecoming for a bishop to show his prior, who was his equal in family.

"What of it?" Prior Godfrey said, "it is in the Jews' part of the book and can be said to be dirt only in a manner of speaking."

Bishop Grandisson cared nothing for Prior Godfrey's family, but he was loath to remove him again, to make such notoriety public. Besides, dismissals, as everyone knows, only leave gaps filled in by other jackals. Bishop Grandisson became resigned. Superficiality is the common vice of bureaucracies, and not its worst. In Bishop Grandisson's rule over many monasteries he dealt with worse: gaming, hunting, whoring, incontinences of all kinds, lasciviousness, drinking, and praying in such a manner as to convey the opposite effect of belief and piety. No highborn could bribe Bishop Grandisson with the gift of a relic or the promise of advancement. And a fool could not worst him with his foolishness. He learned to deal with Prior Godfrey.

Will followed the brethren from the necessarium to the refectory and was gratified to see that the midday meal was considerably ampler than breakfast had been: cheese and bread and eggs and beans and oysters and a glass of mead. The meal reconciled him to other losses. "Now this be more like what my stomach wants," he thought, but he didn't enjoy the thought for long. The habit of recrimination took root early, and he imagined Brother Harald looked suspiciously at him. He searched the other faces, but no one else's looked perturbed. Brother Anthony left all his food but his one cup of mead and a slice of bread. Brother Stephen ate only half of what was given him. Brothers Walt and Ralph looked fondly at their empty plates when they were done, but otherwise seemed cheerful enough.

Nor did Will see a face to his liking on this first morning. He never could tolerate young old men like Brother Ralph and Brother Walter, and Brother John was still a lad with rapt eyes set to become a saint before he was twenty; and Brother Benedict moved his mouth, small as a cherry, in such a way Will knew he could never abide his company. Each man had his tic or wrinkle that set his nerves on edge, and he wondered why he had come there.

After the meal they went out into the garden where Prior Godfrey preached a sermon against accidia, "the midday demon, the little voice that will tell you that all is vanity, that God sees not our work, nor our reaping and sowing matter, nor reading nor copying nor monks' learning. There be those who slander the monks and say he is a sleuthful man, for the times are against the Lord. But Christ loves the labor of the monk and the Augustinians have wrought well with their wool trade on English grounds. The laborer is worthy of his hire and a monk's labor is trebly worthy."

Brothers Ralph and Walter looked singularly alike in spirit, as they listened to the sermon, and a thing like that is apt to make each man look less serious than he might be. Brother Ralph had the sharper glance and more knowing air. Otherwise, both seemed genial and candid, and accustomed to monkhood. That is to say, they had known no other life, desired no other, and believed that fate had done wisely with them. They had come as babes, though at different times. Now being the oldest residents at Bodmin, having seen three priors come and go and a score of brethren, they enjoyed each other's friendship by virtue of similar experiences and similar temperaments. They never quarrelled. They had achieved a state of communication untroubled by the baggage of language, even though Brother Ralph liked very much to gossip and gossiped on every possible occasion, gardening, reading, praying, and washing his hands in the necessarium. He whispered news behind Will's ear as they promenaded in the cloister, and whispered news from behind his prayerbook to whomever, as they knelt in the choir box. Brother Ralph gossiped in his sleep. He spoke aloud in the dark like a possessed oracle imparting to the air and all who stayed awake to listen, information about what dignitary was about to visit Bodmin, what Moll the laundress had said, what the king's mistress was like, what discrepancy Bishop Grandisson had found in the books, whether Prior Godfrey would be removed again, whether the wool trade was succeeding or failing, whether war would come this spring, how it went in neighboring monasteries, who had died, who had wined, who had wived and who had been caught and punished.

Brother Ralph's nocturnal speeches had been brought to Prior Godfrey's notice several times. One afternoon following the midday meal, there was a sermon and debate on whether talking in one's sleep violated the vow of silence. Brother Thomas pleaded guilty and offered to have his tongue removed. To Will's surprise, Brother Ralph took a hard line and said that a monk who practised his vow properly would not speak even in his sleep. "Even had he a nightmare he will not call out but swallow his tongue to keep himself from speaking out. A monk that speaks in his sleep is the bait of Satan." Brother Thomas was crushed by such a judgment and could not keep his head erect, but he made a good recovery by the evening meal and appeared with a cheerful patch of red on each cheek.

Brother Benedict could not abide Brother Ralph's speech, rendered in his lowborn tongue. Nor could he abide Brother Ralph's complexion, "dirty-dark," with yellow eyes. Brother Harald smirked as usual, more accustomed to sin by innuendo than by commission, but Brother Stephen said stonily: "If Brother Ralph likes the taste of human tongue and if he is not prepared to feast upon his own he should not recommend that of others."

Brother Stephen was never sparing in his censure. Will heard Brother Harald call him "a little Jonah cast up by the Irish Sea." Brother Stephen was barely five feet tall with dainty hands and dainty feet and coal-black eyes and a smoldering tongue that darted like a snake's about your ears when he spoke. He never slurred or praised and said candidly there was nothing on earth worth his praise. "It is nought but a mudhole that sucks and bubbles about your feet."

"Do you not like the sunshine?" Will asked him once.

Brother Stephen put his hands inside the sleeves of his cape, and for all his size, looked imposing. "A man who reckons prayer as praise means to buy off the world and take a cheap recompense."

Will puzzled over this speech many times. There was a hint of something marvellously austere about it that was belittling to a man like himself. Brother Stephen always spoke this way, to the point and never waywardly or frivolously, but always with a suitable bitterness that, for all Will could see, came from the air itself.

Brothers Ralph, Walter, and Namlis the hunchback, had the distinctions of seniority, for they had been at Bodmin longer than the others, almost from infancy. Brothers Harald and Stephen enjoyed the distinction of merit in that they fulfilled their vows to perfection and were allowed to lead in prayers and give readings; Brother Benedict and Brother Anthony who knew the Bible, and Brother Claude who knew Arabic, and Brother Bernard who was the archivist, enjoyed the distinction of culture; while Brother John enjoyed the distinction of youth and the uncared-for- distinction of being Bishop Roundsleigh's firstborn son. And so at Bodmin, as everywhere else, were these ways of judging merit.

The morning before Will was to make his profession, he was left to wander by himself. Indecisiveness and muddle followed him about. He sat down by the fishpond to straighten out his thoughts, his brain adazzle with lectures and readings and having heard little but the word of God since he had arrived. He scratched his head. "It is a question, after all, if heaven be man's proper element. Nay Will," he chided himself, "you cannot doubt the joy of eternity. See how the fish swim about in their element, yet tomorrow at mealtime they will be in thine, without a view of heaven. Marvellously innocent of you," he said to them, "to go about your watery business careless of your souls."

He caught sight of Brother Namlis fishing on the opposite side of the pond and came around to stand beside him, for politeness sake, for it was as little to converse with a man who had no tongue as to converse with the fish.

"You seem a good fisher," he said courteously. Brother Namlis could only smile and nod his head and blink his eyes.

Will thought it a hard fate for a man to be so homely, with a hump, and without a tongue. Still, he seemed cheerful enough, and Will was as glad to prattle to him as to the fish. "I tell you what I think," he said. "I do not think Namlis is your Christian name, if I must tell you truly. My dog had a better name and was known by all as Rug, God bless her soul." Her image appeared before him, leaning starboard in her old age, and he began to cry and craved a word of comfort for his homesickness, even from a tongueless man, but Brother Namlis became more distressed than Will and it was Will who had to do the comforting. "I tell you what," he said, "the tongue's not worth much in man anyway. Here was my dog Rug and she could not speak yet I loved her full and here was my wife who spoke right well and we quarrelled the whole day of it. Had you ever a wife?"

Brother Namlis smiled slyly, but shook his head.

"That's a good man," Will said, recovering his equanimity. "You will be with the angels, as Aquinas said, no doubt. What need has a silent man for a wife. That end works harder than the other end. It is not worth a bet to say whether a married man quarrels or beds more. If one end is not wagging, the other is. Though I trust they did not cut off your other end as well."

Brother Namlis tossed his fishpole in the air with glee, and laughed, but his laugh, like his cry, was a terrible sound to hear and it took Will aback. Still he was content to make a tongueless man so merry, and he warmed to the subject of a sermon. "I say with the preacher, God alone knows why He made woman and maybe He knows it not. You have not your tongue and I have not my wife." With this, to his surprise, he began to cry again. "Truth be, Brother Silence, you be not company for a man without a wife though I like you well enough, and do not mind your hump at all. Think upon it this way, Brother Silence, you may not have a tongue but you have a soul and I had a wife which had no soul though Christ knew I meant her no harm for the lack of it, but seeing I will not be with her in Heaven I thought it best to call it off with her here. Man may cut off either end of you, seeing the angels care not for such clappers."

It was Brother Ralph who told Will a few days later how Brother Namlis had come to lose his tongue. His mother had cut it out.

"It cannot be," Will said, astounded.

"As ever I tell you," Brother Ralph whispered.

"Did ever man hear of such evil," Will cried.

"She said he whined and puled too much. She was nought but a wench who went about the land with any man and she has sent many a babe to a monastery."

That was not the whole of the story, for Brother Namlis' survival had been miraculous in every way. Not content to cut his tongue out, his mother had thrown him down a well. "Along came this ruffian," Brother Ralph said, "drunk with the barley and stops to fetch a drink when he hears this thrashing from down below and fetches it up, believing it is a fish and he will have his supper from it. His mother came running and screeching, for she was for throwing the babe back, but this wayfarer held her off and made off with the babe and brought him here. Never has God done to man what this one's mother did to her own, for his back was broke in the fall."

"God give all women a good black eye," Will said.

Brother Namlis held no such view of his mother, but cherished the few good memories he had of her and prayed for her soul every night. Will waxed loquacious, standing by the side of the pond with him. Talking with a tongueless man had its merits. Will could argue his points without contention. Nor could it be counted for a sin against the vow of silence, since it could not be said that they conversed.

Suddenly, however, a ferocious noise brought the bliss to an end. It was a hunting call, but it came like a clap of thunder and before Will could catch his breath, a band of dogs and horses jumped the wall to the sounds of horns and tally-ho, and immediately Prior Godfrey came running and shouting curses, "Damnye, damnye," with vexation and wringing of hands, pursued by the brethren and calling out, "The devil burn your horse's tail and your own as well, you devil of a baron."

But this was Baron Roundsleigh who was not put off by such a speech. He leaned down from his horse and sounded his horn in Prior Godfrey's ear and said with merry hatred, "You blooksuckin' landleecher, who told you to set my son in your priory. I will have my son or your grounds. Christscabsandwounds, may blood dry on your sores and embalm you if I don't shake St. Petrockes bones loose from you." With that, he drove his horse so hard her hoofs churned up the earth beneath, and he drove her straight across the cemetery, across the hallowed grounds, while Prior Godfrey ran after him and screeched that Christ will put him in hell, him and his hounds and his dogs and his whores, and he will hunt for foxes in the fire. But Baron Roundsleigh had no fear of heaven or of hell, and neither did his lords or ladies or his dogs. They all galloped across the hallowed ground in pursuit of a fox or a whim. Baron Roundsleigh was an atheist and no man could threaten him. His motto on his banner and his breastplate was, "als ik kan." His people had come with William the Conqueror and he recognized no native Englishman above himself, especially not Prior Godfrey who had borrowed from him L 300 on pledge of St. Petrock's bones, in return for which Baron Roundsleigh had the rentals and the harvest from a portion of the manor lands until such time as Prior Godfrey would pay him back the money which, for all Baron Roundsleigh could make of Prior Godfrey's inefficiency, would be never. So he rode across the hallowed grounds where five centuries of saints awaited the resurrection, conscious of his castles on the Rhine, his tin mines in Cornwall, and Prior Godfrey's debts to him.

"God save me from these cocks that neither crow nor generate, these landleeches and bloodsuckers that will steal a man's son as ever the gypsies are said to do."

He caught sight of his son, John, running with the other brethren and called out to him, "It behooved you to be like Ysaac and obedient to your father's ways. The Jew had more from his son than ever I will have of mine."

The brethren held their tongues and ran in silence. Brother Stephen's face cursed as loud as thunder, but never a word was sounded. Brother John swooned. Brother Anthony caught hold of the reins of the baron's horse, but could not hold on. The foxes, the dogs, the horses, the horns and the lords and ladies jumped the wall and disappeared into the countryside.

"It be not so tame here as I thought," Will said to himself. The bell for vespers rang. "Oh! Will, what are you doing here?"

He followed the brethren to the refectory and took his meager breakfast of bread and beer, and thought again, "It is not enough." The thought would not stay down, but floated up again and again like a bloated bubble, though it was the morning when he was to enter the Chapter House and say his profession and be parted from the things he loved, village dances and village laughter, Claryce and Rug and Davy, good souls he had nothing against if truth be told, yet he had pledged to renounce them in order to save them.

He could not accommodate the thought, no matter how he turned it, Christian though he was all his life. It was his hunger that made it look peculiar, he thought, as he knelt among the brethren in the Chapter House and said a prayer in Latin and asked to be received into their community and promised to take his vows and part from the world though he would pray for its redemption. This Christianity, with the eyes of the brethren upon him, was not the familiar one he knew when he tramped through a muddy meadow to hear a preacher say Mass in a clay hut where the farmers stood with their animals and pitchforks and the women carried their babes, where the folk laughed and pushed and shoved forward rudely for salvation.

De profundis demani ad te, Domine;
Domine, ex dudi vocen mean
Fiant aures tuae intendentes in vocem

Will was a man fraught with sincerity, but this tongue was not his and he suffered the travail of a foreign language. Still in his leather pants and jacket of a farming man, he kneeled with confusion and solicited the goodwill of his prior and brethren to permit him to become one of them. He vowed to adopt them as his spiritual family, to serve his year as a novice, to become practised in duty and prayer, to keep his vows of silence, poverty, obedience, and chastity, to set his feet upon the heavenly road, and in all ways to follow Jesus Christ. Throughout his petition, Brother Benedict rang a small bell, and when Will stopped the bell stopped. There was a great amen, and then there was silence. That night Will was given a place to sleep in the dormitory between Brother Namlis and Brother Thomas.

The next afternoon, Brother Namlis took him to the cupboard to fit him with a monk's habit and cowl. He was taught first monastic manners, for the monastery was a way of life, not only accountable for conduct and ethics, but for having a style that was appropriate to it. As with all civilizations, it placed value on outward behavior as a sign of the inward state of mind. Brother Bernard gave him his first lessons as well as that grave man could deal with mundane matters: how to wear his habit properly, how to get in and out of bed with modesty, how to walk with dignity, how to hold his hands and head so as to assume a bearing of gravity. If Will was to be a monk, he must look and act like a monk as well as feel like one.

His second lesson concerned the custody of his eyes and tongue and respect for his superiors. Will was urged to think of his senses as being in the custodial care of his soul. Medieval man sought a state of grace, not a state of nature. After he was taught how to chant and to pray properly, then began his lessons in Latin.

Pater noster, qui es in coelis
    sanctificatur
Gloria Patri Filio et Spiritu Sancto

Brother Bernard intoned, and Will intoned after him. To learn to read was to learn to pray and to chant, for reading was said aloud. "The tongue dictates to the hand," the great scholar Alcuin had said. He who wished to read properly must learn to pronounce and to recite, to sing and to pay aloud, to create an aural chamber in the brain, for sound enforced memory, and language and reading were to be enjoyed sensuously. Brother Bernard's Latin was excellent, but he was loath to correct errors and Will was left to render his Latin in his Yorkshire accent.

The month of May passed for him with increasing interest in what he was learning, except for his stomach. The cattle were put out to pasture and their bells and lowing mingled with the steeple bells. In the village, Clooke, the village priest, led the villagers in procession to celebrate Rogation Days. They carried banners and bells and crosses and went about the boundaries of the village and their land to bless it and to mark it, and on Sundays came to hear Mass in the priory.

Will slept in the dorter with the others, a long hall with a crucifix and a candle at one end of it. Each brother had a cot and a lectern with a Bible and a candle on it, and a partial screen on each side of his cot for privacy. Their places were fixed in the dormitory, as they were fixed in the refectory and in the choir box. Brothers Harald, Bernard, John, Claude, Stephen and Anthony lay on one side, Brother Benedict, and then Brothers Walter, Ralph, Thomas, Namlis, and now Will on the other.

Will wondered that Brother Namlis could lay on his hump and snore with comfort, while all night Brother Thomas called out, "I dareye, I dareye," as he jousted with the devil or carried on nocturnal battles with the English. These were not Rug's snores or his wife's ditties sung in the night to alert him, but in time such noises came to take the place of the family snores he still missed.

He rose at Matins in the dark with the brethren, for a monk's day begins at midnight. It was Brother Harald's duty to light the candles on the steps and in the choir box so that they could find their way. A distant bell tolled. They rose and crossed themselves and commended their souls to God's protection. Brother John carried the lantern, and they followed him into the church where Prior Godfrey waited for them. When the bell stopped tolling, they bowed and said the Pater, Ave, and Creed, they sang the psalms and Deus in Adjutorium and the Responsorium and te Deum and a portion of the Gospel.

They prayed most of the night, while the world slept. Immediately Matins was concluded, the bell rang for Lauds. The continuity of vigil was kept, as it had formerly been kept by the Temple priests during the Night Watch, and by the early Christians who had performed Mass at midnight over the graves of their martyrs.

It was mostly during the Night Office that Will's stomach growled with hunger. His flesh would not give up, but kicked and spit at him and cursed him in his bowels. It stomped about inside of him and demanded food. "If it is not one thing it is another," Will said to himself, "stomach, tongue or clapper." He saw that the battle would not be done until his soul split from his flesh.

Sometimes, in the morning, his stomach flew about inside of him like bats, or bit him like a nest of snakes. With a heavy heart, he looked forward to his quarter pound of bread and pint of beer. At the table, every man looked mean to him, and Brother Benedict who read the Saints' Lives in Latin, had a womanly voice which he could not abide, and he believed that Brother Stephen passed unpleasant judgments on him. In time his body came to trouble him less, but never Brother Stephen.

After breakfast, they met in the Chapter Room to discuss the list of the week's misdemeanors. Brothers Ralph and Walter had been caught gaming again. Brother Claude had dripped tallow wax on his manuscript, and later had hidden Brother Benedict's music sheets and had effaced them in a lewd manner. They listened to the reading of the Rule, for it could not be repeated often enough, and then discussed other business matters. A visit was expected from Abbot Roland, Brother Harald's brother, and Prior Godfrey wished them to learn their chants better, for nothing pleased Christ as much as a musical, mellifluous voice. "Speech is a privilege given to man and not to the beasts. Christ hears what you say as well as what you sing and prefers to hear you sing your prayers, for the tongue knows nought but to speak slander, frivolity, and lewdness." So saying, he bid them good day and retired for his nap.

They went out two by two into the field. Brother Claude, as usual, walked beside Brother Bernard, whom he regarded as a simpleton, but as one with whom he could converse in French, if one could converse at all with Brother Bernard. Brother Claude was from the north of France and was the disinherited son of a lord, and therefore very quarrelsome, while Brother Bernard had outlived his grievances and had little to say. Brother Claude had more in common with Brother Harald, who was also a disinherited son and who suffered from unrequited ambition as Brother Claude suffered from unrequited lust, but Brother Claude had no love for the English and Brother Harald regarded Brother Claude as the Gaul's revenge for English victories.

Brother Thomas shuffled his feet in a palsied manner, but turned each corner of the cloister briskly, pretending he was marching to a martial air. Only Brother John would walk beside Brother Thomas, tempting the fate of the French disease; or sometimes Brother Namlis who, being a tongueless man, was glad for any man's company at any cost. Brother Stephen had a "walking" friendship with Brother Benedict, though no other. Brother Anthony was indifferent to social intercourse and walked by himself. Brother Ralph walked beside Will and whispered to him, "Well, now that you have met Bishop Roundsleigh, you have met the whole holy family of Bodmin."

"What mean you by this?" Will whispered back.

Brother Ralph winked in John's direction. "He is that one's father and he has not forgiven the church for taking his eldest son. First born is first born. He meant to marry him to a lady in France and as you can see he would have made a right fair husband for a French damsel. But he has come here, for his father is a sinful man and he wishes to pray to save his father's soul. But his father cares nought to have his soul saved. He wishes to have his land saved and he wants his son to give him heirs."

"How can it be that the church does not lock him away for his evil tongue?" Will asked.

"No man can do anything with him, for he has jewels and castles and eats at the king's table. He came from France with William's men and holds title to much land. I tell you what," Brother Ralph said, "those who eat English meat and drink French wine do right well in this country."

"But if he believes not that Christ be risen what will become of him?" Will asked.

Brother Ralph was surprised that Will took this view of the matter. "It matters not what he thinks. Christ may burn him right well for slandering him, but as for now he does as he pleases." With that, Will became privy to the politics of Bodmin, to Bishop Roundsleigh's notes against the land, to his secret plottings with Brother Harald to dislodge Prior Godfrey, to the messages he sent to France via Brother Claude to the Jewish usurers, to his attempts to kidnap back his son, to his accusations noised up and down the country side that his heir had been castrated by the church to put an end to the Roundsleigh dynasty and extirpate the French influence.

Will was astounded by such revelations and distrusted Brother Ralph's report. "I came not here for such things," he said to himself, and regretted the pangs of hunger he suffered. He thought about what Brother Ralph had told him and decided to believe no more than half of what he heard.

CHAPTER TWO

THE HOLINESS OF POVERTY

It was a tradition at Bodmin, as at most monasteries, for those monks who could deny themselves further, to set aside a portion of their daily bread for the poor who would come during the week to collect it. Brother Anthony's lips barely parted for bread and water, still a portion was collected from him every nightfall. It boggled mind and philosophy how the flesh stayed on him. Brother John always left something too, and wept at night for the pain it caused him. Brother Stephen left the same amount every day, a third of his noontime bread. Brother Benedict followed an unpredictable pattern, sometimes leaving, sometimes not. It was thought that he had a cancer which caused him to be chary and often irritable. Brother Harald left a small portion on the first of each month, while Brothers Ralph and Walter took turns. One week one left something. and the next week the other. Brother Thomas was sneaky. On rare occasions when the brothers had a whole loaf to eat, he dug out the interior and donated an empty shell.

After Will had been at Bodmin three months, he was provisionally appointed almoner, in charge of collecting discarded clothing and blankets, and such portions of bread donated by the brethren, to distribute to the poor who would come to the gatehouse after the midday meal on Sundays and Thursdays. There was often a small crowd of ten or fifteen men and women, and often with their children. Some accepted alms with gratitude, some with a surly manner, most neither one way or the other, only with hunger and patience, or with hunger and impatience.

In larger monasteries, where huge crowds of poor would gather and where the monastery could afford it, a small number of the poor, usually three, were invited on each day to have their feet washed and to partake of a meal in the priory kitchen. But at Bodmin where only two dozen or so would gather, the custom was reduced to a simple foot-washing on Thursday which Will now administered at the gatehouse, and which Prior Godfrey administered on Sundays on the Galilee Porch, and afterwards invited some of the chosen poor to something more substantial than bread: fish, ale, or fresh fruit.

At Bodmin Priory, there was a moderate amount of social intercourse between the monks and the outside world. Brother Harald went three times a year to collect the tithes and taxes, and Brother Ralph went to market once a month and Brother Namlis went with him four times a year, to purchase thread and needles and cat skins. Under other circumstances, the almoner too went to the village once a fortnight to visit the leper houses, and once a week to visit the other sick. But the previous almoner had died more than a year ago and this duty had lapsed, while the feeding of the poor continued haphazardly, Brothers Anthony, Stephen, and John taking turns.

It was a poor arrangement, for Brother John was at an age when he should not be exposed to women, as some of the poor were, and Brothers Anthony and Stephen performed their task too zealously, bringing all the poor to the Galilee Porch, both on Thursdays and on Sundays, much to the cook's consternation if he had not prepared enough and he would then be in a foul temper. And if the food ran out, the poor grumbled that the monks ate the fat of the lamb. And furthermore, feeding the same poor from week to week encouraged indolence, kind deeds being liable to corruption. No matter that in these times the poor were regarded as Christ's patrimony, and therefore as more blessed and honored than the wealthy and the powerful. They were regarded as the stone that had been rejected, and the cornerstone on which such edifices as Bodmin Priory rested. No matter that in this theological age they were a theological category, that the poor had a share in God's plan if not in the state's. "The meek shall inherit the earth." True it was that Prior Godfrey had no intention of permitting this event to happen, but the intention of the Maundy ceremony was to obviate the condition of poverty as dis-graceful. The poor were Christ's patrimony.

The curious thing about this idea was that it changed the behavior of few people. Almost no one volunteered to become a member of Christ's patrimony. Except for a very few people like St. Francis, no one willingly gave up anything and almost everyone, including the clergy and the laity, the learned and the unlearned, those who spoke Latin and those who didn't, desired earthly comforts at the least, and some desired a lot more. The poor themselves, who were Christ's patrimony, seemed not to care at all about being that, for as soon as the plague made conditions favorable, they seized the opportunity to get out of the category of the meek. The wealthy did not volunteer to give up their wealth and seek to join the poor, and whenever the poor tried to take their wealth from them by raiding the monasteries and churches or manor houses, the wealthy made a great fuss and tried to beat them off.

The scandal of theology is not so much that it affronts human reason as that it affronts human instinct. · The desire to partake of immortality, for example, has never been recorded, even once, as a motive for suicide.

The poor, when the plague came, fled from the land they had been taught to regard as Christ's estate. By December of that year, only a few months later, they swarmed over England and neither religion nor tradition, nor laws passed by Parliament or by Edward declaring it illegal for a peasant to leave the land or to be hired elsewhere but where he was born and had served, not even their honor as Christ's patrimony nor threats of excommunication, not fear of hell or prison, kept them back. That December, when Will left for London, he met them everywhere on the roads as they fled the plague, the grange lands and the villages. In a few short months the feudal order of England had disappeared, but at this moment, under a hot August sun, Will went to the gatehouse with a basket of rolls to feed the motley assembly, so different in many respects from other such groups, for each culture has its own kind of poor, urban or rural, mainly men or women, mainly old or young, mainly black or white.

But it is the poor of the Medieval world which have become famous as "the poor" because we hear little of other poor, nothing of the Hellenic poor and not enough of the Roman poor except that they liked bread and circuses. We hear nothing of Gaul or Parthian poor and only know that the Egyptians and Carthaginians had slaves, but not whether they had poor. Whether because there were more of the Medieval poor, or the poor of other cultures have fallen into a memory hole, or whether because the classical poor were so despicable they challenge even Christian mercy, or not despicable enough and not challenging enough; or because they were not Christian poor and therefore not Christ's patrimony, they have no role in our imagination while these, our poor, are indispensably picturesque to the times. The Ages of Faith cannot do without them.

We see the Hellenic poor in their classical purity, if we see them at all; and the Roman poor as mean and bullying and threatening the Christians; but not as crippled, diseased, starving and dying, with a claim to our sympathy. The poor of other ages no doubt died of famine and neglect, but they seem to have kept their skin and hair, and certainly their wits. A remnant of the human physique clung to them. The Torah says of its poor only: remember them, leave a corner of the field for them to glean, and the prophets say God loves those who help the widowed, the orphaned and the poor. They do not say, Pugh! what a stench of crippled man!

All poor are rarely presentable to the eye. They may appeal to our moral sense, but rarely to the eye. But these poor, our poor, do, though they are the unseemliest lot of human poor in a score of centuries, body wracked as no other poor were. Their diseases, their bodily disabilities of rashes and running sores, cataracts and poxes, humps and withered stumps, cleft tongues and dirty eye patches, became the stock of artists. Greek esthetics could not deal with them, but the canvas of the Middle Ages is spread with the hunch-backed and knobbly-legged, the clubfooted, the blind, the maimed and the halt, the ravaged with fleas and dysentery, bellies swollen with nutritional diseases, shaking with nervous disorders, smelling of rags and animal fat, palsied and possessed of devils, toothless, eyeless, leprous, devil-ridden, dwarfed and elephantine.

"Where do they come from?" Will asked Michael, the gatekeeper.

Michael thought that a peculiar question. He was the kind of man of whom it was difficult to know whether he was witty or witless. "They do not come from anywhere. They be Cornish men. Some say they be always be here like the dirt upon the earth."

Well, Will had seen poor men before, in York, but always they were working men, and the working poor look different from the idle poor or the crippled poor or the diseased poor. Their chins are set in a different manner and they carry a tool in their hands, ready for a job. The artisan who goes from town to town looking for work does not look the same as a crippled man lying in his vomit. Even among the poor, and especially among the poor, distinctions of age and purpose and health are crucial.

"Have they no work?" Will asked.

Michael thought that another peculiar question. "These be tinners and cotters," he said, "and the tin be low this year and the law says the laborer must stay where he was born. If they go elsewhere none will hire them, for it is against the law to do so."

"Aye," a voice cackled. Will recognized the sound instantly, though he had heard it only once before. It was the same as the whip at his back when he had parted from Walt of Landsend at Capella du Temple. "Aye," Walt cackled, and singled himself out from the small crowd, unshaven, skinny in a brown smock and graceless, forlorn hose. He wiped the crumbs from his greying cheeks. "How are you, man. You look right well since last we met. The sadness has left your face."

To his surprise, Will said precipitously, "I eat not more than these do."

Walt laughed unpleasantly. All of Walt's tones, like his hose and his brown smock, were graceless and dirty. Will remembered his voice and felt forewarned. "Aye," Walt said, "but these have not souls such as a holy monk as yourself might have. These have but bellies and a belly is a nasty thing when it is angry. A soul does much for the grace of man."

Will pursed his lips together and defended himself against Walt with silence. He put his towel and bowl on the ground and picked three poor and washed their toes as quickly as he could. He tried to feel proper humility in this humblest of acts, but he felt Walt's eyes upon him like prickers in his skin.

Scabby, shameless Walt was quick to see the look of guilt on any man's face and he was not one to let up on the pressure. "Aye," he cackled coarsely, "you might as well wash this one's feet whose skin is rotted and keep your own soul clean for heaven's sake. But here is not heaven but hard land and these be Cornish men who mine the earth, these be diggers and copper seekers and tinners and clay workers. These be not monk's toys. These be poor who be planted in the ground when they be dead. Their souls are dirty things to see, fed on lice and such crumbs as Will here brings them." He paused, but Will did not respond. Something warned him to keep silent. It was true he could not bring himself to touch the poor man's toe with his naked hand. Such a purple, hairy, bulbous, bewarted thing with cracked skin and pus he had never seen. Will was sure that if it had been his, he would have cut it off rather than have it dangle from the bottom of him and tempt the worms. Walt knew his thoughts and eyed him maliciously. He had a talent for scorn and was working himself up to rhetorical heights.

"If the flesh be not holy here on earth it matters not

that it be resurrected."

Will was not the man to rebuke another for heretical thinking, but combat flared in him. He did not like the way Walt shoved his feelings around and treated himself to airs of spiritual superiority. Here was Will rising at midnight to pray for his soul and for the world, here he was washing the feet of an unknown man with such warts and cracks upon his skin as would scare the devil, and he felt no better than any man, not even much better than the heathen. So Walt had better not give him a faceful of holy looks. "You are speaking heresy," he said.

That was the proper thing to say to Walt. He loved enmity. Accusation amused him. Red splotches leaped into his grey cheeks. "Ssss," he hissed. "You had a better tongue when we met along the way. Now your tongue is clipped with Latin and you speak neither York nor Cornish."

"You will hang," Will said, "or burn." Formerly, he would have said such a thing with misgiving, more to himself in a surly manner than out loud with authority.

Walt, who was one of those who had nothing to lose and no hope of gain, spat back, "Either will do."

Thus began a contest between them, for Walt came often with the Cornish poor, and as often as he came he chided Will for his monk's ways and made Will's work barren, so that he wished for some office other than that of almoner. He never knew whether Walt would be there or not, for Walt came and went as he wished and where he was in between times Will did not know. Walt was one of the great disinherited of the earth, belonging to no place or time, only to obsession and passion, so that no one could account for his coming and going. Heat made him appear, a social seizure, a fit of circumstance, and what took him away no one could say. Walt had neither property nor family, which root mankind in accountability. Only the winds of love and hate blew him about. But Walt was not an amoral force, nor an arbitrary one. He was a calculating one. Fierce winds blew him about, but he chose his direction, and when he blew Will's way he made his day bitter. For Will, who was one of the most unselfish men of his day, could not shrug him away. When he sat in the choir box the next Sunday, on the Feast of Firstfruits, he heard from the back of the Priory Church Walt's wheezing laughter creeping about his Gospel pages, curling and snarling with as much lascivious snap as his wife's voice ever had had.

On this Sunday the villagers joined the priory church for Mass, for they came to give their tithe of the first fruits, and Walt joined them in order to work his propaganda. These people were not the same as the very poor, who were migrants or miners or disinherited sons or freeborn laborers. These were the villagers, villeins who had rented land from the lord for centuries, some cotters who rented only the roof over their heads, the parish priest, Clooke, the blacksmith and officiaries of the village, the bailiff, the miller and the reeve, and sundry servants and serfs to the manor.

This harvest, the villagers brought their tithes more begrudgingly than usual, for a conflict was in the air between themselves and the miller. The conflict had been fanned by a recent event at St. Martin, a neighboring Premonstratensian monastery. By law, the peasants were required to use the lord's mill and oven. Lords, being what they are even when they are a monastery, set the fees for these high and millers, being what they are, would cheat on the weight of the flour. Miller Mehler cheated fiercely and the villagers had taken to keeping secret handmills under their bedding or in the hay. Miller Mehler suspected this, for the housewives were baking more bread than the flour they brought to the lord's mill could account for. He made the matter known to Prior Godfrey, who gave orders to search the quarters of each villein.

This quarrel over the right to grind flour went on everywhere in England, for a mill concession was a great source of wealth. At the monastery of St. Martin, the matter had worsened rapidly because the villeins had longstanding grudges against the abbot there. One night, recently, there was an insurrection, and a group of villeins captured Abbot Denis and chained him to the altar and took the flour from the monastery larder and strewed it all over the floor. "Christ give millers and abbots and Jews a reckoning," they cried, swearing that the work of their hands was being ground in the mills and burned in the ovens of their lord.

Baron Roundsleigh received immense pleasure from this incident. His remarks were heard all over the countryside. He paid Bodmin Priory a visit the next day, taking his hunting party across its fields and grounds, and kicking down three tombstones in the cemetery. "Christ love villeins," he bellowed, and twirled his mace above his head. Abbot Denis took out a deposition against Bishop Roundsleigh and swore he had seen him lead the villeins. The matter came to the ear of Bishop Grandisson at his cathedral seat in Exeter. He had nothing to say in favor of either Abbot Denis or Bishop Roundsleigh, but wrote a sympathetic letter to the abbot, inquiring after his welts and bruises, and a diplomatic letter to Bishop Roundsleigh, reminding him that an attack upon an abbot was a serious affair, subverting the monastic structure everywhere.

The people of Cornwall, villeins and serfs though they were, were a prickly pack of people, apt to flog a priest if they were pushed too far. They were Christians in the same way a man is a Frenchman or a Scotsman, born to it, but none think an accident of birth gives a government the right to cheat its citizens. There was a sort of "treaty" between the villagers and their lord. That is to say, a state of war existed between them, with each class covetous of its rights and liberties. A "liberty" was not an inalienable right, but something won with struggle or bought with money: the "liberty" to trade or the "liberty" to become a townsman. A liberty was a "license" granted by the authority when there was no precedent or custom to cover the situation. A "right" was different from a "liberty." A "right" derived its validity from custom. The villeins had sharpened their wits on these rights, whether they involved a certain amount of firewood from the lord's forest or a certain amount of hay from his pasture, an extra bread or ale at

Christmastime, they knew what these rights were and could be quarrelsome and surly, husbanding every inch of ground that was won. They took each other to court continually, fighting for a half acre of arable land or half a day's loan on an ox or a plough. To prove that a thing had been done before and was custom was the whole of the law. The past carried legal weight, and so the memories of the villeins were very sharp. Where a boundary had been fixed in 1249, there it would remain as long as heirs were alive to testify to it. Where a right had been granted that would allow a peasant to pasture his sheep with the lord's, his sheep could never be pushed out. Year after year, his three or five or eight sheep would run with the lord's thousands, and if the reeve had not a sharp eye to tell the difference, who else would?

In the year of the great storm, when the roofs blew off the priory buildings, the prior was pressed into granting the villeins a half day less in the year to work the priory grange lands in return for helping him restore the roofs, and this routine was established from that time. So scheming and rude and unruly did the peasants appear to the barons and abbots, taking advantage of storms and famines and plagues, like the Jews using the misfortunes of others to better their lot, they would have agreed with Michelet's epithet: "The medieval peasant would have burst but for his hope in the devil."

Such as these came in now from the fields into Bodmin Priory church, with pitchfork and hoe in hand to celebrate the beginnings of the harvest with their tithe offerings. They were barely, but a little more restrained here than when they came into their parish church in the village, for the grandeur of the vaulted ceiling, the oak floor, the nave sixty feet in length and the new stained glass windows, inspired a respect which their square, stone church in the village did not. Moreover, they did not care for Clooke their priest, and brought their pigs and goats to church as much to vex him as to trade. They came to hear Mass at the priory on the special occasions of sowing and harvesting when they needed more than Clooke's prayers. Clooke could say nothing but, "In nomine patria et filia et spiritus sanctus." They did not believe his prayers were as effective as the monks', for they could see that the monks prospered very well while Clooke was a husbandman like themselves and prospered as well or as little as they did.

Though they were more respectful in Bodmin Priory, they still left room for improvement to bring them up to conduct in a modern church. The air was filled with crying babies, housewives shrieking their hellos, men in leather trousers calling out a plough for hire or a pig for sale. Barter never stopped, for they could never cease to be concerned about it, seeing their livelihood depended upon it. Prior Godfrey's kyrie eleison was all but swallowed up in the gossip and cheer and crying.

There was Adam, the larderer, taking account of the livestock gossip, and Peter the gardener with his five sons and their five wives and his twenty-three grandchildren. There was the cook whose shoulders were set above the heads of the others, and his son with his blind eyes and blackened face and Michael, Michael the gatekeeper, sitting upon his two stumps so that he could see over the heads of the others, and Rufus and Luke, and the breviator, and the loathesome miller and his loathesome wife and their loathesome children; and the widowed Moll and her dim-witted granddaughter, and the two widowed laundresses, Ruth and Agnes, who had had a dispute that morning and would not sit with each other; and the unpopular reeve and the neatherd and Joan, his ale-wife.

They were named for their fathers, like Robert Leboren, or named for a place like Walt of Landsend, or named for their jobs like Tyler and Straw, Baxter, Miller, Smith, Tailor, and Cowper. And some were named for places in the village or on the demesne, like Richard Furrough, Dick Assart and William Well, Dick Oake, Walter Woode and Mathew Meadowe, or named for the day of their birth, like Margery Whitsun.

In the back were the other poor who came with a stray hound to hire for money, or their own backs and hands in exchange for some coins. There was great fuss and noise and shoving about, for it was the beginning of the corn harvest and the Feast of Firstfruits, and the villagers came with baskets of oats and barley to leave, willingly or not.

One needed strength for church in those days, for the icy blasts of air that came in through the great church doors in the winter, and for the damp and the noise in the summertime, the smell of mold and bay leaves that made the nose itch so that the place was filled with coughs and sneezes and a shot of snot flung often enough through the air, and loves consummated behind the oak door as well as anywhere else by pubescents who made their own use of the hallowed ground in the summertime, when heat burned away the dread of the dead and the fear of damnation.

Confusion and riot, merriment and piety. Such hardworking people could not afford a sober sabbath. Restraint burst their leather breeches and the women's breasts popped through, their bodices gushing milk and winks. It was the coming together of it all that mattered: grace and nature, salvation and survival. To make up to them for their other misfortunes, God gave them lust and anger and ferocious laughter. And who could say they did not have the better of it in that day, thumping one another on the head and shoulders instead of sitting in the choir box with Brother John and Brother Benedict, bodily exhaustion instead of ennui, coarse flesh instead of spirit, mutton instead of venison. Whose to say? None anymore, for in six months' time most were taken by the plague and the rest ran away.

Brother Claude went to hell gazing upon buxom Bessie nursing her baby, and all his Latin came out crooked. Will saw Walt in the back row, his hot blue eyes shimmering down the oaken walls and the altar and squinting at the stained glass windows. "That man is my enemy," Will thought, though why was hard to say, except that a man becomes an enemy out of winks and nods and gestures and a heap of speculation. His brain became heated with the smell and sight of the villagers and homesickness and memory of basil and ginger and his wife standing in the church doorway with the summer breeze blowing her smock against her warm thighs.

Will sat in his spot in the choir stall, under the eastern window. The sun streamed through down the oaken nave and lit the spot where St. Petrock's bones rested in their ivory coffer under the choir floor, warming anciently beneath the geometric center where the old fashioned Norman tower crossed the stone pavement.

Up to the century before, for three hundred years, the bones had lain in the Lady Chapel and had been a valuable relic for pilgrims throughout England, for in the eleventh century Bodmin was the religious center of Cornwall. The bishops of Cornwall were frequently resident at Bodmin, which was the capital of their see, and William Warlewast, the nephew of William the Conqueror, was Bishop of Exeter. But one day the religious tide turned elsewhere, to Rouen and Compestella, and after the Crusades, as far away as Jerusalem.

St. Petrock's bones were stolen, but miraculously rediscovered at Barnstaple Manor. The relic was secured again by the monks of Bodmin and the prior, determined this should not happen again, put them in their ivory coffer and placed them beneath the choir floor, where the brethren and the prior could watch them almost all the time. It was said that when the prior had the floor's stones removed, the monks had found scratched on the foundation underneath an apocryphal message from the time when the monastery had first been found and hermits had sat like crabs upon the holy ground:

> Master: 'What is the best and worst
>   thing, my son?
> And why do we keep the vow of silence?'

> Novice: 'Words, words are the best and
>   worst thing.
> That is why we keep the vow of silence.'

Week after week, Will occupied the same place in the
choir box, during the Night Office and the daily Masses,
gazing across the noses of Brother Namlis and Brother
Walter to St. Petrock's place, sensing Brother Claude's
distracted eyes and Brother Stephen's silent
admonishments, singling out Brother Benedict's Latin and
Brother Harald's crisp pronunciation. Prayer and place
and posture and hour were molded together. By such
routine, some monks achieved peace, but others let their
thoughts wander; some even raved with inward distress,
and none could say why an order so long meditated upon
and created in spirit's longing for mankind's good inspired
in Brothers Ralph and Thomas nothing better than the
urge to wage a secret duel with their forefingers on the
oak bench between them, jabbing in the palm and wrist,
first one and then the other, mindful of Brother Bernard,
the hebdomadarian of the week, now ascending the altar
while Prior Godfrey rapped on his stall and gave the
signal for Pater and Ave to begin. Brother Anthony was
already on the altar, in preparation for reading the gospel
portion. He fixed his yellow eyes on Brother Ralph and
Brother Thomas and transmitted his message of
disapproval. But Brother Ralph was too old an habitue of
the monastery to care, and Brother Thomas was too
absorbed in the duel to notice. Patches of red flamed on
his cheeks as he slashed Brother Ralph's skin between his
forefinger and ringfinger. "Oi have you," he said as low
as he could, but was heard by everyone. Brother Harald

set his teeth on edge and raised his prayer book in front of his face.

Pater noster, quis es in coeli,
Sanctificetur nomen tuum;
Adveniat regnum tuum;
Fiat voluntas tua sicut in coelo et intera

Brother Namlis pretended to speech and opposite him, Brother Thomas became quite Scotslike as he recited, and all his Latin accents fell out of place. Brother Claude's ear for language had long been destroyed by the sounds of war and shouting. All his consonants clumped about, while Brother Benedict held each vowel a second longer than the rest.

Prior Godfrey made his way through the shaft of sunlight to the altar steps. He was small, but appropriately rotund. Vested in robes, a different stride carried him down the aisle from that of the administrator who made his rounds with St. George tinkling on his wrist, but as Trevelyan observed of the medieval bishop, "Respectability compassed them about." Prior Godfrey believed in the resurrection and salvation, and that it was incumbent upon him to pray for the souls of others, but most of all he respected order and fitness and his office was the texture of his religious personality, coexistent with his administrative duties as a landlord to care for Christ's house, to keep his books in order, to till Christ's soil, to mind Christ's property, for monastic land was sacred. Prior Godfrey cared for the afterworld and he cared for this world. He wrote reports on the state of the crops, on yield from Bodmin land, purchases of further land, employment of serfs and lay brethren to work the land, manumission of serfs, crop yield, percentage of food taken or stolen by the lay brethren, doves, pigeons and falcons poached, sheep bought and wool sold, the tithe given to the priory, profit on the crops from land lent to villagers; interest raised on land lent to villagers; purchases of buildings in the village, the cost of caring for the lepers, the taxes raised to contribute to the papacy or the king, the purchases of relics, hay, tallow; the expense of food given to Michael the gate keeper, Adam the larderer, the cook and the cook's son who ate on the grounds; expenses laid out for repair of walls and buildings; monies raised from rates on crops borrowed by the villagers; monies laid out in robes and blankets, books and guests; taxes collected in heriot from the death of a villager; monies laid out for the burial of a brethren; monies laid out in gifts to other abbots; the cost of hospitality to a visiting bishop; the transfer of serfs from Bodmin land, the purchase of other serfs, taxes collected from the marriages of two daughters of peasants.

Prior Godfrey did not require religious passion to feel religious reality. His society spoke its language for him, like a pledge of allegiance: "In the name of the Father, the Son and the Holy Ghost." And wise men before him had created the other language necessary to transcend its earthly media. The attitudes of the soul, even contrition, remorse, and repentance, have a history. Ancient Manasseh prayed:

Thou, O Lord, according to Thy great
   goodness
Has promised repentance and forgiveness
   to those
Who have sinned against Thee:
And in the multitude of Thy mercies
Thou hast appointed repentance for
   sinners that they may be saved

The psalmist's cry hovers with the eagles. Down below the priest weeps for his people

Kyrie eleison

Kyrie eleison

Cleanse my heart and my lips, almighty
   God,
Who didst cleanse the lips of the prophet
   Isaiah with a live coal

Kyrie eleison
Kyrie eleison

For Thou, O Lord, God of the righteous,
Has not appointed repentance for the
   righteous,
For Abraham, and Isaac, and Jacob,
Who did not sin against Thee;
But has appointed repentance for the
   unrighteous

Kyrie eleison
Kyrie eleison

How well I have loved Thy house in its
   beauty,
The place where Thy glory dwells;
Lord, never count this soul for lost with
   the wicked,
This life among the bloodthirsty.
Unworthy as I am, Thou wilt save me in
Thy
Great
Mercy

Kyrie eleison
Kyrie eleison

Will's eyes drifted from his prayer book to the faces of
his brethren: Brother York, Brother Exeter, Brother
Glastonbury, Brother Lindisfarne, Brother Canterbury,
Brother Lincoln, Brother Norwich, Brother Peterboro,

Brother Bly, Brother Coventry, Brother Leominster, Brother Bodmin. "What readst thou upon these faces, Will, for I see that thy eyes are not moving. Eyes that read, move, Brother William." Will's eyes blinkered at Walt and floated back to his page with a telepathic message of resistance.

Holy Father, Everlasting God,
Accept this unblemished offering
I, unworthy servant, make to Thee,
My living and true God,
For my countless sins, offenses and
    neglects,
And on behalf of all who are present
    here;
And for all believing Christians, living
    and dead.
Accept it for their good and mine,
May it save us and bring us to
    everlasting life

The eagle mounts the air and cries with the priest. We have pinned a message beneath the eagle's wing:

Hurry, God, hurry,
Destruction is all about
Now as ever the lions roar
Terror is in the winds;
Hurry, God, hurry;

Make haste, Deliverer,
Warrior, king, creator and judge,
Haste, haste, O Lord, haste;
Our night of terror is coming
As in the past so tomorrow,
World without end

We praise Thee
We bless Thee
We adore Thee
We glorify Thee
Father of Mercies
Have mercy
have mercy
have mercy,
and make haste

Prior Godfrey crossed himself and bowed to the altar
and bowed to the Majestas and magisterally, even he,
struck his breast three times and confessed his failings,
and chanted in response with Brother Bernard: "Glory be
to the Father and to the Son and to the Holy Ghost."
And he lifted the host and the chalice, cognizant, even
he, of the union of history with ceremony, vested in
robes for the ecclesiastical moment, in the dalmatia and
the chasuble worn sixteen centuries before by the Jewish
ephod as he led away the goat selected to redeem man:
"May the gift of the moment become for us an
everlasting remedy."

Inadequate goat! Inadequate man! Inadequate priest!

The psalmist's cry hovers in the air with the eagle. The
smell of death hovers in the August air. The eagle's eye
is hot and waxy.

"As it was in the beginning, is now, and ever shall be,
world without end." Brother Bernard chanted, and the
brethren sang amen.

The shaft of sunlight came in through the eastern

window, over the altar, over the raised host, over the sanctified stones. Prior Godfrey received the response and the language of pleading as his birthright, and grasped in his inadequate mouth an inheritance of spirit.

The villagers spilled out the doors on to the Galilee Porch. The sky had become overcast. They left their offers of wheat and barley and beans and apples. The poorer poor stood in a tight circle and watched the coffers fill up. They bartered vociferously, their working time for an article of clothing, a tool for some gleanings from a field. Robert Leboren, the cotter, stood with these poor and tried to trade his labor for some coins.

No matter what their vitality, the got nothing or very little, for every man who worked above the ground knew that he who worked below had nothing to give when the land was worn out. Still the poorer poor pressed and shrieked like diseased hawks, until the village poor tired of them and went away.

Walt went with the villagers, to plead with them outside the priory walls, to berate them for ignoring the other poor. He ran among them like a sheepdog with a leather pouch hanging by his side, with his Gospel in it.

"Brethren, I call you brethren, for never was Jesus a monk and all the poor were his brethren. It is not fit that you leave your food for the monks to eat when these poor stand by your side with eyes in their tongues and hunger in their eyes. You leave your food to ·feed the fat sheep while the lean sheep starve by your side."

He ran among them with arguments and pricks of conscience until Richard Furrough's wife pulled up short and gave him back:

"Hold your tongue. I will leave my food where I will. You know we leave our food for the monks for the law says we must and the monks will pray for our souls."

Walt shrieked back at her, "Have you never heard that God needs not your sacrifices. Have you never heard the prophet say that all the Lord wishes of you is to love Him and to help the poor and that that is the whole of it."

"Nay, I never heard that," the housewife said. "I tell

you what I have heard, Walt. I have heard it said that if I do not do my duty by Christ my soul willl burn in hell for eternity, and I tell you that is too long for me to burn."

"She cares not to burn even for one night," her husband said.

That sat well with them, for they resented being bullied by Walt for what they saw as common sense. They resented the tithe, but unless famine or desperation caught them, they did not care to clash with the authorities. As long as they had their margin for survival, they sought no conflict with the powers. When the yoke was easy, when the sheep dropped well and the cows calved safely, candles and masses and chants were well enough left alone. But in a bad year, ten percent of a poor harvest could bring a villein's family to starvation. So one year they minded less, and one year they grumbled more and passed such wicked sayings as, "What the prior's doves leave, the bishop's sheep take," or "Between the dove of peace and the gentle lamb, a man need not die to go to hell," but neither the church nor the king listened to the grumbling, nor knew the difference from one year to the next.

Nor did Walt disapprove of the tithe and the church's due. He disapproved that the monies collected went to support buildings and landholdings, wars, and travel. What is the profit of a golden altar and a gilded text when the people lack food for their bellies."

There have always been a few such voices. They create a ripple of conscience in their time, but their influence is short lived. History is too much a matter of pomp and circumstance. Where there is much gold, there is much influence, and that is where history is made. Where there is a great civilization there is much taxation, for a great civilization, even when dedicated to salvation and to saving the world, is an expensive item.

How fared the Church as a landlord?

This was the tax system: There were three tithes on the peasant: the great tithes of crops and cattle, a tenth of this yield: the increase of his cattle, the produce from his garden, and a tenth of his wages paid in coin, if he were a laborer. In Bodmin, this tithe went to the parish church, while the tithe of the firstfruits went to the priory. But the village priest, Clooke, got little profit from this tithe, for he himself had to pay a tithe and taxes to Bodmin Priory, for the land he farmed, as well as pay taxes to the church in Rome. As with the other villages, he paid a land tax to the priory, which was his legal landlord.

In practice, the peasant owned the land, but the lord owned it in fact and in legal theory. When the peasant died, his land reverted to the lord. To inherit it back, the peasant's heirs had to buy it back. A peasant's family might work a piece of land for centuries and not own it, as the Abbot of Burton told his protesting serfs that they owned nothing but their bellies, and so curious is history that an inventory of a peasant's holding in 1293 shows his possessions to have been a bolster, a rug, two sheets, a brass dish, a trivet, and his belly. Except for the ruling classes, taxes were an implacable condition, and the ruling classes seemed always to be in need of huge sums. No matter how broadly based the tax system was, there was never enough money. There were taxes such as the merchet, which was a tax to be paid if a daughter married into another manor, for it was argued that her husband's work was lost to the manor on which she had been raised, since she went to live on his manor. There were taxes on roads, on rivers, on bridges and harbors, on gates and entrances and exits. Whoever owned the land where the tolls were, church or king's vassal, collected the tax. There were taxes to be paid for burials, weddings, communications, and there was tallage, the most hated tax of all levied on serf and Jew for special occasions when the ruling classes were more in need of money than usual, for state occasions, coronations, and royal weddings.

Cheating was immeasurable., How was anyone to know if the peasant gave his tithe truthfully? Who could count the eggs his chicken laid, or how many beans he had harvested that year? Though he feared hell, the peasant cheated. He cheated the miller and he cheated his lord. The Church feared for his soul, and a system of taxation arose to ensure the peasant's passage into heaven. This was the heriot, the second nmost hated tax. When the peasant died, it gave the lord of the manor the right to the peasant's best beast, and often his best cloak or brass dish. The mortuary gave the village priest the right to the peasant's second best beast, which often left the peasant family without an animal to pull its plough, or a cow or goat to milk. Dying was dangerous.

Like Walt, there were other protesting voices, on rare occasion among the lords themselves. It is told how St. Hugh of Lincoln's steward went to claim the ox from a recently widowed woman. She went to the bishop and beseeched him to restore her ox, for she had no way to care for her orphaned family. He granted her request, but his steward, taken aback by this, reminded the bishop that if he was tempted by charity of this sort, he would soon not be able to hold on to his land.

There are names and deeds and anecdotes, usually noted in the margins of history, incidents in the flux, which leap from the pages as a cry against the times. It is said that the Bishop of Lincoln leaped from his horse into the mud and filled his hands with clumps of earth, and cried to his steward, "This, this is the way I hold my land."

How fared the Church as a landlord?

In the year that the plague came to England, one Giovanni de Mussi wrote in the Chronicle of Piacenza: "It is now more than a thousand years since these territories and cities have been given to the priests and ever since then the most violent wars have been waged on their account, and yet the priests neither now possess them in peace, nor will ever be able to possess them. It were in truth better before the eyes of God and the world that these pastors should entirely renounce the dominium temporale: for since Sylvester's time the consequences of the temporal power have been innumerable wars and the overthrow of people and cities. How is it possible that there has never been any good pope to remedy such evils and that so many wars have been waged for these transient possessions? Truly we cannot serve God and Mammon at the same time, cannot stand with one foot in Heaven and the other on Earth."

There were court fines and fees and taxes to be paid to be released from vows, for sins, for penance, and there were foreign taxes called Peter's Pence that went to Italy; and taxes Bodmin Priory paid to the papacy and to the king, but tallage was the most hated tax of all because it was the sign of the serf's condition. All the other taxes, hard as they were, were rooted in the legal system and tradition, but tallage was arbitrary. It could fall on Jew and serf at any time or whim. Tradition gave the peasant a sense of security in the system; tallage took it away. The serf could, if he managed to save some money, buy his way out of his condition, but since he had no land or status to barter with, money was the coin of his salvation.

It was not only the rich churchlords who milked the sheep, but the parish priests as well. Our favorite good man, Bishop Grandisson, complained of such as Clooke:

"Such men do more than suck the milk and clip the fleece of Christ's sheep and carry the spoils away. For I believe that, in all this man's time, he hath not fed a single poor person in his parish from his tithes, nor intoned a single anthem in his church, nor once worn the clerical habit, nor restored the ruined parsonage, nor ever vouchsafed to see my face, his overlord and pastor, unworthy though I be. Wherefore I do as best I can after God's pleasure; the rest, which I cannot do by reason of those who uphold such folk, I commit to God, and lay the burden on your consciences."

"Fearest thou not hell?" Clooke jeered at Walt.
Now Clooke was an inbetwixt, scarecrow sort of man,

with a head of hay for hair, put where he was by Bishop Roundsleigh who had bought the incumbency for him, in return for which Clooke said Mass in the bishop's own chapel, when called upon to do such service. Then he was given a meal to eat with a cloth upon the table. He exhorted the villagers to remember the bishop's dead and burned candles and said Mass for them, and grieved for the bishop's son.

Clooke had been one cause of contention between Prior Godfrey and Bishop Roundsleigh, for Bodmin Priory owned the manor and claimed the right to appoint the parish priest on its own lands, but Baron Roundsleigh said that Augustinians could not appoint a parish priest because Bodmin Priory had first been Benedictine, and it was the custom for the Benedictines to appoint the parish priest. Thus the village had been without a parish priest for several years, while letters went back and forth to the papacy. Prior Godfrey cared not a whit who the village priest was, but he knew that Baron Roundsleigh had designs on Bodmin Manor. He claimed title to it through William Warlewart, his ancestor, who had come with William the Conqueror, while Prior Godfrey claimed the land belonged to the priory by right of a deed given by the hermit Geron to St. Petrock, who had fortunately laid his bones down on the manor before William the Conqueror had been born.

Walt hated Clooke worse than he did the monks. "Hell!" he jeered at him, "I tell you what, I fear you more than the devil."

'You will have a short life of it," the tiler said to Walt, more as a warning than as censure.

"You should content yourself with Christ's mercy," Clooke said, but with little vigor, for he was in terror of Walt. The sight of Clooke in a good leather jacket and a gold crucifix on his belt put ashes in Walt's mouth. Better a straightforward upsidedown hypocritical monk than a priest who knew only two lines of Latin to save his neck with. "Mercy," he screeched at him. "Mercy," he bellowed. "Mercy," he laughed contemptuously. "We need not mercy, for we are hardy enough to do our own work. Give us justice and mercy will follow fast. Justice, justice, thou shall follow, as the prophet said, just laws and just taxes, and we need not mercy." He spat upon the ground. "What has a laboring man to do with mercy when he must first seek justice."

The villagers had heard it all before. They did not question the truth of it, for they could see well enough for themselves what their humanity deserved. Up and down the countryside the jingle was: "When Adam delved and Eve span, who was then the gentleman?" The truth was the truth of a fairytale: the heart responded, but there seemed to be no scheme in reality which did.

The sky was overcast. A wet, chill wind was blowing. The villagers were getting hungry. Moll, the laundress, stood behind her dim-witted granddaughter, and clicked her broken teeth at Walt. What had Moll to do with Walt's sermons? Her husband had died and had left her a plough, an ox, two sheep, and some chickens. The church had taken her ox, and her plough was no good to her without it. She had sold her strip of land and her plough to her son in return for his guarantee that he would feed her two meals a day for the rest of her life. A short time later he caught the pox and died and his wife ran off to London, leaving an infant in her care. The sheep had long been slaughtered for food. The chickens were pampered in every way, but aged and died just the same. She shared her room with her granddaughter and gathered firewood for others in return for food, and slept on hay. The room had no chimney, as was the case with all the village houses, and their faces were black from smoke, like a coalminer's, and their lungs just as bad. Moll's husband had been a villein, but Moll was now a cotter, and like Robert Leboren owned only the roof over her head. Robert Leboren's family had held the rank of freeborn for three generations and though free, he was poorer than the serfs or villeins in Bodmin Village. The villeins envied him his freedom, but they did not respect him. Like the lords, they too respected land. Some of them "owned" a good deal of land, though ownership was provisional, for in medieval legal theory only the king and the church could own land, and they were bitter rivals for it. But a de facto ownership was recognized among the villeins, and respect was given accordingly to those who owned more of it or, more to the point, had more acres to work. The villeins might have common hatreds; but they still had contempt for the poor among them. It was this disunity among the disinherited that aroused Walt's fury more than the facile piety of the monks. Like the prophets, he flogged his own beasts worst for their failings. He almost spit straight into Moll's face, who stood behind her granddaughter, her hands on her shoulders, the both of them stumpy and lumpy, with broken teeth. "But, say, Walt," she said, "say in truth, fear you not hell?"

"I fear this hell," he screeched at her. "I fear that sin that will look upon a starving man and not give him a morsel to eat. You know right well who our poor are, Cornish people as yourself, but you turn your backs upon them, even as the priests and the bishops do, for they feed them not enough to keep skin upon them. You are worse than the monks, and you will go to hell with them and burn right alongside."

"Aye," Moll said, for she hated to be reminded of poverty or of hell. There was not a person there who had not known hunger, for in every generation there had been a famine. "We be not hard people, but we be afraid for our bodies and our souls, and we fear hell more than you."

"Aye," Tyler said, for she summed up the argument for them. Words were wind, hunger was real. He turned away. The rest followed, and Walt was left standing alone in the dusty lane.

Moll's argument affected Walt, for he believed in the afterworld, in heaven and hell and purgatory. Though he jeered and snarled and spoke coarsely, he also prayed to be saved and worried about the condition of his eternal soul and that he risked it for ingrates, who "knew not where and what salvation was." He sensed the cosmological split, and it tore him because he could not heal it. It worried him that he had no answer, and he was inclined to accept his damnation. Skinny, unshaven, uncouth, dirty, he stood up like Job. "But this I do in thy name," he said to Christ, "and if you slay me, slay me."

He disappeared the month of August, and Will hoped that he had taken flight for good, though he did not think it likely. Moreover, Walt occupied his thoughts: how he happened to be among these poor, what his business was, what his aims. Though he counted him for an enemy, he was curious about him and he asked the gatekeeper, Michael, questions time and again, but Michael was not given to speculations about anything. Michael viewed the world as a horse with blinkers does, looking straight on the road.

"He be Walt of Landsend," he said.

"I know that," Will said impatiently, "but what does he here?"

Michael thought that was a peculiar question and no way a man could answer it.

The poor seemed not to miss Walt when he was gone, nor to take notice when he was with them. As with Michael, to them he was Walt of Landsend, and that seemed enough. They continued to come regularly Thursdays and Sundays. Sometimes ten, sometimes thirty, and why there should be more or less of them from time to time, was equally mysterious. Some that came more regularly than others, Will began to know and to talk with. There was one, a long strapping man with a blackened face from chimney smoke. He brought with him his three daughters who ate while he watched.

One day Will asked him why he did not eat too.

"Did you ever think, man, that if such a big one as myself had his full there would be no food left."

"Then what do you live on?" Will asked aggressively.

"You have come recently?" the man asked.

"Aye."

"What were you before?"

"A Yorkman and a villein, sometimes a preacher as well. I have a bit of learning and have wrote a book."

"Hast thou?"

"Aye."

"What be it about?"

But Will had lost his desire to speak about his former life. "It be about God's people, as you and I," he said shortly, and began to turn away. The man caught him by his sleeve. "You look to me like a good soul," he said, "art thou a good soul?"

"I cannot answer you as you might like, but I believe as God gave me life and as I live yet to see my sweet sheep dog, I believe that my soul means you well."

"I thank you for that. I believe you do mean me well, as Christ means me well. Did he not teach us to regard the lillies of the fields, and that God made the heavens and all the fowl, and the vines for all mankind."

Will was taken aback. The argument was proper and cunning, and Will knew who had taught the man those words. Still, he asked, "Who taught you to speak like that?"

"You know right well," the man said, and began himself to move away.

This man, called Robert Le Boren or Robert Leborn or leBourne, was free born and a cotter, which is to say that he owned a one room house, its walls and a spade. He had no plough or beast and sold his labor for coin or food. Sometimes he helped at mowing or shearing time in return for a round of cheese. He had learned to read, and had read the Bible because he thought it would give him power over affairs.

Will did not see Walt for many weeks, and the summer came to an end. The records agree that the weather in Cornwall for the year, 1348, was unusually windy and wet: in short, dank. Omens and rumors and birds and oppressive thoughts circulated in the chill. Pilgrims came with bad news from Europe, and everyone waited for the worst to happen, not knowing what else to do.

Throughout history, chroniclers have noted that plagues are presaged by abnormal weather conditions. Some students of the subject scoff at the idea of a connection between the movements of the microscopic world and the atmosphere. Others, equally eminent, believe there is a relationship among all phenomena: falling pressure which stirs bacterial activity; heavy wetness which covers the earth like a mildewed blanket and influences the microscopic life beneath the soil, beneath the stumps of trees and bushes, and leaves fleas and mold clinging to the wool of sheep and in the tails of cows---and pushes the microscopic world to heave and set forth on an imperceptible migration around the world, from nation to nation. In 1346, just such an intensity of atmospheric activity was reported everywhere, from China to Scotland: meteors, floods, earthquakes. Western man, heir to the Bible, compared the coming catastrophe to Noah's flood. It was the only metaphor he could avail himself of for a tragedy of such dimensions. The chronicles of the times are filled with references to the Deluge. The Black Death, when it came, exceeded the limits of human knowledge. It exceeded the limits of faith. It only did not exceed the capacity of humankind to endure, and the children of Noah, set adrift on a flaming land, clung to God's promise not to destroy them utterly.

The news that the plague was in England arrived inauspiciously at the end of September. A beadle came on horseback to say that two monks were dead of it in Somerset.

"I trust you came not from there yourself," Prior Godfrey said snappishly, and did not offer the man so much as a glass of ale to detain him.

Little was done in the way of taking measures. Brother Anthony continued to say the psalms and the Gospels without perceptible difference, neither faster nor slower nor more volubly. Brothers Ralph and Walter looked penitent, but soon went back to dicing devoutly. Brother Benedict received the news as a sign of God's chastisement. Brother Thomas had a very bad dream that night. He woke between Lauds and Prime and walked around in circles, making a petition against the devil. But it was Brother Claude who suffered the most, he who had been whacked from his horse with the weight of a hundred pound sword, he succumbed to terror. There was nothing left to his face but bloodshot eyes and grizzled cheeks. He did not fear to die in battle, but to die of plague against which no suit of armor could prevail, sucked the marrow from his bones, for a man may fear a type of death more than death itself. Will himself tried to think more kindly thoughts of his brethren, to be more tolerant of Brother Stephen and Brother Thomas's calling out at night.

But as no other deaths were reported, the sense of terror was soon dulled, and habit and daily routine reasserted themselves. Will found Brother Harald more of a nuisance than rumors of evil.

One day Brother Harald asked Will how he, a married man, came to give up his wife and become a monk.

"It is a long tale," Will said shortly.

Brother Harald had an equally long nose for suspicion. "Was she a fornicator?" he asked, without ado.

Will was not a man who could lie outright, but he did not feel obliged to tell Brother Harald the truth. "In a way of speaking," he said.

"What means that?"

"It means she fornicated with her soul."

Brother Harald knew the answer was an evasion. He was curious, but he did not press further.

Great flocks of birds flew through the wet skies and unpleasant moldy odors rose from the earth. Will continued his duty as the almoner, but he felt less and less suited for the task as he sensed the distance between principle and practise. The poor were Christ's patrimony, but Will felt a growing disassociation from them with each passing week, and wondered if he were being afflicted with hardness of heart.

He did other jobs around the monastery. He cleaned the columbarium for Prior Godfrey, tended his private garden and helped Brother Anthony in the cemetery. Some of the inscriptions were in Latin, some in Norman French. Some of the crosses looked strange to Will and he wondered if these were Christian dead that lay beneath them. Brother Anthony never spoke, and Will could not ask him. Brother Anthony squatted among the tombstones on his spidery legs, plucked the weeds, and recited the psalms between his teeth.

In the middle of the month, two pilgrims from Santiago de Compostola asked for hospitality. Prior Godfrey did not think it wise to entertain strangers, seeing how grave the times were, but it also was unseemly to set aside the rules, though these two pilgrims were as unspiritual looking a pair as he had seen, decorated with shells from the Sinai, crosses from Bethlehem and keys from Rome, with skinny, dirty calves and uncombed hair. One might suspect them of a thousand kinds of misdemeanors. The thinner one swung his shells with a jaunty manner, and the broader one carried his staff like a mace. They might have turned up in Provence as jugglers or drifters without homes or destinies, the sort of people who make up a portion of the world's population at any time. Settled society and they have instant disrespect for each other. As marginal people, they develop qualities of deference and watchfulness, and pay their way by amusing others.

They came into the Chapter Room, after the evening meal. Brothers Anthony and Stephen retired, as they always did when company came and the privilege of conversation was given, for they did not think the world had anything to tell them. Brother John felt it respectful to keep quiet, and Brother Namlis had no choice. The rest were eager to speak and to hear, for even in a monastery curiosity about the world is hard to forgo.

One question was uppermost: how does the plague? The pilgrims had been to Jerusalem and through the Crimea, had crossed the Pyrenees and had been to Spain. How was it in the world with the plague?

"It spreads and spreads," the first pilgrim said. "You is fortunate here in Bodmin."

"Aye" Prior Godfrey said, who believed that was true in all ways, "for it is not likely that the plague will cross the channel."

"It goes where it likes," the pilgrim said, wondering at this prior's confidence. "We have met with such as have told us that in China and Tibet the plague has been." Though the news was dire, he gave it with gusto, for to be news-less was a state worse than the plague.

"How does the plague in France?" Brother Bernard asked.

"They say not half the people stand upon their feet in three month's time. It has come to Paris and all who can have fled and all who have not fled are dead, or have been burned by the people."

"Men are given to much exaggeration," Brother Benedict said haughtily through his pain. "Plagues have been and plagues will be."

"No doubt," the pilgrim said, falling back upon the policy of agreeableness. Cautiously, he tried another tack: "Some say it is the time of the antiChrist."

"No doubt it is," Prior Godfrey concurred, for how else explain the ignobility of the pope in Avignon, who opposed the policies of Edward 111.

This pilgrim, seeing how matters stood with Prior Godfrey, told how Clement had come to the aid of the Jews, and the second pilgrim added to the fire: "Have you not heard of the bands of men that roam about the cities, disrobing in public and whipping one another and crying and praying?"

The first pilgrim added what he knew of this. "These say that as man sins by himself he can punish himself," at which Prior Godfrey exploded, "Sayest thou!"

"Not I," the pilgrim said quickly, "I know that Christ alone binds and looses, judges and punishes, but these brethren say," he said cautiously, "that each man has the care of his own soul and so may do with it as he wishes and they whip one another right sturdily for this thought."

"None can whip them harder," the other pilgrim laughed.

"And where they go," the pilgrim continued, seeing he had their attention fixed, "there the people fall upon the Jews, for they are so stirred up by the talk of these who march without their clothes though the pope has said the people might not kill the Jews they kill them right well for they would rather listen to these others."

Prior Godfrey was disgusted, but not surprised. Anything was possible with Frenchmen and Italians.

"What might be the good of it?" Will asked.

"It amazes that they are given liberty to preach," Brother Benedict said.

"Nay," the thin pilgrim said, "everywhere they are chased and none in authority give them liberty, but their numbers swell. We met a pilgrim who had come from Paris and he said that not one less than ten thousand gathered before Notre Dame one Sunday and those that watched on were glad for them though afraid to join. It is because they say the Church cannot stop the plague and never has there been such talk of heresy."

The brethren were amazed to hear this.

"Many there are," the thin pilgrim went on, "who join these flagellants as they be called, in penance and prayer, knowing not what else to do, for they say the Church and the doctors alike have failed them."

"In Paris anything is possible," Prior Godfrey said.

The pilgrim was impressed by the effect of his speech.

"The priests have refused to give the rites to those that die of the plague, and the pope has declared that if we die without the rites it will not bar us from heaven. Seeing how he has now declared this, men now say the rites are nought and it matters not one way or the other. In all the cities fires have been set to drive away the plague but it abates not and the people stay in church all day and pray and it abates not. Nought abates it, though the people whip one another and pray all day and weep upon their knees."

Prior Godfrey believed the problem was the French. Brother Claude glared balefully at Prior Godfrey, but Prior Godfrey believed that such acts were as unenglish as Brother Claude was. Europe was to him what the city is to the confirmed countryman. Not one street lay straight with another and none of the signs were useful.

Their cathedrals looked sinister and their climate bred diseases. It had no brace. It vexed him that so many of Bodmin's brethren were from Europe. It gave his priory unfamiliar mannerisms as well as unfamiliar speech. He could not remember to have heard Brother Anthony's natural voice, and he often felt not at home in his own priory on his own land. Oh, Brother Benedict! May thy cancer swiftly take thee and bring Prior Godfrey an Englishman in thy place.

"What be the talk in Spain?" Brother Harald asked practically, seeing they had come most recently from there. The question brought a light of amusement to their faces.

"In Spain they read the book of Juan Ruiz and say the priests may copulate as good as any man, and some say even better."

Prior Godfrey paled, but responded sturdily, "I doubt it not, seeing how they live among the Jews and Moors."

"Aye," the first pilgrim said, "but they war against the Moors and will not marry with them. The plague has come to their aid, for it do drive the sheep southward through the Moors' pastureland, and bless me if the Christian sheep do not drive the Arab horse from his own home."

"Some good there is then," Prior Godfrey said, "but I have heard that the wool of this benemerino sheep is now to be found in the markets more than English wool. It is a wind that blows both good and bad."

"As winds be," the second pilgrim said, "for the plague drives the price of wool up everywhere and whether this wind be good or bad is a matter of whether you run with the wind or against it."

"If the sheep do not sicken and the wool be gathered it will be good for them that gathers it," the first pilgrim said.

"There is talk that two Jews in Basel confessed to spreading the plague," Brother Harald said.

"Aye," the bigger pilgrim said, "put to rack and told how they did spread it through the wells and signed the confession which was known everywhere within the day."

The thinner pilgrim added to this. "In every city good Christian folk have taken arms against them for their wicked deeds."

"And the Jews?" Will asked, "what say they?"

The pilgrims laughed. "Why, good brothers, what matters? They deny it and bite one another with confusion."

"So let it end here," Prior Godfrey said. "England is safe, for there has been scarcely but a case in Somerset. And if there be no Jews the plague will not spread."

"Aye," the second pilgrim said, and winked compliance, "good it is to be on English ground again."

That was the proper note on which to end their talk. Their souls were satisfied. They had shared their experience of the world with the brethren, and when Brother Ralph, who was going to Noir-on-the Coast in the morning to do the marketing, invited them to journey along, they accepted the invitation with alacrity. It was more good fortune than they could have hoped for and Brother Ralph, who was to be accompanied by Brother Namlis, was exuberant at the thought of more gossip. They bid each other good night in high spirits in spite of the fact that they had spent the evening exchanging somber news.

CHAPTER THREE

THE ROAD TO NEWOOL

Maream, the horse, was taken from the stable and hitched to the wagon, for she knew the road to Noir-on-the-Coast better than the other horses at the priory. She had been pulling Brother Ralph there for seven years, as well as running other errands for the brethren. She was a great favorite at the priory, reliable and rarely balky, always happy for an outing in the countryside. The old almoner who had died had put a bell on her forehead and the sound accompanied her wherever she went. When Michael the gatekeeper hitched her to the wagon in the morning, she stomped and steamed with anticipation, while Brother Ralph and Brother Namlis climbed into the front of the wagon and the two pilgrims climbed aboard in the back. Brother Ralph and Brother Namlis would be gone three days, a day to go to Noir-on-the Coast, known at that time as Newool-on-the-Lerin, a day to do the marketing and a day to return. Brother Ralph was supposed to mind his vows of silence outside the monastery walls, but he minded them no more than inside. Nor did he think of the outside world as corrupt anymore than a housewife does when she steps outside her home and goes to market. Bodmin Priory was his home. He was happy when traders and villagers regarded his status as special, but not surprised if he met with the other kind. Sour faced buffoons! As long as they did not threaten him he was content. One could pass through places where the villeins threw sheepdung and bees nests at the monks.

In all things, even in matters of the spiritual life there

is an ebb and tide. The 14th century was not as high in spirituality as the 12th had been, but it was not as low as the 10th. It kept a middling course in matters of corruption. It was not the sinfulness of the monks that was resented, for medieval man understood sin as well as anyone else; it was their seeming uselessness which the peasant did not understand. Serfs and villeins were in the fields, scything the hay for Bodmin Priory and they did not look up to greet the wagon as it went by.

"Surly peasants," Brother Ralph thought, but a holiday soon erases anxiety. It is a trick of nature's to divert the bile. Brother Ralph and Brother Namlis were in good spirits as they travelled across Bodmin demesnes in the wet, morning air. The insects hung over the heath. The sky was low and humid. Brother Ralph commented on everything he saw: the sky, the clouds, the sultry air, the moors, the woodlands, the wagons they passed on the road, the state of the hedges, the land bounded by sod or stone walls, so old, so sunken into the earth they looked to be part of nature and not put there by man at all. The two pilgrims lay in the back of the wagon and whistled and passed winks. The wind blew over the wet landscape, fetid to the sensitive nose, but it blended with the smell of the cut hay which, of all odors, is the most reassuring of the earth's bounty and of the morality of husbandry. Brother Ralph chattered to the pilgrims and to the universe at large. Brother Namlis did not think that Brother Ralph's worldly talk went with the wind and the sound of the scythes and the rumors of the day, but he had never put any man in his place, nor could. He bore with the gossip about sheep and hay and the cost of wine and the price of a new altar cloth and the gossip about the coming visit from Brother Harald's Brother, the great Abbot Roland. "Twill cost a penny to be host to that one," Brother Ralph said, "and I must ask you why he chooses to travel in this direction and not another? I will tell you why. He wishes that one, our own Brother Harald to be the prior here."

Brother Namlis had no tongue, but he had a brain. He had heard this rumor before. Things might not be as good as they could be, but they were far from being as bad as they might be. Monastic politics, as other kinds, rested on personalities, and often came down to whether the helmsman could steer. Brother Harald would steer too well. Every spirit would be made straight, and Brother Namlis believed that his was meant to be crooked. He did not believe he was bound for heaven, and had settled his mind on purgatory since he could not manage the idea of hell at all. Its terrors could not even come into his mind, unlike Brother Claude who fought them daily in place of infidels. Brother Namlis was used to humps, and had worked out a way of living where he could be at peace with his vows and his nature. The balance was necessarily delicate, and a change in administration could upset it. Monks regard such changes as any household would regard a new head coming to rule over it: the old accommodations have to be discarded, and it takes years to work out new ones.

The wagon came into open fields where the hay harvest was finished and the sheep had been put in folds and the cattle had been put to pasture. Brother Ralph dropped the matter of Brother Harald, which was idle speculation, and addressed himself to the economy of the sheep. "A goodly sight for a Christian man. There is nought that a sheep can do that is evil, and I do bless the sheep as I am upon this wagon. I thank Christ and ever shall, it is the sheep has paid for all. They say the price of cloth this year is risen and that the Flanders merchants howl for our wool. What say you?" he asked the pilgrims, calling over his shoulder, "how is the price of cloth in Flanders?"

The bigger pilgrim scratched his dirty hair, pressed for an answer, not because he had not taken notice of the price of goods, but because it was seldom wise to be too specific in his answers. "As I live," he said, "I wear but leather myself and have yet to have a piece of wool upon my back."

"Sayest thou! What! Have you no use for the good cloth the holy men labor to make?"

"Aye, I have use, but not money. A piece of leather

goes a man's life. It wears not out as it wears not out upon the beast."

"Say you wool wears out upon the beast?"

"Not as God gave the wool to the beast, but as man weaves it. As God gave the wool to the beast, no doubt it is suited to last the beast's life, for never have I seen a sheep without his wool upon him except those that be clipped right close."

Brother Ralph would not be worsted. "You wear not the pilgrim's sackcloth," he said, finding fault where he could.

"Aye, I do."

"Dost thou?"

"Aye, see you not my sackcloth?"

"I see not your sackcloth."

"I wear my sackcloth where it holds my spirit up best," he laughed.

"He wears it upon his cock," the other said.

Brother Ralph clicked his teeth with disgust. "Much good it does him there."

"It does me much good, for sure it is Christ's punishment for longing and I suffer most hardily."

"Aye," the other said, "his is a right goodly sackcloth. You can well believe such a sackcloth was a rare piece in Jerusalem."

Brother Ralph changed the conversation again. "See you that sheep there with her udders full," he said, reining in the horse. "Jesu love me as ever I did' see such bags upon womankind, and her young is not about for what I can see. Poor mother to stand with such full bags. Poor womankind. Poor sheep standing in the field with her bags bursting. What say you, Brother Namlis, if we help ourselves to a drink, for there is no animal so good for Christian man. I for God's milk," and he climbed down from the wagon and hitched his habit over his ankles as he went after the sheep.

"Good sheep," he called to her, "holy udders. God knows you will be good to a holy man, for I have not had fresh milk this time it makes a year."

The sheep was flattered, but cautious and eyed his

outstretched hands. "Good monk," she said with a benevolent eye, "As God made me He made me for my young. I have not Thor's spigot."

"Good sheep," Brother Ralph said, "thou art beloved of Christ and holy to the Christian man. There are those I have heard who worship the cow and I have heard it said that once there were those who worshipped the bull and the Jews are said to worship an ass, but we have glorified thee full well."

"Good monk," she said, "I care not to be worshipped, for worship leads to sacrifice," and she moved coyly away.

"Good sheep," Brother Ralph said with an outstretched hand, "know you not your shepherd."

"Aye," she said, "He who created me."

Brother Ralph called to Brother Namlis to come and help him but Brother Namlis, who was a trusting soul, knew it would be injudicious to leave the wagon in the care of two strange pilgrims. Brother Ralph, who was not a trusting soul, forgot. Was ever man led so astray by a female? He beckoned again to Brother Namlis to come and help. Grudgingly, against his better judgment, Brother Namlis climbed down from the wagon. The sheep remained intransigent. Her milk was not for man, monk or pilgrim. As stealthily as the two approached, she coyly moved off. Their mouths watered, but she remained resistant. She flicked her tail and rolled a watchful eye, her milky jewels beyond their reach. Oh! sheep, oh! mother. Brother Ralph felt his lips curl about her udder. "May every good woman carry such a bagful. Come, Mother Maree, hast no mercy for a thirsty monk that does the work of heaven."

It was Brother Namlis who sensed the danger as they made their way further and further from the wagon. His ears flicked, but he could not tell Brother Ralph of his anxiety, but premonition hit him full force. He ran and leaped for the wagon as the big pilgrim seized hold of the reins. He clung to its side with his gnarled strength while the thinner pilgrim hit him on the head with his fist. Then Brother Ralph abandoned the sheep and came running. "Hie, fie," he called and ran after the wagon, pitching stones and rocks. One hit the side of the wagon, one hit Maream in her ear, one hit Brother Namlis on his hump, and one hit the reeve who came running with a shovel. The pilgrims perceived their danger and jumped from the wagon and scattered.

"Christ slay the man who will steal sheep," the reeve cried.

"Nay," Brother Ralph said, "canst not see we be men of God. These pilgrims made foul game of us."

The reeve squinted a pair of cunning eyes at him.

"We be monks of Bodmin," Brother Ralph said, "and this be Bodmin land. Know you not Brother Ralph?"

The reeve raised a scoffing shoulder. "I know sheep. I know land and sheep and the price of wool."

"You be a reeve after a monk's heart and I will tell Prior Godfrey you guard his sheep well." He set the wagon right under the watchful eyes of the reeve. "What think you of this world?" he said to Brother Namlis as they moved on, "a pilgrim that will steal a monk's wagon! It is the time of the antiChrist for sure, as all say it is and a great blackness is about to fall upon us."

Brother Namlis ignored him this time. His hump now had an extra swelling, and he was dumbstruck with bad luck.

They came to St. Martin by nightfall. They did not care to stay there, but they had no choice. St. Martin had not righted itself since the trouble with the flour, and the monks as well as the villeins in the village were in a mutinous mood, each for their own reasons.

Abbot Denis was a bit of that earthly clod the church could never shake from her doorstep, the gluttonous, lecherous monk. Where Prior Godfrey kept a falcon, Abbot Denis kept hawks and hounds. Where Prior Godfrey had grown reconciled to chastity, Abbot Denis remained unrepentant. Where Prior Godfrey kept books, Abbot Denis kept concubines. Where Prior Godfrey was fanatical about cleanliness, Abbot Denis was dirty in his personal habits, and the monastery reflected his leadership. The plates the monks ate from were dirty.

The season's various puddings and meats were encrusted on them. The hay on the refectory floor was smelly with age and refuse and venison fat. The cloth on the tables were stained with mutton grease. The habits the monks wore were wormy and licy. Unlike the monks of Bodmin whose habit was black, the monks of St. Martin wore white. When clean, they looked grand; when dirty, their sins of gluttony were apparent.

Abbot Denis was the eighth son of a French bishop. His father had bought him the abbot's position when he had reached puberty. St. Martin was already an example of institutional sloth, the kind of fate that can overtake any asylum pampered by society. When Abbot Denis came to reign there at the age of fourteen, St. Martin slid giddily and altogether toward indulgence and cynicism. The seventeen monks beneath him passed from covert to overt dissipation. While Brother Ralph and Brother Namlis wore their habits when abroad, these did not. They shed their habits whenever they left the monastery grounds, and they left the grounds whenever they chose to, and went wherever they wanted to, taverns and elsewhere. Bishop Grandisson received letters of protest from neighboring villages regarding the safety of their wives and daughters, and one letter hinted at worse. The villeins threatened more reprisals if the abbot was not removed. They threatened to tear St. Martin down stone by sacred stone.

Even the brethren of St. Martin threatened to rebel if Abbot Denis did not mend things sufficiently to quiet the rebellious mood of the villagers. They sent a Brother to consult with the reeve of the demesne to organize matters better, to give an accounting of the peasants' sheep to them and to pay them for their portions of wool. They cleaned the hospital attached to their monastery. They made a donation to the parish church and bought the priest there new robes to wear. They dismissed the old miller and put a new one in his place and, most importantly, they swept out the old hay and set down new hay.

They improved many things, except Abbot Denis who

had lived through three attempts on his life, six attempts to remove him, innumerable scoldings and abuse, all of which had convinced him of the impossibility of reform. Abbot Denis was not wise or learned or temperate or continent or moderate in speech, or anything an abbot should be. He did not even have a sense of humor. He was a sullen man, without sufficient temperament to be pompous, though he tried. Everyone wished him elsewhere. His father had sent him to England, and had committed simony on his behalf. His brethren sent a letter to the abbot at Premontre in France, recommending that he be made an archbishop, but the abbot of Premontre wrote to Bishop Grandisson that he was pleased to hear that Abbot Denis proved to be an asset to English religious life. Bishop Grandisson reminded the Abbot of Premontre how much the spiritual life of France would be enriched by the presence of Abbot Denis. Then the abbot of Premontre was taken away by the plague, while Abbot Denis continued in his office where he had been for fifty years, evading all cosmological and terrestrial furies that laid low so many others. He buried with grace, within the year, thirteen of the brethren. The four who survived left St. Martin and joined a sect called the Luciferians.

Two months had passed since Abbot Denis had been chained to his altar, when Brother Ralph and Brother Namlis arrived, but the event still consumed Abbot Denis' thoughts. What said Bodmin Priory of this matter? What thought the other monasteries? Would they join him in raising an army to crush the rebellious peasants? He reminded Brother Ralph how all the brethren of the religious life shared a spiritual relationship, and glossed over the suspect nature of his house as "alien." Abbot Denis was not many things, but he was bold and he dared Brother Ralph to confront him. Brother Ralph was many things which no one gave him credit for being, among them subtle and he did not rise to this invitation. "It is the time of the antiChrist, no doubt," he commiserated loudly," and he told Abbot Denis about their misadventure with the pilgrims but Abbot Denis knew how rarely loved he was by Augustinians and lapped at this speech with untrusting eyes.

Brother Ralph tried to divert him and told him of the pilgrim's news of plague and heresies and flagellants, but Abbot Denis didn't care a straw for any of this. Brother Ralph looked down the refectory where the other brethren sat, now disguised as angels, and lowered his voice: "It is not for us to judge that Clement protects the Jews, but in this matter he has set himself against the wishes of the people. There is rebellion everywhere, even against the pope." This laid a broad foundation beneath Abbot Denis' view of things, and he saw the act of spite against him in international dimensions. "The less is known of matters in these times the best it is," Brother Ralph said and bid Abbot Denis goodnight with the satisfaction of believing that he had played a skillful part.

He was not loath to brag of it to Brother Namlis the next morning when they were on their way again.

"Ha ha ha ha ha ha and aha," he laughed. "Didst ever see such a houseful of demons. I warrant they fell into mayhem afore the wagon passed out the gate."

Brother Namlis preferred to presume the innocence of mankind whenever possible, but he knew this would prick Brother Ralph to greater heights of denunciation, so he kept a noncommital countenance.

They met two carters along the road, one pulled by horses carrying bolts of cloth and headed for the market in Newool-on-the-Lerin, the other pulled by oxen and carrying sacks of wool and headed for the port of Bristol. Brother Ralph's eyes registered the cargo on every wagon that they passed. He had been instructed to buy cloth from Ghent or Brabant, "not English cloth" as Prior Godfrey put it, for Edward received his revenue from the cloth that was imported, and not the other way around. Prior Godfrey supported these taxes in support of Edward's claims in the Hundred Years' War, of England's claim to France, and her claim as leading exporter of wool to the cloth markets of Calais, Ghent and Flanders. War makes money, but only if you win. In the meantime, it costs money.

Embroiled in the moist summery air that hung too low and stayed too long and that oppressed with thoughts of the plague, blew the winds of social change, as always confusing, laying some low and raising up others, and sometimes not those who expected to be raised. Sometimes those who never had a thought of changing their positions, were pushed up or out or sideways, or suddenly got a voice when no one had ever heard from them, or suddenly parted company from an old position and took quite another direction or split off altogether and disappeared, as if Proteus were the god of history; so that it is never easy to know who or what, or even when, to support.

Brother Ralph nudged Brother Namlis on the shoulder to look yonder where the walls of Newool-on-the-Lerin rose. The ground alongside the road was rapidly becoming moist. A trickle of water ran that soon swelled into the river Lerin that circled the walls that circled Newool-on-the-Lerin, that carried the odors of hogs and dying chickens, butchers, tanneries, and dyers.

Medieval towns were famous for their noise and color and confusion, liveliness, lustiness and famous, most of all, for their evil odors and their dirt. No great city of antiquity, not Antioch or Carthage, smelled like London or Paris in the Middle Ages. We do not know whether Athens or Constantinople suffered daily from internal disorders, self-generated by body lice. We see the one in her Attic grace set against her chaste hills, with Pericles orating from a pinnacle; the other winding exotically through Byzantine streets in the twilight of the Roman era, Alexandrinely seducing the Latin crusader with oriental scents. Athens arouses thoughts of virgin winds, philosophers treading her streets with noble gait, poets, playwrights and tragedians; Constantinople, city of political wars, arouses thoughts of skills and sex, pomade, musk oils, the scent of roses pressed into the armpits of ladies.

But a good earthly medieval city! Offal, dung and blood! The market square, the executioner's block, the winding streets! The overhanging balconies! The slops thrown therefrom! The towncrier, the screeching shrews, the lepers, the lepers' bells, the sheep, the pigs, the geese. No elegance whatever. Backwoodsmen turned bourgeousie in coats of arms. London or Norwich, York, Calais, or Ghent! We hear the names and think of vintners, mercers, haberdashers, burghers, merchants, carters, weighers and dyers. The syllables bring to mind the economic and industrial revolutions, the profit motive, the ploy of parliamentary power, all the seamy developments of civilization that apparently missed Rome, Antioch and Jerusalem.

The name "Newool" at one time boasted of something more classical: Noire, or Blacktown, in memory of the bloodshed there between the Saxons and the Normans, for possession of the place. Even earlier, it had at first been called Newall, by the ancient, ancient Saxons, in deference to the Danes who had built a wall on top of the Roman wall that had been built there by the Romans to protect themselves against the Picts and Welsh who took so long to go away. With the sea to their backs and the wall to the Welsh, first the Romans thrived in their small encampment, and then the Danes in their larger one, until the Normans came and drove them out. A vassal to William set up a victory stone on Christmas Day and renamed the place Nouelle, carved into the slab of stone beneath a French cross beneath the Roman date, Dec. XXV, CLXVl. The Normans built a Norman church as an expression of their gratitude and a Norman castle for protection and then claimed the surrounding land, the woodlands, the marshes and the river, which they called Le Rin.

For two hundred years Nouelle remained a wall and a stone with a cross and a date on it, and a castle with a keep. As such it prospered very well. The barons changed their crop from barley to oats to sheep, keeping up with the times, until the crusade of 1248 when the Baron Neufhenser pledged himself to St. Louis, and his castle and his sheep to the creditors in Florence in order to raise an army befitting a Norman baron. Neither he nor his army returned to England. An illegitimate son and a determined wife were left to deal with the creditors. He was inept, she was zealous. She burned out three husbands in an effort to find one who could defend the place, and finally took to armor herself. Her peasants rallied around her, stirred by her temperament and the promise of two acres of land to anyone who fought. They held the creditors at bay for thirty years, until she died in the saddle, when the creditors pressed their claims again while the peasants now claimed half the land and preferred to serve a French baronness rather than Italian merchants. The rights of armed struggle fought with the legal machinery. In those days, creditors had a hard time collecting on their loans. Their debtors either defaulted or ran their creditors out of the country. In 1300, Edward 1 promised to settle the peasants' claim, to give them a royal charter to the place if they would help him fight the Scots. Once again, the peasants went to war, the sons and the grandsons of the peasants who had helped the baron's wife, and the great-great-great grandsons of the peasants who had pledged their lives to Baron Neufhenser in return for a piece of Jerusalem.

The present peasants rebuilt the old wall, though the Welsh were by now quiescent and had retreated north behind another wall. In honor of their victory and their royal charter to found a city to trade in wool, and to expunge the French and Roman influence, they threw down the ancient slab of stone and renamed the place Newool. As such it thrived for another two hundred years, looking outward across the water to Europe rather than inland across the marshes and the woodlands to the Scots. Its situation beside a river and alongside the channel was propitious.

Egypt! Paris! Rome! Jerusalem! Cities founded on high bluffs for protection, or along waterways for commerce, or as places of refuge where the dead await the resurrection or where the living find refuge by grace of the law, cities of sanctuary where a criminal can escape vengeance or a man get a foothold in freedom:

And the cities shall be unto you for refuge from the avenger....Ye shall give three cities beyond the Jordan and three cities shall ye give in the land of Canaan; for they shall be cities of refuge. For the children of Israel and for the stranger and for the sojourner among them, shall these six cities be for refuge....But if the manslayer shall at any time go beyond the border of his city of refuge, whither he fleeth; and the avenger of blood find him without the border of his city of refuge, and the avenger of blood slay the manslayer; he shall not be guilty of blood; because he should have remained in his city of refuge.

Medieval English law likewise provided that if a serf could make his way to a town and remain there for a year and a day he could escape his lord. Burgers, merchants, guild masters and craftsmen, tanners, grocers, saddlers, stitchers, smiths and drapers, hungry for labor, gave their protection and many a serf preferred the mercer's mercy to his lord's. The bargain was struck between the serf's desire for freedom and the towns' need for masons. The medieval city grew out of commerce and trade and lusty greed and love of liberty. In her heyday, the medieval town was a whore. Men lusted for her and paid for her in coin and she gave herself to every newcomer. She became famous for brawls and smells and taverns and the rules of the bawdy house, the brothel on the frontier of every man's imagination.

Newool had just such a hectic atmosphere, the air of a boomtown. Graingrowers, butchers, spicers, fishmongers, and tavernkeepers had a common goal and kept a jaunty pace in the winding streets. Newool was the first town in Cornwall to sell homemade cloth spun from English wool and this quickened the foot and the laughter, the vision and temper of its citizens. Wharves and warehouses sprang up on the channel side. Boats came from Bologne and Cherbourg. On the land side, carters passed in and out of the town gates from sunrise to sunset, swelling the town's money with tolls. Prosperity calls to prosperity. Traders came from Somerset, Dorset and Wilts. Barter merged with commerce; coins passed everywhere, and whoever got a coin by barter or labor was able to find a place in the town and purchase his franchise of liberty. Mankind found a new lease on life.

Money makes money. Prosperity loves prosperity. Newool guaranteed Edward an annual rent of L 55. In return, Edward gave Newool the rights to collect his taxes from the surrounding land and villages. In years, when the tax collectors were successful, Newool made money on its rent to Edward. It was a form of speculation, but it was not called usury, for every Christian knew that that was forbidden.

Ten years later, Newool guaranteed another annual sum to Edward, and in return "bought" the right to collect the tolls on the roads, the river, the docks, and the gates. In years when the traffic was high, the amount collected was doubled the annual sum given to Edward, but neither was this called usury. By means moral and Christian, the town's treasury grew. In time, Newool bought the land surrounding its walls, bought the marshes and the woodlands, bought the river and the mills on it and, of course, bought the Norman castle. In time, a wealthy merchant of the eighteenth century, descended from a wooltrader who walked the streets of Newool as Brother Ralph's wagon passed through the Head Gate, bought the castle and gave it to his French wife as a wedding gift.

Inside the town walls much building and brawling and trading. A new church, St. George, with the name of promise, was being constructed in the new architectural style so handsomely funded by the wool merchants and so named for them as "wool churches": ribbed vaulting, an apse, a clerestory, and stained glass windows commemorating the guilds and the merchants who had contributed generously to the church. There was a window donated by the Guild of Drapers, and there was a window with the heads of three councilmen drawn as

Peter, Paul, and St. Jerome. The brass effigies of William de Staple, the prominent wooltrader of Cornwall, and his wife Matilde, had been laid to rest in a private chantry; and citizens who stopped to watch the progress of the building traded jokes with the masons about how in England wool was turned into stone which would be a monument for the ages. New two story houses made of oak were being built, and in the center of the town was the auspicious guild hall which rose as high as St. George's steeple.

Brother Ralph whipped Marean with anticipation and spurred her on. The numbers of carters that passed them on the road in both directions doubled and trebled. Living intensified. The river ran faster, broader, deeper. Two great mills for grinding flour and a fulling mill for beating cloth straddled the river, and a windmill sat on the banks, while the millers sat atop the platforms on the mills and poured the precious grain over the millstones. The butchers, the tanners and the dyers, made to practise their trades outside the walls because of their foul odors, ranged themselves along the banks of the river. Sheep and hogs bleated as they were being slaughtered, giving hide for the tanners and carcasses for the butchers, while the dyers stirred huge vats of blue, madder for red and grain for scarlet, saffron and green and brown, which they emptied into the river so often that it ran like a ribbon of many colors mixed with the blood of the slaughtered sheep. The town's scavengers, who collected the refuse into carts, dumped it into the huge ditch which circled the wall and served as a moat, where rose every manner of odor from the garbage of the human race, to mingle smells with the cries of the animals anticipating death and with the sounds of the lepers' bells warning the human race of the presence of disease. Overhead the preybirds circled in patterns of lowering flight.

Brother Ralph paid the toll to cross the Head Bridge that spanned the river and paid another toll to enter the North Gate, and directed the wagon straight to the center of town, knowing where everything a man could wish for in the way of fish and flesh and meat and wine and wool and dice could be found.

Marean knew the way too and needed no prodding. Neither sheep nor pig stopped her trod.

The center of Newool was a large gridiron of blocks in the shape of a compass cross. In this center, where the four directions met, engraven into the street was the town's crest: a lamb, a sack of virgin wool, the fuller mill, and the dyer's vat; and underneath the crest was the town's motto: "The Sovereign Merchandise and Jewel of This Realm."

The sheep is worthy of this veneration. Among the oldest of man's domesticated animals, she is woven into the history of civilization and this story cannot be told without her. She accompanied Abraham and Jacob, and was sacrificed for Isaac. She kept the shepherd company in his lonely work. She accompanied the nomads of the desert in their search for settlements. She kept man company in his solitary watches for the raiders. She developed in him mercy and protectiveness. In due time, from her tender body was born the industriousness of the modern world. Well may she be called the lamb of God.

On the west side was the Guild Hall where the town council met. The lower story was framed in arches and here the traders set out their wares. From the central beam of the overhanging porch hung the town's great weighing machines. On the east side rose St. George, with its three decorated arch doors, which no other church in Cornwall could boast. In one arch stood the Virgin Mary holding her infant Jesus, in the central arch stood Jesus holding a lamb in his arms, and in the third arch stood St. Godfried of Finchale, patron saint of merchants, holding the scales of justice.

On the north side was the town well where the gossips and vendors clustered. To the left of that was the stockade for criminals, where teasing brats gathered; and in the angle between the north and the west streets a cockfighting pit where gamblers and gapers crowded; and close to that a cookpit where the housewife could bring her meat to be cooked while she sallied elsewhere.

Between the town's two great edifices were ranged the lesser buildings and the carts of the traders.

Brother Ralph drove the wagon down Spice Lane in a state of hilarity, and even the mild-tempered Brother Namlis grinned with his big, brown teeth. Never did he wish for anything so much as to get up at that moment and shout to the horse, "Hie, hie, hie and fie, giddap, you old brown mare, ride, ride, ride through the town and the devil take the care." Marean read his thoughts. Being old and well trained to Bodmin Priory habits, she made straight for the tavern. Not that Brother Ralph was a drinking man or that Brother Namlis was a gambling man, but they left it up to Marean and put their consciences on her tail.

Inside the tavern, the ale flowed from brown barrels and Betty the Brewife measured the cup carefully. Brother Namlis got his pint and Brother Ralph found the gaming table with six yeomen at hazard. He watched until it was ill mannered of them not to invite him in, and he declined until it was ill mannered of him to refuse any longer. "Now, Brother Monk," they said, "how does the dice in your hands." His dice did very well. They rolled and crackled and kissed the oak table while Brother Namlis watched Betty the Brewife, whom he hoped liked humps.

Brother Ralph measured his sinning carefully. He played for an hour, won a negligible but pleasing amount and left in good time to bet his winnings on a cockfight, which he lost, for it was dice he knew best. Brother Namlis was sorry to leave the sight of Betty the Brewife, but outside was almost as good as inside, such women there were who immodestly sold threads and things from covered baskets, apples and strawberries and such sundry fruit. He feasted his sight on them all, pockmarked, toothless, aging, belly-swinging, flabby breasted, and those who walked with their breasts tilted and their mouths so drawn with a stylish pout it made him shiver.

Nor were the women the whole of the sights. Within the afternoon, Brother Ralph and Brother Namlis witnessed the stoning of a ship, saw a man stabbed in a brawl and left to bleed in the streets, a child's arm torn off by the spokes of a cart's wheel, and a wife trampled by a runaway horse and the horse itself flogged to death and left to die outside the Head Gate, as flies picked its sweetly dying flesh.

"Let's to the cloth and return," Brother Ralph said, now that he had had his fill of dice, "for there is little else here for the good monk," and he directed Brother Namlis to the cloth counters underneath the Guild Hall porch.

"What seek you?" the merchant asked.

Brother Ralph had at his disposal three or four personalities: the monk, the prattler, the put-upon gambler, and the shrewd trader. He cast his eyes upon the cloth laid out. He fingered this one and he fingered that one but would not say one thing or another. Finally, when he had tried the merchant's patience with so much appraising, he asked, "What be this cloth?"

The trader appraised Brother Ralph in turn, taking into account his monk's clothing. "As Christ rules our land and we be good Christians, this be English cloth."

Brother Ralph was not impressed. "I seek cloth from abroad," he said.

The trader said less piously, "Seek. It will not be found in Newool." Brother Ralph reworded the matter. "You can not mean there is not cloth from Ghent or Brabant to be found in Newool."

"Aye. There is not such."

Brother Ralph said, "We pray for all good Christian souls, for they say winter will come fast this year and will be hard."

The merchant said, "Neither Christ nor winter sets the market for cloth this year, but plague. Hast thou not heard it? There be no hands to weave and that which was woven six months ago in Flanders or Brabant, men are afeared to put on their backs for those that wove it are dead, and now English cloth is in English markets."

Brother Ralph said, "We pray at night and oft times the chill rises from the floor and up our robes so that a monk cannot pray rightly as befits the saving of souls."

The merchant lowered his voice: "We be not like the Spaniards. We will keep our wool for ourselves and not the king's treasury. I tell you what. I have cloth that came by boat but two months ago woven in Brabant where now is said the plague rages. This cloth I will sell you at last year's price, for cloth is risen, and you may bless me for my honesty, for I know not if such honesty will purchase me a place in heaven," and he unrolled a bolt of cloth. "Here it is. It looks not different from other cloth."

Brother Ralph examined the bolt with his eyes, but not with his hands. "How is it known if there be plague on it?" he asked.

"It is not known. It is only feared, for none know how the plague passes, but the boat it was on was chased afterwards from Lizard Head to Eddistone Rocks because plague was on it. But it may be there was no plague aboard the boat though two bodies came washed ashore in Mullion black as night and men care not what the captain says that they died not of the plague."

"How come you to have this cloth?" Brother Ralph asked.

"If you trust me not," the merchant said, "trust not the cloth," and he unrolled a third bolt. "This be English cloth. Clean. No plague in it, for there be no plague in England. It cost twopence more by the yard, but it will not sicken you."

"I tell you what," Brother Ralph said to Brother Namlis, "I trust this merchant, for he seems to be a good Christian man," but he said to the merchant, " We will return to Bodmin and ask our prior how he judges, and with his permission we will return to you in a fortnight. It may be by then the disposition of the cloth will be known and with God's mercy the price of this cloth will come down as well, for we be monks that live by prayer and not by trade."

The merchant said he did not hope to see the price come down until the world righted itself. Brother Ralph, for his part, had no intention of leaving Newool without his bolts of cloth, and he moved away to test another trader.

"Seek, seek," the merchant shouted after him, "you will not find this year's cloth from abroad, for none will take it, nor would I put last year's cloth from Brabant upon my children's backs."

Brother Ralph moved away with an injured air, common to all bargainers. He and Brother Namlis sauntered through the archways under the Guild Hall Porch until he believed they could not be seen by the merchant anymore. But before he could manoeuver any further, the cry of danger was sounded, shrill whistles and shouts came up from the waterfront. "Boat, boat, boat, boat from Calais. Good citizens, protect yourselves. Ship from Calais."

The crowd responded instantly. Transformed, the social head reared itself collectively with the sense of danger. As one body it ran in the direction of the wharves. The square was immediately emptied of everyone except the traders who stayed to watch their wares. Dogs, children, horses ran. Citizens ran with upraised, menacing hands.

"What means this?" Brother Ralph asked a merchant.

"It is a boat that is thought to have the plague abroad her and has asked to land here."

"Nay," the town shouted, and ran with javelins and bows and arrows and flaming torches.

Now even a man who has lived an adventurous life, chasing whales or hunting bears, may not be prepared for the sudden uprising of a town. How much less Brother Ralph and Brother Namlis, whose lives had been passed within monastery walls except for such marketing holidays as this one. Though they believed in the devil and in hell, they had yet to meet a demonic force.

The trader warned them not to stand in the way of the crowd. The very dogs of the town ran, with their tails between their legs, depressed with fear. The town crier climbed to the top of the Guild Hall Porch and kept up his warning.

But not everyone ran. The culprit in the stocks could not. The gamblers did not, for they never leave their game, and the tavern keepers stayed to make ready their barrels of wine for when the traffic would return.

"How know you the plague is on her?" Brother Ralph asked someone.

"Aye, it is," this citizen said. "She is from Calais, and there has been word up and down the coast that men have died aboard her."

"But if there is not?" Brother Ralph asked.

"I care not," the man said, "no one will go to enquire."

True. The ship sat out in the harbor for half the day, while the town kept watch. It bobbed and sparkled in the water, as any boat in a harbor will do. It was hard to find her menacing. Her lines were etched in the sunlight, her poop deck and flag breasted the air. The glittering gold of her name, The Mary Gallant, flaunted her flanks, while from her deck was heard the cries of her sailors torn away by the wind. She sat in the harbor until the tide took her elsewhere. She was heard of now and then, here and there, and then was heard from no more.

Brother Ralph hastened back to the first merchant and bought the English cloth from him, and told Brother Namlis to purchase his threads and needles. "It must be this way, for to return with nought would not be good either, for who can say what the next month will bring."

It was a sensible decision, but Prior Godfrey did not see it this way. Brother Ralph and Brother Namlis piled twelve bolts of cloth on to the back of the wagon and directed Maream towards Head Gate. Brother Ralph spoke little on the journey back. "It is not a good world," is almost all he said. Brother Namlis' lips were dry, but he felt no thirst and no urge to drink. The twilight was warm and wet. The cries of the animals being slaughtered along the riverbank became distant. Overhead, the birds of prey passed on in the direction of Newool.

The genealogy of Newool's name should be brought up to date: Within six months of Brother Namlis' and Brother Ralph's visit, the population of this town was reduced by half. The measure of not permitting ships to come into the harbor proved to be ineffective, for the plague came to Newool down the inland coastline. The trader who had sold the cloth to Brother Ralph was dead, the tavern keeper was dead, Betty the Brewife was dead. Of the men Brother Ralph had gambled with, five were dead. Of the people who had run down to the docks to keep the ship from Calais from landing, half were dead. The dump carters dragged their bodies to the ditch outside the town walls, and in three weeks the moat was filled with two thousand bodies, and the birds walked boldly upon them.

The town council ceased to meet. The fragment that remained could not sustain the town. Three priests were left to minister to fifteen churches, and St. George was never completed. The stained glass windows and the oaken carvings were eventually removed and placed in other churches. Prosperity drifted elsewhere. Grass grew over the town. The ditch was filled in with drifting land. The wall crumbled little by little, and little by little the town disappeared until a new landscape formed itself: a picturesque one of a coastline with a castle in the distance. The place was named Noir, and it is thought that this name commemorates the Black Death that came there in the winter of 1348.

Today, there is a new slab of stone that stands on a sandy dune, a mile marker with a legend carved on it, Noir-By-The-Coast, 3 KM., looking more like a tombstone than like the auspicious beginnings, or even the unfortunate remains, of a town. Its present name is a corruption, like its history. The moral of all this is not to point to Ozymandias or to the vanity of human endeavor, but to the uneasy alliance between nature and civilization.

These thoughts affected Brother Namlis, for while he could not speak, he was not beyond sensations of profundity.

But rumors of world fatality are not grasped by everyone all at once. Prior Godfrey refused to believe that the ship carried plague. "It carried cloth of

Brabant," he berated Brother Ralph, and screeched at him, "Aye, the price of wool will fall and the price of cloth will rise and you will take to mending many a hole in your habit, for where will you buy cloth if you cannot sell the wool abroad. A good thing that merchant did with you. They made you believe there was plague in the cloth, but there was nought but good cloth from Calais where Edward has established his market, and these men of Newool that will not let this ship land be not Englishmen but devils."

Politics will make any man choleric. Prior Godfrey, like other churchmen of his day, regarded the rising towns with distrust, for they beckoned to the serf and even to the free villein, and if every man left for the new towns, who would work the lord's land? He had lost three serfs to Newool within the last half dozen years. He had claims against the town, while the guildmasters defied him, saying they had a writ that such and such was free born, or that such and such "had bought his blood," meaning his freedom. They believed what the serfs told them, and were made arrogant by lawyers and charters, and they did not hold with tradition but what was written in a charter. Like everyone else, Prior Godfrey said the times were bad. The times were oozing, like clay, into other shapes. The times would not stay as he wanted them to stay: landed and Saxon and under the governance of the Church. Bodmin land was not clay to him. It was consecrated ground, it was hallowed ground, it was holy ground, it was churchland. The odor that rose from its grass after a rain was not like the odor of other grass: it was incense. Such lands as his were being bought up by laymen, merchants who had made fortunes in wool, who bought money from London bankers, from Lombards, from Jews in Paris. Their abbots themselves sold off portions of their manor lands to buy other land, more land elsewhere, to buy relics to attract pilgrims, to hire masons and carpenters to bring their churchs up to date, to add wings and walls and chapels and windows commemorating deeds and people. And they all went into debt, sold relics to pay off their creditors, sold statuary and mortgaged off their crops or gave out on loan acres of fields. Usury rotted the foundation of their buildings. The earth would not stay still. It was infected with invisible forces that were changing its nature everywhere.

The wool had been pulled over their eyes. The twelve bolts of plain English manufactured cloth had been bought, the money had been spent and was gone. The next day Prior Godfrey delivered his midday sermon on the evils of dicing, the wagging of monks' tongues in the world about, the contumely of the French, and the robbing of Christ's treasury for the pleasures of the world.

Only Prior Godfrey did not believe Brother Ralph that the boat from Calais carried plague. The other brethren did. Conviction that the plague would come to England came to them with this piece of news. But nothing else changed. The quotidian held them in its grasp. The days continued with their patterns of prayers, study and work. This ritual was so old it could not easily be dislodged by bad news. Though all but two would be dead within six months, their imaginations could not encompass it, for they could not imagine what had never happened in the world before, and the world, as everyone knows, is very old and has seen many things and is not likely to see something it has not seen in the past.

Plague too is very old, as old as the world is old, seemingly bred into the very nature of the universe as part of the manicheanism of creation: plague, which brings not merely death, but the death of social orders and institutions, villages and cities, which brings death in such numbers it sweeps away the times, which combs the countryside and gathers up the living and drops them in attitudes of disaster, distorted flesh and pain which extinguishes human sympathy and makes man know that death is very real and putrefying, and not an eternal sleep.

Brother Benedict did not think the plague could be as bad as his cancer. He had been dying for two years, and the world had not changed. The plague could not be as bad as his disillusionments. As he became sicker, he became more insistent on not being touched, on doing for himself, putting his marker in his Gospel with precision, folding his robe with purifying carefulness. Those who wished to help him were rebuffed. A sullen disappointment seemed to have afflicted him which he could relieve only by persistent attention to his purity and independence.

The coming plague, in all its documentation, was less real to Brother Harald than his hypochondria, which was a daily struggle to which he expected no end. Rumors of the plague gave him a pinprick of fear, nothing comparable to the terrors he had lived with from his childhood. There was no known cause or origin to these terrors. Monastic life had not caused them, and could not cure them. Almost daily, the terror would come upon him anywhere at any time: reading, conversing, eating, praying. It lasted only minutes, it came only once or twice a day, but the conviction that his heart was about to stop, that a blood vessel was about to burst in his brain, that a force was about to deprive him swiftly, utterly and thoroughly, ruled his life. He did not identify at all with Brother Benedict's symptoms. He did not imagine himself withering away or weakening slowly. He was simply seized by the catastrophic and believed he was about to be destroyed, like a tree blasted by lightning, its nature twisted from its original design in an instant. The terror was too much for any book or prayer. He could utter nothing in the presence of it.

Inevitably, he was none the wiser for it, for it surpassed all understanding. He could not tell anyone about it, for there was no language for it. So he had endured into his fortieth year, and went about his business, and when he had to, went about the manor lands to collect the tithes and learned to live with himself as Caesar learned to live with epilepsy, not cancelling any battles. Though Brother Harald passed through living death once or twice a day, he had no spells or fears as he rode to the Cornish Heights, as far as Wodesbridge on St. George's channels, everywhere hearing the rumors of the plague. He spoke with reeves and overseers and kept a tally of serfs and villeins, who had died, and who owed a death tax, and whether any had daughters who had married off the lands and owed taxes for such; whether any had given birth and how many were in the litter; whether any had run away and if any had conspired in their escape. Without him, Prior Godfrey could not have kept his books.

This year he brought back other news: everywhere on Bodmin Manor the sheep lay dying in the fields, and that was known everywhere. The laundress had told the cook; the carrier who bought their hay confirmed it to Adam the larderer, Poll screeched it one day into the air and Michael the gatekeeper, who never had anything to say, one day said to Will, "There is plague in London. Aye, there is plague in London, and on the grangeland as far as Bristol. It be all about the Cornish Heights. There is plague everywhere in England now and not a spot to stand on."

Will hushed him and Michael looked quaintly back at him and gave him a smile full of bad teeth. Not the prior, nor anyone else Will knew, had anything to say on the matter, except, "Pray it comes not to Bodmin." And that is what Will said to Michael.

Walt reappeared and confirmed the rumors. There was plague in London, there was plague in Bath, there was plague in Southampton. "There is plague here," he said gleefully. "Your walls will not keep it out." Will ignored him.

Prior Godfrey brought the matter up at the next Chapter hour. Brother Stephen spared nothing of his Celtic wrath. "There is nae plague in Cornwall and if there be plague or not, we forsake not our Christian duty."

None of the brethren opposed him. Brother Harald put down this compliance to spiritual diplomacy. Brother Bernard suggested they write to Bishop Grandisson for instructions.

Bishop Grandisson answered in a manner that left them little room to manoeuver in. "If thou be not Christians in time of trouble, what means thy Christianity?" He forbade them to suspend the Mass for the villagers, and he forbade them to suspend the Maundy. He reminded them of their obligations to the poor. He conjoined them to continue with their Christian lives with even-ness and certainty in the outcome. And to be certain that they would, he informed Prior Godfrey, that he would pay a visitation before the year was out.

Prior Godfrey hedged on these instruction as much as he could. He moved the Sunday Maundy to be held at the gate and conducted by Will alone.

So Will met twice a week now with the poor, and they looked never worse.

"Aye," Walt laughed, following his glances, "they're disgraceful to the eye. Shitty-smelling and vermined, and though I am their priest I tell you I would not trust one of them to my turned back. This one would pick a flea from between the cracks of my ass and sell it for priest's gold. But I tell you, man," he moved towards Will, for Will kept backing away, and so began a dance between them, "I tell you, man---stand still and do not hop so---I tell you I do love them, for their suffering is deeper than their dirt. Nail you to a place, Will," he shouted at him, "and hear my words. A scrubbed man is a different man. Soap is grace, Will." Poor Will kept moving backwards. "Pox on you, Monk," Walt shouted at him, "do you not know there is a storm coming?"

"Mean you the plague?" Will asked.

Walt blinked his eyes impatiently. "I mean not your plague. Famine is plague enough for us."

"Plague kills quicker."

Walt cackled with dirty laughter. "Look at my flock. The poor are the first trampled by the horses of the apocalypse." He howled with malice, but still Will moved away.

In truth, it was difficult to absorb Walt into a social pattern. His nervous system was keyed too much to a single resolution. His moods flashed from malice to anger to cunning. He was too intemperate, too combustible for social intercourse.

"I will not stand and dispute with you," Will said, "I must return."

"Aye," Walt said scornfully, "aye, return," and he flung the empty basket at him. "And return next Sunday with it full up. We are always here."

Will would not stoop to pick up the basket. He returned without it, and when Prior Godfrey asked him the next morning where the basket for the bread was, Will told him he thought it best not to bring back into Bodmin what had been outside its walls, considering the times.

For the second time, within a week, Prior Godfrey was astonished at a spendthrifty act. "And what shall we carry the bread in?" he shouted. Will surlily offered to carry it in his blanket. "Do!" Prior Godfrey said, but the next time Will left that outside too, for Walt snatched it up with a, "We thank you, we thank the prior, we thank the good monks, the sacristan, we thank the baron and the bishop."

"Enough!" Will cried at him. "I am not your enemy nor any man's enemy that I know of."

Such a note was in Will's voice that even Walt paused. "Nae, man," he said more kindly, "not in your flesh, for I know you for a good man in your heart, but in your habit and in your manners it is otherwise. The cage you sing in is befouled, worse than this man's dirty flesh which so offends you."

Will was not pleased with himself that human misery disgusted him, but a man who has a hole in his face where his eye should be is not pleasant to look at.

Seeing Will's struggle, Walt relented. "Aye," he said, "so it is. My heart is torn with love of Christ and with hatred for his monks, for they eat the fat of the land while the poor eat from a basket. And Will, though I am mean to you, I like you and I would have you with me and not against me."

Will went back in silence. He faced the problem that night of being without a blanket and in the morning had to request another. Brother Namlis, to his regret, took the matter up with Prior Godfrey, for no such thing had happened before. Blankets wore out, indeed on occasion mysteriously disappeared, stolen by thieving servants, but never had one simply been dropped. "You are mad, Will," Prior Godfrey screamed at him, "Bishop Grandisson will accuse us of unworthy spendthriftiness."

"Nay," Will said, "I gave it to the poor."

"Commendable," Prior Godfrey spit at him, "but how will you cover your own body. And will you give all our blankets away? There are more poor at Cornwall than there are blankets in Bodmin. You must ask that man Walt to return the blanket. I tell you truly, Will, I have had it in my mind to sell St. Petroke's relic for tallow wax, so poor have we become with the price of things and the taxes never letting up. You will shiver this winter."

"I will shiver," Will said sullenly, and reminded Prior Godfrey that it was not wise to bring a blanket back that "might well have been touched with fleas and what not."

Prior Godfrey swallowed his wrath and any sermon he might have delivered to Will on committing the poor to God's Providence who was wiser in handling these matters than man could hope to be. "You are right," he said, biting back further comments, and walked away.

But the next day, in the balmy, summer's end garden smelling of basil and thyme in the midday sun, Prior Godfrey delivered a sermon on the evils of parish priests "who flee from the cities on feast-days and poach upon God's grounds and lure the sheep out from within the monastery walls and do such unseemly things that everywhere men cry out against them as abominations in the holy land. It has been said close by that one such parish priest who calls himself Walt of Landsend and a pack of Cornish men as he controls broke down the gate to St. Martin and made off with the gold from the altars. The times are wicked and brethren who desire peace must arm themselves to do Christ's work and battle for him and scatter such as be lice from our clean selves. Christian folk take from such priests pernicious examples of the sins of gluttony and greed, for these priests who cannot read their Latin take the gold from the altars and the bread of heaven from the monk's table."

Prior Godfrey could hardly catch his breath, his words flowed so fast. "And I have heard it said that this Walt sups more splendidly than kings though he goes about the countryside dressed in rags to win the fold and cries up poverty and down with the monks. Such is his masquerade as the Gospel says is a wolf in sheep's clothing. And such was not Christ's way. Christ suffered in silence. Christ bore his pains with grace and clamored not with noise though the spear pierced him right hard so that he fainted. Though the Jews spat and the spear struck his side Christ cursed not his enemies. In this way we see that this Walt and his band are not true Christians or of true Christian fellowship." He paused at last.

Will who claimed he had no love for Walt, warned him that a sermon had been preached against him. Walt denied a part in the St. Martin affair, but he might as well have had a part, for he openly declared his sympathies.

"You must see that it is a sin to rob the gold from a holy altar," Will said.

"I see it not," Walt said curtly. "Christ had not a gold altar, nor statues and lace and such. He preached against the priests that walk in long robes and sing through their noses and burn incense. He preached for the heavenly treasure. Earth must do for earth and where men starve, gold will not do, for we cannot eat it. I say no more. My tongue is tired." And to Will's astonishment, he walked away, for when had Walt ever turned his back on a good lecture.

Will tried to puzzle it out with Brother Namlis in the cloister walk. "They be not as the prior has said," he said. "Though this Walt has no love for monks, I do not think he is an unchristian man and yet it is beyond me to see why he dislikes us so. Here are you and I no different than this Walt. None can be more saintly than Brother Anthony or Brother Stephen. None can call them wealthy. They eat not a bird's worth of food for the day. And Brother John has yet to feel the sap of anger rise within him. Now there may be among us some who pray not as hard as they should, who keep not their vows too firmly, but all men cannot be cast in the same mold and there are some here who are better here than out there, for Brother Harald would be unkind wherever he went, and so I think it is a wise Providence that sends him abroad only now and then. Surely, Walt has not thought out the matter in all this way."

When Walt disappeared for a time, it seemed to Will that the better arguments were on his side. When he brought the food to the poor in whatever container he could find, what vessel the cook or the larderer or Brother Namlis found for him, it seemed merciful and fit and right, and the monastery seemed vindicated though the poor seemed never to change one way or the other, and he could never say what was in their minds. The one that was called Leboren said little more to Will.

The days passed and his thoughts worked and reworked themselves, for how a matter of injustice is perceived depends upon many things. Most people can perceive it, but a passionate reaction to it comes from somewhere else. Bishop Grandisson was conscientious, but St. Hugh of Lincoln was passionate, though the same religion had bred them. But Will's thoughts were soon distracted elsewhere, for a breviator cane from a Benedictine house in Dorset with the notice of death of two brethren there. Will received the roll and gave it to Brother Bernard to read it to the brethren and make copies to distribute about the countryside, as was the custom with the death of brethren.

"You have been about?" Will asked the breviator. "What is being said?"

"Nought is being said for none know what to say."

Michael the gatekeeper was given orders to admit none but the carriers and the breviators. Prior Godfrey dispensed with the Aspergis that Sunday and sent word that the villagers were not to come. The brethren sat in the choir box in their order: on the north side, Brother Harald, Brother Benedict whose cancer drew less attention now; Brother Anthony who was unchanged by any news, Brother Walter who was immune to any disturbance, and Brothers Namlis and Will. On the south side Brother Claude whose face grew darker each day; Brother Bernard who had copied the death notice with a tremor; Brother John who had fled the world and was soon to die; Brother Stephen who believed in God's will, even if it brought the plague; Brother Ralph whose temperament did not invite pessimism; and Brother Thomas whose nightly terrors increased but whose daytime demeanor became more jovial. The huge church was gloomy and seemed preternaturally empty without the villagers. The brethren found, to their surprise, that they missed the noise and the shrieks and calls which they censured in their prayers. When the breviator from a Franciscan monastery in Somerset deposited his roll ten days later, which contained the news that three brethren there had died, Will was careful to take it from him without touching his hands, and though he invited him to eat, he did not linger in his company. Prior Godfrey told Brother Bernard not to make out copies for the poor to take about. "For the deaths of the brethren are the concern only of brethren and have nought to do with other folk."

News was heard from Michael the gatekeeper who heard it from the carriers and who told it to Will that there was plague in many monasteries, there was plague and more plague everywhere, there was plague in Somerset and Dorset, and it was said to be in Cornwall. For the first time Michael said more than he had to: "There be those what talk of leaving the land. Who will there be to carry on work that must be done?"

This rumor, anyhow, was considered irrelevant, for if there was plague everywhere, where was there to run. In a month's time, death rose from the ground and fell from the air, not in such multiples as was heard to be in London, but one heard of a child in Launceton who died three days ago and one heard of a housewife in Taunton who was found dead in the meadow where she was milking her cow, and one heard of a pilgrim who was found on the road with a blackened face and a black tongue sticking out from his mouth. None ventured anywhere now except for the most important mission. The brethren quietly drew their circle of safety closer about them, sealing themselves off as much as they could from visitors and strangers. Pilgrims and wayfarers found the doors locked. Michael received his instructions. The only exception to be made was for Abbot Roland.

Will noticed that the collection of bread was cut by half. Brother Harald and Brother Claude, Brother Thomas and Brothers Ralph and Walter ceased to give. Of those who continued, none looked with accusation at the others who ate everything from their plates and left nothing for the poor. Brother Harald did not withhold the poor's portion out of lack of charity, but because his practical nature told him that the poor must be driven from the gate sooner or later.

Will went to the gate on Thursdays and Sundays with a sinking heart for the little that he carried with him and for the look fixed upon him of hungry people with hostile eyes, searching for an explanation to his empty baskets. Brother John and Brother Namlis, Stephen and Anthony lay aside more as the others lay aside less. Yet the less became too much for the more. More poor gathered, as plague and famine drove them from elsewhere and they snatched food from each others' hands, snatched them from the hands of children and bit the hands and cheeks of anyone who took a piece of bread from them. They clawed and pried the bread loose from each other. Walt appeared among them again, but had no greeting for Will. He ran among his poor with a stick and beat them for their bad manners. "Brethren," he shouted at them, "best we die together than we destroy one another. I will beat any man who takes the bread from a child."

At the next Chapter meeting, Will declared that it must not continue. "Nay. The portions must be increased again."

"What then, Brother Nice," Brother Claude squinted at him, "do you not know that the time is coming when we will not be able to purchase for ourselves?"

Brother John, who never spoke even when given

permission, reminded Brother Claude of the miracles of loaves and fishes and of Jesus' sermon on the lillies."

"Lillies do not eat bread," Brother Claude sneered at him.

Brother John did not feel rebuked. Unnoticed by the others, he had already disciplined his nature to accept rebuffs. Monastic life both exhilarated and disappointed him. To save what he could of his enthusiasm he had to carefully weed out the disappointments. He was hardier than anyone thought.

When we contrast this with Brothers Stephen and Anthony, whom everyone noticed and agreed were saints, we see that saintliness can be arrived at from opposite ends.

In spite of his hard words, Brother Claude increased in fervor. He took to fasting and wearing a hairshirt and crawling the length of the nave on his knees. Prior Godfrey was disgusted. Brother Claude belonged in some other monastery, perhaps a Spanish one, but not an English one.

It was Will, howver, who troubled Prior Godfrey most. His habit did not fit him properly. One shoulder slipped continually, exposing his boney yeoman neck. He did not walk properly. His tread was always to be heard. His stride made his habit swish and swing around his ankles. "You should not alert the world to your coming," Prior Godfrey said. In addition, Will's Latin was as bad as Cornish English and showd no sign of improving. "How is it you have left off learning Latin," Prior Godfrey asked him.

"I have taken to thinking," Will said, pretending not to understand that he was being rebuked, "and I cannot do both at the same time. My thoughts occupy me much."

This ingenuousness did not recommend itself to Prior Godfrey, who put it down to the nature of the Yorkshire man.

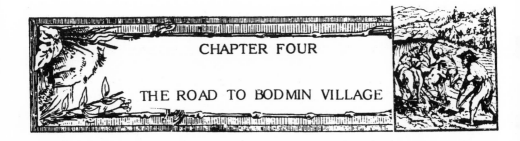

CHAPTER FOUR

THE ROAD TO BODMIN VILLAGE

At this time Prior Godfrey had the unpleasant task of bringing a writ against Robert Leboren, counter charging his claim to freedom. The ambiguity surrounding Leboren's claim arose from the fact that his grandfather, who had been a serf on Bodmin manor, had run away to Dunstable Monastery and there, through one contrivance and another with the Jews who were then in England, had raised coin and bought his freedom. He had borrowed money, and when the Jews were sent from England, Leboren's grandfather had been left with his money and no one to return it to, though legally it should have reverted to the king, if the king had known about it. But he did not. Still it was said everywhere, as these things go, that Leboren had perfidious money on him. He hid it and denied it and denied it as many times as the Abbot of Dunstable charged him with it and threatened him with excommunication. He denied it for three years, and in the meantime traded quietly.

At the end of this time, there were six other serfs on the manor of Dunstable Monastery who had, willy nilly, collected coins when the abbot was in need of money to pay for a new altar. For this he intended to send his sacristan to the Italian creditors in London to raise the money when Leboren and these six serfs reminded the abbot that it was perfidious to deal in usury and offered, for their love of Christ, to give him the money for the altar without charging interest, for that would have been usurious, but only if he would make out a writ releasing them from tallage and serfdom.

The Abbot of Dunstable turned red. His breath hummocked in hs throat. The swine! To tell him what was sin and what was not! "How came you by this money?"

"By Adam's sin and punishment," they said.

They fought and wrestled and struggled for months. The Abbot of Dunstable would not be had by serfs. He ordered his sacristan to London. The poor man was found the next morning with his toes cut off.

"I'd as lief go to hell as be beaten in this matter," Leborne's grandfather said.

The gilding on the altar chipped and cracked and became altogether uncreditable. The time came when Edward 11 was to visit the manor, and word went out that the buildings and movables and carvings and sculpture and chapels and windows should be cleaned and the abbot sent his reeve to London, but the man disappeared. Then the Abbot of Dunstable accepted the offer from the serfs.

But in an ignorant moment, Leboren's son returned to Bodmin Manor where he had been born, thinking his father's purchase made his freedom legal everywhere in the realm, as well as that of his children. But the right of serfs to make wills was in dispute, for the children of serfs were held to be "sequela" or "litter", that is, not human, and therefore not entitled to inheritance, which was a human privilege. In this matter, the Church went against the barons and upheld the right of the serfs to make wills, but Prior Godfrey considered the church to be in error in this matter since "the pope sits not where he should sit, but sits in Avignon and has French advisors and French counsellors to instruct him in English law." Leboren said that Prior Godfrey had the spite of the times in him, fear of the plague and contention within the church. He said, as people always say when misfortune hits them, that the times had gone sour and each man's life had become a pawn.

The problem for Prior Godfrey was whom to send to the village with the writ, and furthermore to take the inventory of the village, for it was heard from the pudding wives that the people were in agitation. Adam confirmed this news:

"They do gather twice a day to say the Mass and for all that Clooke knows no Latin but bibble babble they be pleased to have him light a candle and blow the smoke about. It has been heard that there was a death in Barnstaple, and none will take the wool there to be sold."

This was vexing news. Prior Godfrey reconsidered the wisdom of the measure he had taken, that the villagers not attend Mass at his church on Sundays, for it now seemed best to keep the gossip close at hand. However, a counter measure now would be suspect and even dangerous. He struck his forehead and went immediately to Brother Bernard's carracel, where that monk sat in his accustomed place. "Your accounts, Brother Bernard. You must bring me your accounting books and we must have an account of the village."

As sacristan, Brother Bernard worked on the Bodmin rolls twice a week in the Scriptorium. This was the great daily chronicle kept by many monasteries and manors, the insuperable data of their lives: what they ate, how many candles were burned, what taxes were owed, who died, who was excommunicated, what was paid for heriot, what for merchet, and so on. It is called "rolls" because those budgetary accounts were written in rolls of parchment before the book was invented, but they constitute a Book of Life. Into Brother Bernard's roll went the name of each villager, tithe owed and paid, taxes owed and paid, boondays, land owned, inheritance taxes, size of croft, numbers of chickens, lambs, sheep, oxen, commutation of labor services, coin paid to the reeve and miller, relics sold and bought, wool sold, merchandise bought, fees collected from court trials, fees on poachers, damages caused by Baron Roundsleigh to the cemetery and otherwise, cases of incontinence, adultery, illegal children. Christ's work, for abbots and priors, was largely estate management and no monastery could manage without its ledgers and accountings. In Bodmin Village at this time, the tax scheme was as the following:

Name	Land	Labor per annum	Tax per annum	Tithe
Clooke the Clerk	20 acres	service as parish priest 2 days a week to manor, & all boon days.	4S 6P	His best lamb & 2 doz. eggs
Adam the Larderer	50 ac.	3 days per wk. in priory, & all church holidays & other special occasions	6S 7S	1 lamb, 3 hens, a sack of beans
Wm. White the cook	38 ac.	1/2 day, 7 days a wk gives his son, also for special occasions		1 lamb, a sack of flour, 3 sacks of beans
Simon Smith the smith	15 ac.	3 days per wk on the lord's fields, 6 boondays	6S	"	"
Henry Cupper the carrier	14 ac.	1/2 day every day	2S	"	"
Simon Mule- ward the carrier	22 ac.	"	"	"	"
Michael the gatekeeper	free- born	services pd. in coin, every day at Lord's gate	"	commuted 2S
Moll the widow	6 ac.	2 days per wk, all boondays, incl. granddaughter's work	"	1 lamb at Eastertime, 1 hen, 3 sacks of beans
Wm Osborne gardener	free- born	3 days per wk in the lord's fields, pd. in coin	"	commuted, pd. in coin, 3S.
Hugh Alyn pudding wife's husband	17 ac.	3 days per wk. all boondays	3S. 1D.	1 lamb, 2 hens 2 doz eggs, 2 sacks of beans
Rosey, the brew- wife, widowed	free- born		4S	12 barrels of ale
Robert Leboren	free- born		6S	2S 1D

Some may note an inconsistency in this tax structure, but it is not more inconsistent than other tax structures. It was noted then, as now, that the tax system was peculiar, shaggy, lopsided and misshapen, if not downright unjust. This was because it was rooted in customs which could not be easily disposed of. Sometimes, one simply had to jump from one's horse, as the Bishop of Lincoln did, and cry out, "This is how I hold my land." But the legislated past was on the side of Prior Godfrey.

Whole schools of lawyers labored then as now to correct the tax thing, but the tax thing proved impossible to correct. We may marvel at ecclesiastical heads taxing Moll the Widow as much for her six acres as Simon Muleward for his twenty-two, or taxing William Osbourne who owned no land at all, or taxing Robert Leboren who owned a one room cottage as much as Dan the Larderer who owned fifty acres, but who today thinks he's justly taxed?

Brother Bernard gave no signs, as we might, of reacting to these questions. He sat in his carrel in the Scriptorium, his long legs tucked and folded under the oaken stand, his quill in a bottle of dye and the Bodmin customals unrolled before his particularizing glance. His observation fastened upon other trifles. He knew how much timber there was in Bodmin woodlands, how many rabbits had multiplied, how many fish had spawned. He could watch two raindrops course down a window and measure their orbidity, pace and landing. He kept account of everything: amounts of rainfall, average temperatures, yield of corn, runaway serfs, numbers of candles burned. He could discriminate the difference between two peas in a peapod. Like the old Saxon chronicler who bemoaned the toilsomeness of the office of chronicler which imposed upon him the duty of not neglecting "anything that might prove useful, not even a mouse trap, nor even, what is less, a fly for a hasp," Brother Bernard was the "compleat householder." To this mild mannered man, to the combination of his long days and avid observation, his conscientious and laborious record-keeping, his absentmindedness, his love of solitude and idle watching, we owe our knowledge of this past.

The Knights Templar are credited with having developed the first sophisticated accounting book in their effort to deal with the costs and charges of the Crusades and with the accounts left by the Crusaders. In England, the Domesday Rolls, kept from the time of the Norman Conquest, have acquired their just place in history, but it was the Winchester Rolls which were the earliest to be systematized in England. Brother Bernard began his rolls in 1327, the year of the accession of Edward III and practically the year in which Bishop Grandisson came to Exeter. The sacristan before Brother Bernard kept the rolls from 1310, the year in which the Knights Templar met their doom in France. The sacristan before that, one Brother Hugh, had kept the rolls for only ten years, from 1300-1310, having initiated them in celebration of the first jubilee year. Earlier than this, the rolls dribble into half articulated statements, smudges of observation, without usefulness for the historian.

It is with Brother Bernard that the Bodmin Rolls come into their own. Given his meticulous nature and his scholarly innocence, he recorded everything and left the record of his civilization, which was left to Will to finish.

The homely mortar of culture, housekeeping and management, is taken for granted, and record-keepers such as Brother Bernard are historians without glory. Most of us would rather visit a museum than read an accounting book, would rather visit a cathedral and have our souls stirred with its splendor than be inundated with daily thinginess. Brother Bernard entered Bodmin as a young man in search of God and in need of spiritual comfort. We do not know if he found these, but he left us, his heirs, his accounting book, matter enough for spiritual contemplation.

Similarly, Prior Godfrey never acknowledged his debt to Brother Bernard, but simply called for his accounts, as it was his right to do. He then perused them for the year beginning at the previous Michaelmas, sensitive as he was to the coming visit of Abbot Roland. While Abbot

Roland had no authority over Bodmin's budget, his reputation was so august that Prior Godfrey wanted to set his records in order to assure himself of his administrative skills as a way of acquiring the necessary psychological weight for the coming visit. Going over the accounts, he fastened upon the matter of Leboren as an untidy loose string in the legal machinery of the manor.

It is the impulse towards efficiency that sets such motions in order. Prior Godfrey deliberated a day about whom to send on this mission, and decided to send Will, unprecedented as it was to send a novice. But the times were unprecedented. Go down the list! His bailiff was in Barnstaple with a writ against Bishop Roundsleigh for damages done to the cemetery grounds; his reeve was on the grangelands; Brother John was pubescent and vulnerable and, moreover, liable to be kidnapped back by Clooke the priest, who was Bishop Roundsleigh's man; Brother Thomas was deranged; Brother Harald was on the grangelands with the reeve; Brother Claude was not to be trusted; Brother Namlis could not speak; Brother Bernard was absentminded and might wander to the wrong village; Brother Walter would never speak; Prior Godfrey had taken away the privilege of leaving the monastery grounds from Brother Ralph; Brother Stephen and Brother Anthony would not approve of this mission and would refuse to go; and Brother Benedict was in too much pain to walk.

Will was sent. He left after Mass and a little breakfast, and followed the footpath through the pasture and the meadow. A haze of morning summer heat lay on the fields, a silvery, half dewy, half podseed atmospheric sloth. The air had a perfume in it that makes a man think embarrassing thoughts, and Will's thoughts spilled out over the countryside. Ah, Will! World lover, wounded by your worldly wife. She lay by your side as close as Adam's rib, when the heavens were your covering. Langorous Will! Regretful Will! No sooner did he think these thoughts than a shadow ran beside him, the shadow of the gone years that lay inside his brain, as powerful a sensation as any he had ever had, so that he wondered why he could not reach out and touch the shadow that walked beside him, the shadow of his sensuous past. He had loved his wife in that past, and a man who has once loved a woman and cannot get her ways, domestic and sexual, out of his mind, will hate her if he strives not to love her.

"You are not that man anymore," he reminded himself, remembering how he had passed this way three months ago in leather pants and vest in the ringing of vespers, seeking to shed his Yorkshire self. "You are not that man and it behooves you to remember your gait as Prior Godfrey has taught you and not to slump. It behooves you to walk in Christ's time and not your own." He shifted gear and arranged his walk to accommodate these thoughts, so that he could enter the village with the air of purpose which befits a man of the habit who carries a legal writ. But like most human beings anywhere at any time, he would rather not have been the bearer of bad news, but seeing that he was, the mundane past seemed lighter than the spiritual present. Dichotomous reality took revenge on Will: a shadow walked beside him.

Bodmin Village was in the distance, a lane of cottages and crofts, with the perennial river running beside it, the sheep in the field, the smell of dung and hay, apples and marigold, daisies and thyme, basil and mint. One could tell what the season was by whether crop or cattle were in the field. One could tell the season by the odors on the land.

The village was not a small version of the town. It was an altogether different social unit. Its economy was agricultural, not trade. There were craftsmen and officials, such as the bailiff and the reeve, but there were no tradesmen and rarely a guild. The legal basis of rights in the village rested on custom. In the town it rested on a charter. Hence, the villager was conservative, "backward-looking," from whence he derived his rights; while the townsman came to suspect tradition as a deterrent to his "liberties" which could only be granted and bought, created "newly" to meet the new situation. Thus the townsman came to depend on law and books. He nourished the growing profession of lawyers as he won the right to establish municipal courts and town councils, while the villager's case would be tried by a different body of men, the ecclesiastical or the manor court. Legally, the village and the church belonged to the feudal system. The villagers were as expert at law as the lawyers of their day, for they were just as zealous of their rights as burghers and tradesmen were. But their rights were rooted in the past and their memories were an adjunct of the legal framework, and the personalities of the villagers, as those of the townspeople, were partly shaped by their legal status.

Will went to the church first, to pay respect to Clooke because good manners told him to do that. The villagers were still there, and all heads turned to look at Will. As sometimes happens in such a situation, for no ostensible reason, a psychosis of estrangement rose out of nowhere. Will felt conspicuous and out of place, disjointed and peculiar in his monk's habit. The shadow of his former self became more insistent. He missed his brother, Davey. He missed Rug's shaggy body and her leanto walk, braving every hillside storm with him. God keep you, Rug, Will thought, as he took his seat, feeling displaced in the church, Christian though he was.

Clooke, the clerk, was flattered by Will's appearance, though Will intended him no flattery, only elementary respect. Nor should Clooke have been flattered, seeing he was Bishop Roundsleigh's man, as could be seen by the appointments in his church: the tapestry on the rood screen depicting the conquest of William the Conqueror with Bishop Roundsleigh's ancestor leading the troops, the alabaster statue of the Virgin Mary bearing the likeness of the bishop's grandmother, and the stained glass window with the portrait of Bishop Roundsleigh in knight's armor, combatting a three-tailed devil who bore the likeness of Prior Godfrey.

Clooke, out of his peasant leather clothes and in vestments, stood beneath the glorious windowed allegory of man's struggle with good and evil, through which streamed the September sun giving Bishop Roundsleigh's mitred face a wash of ochre gold.

All ninety mature citizens of Bodmin were in the church that morning. They flung themselves upon hope in extremity, conscious as they were that their lives were not what they should have been, often fornicated, often gossiped in church, often slept through prayers, often ridiculed Clooke, and more often never went to church. Now they were rarely out of church, except to eat and sleep. Like everyone else, they thought of God mostly when things went wrong, relegating Him to the compartment of disaster until He naturally got a bad reputation.

On the one hand, they felt reprieved seeing that there was still no plague in Bodmin, wondering if, like Noah, they had been set apart for survival, and praying it was so. On the other hand, the news was not yet so bad anywhere that prayer might not help, unlike in Europe where prayer had never helped. But they had sore doubts about Clooke who only knew "in nomine patria et filia et spiritus sancta," and made the rest up as he went along. But since he was Bishop Roundsleigh's man, they were advised to let well enough alone. It would be easier to remove a Roman wall than to remove Clooke.

They instituted triple Masses, though rumors reached them of other remedies. It was heard that the pope in Avignon sat surrounded by six vast vats of boiling water, from which rose a constant vapor which was supposed to purify the air and which kept the auditors at bay. Almost anything was considered likely to help, and in the end everything failed. By that Easter the village of Bodmin was gone. The door of the parish church flapped open in the winter wind and no one came to shut it. Bishop Roundsleigh gazed from the stained glass window at an empty church for centuries to come, and fought Prior Godfrey to no avail. Within three months, Moll's granddaughter was killed by the villagers driven crazy with terror and the deaths of their children. The voice of Richard Strawyer, whose wife and three children died within a week, cried out that the devil must be destroyed, and the villagers passed from the worship of Christ to murdering their neighbors without a change of constitution. Moll herself survived the plague, but she remained deaf from the events of that night, hearing nothing more of the world but the voice of her granddaughter calling for help.

This morning they sat in church and prayed to prevent this future, though it was no more than three months away. One would have thought that a hint of something so close would be upon their faces. But the only expressions they had were resentment towards Will for being there, and after church they jostled him in the street. It was guessed what he was doing there, for they had a sharp nose for legal affairs and no love for any who came on such errands. Richard Strawyer said, "Never in the realm of the land has it been heard that a man's grandson has lost his freedom once bought and paid for with coin."

"Aye," Cupper the carrier said, "but the custom of one manor does not prevail on another. His grandad bought his blood on Dunstaple Manor and it prevails not on Bodmin manor."

"The custom," Robert the Reeve said, 'is for each manor and Leboren should have stayed where his grandad bought his blood."

"Aye," mocked Joanna, Leboren's wife, a stoutish woman with a blackened face from the cooking pit, "and what freedom is it if a man can't move about?"

"It is law and custom," the reeve said," "and each manor goes its way and you must abide by this."

Joanna almost swung a child at his head, "Aye," she said with fury, "and me and my man will go ours," and she walked away, a child in her arm, one at her skirt, and one by the hand. "Good day," Leboren said, "I will go with my family." He carried his Bible in the crook of his elbow and struck an aloof pose, one he felt proper to a man who could read.

Will was dismayed to see that Leboren, whose name he had not known, was the man he had spoken to outside the priory gate. As any man, Will was hoping to find the man he had to bring a writ against to be unlikeable and deserving of punishment.

"What say you of this talk of plague," Leboren asked Will.

The topic was singularly not uppermost in Will's mind at the moment. "I suppose we must pray it comes not here," he said sententiously.

"Aye," Leboren said, eyeing him, "have you no other recommendations or advice or remedies?"

"I have not."

Joanna clicked her teeth. In deference to this, Will and Leboren walked the rest of the way silently, Joanna with a child in her arms, and one by the hand and the other at her skirt, and Leboren with the Bible in the crook of his arm.

"I have read the Bible," he said after a while, "and I have read that there has been plague among the children of God."

"There has been plague always," Will said ineptly.

"So it seems, which is a strange thing if you consider how much praying man has done to be rid of it."

Bodmin Village was laid out along one main road through which the sheep could be driven, and they followed this to Leboren's house in further silence, for Will felt that Leboren was prodding him and he surlily resisted. Will understood the reservoir of doubt that lay underneath everything, but he had no mind to say it to a man he had a writ against.

As they came to their cottage, Joanna pushed in before her husband. Unlike him she made little show of manners. He made a show of manners because it amused him to do so, but the things which amused him did not amuse her, and vice versa. She was sullen because she could not say she "had fields," and he said that "fields were not worth worms if a man could not stray from them." She said she had no wish to go anywhere. "I had no thought to marry a travelling man."

Her mockery was a gnat on his tail.

"'Taint travelling, but being," he quarrelled.

"Being?" she mocked, "how is it being if you have your freedom but no land," and so on and on between them the whole of their married life.

In Will's presence, Leboren lay low and played cool, while Joanna's shoulders let it be known that she'd be damned if she'd let a cockless rooster crow to her man. So it was turnabout and turnabout with these two, smirks and eyebrow lifts, and "I told you so" glances. After Will was gone, Joanna said she'd laugh her head off if she had to pull a plough on her back to pay the court fees to the priory, "though you win your case." And Leboren said drily, whittling on a piece of wood, that if she were so hot for fields she should not mind to pull the plough on her back for them.

It was peasants such as these who had given rise to the metaphor of the black rage, for their skins were always black from the smokepit in their huts. The poor did not have chimneys in those days, and the smoke settled everywhere: on the table, the chairs, the mats, their faces and in their lungs. They came to be the color of smoke, and when they quarrelled their faces turned even darker.

This room was not unfamiliar to Will, except for one piece of furniture in it, which was a rocking chair. Otherwise, there was the immemorial straw pallets, the one woolen blanket, a table, a brass pot, a candlestick, some wooden plates. The unfamiliar item was a rocking chair over which the three girls fought as to who should have the first ride in it.

"Not any," Leboren said, "for we must let our guest try it first."

Will declined the favor. The thing moved about by itself. His fear was flattering. "Try it," Leboren urged. Will refused. "What," Leboren said, "if a child can work it, why cannot a grown man?"

Fear is not respectable and Will remembered his writ and his errand, and so hitched up his habit and carefully lowered himself down into the thing. But the chair moved away from him and he jumped from it in alarm.

"Control it," Leboren said. "You must work it with your own feet," and he gave Will a demonstration. Curiosity replaced fear. Nor was Will the man to hold out indefinitely for the sake of dignity. He got back into the chair and this time managed it.

"How came you to think of such a strange creature?" he asked.

"One day I was looking at my scythe and thought how would it be to set a chair upon it. I made such a chair with but one curving piece in the center, but it fell to a side. Then I thought you cannot make a wagon with a single set of wheels and how it must have an axle and so on."

"You are a clever man," Will said.

"Aye," Joanna said, with a glinting voice.

"You are a good man," Leboren said, pressing him. Joanna kept silent. Will understood. He rose from the chair. "I mean you no harm," he said, and laid the writ on the table.

"Aye," Leboren said, "leave it where it is. It makes no difference here, for the Gospel says in Christ all men are free."

It is strange what different messages are read from the same book. Here Prior Godfrey and such as Brother Benedict and Brother Harald read the Gospel everyday, but when such as Leboren quoted from it they pressed their lips together and said that the times had given every man the Gospel to read as a weapon. Will felt the cutting edge. He sat upon it. It rocked beneath him. He could not steady it. He felt the cunning of Leboren's words and felt the cunning in his eyes and the watchfulness of his family, their balance between courtesy and hostility.

He returned to Bodmin Priory by twilight. He heard the Vesper bells, but he felt little anticipation in passing through the gate this time. He understood very well now why Walt execrated his order, but when he stood at breakfast the next morning in the refectory and saw the faces of his brethren he could not judge them guilty of inhumanity, except perhaps Brother Harald. None carried the corporate image on him. Certainly, Brother Namlis wished no man ill. Surely a man who has been so injured by his own mother had a right to a little hatred, but Will had never found any in him. Bodmin had given Brother

Namlis refuge. Will could not feel Walt's rage at this. He felt as many before him, and after him have felt: that he lived in a world not of his own choosing and was the bearer of confusing messages. But when he heard a week later that Leboren had bolted for Newool, he thanked God.

So his thoughts came to him in confusion and contradictoriness, and no one thought lay smoothly for long.

CHAPTER FIVE

THE TREASURY OF HEAVEN

Abbot Roland's visit anywhere in the Europe of his day caused a moral excitation. Some said the mantle of St. Bernard had fallen to him.

To celebrate the occasion of such a visitor Prior Godfrey preached a sermon on the treasury in heaven, based on the latest spiritual enunciation. In addition, he gave the cook, Adam the larderer, and the pudding wives special instructions for the preparations of meals, and sent the bailiff to retain a victualer on behalf of the meats to be served. He ordered a fire to be set in the calefactory though it was only September, and the lambskins and the fur capes to be taken from the closets and set out for the use of Abbot Roland and his company: his secretary, a scribe, a servant, and the abbot's physician who was said to be a converted Jew. Preparations for sermon and ceremony were done on behalf of Bodmin's prestige, preparations for warmth were done on behalf of the abbot's famous fraility.

It was a thing often forgotten about him in his presence, and when remembered was for the sake of underlining with legendary awesomeness his personal and public achievements.

Abbot Roland was one of those who suffered from multiple disorders: a spinal defect, stomach problems, migraine, inexplicable fevers, an undiagnosable form of arthritis, and having suffered from them practically from birth, had acquired the elaborate gentleness of the sick child. He had learned at an early age to suffer unostentatiously.

His complexion was pale. The veins on his forehead were visible under his sparse hair, his shoulders were narrow. He was barely five feet two, always cold, his toes, his fingers, his bones. Except for his shawl, he never yielded to the temptation of physical comfort, or to the need for varieties in food, and had eaten the same meals every day for thirty-five years. His private room was the traditional one for a monk: stone and square, with a narrow bed, a reading lectern, a candle and a crucifix. He wrote, standing at his lectern: his accounts, his state letters, his personal correspondence, his treatises on the nature of God, love, man, etc. As with other monks or philosophers of his time, it was a novel experience to read or think while sitting; tradition was still in favor of the discipline of thinking while on one's feet.

In the autumn of every year, since he had become a monk, he retired for forty days to a retreat in the Jura Mountains, where he enjoyed the silence and the space he seemed always to crave, as if the breath allotted him by the religious world for his small frame was not sufficient. This season was the first in fourteen years he had not gone to the mountains, but came to England instead. He was pleased to be back in his native land, but felt he had missed a step he would not recover. He felt the wound of not being in his adopted landscape which had ingratiated itself into his spiritual year.

Though it escaped the attention of his biographers, his survival through childhood was wholly unpredictable, and wholly unpredictable his moral survival. In another tradition, he might have been given to the herdsman to be disposed of in the forest. In his own home in the family castle in York, his father had left him to his mother and his mother had left him to a servant. As is sometimes and also unaccountably the case, this one had compassion on his skinny, knobbly legs, his malformed back, and his unfortunate face. Being ignored, herself useless, elderly, childless, homely, she became his companion. A mat was set in his room for her to sleep on. She died when he was fifteen, having lived long enough for her to accomplish the work she had to do. The church was the next step. When the servant died, his parents could think of nothing else. At that time, the single piece of good fortune that could happen to an unpretentious, homely but intelligent youth, was to come to the attention of a wise teacher. Roland's potential, housed as it was in a sickly adolescent, was not wasted on Abbot Thomas of the Cistercian Monastery at Fountaineville, outside York. He nursed him and tutored him and within five years, though Roland did not grow another inch, he had mastered Greek, Latin, and Hebrew, and his life's pattern as a scholar was set. But Abbot Thomas decided there was more to be had from his student, and sent him to study in the papal court where he could learn church politics and ecclesiastical diplomacy. Roland also discovered that the climate in France was beneficial to his health. In spite of this, he asked to return to England, but Abbot Thomas, having learned that the climate in France favored his pupil, refused the request.

As is so often the case with a decision that seems temporary, it became permanent. Abbot Thomas aged and died in the Abbey of Fountaineville which he had not left for fifty years, and Abbot Roland did not see him again; but he had received from him the necessary brace to withstand the nature of the papal court. Roland arrived in Avignon, the corpuscular heart of Christianity in 1313, at the age of twenty-three.

Whatever else may be said of its spiritual atmosphere, Avignon was in many ways an average Medieval city, enclosed by the usual walls, possessed of the usual muddy streets, bad air, bad odors, narrow lanes, badly ventilated houses and exorbitant rents, by crafts people of all kinds, butchers, goldsmiths, furriers, masons, musicians, book illuminators, and many, many lawyers. Finally, the usual suburbs and settlements sprang up outside the walls, pushing the city into the countryside with sprawling cosmopolitan pressure.

The popes came in 1305, bringing to a provincial Provencal town the international and urbane climate attendant upon the papacy in those days. That the popes came here, into the heart of the heretical Midi which they had labored to extirpate and had all but destroyed by 1251, leaving only the arches of the Pont St. Benezet, is surely an irony. With them came guards and servants, couriers, usurers, prostitutes, thieves, bureaucrats, financiers, diplomats, ambassadors, pimps, artists, scholars, and foreigners of all sorts. The Germans formed a confraternity, the Italians founded banking houses, the Tuscans a school of painters, and the French an establishment of architects.

Guillaume Mollat, in The Popes of Avignon, gives three hundred as the number that were usually in attendance upon the pope: over a hundred knights and squires, doorkeepers of various kinds: third-hand porters who opened and closed the first ring of outside doors, second-hand porters who opened the second ring of inner doors, and the master-porters who opened the first ring of doors to the pope's private chambers; sergeants-at-arms, varying in number throughout the century from 23 to 72; thirty-two chaplains who sang matins at midnight and bore the cross before the Holy Pope when he rode on horseback or appeared in procession; a subdeacon who read to him at mealtimes, and a priest who handed him the psalter when he wished to recite Vespers; chamberlains and kitchen staff, scribes and notaries, wine butlers, two masters of the buttery who bought the corn, bread, salt, cheese, etc., and one who handed the pope his napkin when he wished to wipe his hands; three masters of the stable with a staff of stable-boys, grooms, mule-drivers and carters; a furrier to arrange for summer and winter wear; a gaoler to keep guard over the papal prison, 43 moneychangers and one Master of Theology. Mollat computed that for the year 1329-1330 alone, "John XXII spent almost three million gold francs on the maintenance and payment of members of his staff," compared with the expenses in that same year "of the king of France, the queens, the duke of

Normandy and the duke of Orleans together, whose combined expenses were 265,873 livres, 5 sous, and 3 deniers.

> "Unholy Babylon, thou Hell on earth, thou sink of iniquity, thou cesspool of the world. There is neither faith nor charity nor religion, nor fear of God, no shame, no truth, no holiness, albeit the residence within its walls of the supreme pontiff should have made it a shrine and the stronghold of religion."

So said Petrarch, but Daudet sang of the same place in this way:

> "Avignon! Avignon! on her mighty rock. Avignon! the joyful ringer of hills whose stone carved belfries, side by side, point heavenwards."

But St. Bridgit of Sweden and St. Catherine of Sienna sided with Petrarch and regarded Avignon as ravished by the sins of simony, avarice, pride and luxury, and wished the city "to be torn out by a plough and purified."

How are we, being neither Italian nor French nor Swedish of the fourteenth century, to make a judgment? We must take note of wealth, for wealth is always consequential in the influence of good and evil, and the source of wealth, at least in the fourteenth century, was explicit in the taxation system. Couriers and courtiers came constantly to Avignon from foreign countries, hot with messages upon their lips. Vatican ambassadors and papal nuncios were discharged across Europe, visitors flowed into the city continually like the River Rhone, bearing the gifts of loyalty. Merchants, traders and usurers came and went between Venice and Avignon, and tax collectors went out to the corners of the Continent to gather in the blessings of the lands.

This economic and spiritual world, like any world into

which one is born, seemed as solid as the Roman bridges on the river. No one anticipated change. No one ever does. The towers of the papal palace rose higher and higher on the Rocher des Dams. More churches and monasteries and cloisters were pressed into the city behind the walls, and when the city could not hold another building the palaces of anglophobic cardinals sprang up along the banks of the historic river, where cardinals and pontiffs sailed on their magnificent barges hung with banners and bunting.

The spirit of the age was formulated in the architecture of the papal palace: arches formed of the largest machicolations in the world, every gate defended with its portcullis, every wall crowded with parapets. "If it was the home of the Vicar of Christ," Y.A. Cook commented, "it was very clearly also meant to be the fortress of the Church Militant here upon earth." And at this it was successful. For ten years of siege, Pope Boniface XIII held out behind these walls.

When not besieged, the popes sailed under St. Benezet's Bridge, past Notre-Dame Des Dams, past the papal palace, past the Hotel Des Monnares, and past the papal mint, while friars and papal guards stood in the squares and sang Latin chants as their barges went by.

Daudet wrote: "He who did not see Avignon in the days of the Popes has seen nothing. It was unrivalled for exuberance and mirth and endless feasting. From morn till eve, processions and pilgrimages filled the garlanded, flower-strewn streets."

Up this river sailed Roland, arrived from the sober English Cistercian monastery, outside York. Shyness protected him at first. Then his various sicknesses aided him. His stomach could not hold down the rich foods, the venison, the puddings and the wines. His arthritis made it impossible for him to hunt. He suffered seasickness on the canopied cruises. His knuckles were too gnarled to wear rings. His body suffered calamitously when he was fitted with heavy robes. He developed a humor about his inabilities. "It seems," he wrote Abbot Thomas, "God wishes me to go only in sackcloth. I am achieving a reputation for piety when it should be for infirmity, for there is no doubt that this manner of living in Avignon calls for great strength and fortitude. To live in a palace such as the one I am now in, serving as secretary to Cardinal de Garves, tests one's physical as well as spiritual skills."

Roland wrote regularly to Abbot Thomas for twenty years. His letters are our record of life in Avignon from 1313 until 1333, when Abbot Thomas died, and the letters ceased. Roland sent his teacher not only personal observations, but philosophical and theological observations, for Roland had a "weakness" for philosophy. To Aristotle's famous dictum, "man seeks to know," he appended "God," and wrote his comments on the life to be met with in the corridors of the cardinal's palace.

"Seeking and knowing are not the same," he wrote.

His style was aphoristic. He set down notations, each one as a commentary upon the next. "It is difficult to record the soul," he made a note of that somewhere, "therefore, simple language is recommended for this. For who has not observed an animal seek food and not find it. Thus, men may seek and not find or know. To know is a gift. As some are more gifted in the knowledge of mathematics, so some are more gifted in the knowledge of God. Gifts cannot be explained. But they can be accepted and used. But an unwise gift which its receiver misuses can be an affliction. And he who misuses a gift from God betrays its giver. He who uses a gift to betray its giver has violated the spirit of all charity. As it is said: cast no stone into a well from which you have drunk good water.

The manner of knowing must be appropriate to the thing sought to be known, for one cannot know the way of the stallion with the same methods of knowing the way of the ant. And the manner of receiving a gift should be appropriate to the gift that is given, for surely the gift of God requires a manner of reception different from the gift of earthly goods."

He wrote, as he always did on such subjects, standing by his lectern with his shawl on his shoulders and his fur slippers on his feet. Even after Abbot Thomas died, he wrote tracts and treatises as if he were writing them to him, as though this old and now dead teacher were an axis around which his mind and soul rotated so customarily that Abbot Thomas' death made no difference to his spiritual tropism. Apparently, a small man such as Roland can be nourished by one good teacher and a good servant.

He pointed out to the dead Abbot Thomas, that verbs of knowing were not synonymous. Each suggested modes of knowing, For example, "to experience breathing" was not the same thing as "to meditate upon breathing," "to contemplate the act of breathing" was not the same thing as "to experiment with breathing," "to breathe ritualistically--panting in patterns" was not the same thing as to construct a syllogism, such as "I breathe, therefore, etc." Hence to experience God was not the same thing as to reason about or to contemplate or to remember having experienced. How different was breath to the sick man who struggled for it, or to the mountain climber who was unselfconsciously conscious of the sweet air, or to a person breathing unselfconsciously. "The mode of reasoning," he wrote, "may be the least valuable way of knowing. Hence we cannot say that man alone can know God because only man alone can reason about God." Here he appended a statement from St. Bernard: "But it matters what sort of generation it is which receives consolation from the remembrance of God."

In 1333, Abbot Roland was offered the position of Cardinal and urged by friends to accept it, seeing that there was such a preponderance of French cardinals and so few English ones. That was the political argument, one which Prior Godfrey ruefully resurrected on the occasion of Abbot Roland's visit to Bodmin Priory. To refuse wealth and power is always suspicious, and the cardinals at this time were very wealthy and being very wealthy were very powerful. Cardinal de Garves himself owned no less than fifty-one establishments, and over two hundred horses housed in a dozen different stables. So wealthy were the cardinals that even the popes borrowed money from them. Nevertheless, Abbot Roland apologized with subtle grace, "that his failing strength would not allow him to undertake the strenuous career of cardinal and he asked instead permission to establish a Cistercian monastery in a pocket of land northeast of Dijon and Vesoul, an outcropping in the Jura Mountains, surrounded by the four rivers of the Rhine, the Doubs, the Saone, and the Rhone.

After founding Mount Saint Bernard, he established his yearly retreat each autumn and was pleased to discover that he could stretch the meager resources of his body. "Habit," he wrote the dead Abbot Thomas after his first retreat, "is a great consoler and a bad teacher. It allows us to assume our limitations. I may not be strong enough to eat venison and dainties or to return to York, but I am fit enough to live on roots and berries." This was to chide Abbot Thomas for having refused his request to return to England.

In the winter of 1323, Abbot Thomas had a stroke and foretold his death. He lost his ability to speak and to write for about three months. He made a partial recovery so that he could write a letter to Abbot Roland, in which he advised him of his illness and his coming death, and forebade him to sorrow or to return. "Your destiny is to stay," he wrote. "I leave an heir for the world in you, and in how many ways is this to be preferred to a school of many where one's spirit is divided like the robe of Jesus." He ended his letter by describing Fountaineville and how it had weathered over the years, the gardens the rose-colored stones, the fountain, the birds peculiar to the place. "No man can wish for more than to die among the things he loves."

Abbot Roland did not return, but homesickness surprised him with its tenaciousness. He longed for England, he even longed for the climate that was inimical to him. He mourned for Abbot Thomas and for the collisional feeling of spiritual abundance in himself and spiritual uselessness in the corridors of Cardinal de Garve's palace. But he stayed because his teacher had asked him to, and he witnessed the rules of Clement V,

John XX111, Benedict X11, and Clement V1, and matured, his piety hedged round by history. In the earthly Jerusalem, he was sometimes impatient but never incautious, often frustrated but never stopped. Once he had been driven into a state of such anger he lost his hearing for two days. After this he practised even temperateness until he died. He had enemies, of course, and they branded him dispassionate. Commenting on this to Abbot Thomas, he wrote, "Nevertheless, there is no justice without wise administration."

In his honor, Prior Godfrey preached a sermon from the oaken pulpit in St. Bodmin's Church, beneath the eastern window. It did not look as grand this morning as he could have wished, for the light was dull owing to the weather, but the interior of the church with its statuary and golden candlesticks compensated for this. Prior Godfrey looked over the altar railing at the brethren, the priory servants, and his guests, the papal nuncio, the chamberlain, the scribe, Abbot Roland and his peculiar doctor. A sense of their foreignness struck him, but he mastered it and began in good voice. "There is in heaven a great coffer filled with the spirits of the good works of Christ's laborers here on earth. Christ gave this coffer to St. Peter and St. Peter keeps it for the good, clean souls who will go to heaven. This treasure, for which Christ paid for with his dear life, accumulates and increases with worth and merit and increases each day with each good deed a man does upon this earth. Therefore, think upon it in these ways, that whatever is done here its value increases in heaven. The good works on earth add to the heavenly store. So it is that a sinful man may sometimes borrow from this treasure to tide him to confession time so that he may not walk in sin till he be confessed. He may borrow and do good deeds in double and pay back with interest into heaven's treasury.

So my brethren, doubt not but that good increases of wealth come from thy works. When the good souls are gone into heaven they may help themselves to Christ's treasure. Be not like the Jews who hoard treasure upon earth, be thou for heaven's treasure and keep you a look out in the last days when there will be a great rush of many people crying that heaven's treasure belongs to them, keep you a look out for deceivers going about for their own profit and crying that for a penny they will buy a piece of the heavenly treasure. Nay, nay, the heavenly treasure cannot be had so cheap. There was a man here in Bodmin Village who bought a false bull from a false pardoner who for a penny told him that he had no more sin and would go to heaven with a clean soul, but when this man came to heaven Saint Peter held fast the gate against his crying though he cried ever so loud, "let me in. I paid my penny to a pardoner and am sinless." "Not so," said Saint Peter, "you paid your penny to a false pardoner and I cannot let you in for your soul is sinful and dirty and it will soil up this clean heaven." Straightway he hurled this man down to the eternal fire and Saint Peter's laugh followed him all the way down. This man lost all hope as well as his penny. Therefore, I say to you, be not like the Jews and take pardon of a false pardoner. It will not avail against Saint Peter. Lay up, lay up your treasure in heaven."

Afterwards, they went into the Chapter Room, where Abbot Roland thanked Prior Godfrey for his special considerations of food and comfort and sermon, and talked about his health, the welfare of Bodmin and of England, and his Brother Harald whom he regretted missing. The amenities over, he came to the point of his visit. Prior Godfrey drummed on the arms of his chair with his fingers, while Abbot Roland discoursed about taxes and figures and death.

Europe was burning! He had the facts of its demise at his fingertips. In Sienna, 80,000 had died in seven months out of a population of 100,000. In Marseilles 50,000 had died. In Paris, 80,000 were reported dead only this past summer. The famous physician, Guy de Chaullac, had written from that stricken city, "Human charity is dead. All fear the plague so that a father will not visit his son, nor the son his father." And in Avignon, in Avignon itself, 62,000 people had died in four months time, only between this past January and April. Eleven thousand bodies had been buried in one cemetery, and the rest thrown into the Rhone. Seven cardinals had died within three days of each other. Palaces stood deserted. The river was glutted with bodies and carrion. Not a soul to be seen in the piazzas. The halls of celebration were empty and one mourned not only human life, but the decay of magnificence, our emblems of our earthly desires and achievement.

As Abbot Roland reached England, Rome itself was destroyed by an earthquake on September 9. Europe was burning! Europe was burning with plague and war and famine. He had come to persuade the religious houses of England to cut off Edward's revenues so that he could not continue his war against France. "Europe is burning!" He cried it hoarsely. He said it everywhere. It was his only message. It was not only moral, but reasonable and right and righteous and humane and even commonsensical for humankind to cease its hostilities. Was it not enough that nature warred on man?

He carried the message to the Benedictine Abbey of Coventry, to the Earl of Warwick, to the Augustinian Canonry of Kenilworth, to the Cistercian Abbey of Combe, to all of England's largest landowners. He carried the message to monasteries and castles, to the feudal demesnes of England. "Europe was burning!" He was obsessed with this old, corrupt, ever-renewing, barbaric and civilized civilization, ever over-ripe. He was obsessed with love and fear for it, and his obsession kept him at a journey that taxed his strength and worried his physician. "Europe was burning!" Europe was sinking beneath the weight of catastrophes. The palaces were sinking, the bridges were sinking, the rivers and the land were sinking beneath the weight of dead bodies. Europe was burning! Europe was sinking beneath its own weight. He went further, into Cornwall, and his secretary and his servant ran after him, and his physician followed him with blankets and ointments and entreaties to return. He waved the arguments away and held audiences with the Bishop of Winchester and the Bishop of Canterbury and Bishop Grandisson in Exeter. And he arrived at each gate too late, already foiled by the nature of things. His reputation for saintliness, hedged as it was by history, had been sacrificed before he had set foot in Dover. To the English he had become Frenchified and to the French he remained English, everywhere respected for his probity and suspected of his loyalties. The problem was to persuade people to do what was good for them, even if their enemies benefitted.

The main source of Edward's funds was the wool tax. The largest suppliers of this wool exported to Europe were the monasteries. The history of this wool tax, which had brought Abbot Roland to England was this: In 1275 the first specific wool tax had been created, 7S 6d on the sack. This tax was afterwards known as the "Great and Ancient custom," and was the occasion for the first conciliar meetings of the barons, which then gave rise to Parliament. The barons met to see what they could do to meet the king's expenses, as the king himself had requested them to do, not dreaming that out of his problem of fiscal management would grow our notions of democracy, of advise and consent to the ruler. No one minded this tax at first, but when it jumped to 40S on the sack in 1294, the "Great and Ancient Custom" became known as the "maltote." By that time it was too late to undo the thing, for never has it been heard of a tax being removed. In fact, by 1348, the tax upon wool was L2 on the sack. One hundred and eighty English monasteries produced wool that was transported to the continent. Lincolnshire, Fountains, Rievaulx, Kirkstead, Revesby and Spalding alone exported 5,800 tons annually, and the tax on this was considerable, quite enough to wage a war. In addition, Edward, to the chagrin of the pope, had been appropriating the revenue from vacant alien bishoprics. To the chagrin of the crown, monies raised from the alien incumbencies in England, passed from the papacy to the French. It was Abbot Roland's task to swim against these currents, to bear in mind that the pope who had sent him to England had once been chancellor to Philip V1 of Valois, who was now Edward's enemy.

"Tut!" Prior Godfrey said and raised a pontifical hand, "all this matters not now that the Jews have confessed to poisoning the wells. The plague will soon end and with it France's fears for another war, for no doubt she will arm herself again once the plague is past," and he declared Clement's bulls against the persecution of the Jews to be pointless.

Abbot Roland fumbled for his shawl. "I plead not for France, but for Europe and for Christendom. What avails it if the Jews burn, Europe will still be Europe, Christendom will still be Christendom, and if the Jews burn we will not be able to raise coin in all of Europe."

Prior Godfrey was not impressed. "Coin may be raised by Englishmen as well," and though he did not say it, he went on to think, "as well as by Florentines, Lombard, and whatever you may call the pope's tax collectors." But he reminded Abbot Roland that one hundred years ago, the king's brother, Richard, Earl of Cornwall who had owned the Cornish tin mines, had been the chief lender in the realm, "though I defend him not, for it is unworthy to raise coin, but it is not a talent for Jews alone and Englishmen can raise coin as well as another. Have you not heard that William de la Pole has stepped into the shoes of the Florentine bankers?" Prior Godfrey imparted this as a piece of eminently good news, "For if coin must be, better it be in the hands of the English than the French, the Florentine or Jew." There was nothing on the economic horizon that he judged disturbing, now that economics and politics travelled in the same direction. He did not see himself as playing the dangerous game of sitting on two stools at once, land and coin. His values were feudal and he did not assume these could be superseded by a temporary flirtation with other forms of economic power. What he saw in the newly rising commercialism was his own chance to increase his land power and the wealth of his monastery "for the benefit of Christ." He could recite Edward's warm commendation to William de la Pole when he made that "merchant" a baronette in 1339: "Because he had made and procured to be made such a supply of money that by his means our honor and the honor of our followers, thanks be to God, has been preserved." He would have rejoiced to see de la Pole's son become Earl of Suffolk, though Prior Godfrey abhorred and denounced usury, as did every good Christian.

Abbot Roland reminded him of the misfortune that had befallen Laurence of Ludlow, the great wool merchant who had first negotiated the hated wool tax for the king, and was afterwards drowned in a ship laden with wool. "For the peasant loses thereby, as you well know, for his profit goes off in the tax."

"Tut! what he loses in the one hand he grasps with the other," Prior Godfrey said. "Where there is wool there must be markets to sell the wool. Where markets are sought, there must be wars to capture them. Wars must be financed. The peasant paid and gained at Crecy and Calais, as well as did the lords of the manors." Moreover, as Abbot Roland knew, wool was traded for wine from Gascony. Where would they obtain wine had they not the wool for it?

Prior Godfrey could not comprehend Abbot Roland's misgivings. In Castile, the king raised money from the wool export to fight the Moors, the same as Edward did to fight the French. Prior Godfrey shrewdly pressed this point. "In Spain the sheep does the work of Christian soldiers. God bless the sheep, for she runs now where the Arab horses ran but a short while ago. How can the king fight the infidel without money and where can he raise this money without a tax. God bless the sheep, I say."

Abbot Roland did not address himself to the broad question of crusades everywhere. He argued against a specific tax for a specific purpose at an inconvenient time. "Would it not be better for England to let the peasant keep the wool and manufacture cloth from it?" Prior Godrey's nerves fluttered at this, but he ventured to say, "We are encouraging as we can. The welfare of our serfs is close to the heart of Bodmin Priory, as is the welfare of our country."

"But England is none the worse, aye better if she keeps the wool," Abbot Roland said.

"Aye, and so is France."

Abbot Roland knew that there were few words that could dispel suspicion once it was lodged in a brain. A diplomat cannot plead his sincerity once his credibility is questioned. He would let the matter rest and see what his visit to Abbot Denis would bring. He could only hope to accumulate hints and to mold them.

Prior Godfrey was glad to see him go, but not to Abbot Denis', whose monastery he suspected of harboring spies, but Abbot Denis welcomed Abbot Roland with the emotion of one in exile. He burst into tears and embraced Abbot Roland, sparing him not a detail about the unpleasant events he had endured in this island. Nevertheless, his table was elaborate, with mutton and venison and fish and hot spiced ale, though not much more so than was usual. Scent and herbs had been laid down in the straw, which was unusual. The linen of seventeen brethren had been laundered but their faces still bore the strain of their cynicism, sullenness and apathy. When Abbot Roland remarked on their lack of spirit for the Lord's work, Abbot Denis told him, "It is all this talk of plague which the English have noised about. We live in an atmosphere of rumor and discontent which saps the joy of prayer."

Abbot Roland made the sign of the cross as he sat down to eat in the midst of this company, reminding himself that a part of his mission was to bring moral support to the alien priories. "Tell them the purpose of prayer is to sap the venom from rumor. They live by reverse motion."

"Aye, we live in difficult times and in a difficult place," Abbot Denis said, glad to unburden himself. "England is a godless country, for all her religious houses. I will not waste your time with talk of this place, but tell me how does the flower of Europe?"

"She is trampled with plague."

"How's that?"

"In France, the plague is not an Englishman's rumor."

There seemed something censurious in this remark to Abbot Denis, not merely informative. "But one cannot believe everything that is said," he said.

"True," Abbot Roland said with carefulness, "but believe this."

"One must sift and choose and think upon the reasonableness of whatever is being said."

"True. It is difficult to persuade people to swim against the current of their wishes."

"Well, as for that, I have heard it said that there are fishes with two heads in the sea, and men on the other side of the world with their eyes slanted towards their ears. Bless me, if I can believe the Lord would create such monstrosities."

"No form is impossible," Abbot Roland said.

"Aha, then you would believe me if I told you I had wings on my shoulders pinned beneath my cape."

Abbot Roland's utensil drifted slowly downwards towards his plate. He was in no hurry to eat. Hunger was not his problem. Being such a small man he could almost exist on air. "I am afraid you have caught me there," he smiled.

"I have caught you there," Abbot Denis said. "There is a limit to everything, even to matters of creation." He flushed with philosophical victory and forgot what his original point was, which was something about Englishmen and the plague. Abbot Roland intervened to help him out. "I only meant that in theory God could create anything, even wings on your shoulders, and that therefore we should be prepared to welcome even that which would be most unusual."

Abbot Denis recovered his thought. "God could not create the Englishman and none can be prepared to love him," adding quickly, "excepting yourself."

"Friend in Christ," Abbot Roland said to Abbot Denis' surprise, "I come not as Frenchman or as Englishman. Be assured, the plague rages every bit as rumor says. In this matter, trust rumor. It cannot enlarge upon the matter. If our generation does not know what it is suffering, what will future generations know?"

Abbot Denis found this outburst unnecessary, for he concurred, a thousand times he concurred that Edward's funds should be cut off. "As for my loyalty to Clement," he said, "be assured that I shall give my reeve orders to let my wool stay in the land, though it cost me the love of the London bankers. In this matter I shall persevere. Trust me. I have an advance on this year's wool from Chaunton. Trust me. I shall return half of it."

Abbot Roland fancied he looked as drained of energy as the seventeen brethren who sat a step beneath him. History seemed to overwhelm the sentiment of righteousness.

"You will surely do that," he said with a dry tongue, and he rose to retire.

"Trust me," Abbot Denis said again, "I will not fail France or the Pope."

Abbot Roland transcended the moment and set a kiss of gratitude on his cheek. "I do thank you," he said. "But now," he held Abbot Denis away with outstretched arms, "I will say the evening prayers in my room. I do believe my old teacher was correct and the climate here is not good for me."

Philip his physician observed the more than usual weakness in Abbot Roland, and followed him to his room. That it was no use to ask him to return, he knew. From the moment they had landed on English soil, he also knew the journey would be irretrievable. And for what good? Did he not know Europe as well as Roland did, and this place as well. From the moment they had stepped ashore and he had heard the accent of this island people, the language they spoke stirred cells in his brain and evoked the disease of memory. He was a native of another kind, one who had been here through others, whose empirical self was trapped in the memories of others.

At fifty-eight, Philip was slender to a fault, tensile. He moved with the inelastic grace of the monk who had outlived his problematic youth and has channeled his inner turmoil into the routine of monastic life, but whose struggle for a spiritual life had all but dessicated him. He was reserved and seemed to have no personal life, he was habitually to be found alongside Abbot Roland, or just behind him, so that he had been dubbed "the abbot's shadow." In his youth, Philip was tormented by any jeer, expressed or inferred. But successive rebellions seemed to erode his personality and his strength, and did nothing to weaken his oppressors. To himself he felt like an animal caught in such a net that its attempts to extricate itself traps it further, and its own efforts to escape destroy it. He could ignore his brethren's jeers now. For one thing, by a mutual absorption of one another, theirs and his antipathies had become sufficiently muted to make life bearable. They had worn each other out. Exhaustion was evident in his brown eyes, but poise too in the way that his black habit fell supply along his thin body, his onyx cross lying authoritatively on his chest. His friendship with Abbot Roland compensated him for the lack of other friendships and justified to him the path life had set him on.

If it is a fault, it was a fault that Philip's bearing was too "monkish," as the secular would say, or "too metaphysical," as his brethren would say, "leaning too much into the spirit of the thing." Had his appearance conveyed only unctuousness they would have found a place for him in monastic life, which had its share of this quality. But his shoulders conveyed a heightened and camouflaged self awareness, and in the monastic world temperamental deviation, particularly the effort to conceal that deviation, invited enmity, particularly too if the deviation took the form of both declarative holiness and the effort to conceal it.

Philip had a rare singing voice which rose above the other voices when he sang in a chorus. It could not be concealed, for merely to hear it was to wonder where this rare sound was coming from. It had both purity and volume and seemed to be immanent in the halls, to come from everywhere at once. Visitors always inquired whose voice it was, and if the visitor was distinguished, an archbishop or a baron, Philip was brought forward to perform alone, and sometimes invited to accompany the visitor to his castle to perform at Rheims or in Paris, and in return he would be given gifts to bring back to his monastery. Because of this gift, he was singled out for many advantages which his brethren could not share. In their spiritual lexicon they believed that for decency's sake, he should modulate his tones and blend them better with their own. Philip wished to avoid invidiousness and would respond: "I am singing for the glory of the Church."

Perversely, this remark aroused their contempt.

Later ages might believe that Philip could have made a wiser response, but at fifteen or sixteen in 1306, the conjunction of "fit" between his response and his condition struck him as so inescapable as to be natural, and so natural as to be logical, and therefore convincing to him. He said it because he believed it, but no one else did. He imitated expressions he read in books and it pleased him to say them. At any rate, there is no guarantee that if he had moderated his voice or had refused to sing altogether, that things would have been different for him. If he had not aroused envy and contempt, he might have only aroused contempt.

In the beginning, however, his voice was a source of great pain to him, not only because of the sacrifice it had entailed but because he could not hear it without reliving the terror of his kidnapping, and this memory evoked antecedent memories of a home he could not return to. In the beginning, his longing to go home was unendurable, his gift a curse, the groundplan of evil for which everyone else flattered and complimented him while he believed himself insidious. He was an animal whose trap is his own nature. Singing, he heard his mother singing in accents and in a language he never heard again, until he came to England. Singing, his father carried him to the altar singing hosannas to his firstborn. Singing, his grandfather kept the beat for him with his hand and accompanied him with spiritual care so that no sound of prayer went awry, mindful of the shadows that accompany error. Singing, their voices transcended his. Singing, they surrounded his soul like the leaves of a fruit. Singing with him now, they would not let him sing with the others.

Eventually the past was muted and became less threatening. Sometimes he would forget it altogether for long periods at a time. Then, some minor event would remind him, invariably something insignificant as a cloud or a certain pitch to a certain voice, and the past would assault him like splinters penetrating his tissues, not so much as memory but as pressures he could not identify, threatening and seemingly unreasonable, causing him terror, depriving him of a sense of direction, causing him vertigo. Such moods could come upon him anywhere at any time. They were as unpredictable as a disease. One awoke one morning and discovered a pain that had not been there the night before. The pain might or might not go away, might or might not be symptomatic, should or should not be taken seriously.

He treated these "moods" as illness and would go to the infirmary or take to his bed until the mood or the threat of it, or the "temporary inconvenience" of it had passed.

Psychological strategies governed his development. Freedom of self, to live without this threat from within, governed all his decisions, survival of the self became the premise of his intellectual and religious thought. His childhood became remote and strange to his present mind. In the long run, reason, with its constructive abilities and claim to reality and sanity, had to triumph over sentiments and memories, or Philip would have spent his life, metaphorically speaking, inside the potato sack that had been lowered over his head when he was first kidnapped, kicking with terror.

He could not say then, or ever, where he had been taken to. A potato sack had been dropped over his head, like over a kicking cat, and that night he found himself in a monastery with three others. In the morning they were fed, put on a wagon and transported somewhere else. During the day, they were separated and he travelled alone in the company of a priest. He identified the place that he was brought to as eretz norte. He did not recognize the landscape, but he had heard stories that it was here where Jewish children were taken when they disappeared. He believed he was as far north as the North Sea, for the air was cold. His fears diminished when he realized he would not be physically threatened, but the thought of his parents' grief agitated him. When his request that his captors send them word of assurance was refused, he suffered his first shock of impotence.

In reality, he was not far from his home, a few miles north of Cologne, on a road his uncle travelled twice a month. A priest had brought him there, who meant to collect the ransom for a debt he had been taxed with by Archbishop Sigismund to pay the usurer, Mose Menaheim. The abbot of the monastery convinced him to let the boy stay and be baptized. The weight of spiritual argument was on the abbot's side and the priest relinquished his interest in the ransom.

Philip was baptized and kept three years. His voice attracted the ear of Abbot Waldheim and at the appropriate time he had him castrated and sent as a present to Abbot Gottfried. Here Philip stayed hardly a year. Abbot Gottfried had no ear for music and Philip could not get along with the other novitiates in his monastery. He made no friends. He was sullen and melancholy, and his voice caused envy and contempt, because it was known that he was a convert.

The problem of Philip's origins would not go away. His brethren confronted him in the cloister as neither fish nor fowl. While the Church strenuously advocated his conversion as a solution to history, it was apparent from Philip's case that his conversion did not solve anything. There beneath tempus eterna, war, famine, plague and plain everyday distemper raged on. Philip lived among his brethren as a brethren among brethren, as the brethren lived at Bodmin, but his brethren sabotaged his efforts at salvation in any way they could. They marked up his songbooks, they put inksplotches on the notes and they distorted their values. One, he claimed, had thrown his Gospel into the fireplace. "It had been possessed of motion by itself," the other student explained to Abbot Waldheim.

Philip's condition as a convert was not unusual. Though the Church welcomed converts, indeed sought them and promised them salvation, it cannot be said, except perhaps for a very few, that any found it. As a rule they remained "converts" even to the fourth or fifth generation. Sometimes it took as long as five hundred years for a "new" Christian to become simply a Christian and what was the condition of their souls in all that time is not known, wandering in spiritual ambiguity through purgatory as they waited for conversion to complete itself.

Philip distressed himself with these questions. His conversion had been imposed upon him but in time he took it seriously, while his brethren did not even take seriously their monastic vows "in the brotherhood of charity." Born to the manor, so to speak, they could not suffer eviction except under extraordinary conditions of sinning. It was rare that anyone simply dropped out of being a Christian or, for that matter, of being a Jew, so much birthright conditions spiritual destiny. His brethren acted on the prerogatives of their birthright. A great many adjectives made up their complaints about Philip: "guarded," "secretive," "unfriendly." These gave rise to other unpleasant rumors, for Philip was guarded and unfriendly, and almost anything could be said about him---"he had arcane thoughts," he "squinted" at the crucifix, "he dipped his fingers in urine" before making the blessing.

Philip did practise tricks, chiefly on himself. He could spend days in which he refused to acknowledge the existence of anyone; he could stop his breath and have fainting spells; he could become deaf for days and hear nothing and consequently could not hear the bells and come to prayer or attend meals or follow a discipline of any kind. Once---the final straw for Abbot Waldheim--he was found on the steps of the altar, gazing at the crucifix, apparently dead. When touched, he fell over like a rock. He was in fact pronounced dead in a short while and only awaited internment, but he recovered in time. So close did he come to real or imagined death that he did not do this again, but afterwards focused on his reading and singing and became very "monkish."

Abbot Waldheim, who was not an imaginative man, regarded this as Philip's last trick. He wrote a letter to his bishop requesting his removal from his monastery, describing him as "intractable," and causing trouble wherever he went. He himself had witnessed his resurrection from death which, in Philip's case merited his quick removal. He was a danger to the spiritual health of the monastery. He was possessed, he was and always would be a "Jewish devil not worth the effort to convert." Abbot Waldheim had no plans for Philip's future or salvation, but with his bishop's approval he packed him off to Abbot Benedict's monastery with the warning, "I doubt that the Jew can be made into a Christian, for his soul resists the truth as the eyes of a bat resists the light."

Abbot Benedict, of St. Boniface's Monastery, was a long standing friend of Abbot Waldheim, and never accepted his judgment in anything. Philip arrived at seventeen, appearing very much as Abbot Waldheim had described him: "possessed, inattentive, perhaps dull, his eyes wandering, incommunicative, unpleasant, sometimes violent." Abbot Benedict distrusted all these statements; he distrusted Abbot Waldheim, and he abhorred such methods that were taken to convert the Jews as had been taken with Philip. His intentions were to make amends as soon as he could, but as he became aware of Philip's condition he understood the difficulties and for the time had to content himself with letting Philip be "until time should reveal a calmer nature."

In time, Philip did mend and became attentive to his monastic duties, but he made no friends. Abbot Benedict believed that even in a monastery, social attachment was good. Philip ate silently, he read silently, he walked in the cloister silently, he worked in the garden silently. His voice was only heard when he was compelled to sing. He was both compliant and withdrawn. The voices of his parents and his sisters and his brother still accompanied him, though he knew he would never go home, not even if he were able to go home. He could not sing with them anymore. He could not sing with them in the synagogue if his father asked him to, and he would not explain to them why he could not. For what was the glory of the Church was the shame of the synagogue.

He had been converted in every part of himself, in the secret parts of his body and in his tongue. He could not be recognized as a Jew by anyone, not even by Jews. Three recently had come to talk with Abbot Benedict on the matter of a loan. They passed him in the garden as he worked, and did not recognize that he was a Jew. They spoke among themselves, but not to him. They did not know that he could understand their language. He could speak it, but he did not. He would not open his mouth. How startled they would have been! He could not open his mouth, but he prayed that God would open their eyes so they could see into his heart and gather him up. If he could be healed! Made whole again. If his parts could come together! Nothing was too difficult for God, Healer of all afflictions. Could He not heal history and return him as a full Jew?

One afternoon, Abbot Benedict stopped him in the cloister to speak about his parents. Philip began to tremble. "You must know your parents suffer," Abbot Benedict said. Philip's trembling became violent. Abbot Benedict was sorry he had spoken. "I do not wish to go back," Philip said. "I will bear their suffering on my conscience." He looked down at the mosaic floor with its elaborately worked unfolding of New Testament deeds.

Abbot Benedict went away, troubled. What was done could not be undone. Perhaps worse harm could come of trying to undo the past. He decided that he must change the course of Philip's development and do what he could so that Philip could enjoy a full Christian life. He must not be left to drift anymore, betwixt and between. Having been so wounded, it was no cure to be left to subsist on the periphery of Christian life. Abbot Benedict took personal charge of him and attended to his education. Philip proved responsive. He advanced intellectually, but he still kept distant from his peers, in time incurring the worst of social reactions: contempt and envy.

After two years, Abbot Benedict wrote to Archbishop Sigmund for advice, detailing the matter of Philip's background and requesting with due respect to all the difficulties, that Philip be returned to his former life. Archbishop Sigmund had more of the official conscience than Abbot Benedict, and he responded in kind. "Christian piety accepts the Jews who, by their own guilt, are consigned to perpetual servitude because they crucified the Lord. Through baptism are they redeemed from this servitude. Would Abbot Benedict wish to consign one back to servitude whom fortune has rescued and given the grace of freedom and eternal salvation?"

Abbot Benedict's doubts subsided for a few months, but they revived again, and he wrote again, this time requesting Archbishop Sigmund to examine Philip personally and if he would do that, whatever the decision, there would be an end to the matter, for it could not be borne with any longer.

Philip was gone a week, and returned bearing a lengthy response from Archbishop Sigmund:

> "Having done that which always enriches the Church with a new child, we send back to you as a Christian our dear son, Philip, the bearer of this letter. We have caused to be added to this document also that which we have heard from him, the substance and sequence of his story, for it is pleasant to relate the wonders of God. We have tried him and have questioned him in every way and we are assured that he is in the Faith. Since, however, a new plant of this kind should be strengthened not alone by the dew of doctrine, but also nourished by temporal benefits, so that God may show him an increase, we order your fraternity so to arrange matters that he be provided with

such advantages and preferments as to advance his position in life and sweeten his departure from his enslavement so that he not be forced, from spiritual or temporal want, to look backward, as you have complained of him, but to steady his gaze and be encouraged to look forward to his salvation.

As the soul is superior to the body, to that extent are things spiritual preferable to things temporal. We could not look with favor upon the return of one to slavery and servitude when he stands already within the door of the Church and has taken a step upon the path to freedom and eternal salvation. We rejoice that he is akin to the angels and is a jewel in the Crown of Our Lord."

Abbot Benedict took heed and sent Philip to the University of Paris to study medicine, to give Philip's intelligence and personality a wholly different direction from the monastic one, for Abbot Benedict wisely considered that Philip's morbidity might be due to this environment as well as to his estranged past.

Philip was released from his monastic vows, but he continued to wear the habit at the university. The atmosphere was wholly different here from the monastery, but so contentious as almost to frighten him. Everyone here laid claim to his soul. The privileges and the curriculum of the religious classes were contested, while the Orders assailed him with arguments against reading the new pagan literature, lyrical poetry, the "new sciences." The best of these religious could not value empiricism as the means to redemption, or experimentation as a foundation for morality; the worst were careerists who protected their priestly positions.

The idea that the university is the place for the contemplative life is a contradiction in terms, for nothing breeds contention like ideas. Bickering is the disease of philosophers. Thus the University of Paris, when Abelard taught there: ". . .within a few days after I began to teach dialectic there, with what envy our master began to grow green, with what grief to rage, is not easy to express in words."

Thus, also, Pelagius, On The Vices of Masters: "Moved by envy, they scorn to admit well-prepared subordinates to professorial chairs, and full of arrogance, they despise others and censure their utterances unreasonably. They teach useless, vain, and sometimes false doctrines. They are dumb dogs to bark, as Isaiah inveighs against them (66:10). Seeing the faults of peoples and lords, they keep silent lest they displease them, when they ought to argue at least in secret---which they also sometimes admit to do because they are involved in like vices themselves. And although receiving sufficient salaries, they avariciously demand beyond their due or refuse to teach the poor unless paid for it, and want pay whether they teach on feast days or not, or fail to lecture when they should, attending to other matters, or teach less diligently."

The atmosphere was contentious. The scandal of the Knights Templar pervaded it and condensed everyone's thinking, bordering as it did on so many areas of concern: religion, politics, economics, heresy. The scandal of the Grand Master of the Knights Templar being tried for "confessing that at his reception he thrice denied Christ, thrice spit on the Cross and once on the ground," intelligently aroused cynicism in most Christians. Kings in need of money were apt to burn anybody. Even the pope was skeptical and attempted to intervene on behalf of the Grand Master. But persecution was lucrative in those days, and the pope's powers were limited. The Dominicans had grown in strength and were to be seen everywhere during this time, intellectually competent, self assured and useful while the Franciscans, deprived as they were of any significant part in the Inquisition, contented themselves with lyrical introspection and with carrying on their warfare with the university faculty for the soul of man, "holding classes," their secular faculty charged, "when the faculty voted to retire, in order to influence the students in their absence." In the end, Jacques de Molay, along with other brothers of the order, was burned practically beneath Philip's nose.

He did not go to watch the proceedings, though everyone else did, but he was immersed in their writings about heretics. Into his searching hands fell all manner of literature, particularly the records of Jews who had converted to Christianity and had relapsed back to Judaism. From an anonymous Parisian journal of the century before, came this!

> In that year, 1268, a certain accursed Jew was seized; he had been a Christian for twenty years or more, had taken a wife according to Christian law, and through her had sired Christian children, of whom he subsequently caused two to be circumcized and to Judaize with him. On Sunday prior to the Feast of St. Vincent, at St. Anthony near Paris, with a multitude of good men in attendance--for those who attended received major indulgences from the bishop--the accused was stripped of orders by the bishop, was degraded, and was turned over to the secular court. On the following Thursday---after he had chosen for himself fire rather than to return to the Christian faith, asserting that if all the kindling of Paris were gathered and ignited and he be thrown into the midst, he would not be burned by that fire---he was led into the square where hogs were sold in Paris and there, bound fast, he was totally consumed by the fire, so that nothing remained unburned either of his body or of his limbs. Then his ashes were strewn throughout the adjacent fields.

A second case was even more desperate

April 18, 1266, with God's grace we preached near the Mare-du-Parc, where the clergy and people of Rouen had collected after marching thither in a procession. Here we adjudged and condemned as an apostate and an heretic one who had been converted from Judaism to the Catholic faith. He had again reverted from the Catholic faith to Judaic depravity, and once again baptized, had once more reverted to Judaism, being unwilling afterwards to be restored to the Catholic faith, although several times admonished to do so. He was consequently burned by the bailiff.

The Register of Eudes Rigaud, Archbishop of Rouen.

Philip was surrounded by a century of conversions and relapses and re-conversions. What could one tell from the record?

Believer: There is a major proof for our faith in that there is no people lowlier than the Jews.

Unbeliever: Precisely the opposite! It is a major proof of our faith, that we remain steadfast in it nonetheless.

Biblioteca nazionale, Rome, Hebrew ms. no 53, 24b.

For Philip there was no longer any question of relapse, but he was driven to justify the path he was on. For him, as for Paul, only that Jesus be the risen Christ, he too would be justified, redeemed from his flesh with a magnanimity of compensation.

He asked himself, why the Jews who believed in the resurrection of the flesh, did not believe that Jesus was the Risen Christ. This argument raged throughout the century in disputations which had become popular literature: their Messiah was not divine, their Scriptures did not require him to be divine, their prophecies foretold that when the Messiah arrived he would be concerned with the affairs of the earth. Some held that the Messiah had to do with the Resurrection of the flesh, but that this had to do with the end of history when the dead would arise and take their place in the Eternal world. Others disputed this. Upon close inspection, there were many ideas concerning the Messiah, the Resurrection of the flesh, the nature of the afterworld, among both the Jews and the Christians. Some believed the flesh was resurrected soon after the body died; others believed in a general resurrection at the end of time; others were vague about the when and the how, but were quite clear about everything else. The prophecy was not precise. Even Pope John XX11 had become lost in its maze of contradictions and had to be condemned for heresy.

A cruel thought occurred to Philip: whether in the Resurrection the flesh was made whole? Did the lame and the deaf and the halt and the blind enter into Eternal Life with the stigma of their earthly condition upon them. This, at least, he ruled out. For if the Eternal Life did not heal the wounds of earth, what else could be its function? No blemished sacrifice entered into the Kingdom of God.

He turned to the writings of famous Jewish apostates, who had not relapsed: Nicholas Domin, Pablos Christianos, and his famous contemporary, R. Abner of Burgos. He turned finally to Raymond Lully, intriqued with the gossip pertaining to his birth. Some said he was born of a Saracen father and a Jewish mother. Some said he was born of a Jewish father and an Albigensian mother. Learned in all these traditions, in the mystical writings of the Jews and in the philosophical writings of the Arabs, he was an authoritative Christian.

After Philip finished his studies at the University of Paris, Abbot Benedict secured a position for him as Cardinal de Garve's physician in Avignon, but the city was no longer the center of religious discourse. It was by this time a thoroughly politically embattled city suffering the vice of luxury like a snake coiled around it. As Philip walked along the corridors of Cardinal de Garve's palace, such convictions regarding Christianity weakened before this confrontation with the earthly form of the religion. By comparison now, his life in the monastery, unhappy though it was, seemed more suited to him, more suggestive of the religious reality he sought than the papal city. But his temperament, he knew, was not suited to monastic life. The virtues of cosmopolitan life are intensity and variety, and these Philip needed to exhaust him. He needed to be exhausted by the world.

It is often assumed that the castrato loses sexual desire. The hell is otherwise, as Origen learned to his embarrassment. He retains desire. What he loses is effective ability. In time, Philip learned to master this unique condition of having been given an unworkable set of rules for his salvation, for the Church abhorred crushed privy parts as much as the synagogue did, and regarded the removal of testicles as bad as the removal of foreskin.

Abbot Benedict had also informed Cardinal de Garve of Philip's voice, and his reputation was established. In a city like Avignon particularly, where the arts were esteemed, his voice very soon attracted attention. He sang at lavish dinners and was part of every papal ceremony. As with everyone else, he became addicted to the flattery of being wanted and of being presumed serviceable. But the flattery soon enervated him. · The buried tension arose again between his self flagellating "I" which understood that the condition of this gift lay in deformity and his estangement from a ˉworld which could ignore the conditions of a gift which humiliated him. Moreover, he was rarely asked to practise the medicine he had been trained in. When real illness struck a member of the cardinal's family, paralysis or a tumor, the cardinal called in the Jewish physician from Toulouse. Philip's function was to purge the cardinal of the bad effects of his indulgences. He complained to Roland, "The only time I see him clutch his cross is when the passage is painful."

Roland's refusal to accept the cardinal's cap influenced Philip deeply. The offer was political enough, courting English friendship with an English cardinal, with scarcely the courtesy of recognizing Roland's nature. He refused, not because he felt slighted by the obviously political nature of the offer. In fact, he weighed that problem carefully. He refused because he understood the limitations of power, its inhibitions with respect to trust, its inevitable complicity with luxury and justification by pomp, its inclination to delusion and self devourment, its inflexible and limited parameters in the field of moral action, for of itself power has no vision, only force. No one could say how he came to know this. No one had ever observed him to read a book on this subject. He seemed to have been born knowing this. Unlike Philip, the knowledge caused him no strain. Sometimes he was caught offguard and became impatient, indignant, even angry. But he never became confused.

He left in 1333 to establish his monastery in the Jura Mountains, and Philip remained behind in the service of Cardinal de Garve. The situation soon became untenable for him. There was no infinitude of distraction any longer. Avignon, with its intrigues and luxury, was routine by now; his medical attentions were debasing; his singing had never been a pleasure to him. He had not become accustomed to the wound of himself. But he wanted no more searchings, no more forays, no more crises. He wanted plain and simple rest. His everlastingly bruised soul required and deserved a home.

He thought again of monastic life and explored the subject with himself, and in letters to Abbot Roland, who responded that his was "a plain and arduous monastery, Cistercian, plain singing, little ornament in art or music."

"I am relieved," Philip wrote back. He confessed his fear of being ill suited to the monastic life, "but then what life am I suited for?" Thus, he finally confessed everything, his origins, his early years, his condition. "Believe me, I pray fully with all my heart," he wrote Abbot Roland, "that my sacrifice was not in vain, that I never discover its vanity, but I cannot believe that Christ asks such gifts of us."

That winter, Abbot Roland suffered a particularly painful attack of arthritis and asked Philip to visit him. "Come and stay for a while. At least, help me bear this winter. Believe me, it is I who needs you. It is enough if you come as my doctor and ease my pains. You will not stay more than you wish to. It is enough if we are friends. Believe me when I tell you, as St. Bernard wrote, there is a grace of nature common to all mankind, and one who shares with us in nature has his share in grace. You are free, my friend, to come, to stay, or to go."

Philip stayed. He ceased to contrive at conviction, but he also ceased to be tormented by the lack of it. Monastic life did not abuse him any longer, and he found a place in it. Christian life simply carried him along until he became a part of it.

But the habits of psychological conservation were very strong in him. He repulsed change. Routine gave him confidence. The unpredictable threatened, and he did what he could to frustrate the plans for this journey. Even en route, on every step along the way he warned and pleaded with Abbot Roland to return before it was too late.

"Too late for what?" Abbot Roland chided him. "It is already too late." He put on his furry slippers. "Yes, this English climate has produced a race of stalwart souls, and I am to be counted among them. All my life people have thought that every day that I lived was a miracle. See how I multiply miracles."

"There is a boundary to everything, you once told me," Philip said. "To suffering. Even to miracles, I think."

"Did I teach you that?"

"Not quite."

"Well, then, I am not in danger of contradicting myself, and we can take a step further."

Philip saw that he could not change Abbot Roland's mind and left his room, angry with a world that was too much for human beings.

Abbot Roland lit a candle and placed his crucifix next to it. He would not say so to Philip, but he felt weak, and he did not care to die. This time, in years past, he would go into the mountains "to exercise dominion over his nature," he would say. He meant to conquer his frailties, his physical weaknesses, and especially the unpleasant voices that accumulated from libraries and corridors and missions. In the mountains, along any stream, watching a chipmunk, he recognized the essential element of his faith: that the world God had created was good, and in its goodness was God justified.

He missed the journey this year, the renovation of his soul and the thought of the rest of the way through England that he had still to go, dismayed him: Somerset, Gloucester, Hereford, Worcester, Leonminster, Yorkshire. He pitted his spirit against the times and prayed that he be equal to the task.

Lord, Jesus, enlarge Thou me in love that I may find room in my heart for this earth, as I have found room in my soul for Your kingdom. Enlarge Thou me, that I may find peace in this earth, and I will find peace in Your Eternity. If it is Thy will to bring me home, Thy will be done," he said, and blew out the candle.

CHAPTER SIX

DENARII DEI

This chapter could not have been written without the help of the chronicler, Mathew of Paris, as well as others, who wrote approximately one hundred years before Will was sent to London while the plague was raging there in the December of 1348, charged with Prior Godfrey's instructions to borrow a certain sum of money from certain parties for certain reasons which had to do with certain sums of money he had borrowed in previous years from Bishop Roundsleigh, which he now moreover owed to the papal collectors, because of certain sums of money he had withheld from last year's taxes for certain reasons which had to do with the buying of more sheep to multiply the sacks of wool to be gathered which would allow him to borrow further sums of money against the wool as collateral.

In 1253, Mathew of Paris, monk and chronicler, wrote: "The whole world knows that usury is held to be detestable in the Old and New Testament, and is forbidden by God. Yet now the Lord Pope's merchants or moneychangers practise their usury publicly in London to the disgust of the Jews." Mathew continues: "And if, by chance, thou wilt pay the Papal usurer the principle of the money which thou hast now in thy possession, within a month or less of the day of the borrowing, he will not accept it unless thou pay him the whole hundred pounds. This is worse than a Jew's condition, for a Jew will receive the principal courteously whensoever thou shalt return it, with only so much interest as is proportionate to the time for which thou has had it in hand." Mathew writes on: "From that time forward (1229) the land of England had never lacked certain Ultramontanes, who style themselves merchants, most impious usurers, who seek nothing else than to ensnare those men in especial whom the Roman Court is pressing for money."

Another Bendictine chronicler, Oxenides, bursts with similar resentment: "Usury being forbidden in both Testaments is now practised almost as a lawful trade by those usurers of the Roman Pontiff who are called 'merchants.'" In 1258, he wrote: "The plague of usury...did so ensnare the English religious houses that there was no conventual house, nor cathedral, nor any so modest foundation but that it was involved in so many debts as made it despair of acquittance at any time."

And Pope Innocent 111 candidly admitted that "not a church in Europe would remain standing but for usury," while Archbishop Pecham gives us this sobering account of the awesome abyss that gaped beneath the feet of ecclesiastics:

> To the most Holy Father and lord in Christ, Nicholas, by divine providence supreme pontiff of the Holy Roman Church, his poor little brother John, priest of Canterbury, sendeth greeting, falling down with all reverence and kissing his holy feet.... there hath lately reached me a letter of execution, horrible to see and terrible to hear, whereof the final purpose is this: that unless, within a month from the feast of Michaelmas next coming, I pay fully and completely to the merchants of Lucca, from whom I borrowed at the court of Rome, the sum of a hundred marks for a hundred pounds, which I am to pay at the end of the terms I shall be forthwith involved in a sentence of excommunication, and shall be denounced as excommunicate in my own and other cathedral churches, with bell, book and candle, on every Sunday and

holy day....And this, although according to the contract which I signed, I might have secured freedom to myself and my church for an indefinite time so long as I paid the damages and interest to the aforesaid merchants, in consideration of the losses they would incur by my delay....Therefore, most Holy Father, may it please your most merciful Holiness to reach me the right hand of succor and to revoke this cruel letter.... otherwise, I see no other refuge but either to leave this prelacy committed to me, to disperse my household or flock, and to depart as an exile into some distant land, where I may lurk alone in some monastery and bear this anathema with humility until, as God shall give occasion, I shall have succeeded in satisfying the aforesaid merchants from the revenues of my see, in proportion as they can be raised from time to time, or, again, to borrow further from these merchants and, as a borrower, to fawn upon them, and to bear with patience their base speech though, by your Holiness's special mandate, it would be my duty to take strong measures against such lenders, since in these days no other men can be found in England who have money enough nor, in the face of the present change and clipping of coinage, could I borrow elsewhere than from these merchants of Lucca.

Paradoxically, the moral reputation of the Jewish usurer during the Middle Ages was very high. A Norman chronicler, in 1306, describes the expulsion of the Jews from France, and the consequences in this way:

...there are many occasions on which people, however well off they may be, have a sudden need of money, and if they cannot produce it, either lose an inheritance, are excommunicated, or are punished; or else they fall into some great misfortune because they cannot rapidly collect the rents or debts due them; whereas if they could raise the money for a little usury, they would escape. But after the expulsion of the Jews, they could not find any money, except by borrowing it through agents from certain Christians, both clerics and laymen, who lent at such an enormous rate of interest that it was more than double what was charged by the Jews, and who did it in such a way that the debtors did not know the lenders were in possession of their pledges. This was a dangerous situation, for if the agents died or gave up the business, they did not know where to recover them."

In 1480, the Elector of Brandenburg, stated, ". . .at one time the Jews were forbidden to stay in Brandenburg, but in that period the people were worse oppressed by the Christians than they had been by the Jews, so that the latter had been readmitted."

The state of unreality is such that many matters now being fiction, there is no reason why fiction should not avail itself of documentation to rid us of our unreality. Prior Godfrey's problem was similar to Archbishop Pecham's, as it was similar to that of many abbots and priors of that time. The Church demanded a year's income in advance from each monastery, called "first fruits." Prior Godfrey, like so many householders, was always a year in arrears. Instead of first fruits, his were the last fruits. Debt was the natural condition of all the classes in the Middle Ages. Prior Godfrey's iniquities were not deliberate, but like any householder, he found that there was always something to be paid off, bought in advance of having money for it: the new gatehouse or the new east window, his pride and pleasure as he sat in the choirbox. It was not only pomp and status which motivated him, but the simple love of thinginess which clings to the most spiritual of men, but which always costs money. Prior Godfrey was always behind, and he always imagined that he could catch up the following year, like most of us. The more debt he accumulated, the less real his debts became. Like Archbishop Pecham, he too blamed his creditors for this inglorious spiritual pinch. On the one hand, his was a position of authority and wealth and power, while on the other hand he was in constant craven fear of excommunication and was reduced to the ignoble method of cheating Peter to pay Paul. Usury was the black business of the Middle Ages, it was its addiction, its secret and most beloved vice, practised with the most misgiving, not because it was condemned, but because most churchmen rightly sensed that usury was gnawing away at the foundations of the feudal system, and that they themselves were digging its grave. Usury was the irresistible disease. Every ermine robe, every set of jewels, every ivory reliquary, every carving, every stained glass window, every crusade, every war, every state marriage, every coronation ceremony, cost money and was paid for in coin. The fabulous and lauded artwork of the Middle Ages was paid for in the coin that the Church condemned. The reverential works, the inspiring gardens, the church architecture, the beatific cloister pathways, the stately monasteries, all paid for from the pockets of the despised usurer, constituting the most singular collaboration between vice and faith. Usury was condemned by the Church and practised by everyone: Lombards and Cahorsins, who often disguised themselves as Jews to escape the detection of the Church, for Jewish usury, where permitted, was legal and was the only legal usury in the Middle Ages. Usury was practised by Florentine and Venetian merchants and papal collectors from Rome. It was practised by men and women, and women were as adept at it as men.

The problem appears to have been schizophrenic and was schizophrenic, as is all problems resulting from moral delusions, particularly the moral delusions of the powerful classes, spiritual and secular. Power itself is part of the delusion, resting on relationships and connections which in their own turn become part of the process of the attrition of the power of the powerful. Everything keeps changing, even so powerful a force as power. In Prior Godfrey's case, it had been a good number of years that he had always managed, willy nilly, to pay his debts. He had witnessed the excommunication of other abbots for their failure to meet their debts, but he himself had never fallen so low for so long that he did not manage to escape this fate. It was reasonable for him to imagine that matters would continue in this way, that he could keep his balance between debt and credit, allowing him to finish his life with equanimity, and to go to heaven. As with other abbots who were in continual debt, worries of hell brushed his mind from time to time, but he, like the others, solved his doubts about salvation through the Jew. In their stead, the Jew went to hell.

But when Brother Harald delivered his report on the state of the sheep, Prior Godfrey momentarily lost his balance. He took the rolls from Brother Harald's hands and laid them out on his lectern without a response to him. In fact, he crudely waved him down, which irritated Brother Harald. In the past, their roles had been reversed. It was Prior Godfrey who was always intemperate, irritable, quaking with alarm, while Brother Harald exhibited the sang froid which caused Prior Godfrey so much envy. Brother Harald's brain was now in a fever, calculating the possible ruin that could happen to Bodmin Priory. The only cheerful aspect of such a future was the certain excommunication of Prior Godfrey, upon which Brother Harald could reasonably expect that he would become prior.

This humanly indulgence in a fantasy led him to regret that he had missed his brother's visit, for in his mind he already read back his appointment and imagined that it was he who had greeted Abbot Roland and had conversed with him on matters of state. He would have relished the meeting, for reasons of affection and confrontation, the chance to appraise the surprising development of his brother's career. Their parents had viewed it with cynical gratitude, but when they had learned that their son had refused to become a cardinal it confirmed them about his peculiar nature. "Christ rot the runt!" his father had yelled, "there is a place in hell reserved for those who turn their backs on their duties."

But Brother Harald, his father's voice still echoing memorably in his mind, had not been there to greet his brother. It was more necessary for him to do his duty, particularly this year when rumor of plague and what not might permit the reeves and bailiffs to take more liberties than ever. No one questioned the idea that family relations were subordinated to monastic affairs anymore than a general today would think that family matters should call him away from his war; and Brother Harald was as formidable in his protection of churchlands as Prior Godfrey was obstinate in its theories. For all their antipathies to each other, they were one on this issue, though Prior Godfrey frequently found the official presence of Brother Harald, who did everything properly, too much for him. But his advice was always correct. He was the perfect aid or secretary, lawyer, counsellor or minister. His bearing required a portfolio. It was his talent for efficiency which made Brother Harald impatient with Prior Godfrey, who always flew into a temper when his additions were corrected. It was obvious in every way that Brother Harald should be the prior and that Prior Godfrey, being forced to use the man he most disliked, could not be expected to feel gratitude towards him. But when the time came for Brother Harald to take his trip to the grangelands, then Prior Godfrey appreciated him most fully, for in estate management, nothing brings a landowner the sense of security and bliss so much as a competent overseer.

A husband does not rejoice in a chaste wife more than a landowner in a trustworthy overseer, or a master in a servant in whom he has confidence. Go the world over! To surrender some portion of your well being, whether psychological or material, to one who is not trustworthy, is scary. To be cheated is unpleasant, and marvellous is it in the history of human relationships that Prior

Godfrey, who so disliked Brother Harald as to sometimes leave him out of his prayers, trusted him completely with this task.

Brother Harald deserved it. In Wodesbridge he heard talk that plague was in London. He did not move his horse any the faster for that. "What of it?" he said to the reeve who told him, "there's plague everywhere." He bought an air purifier made of a hollowed-out orange filled with vinegar and garlic and kept it at his nose as he went about, regarding with disdain the fires that were being set everywhere to purify the air. "It makes the air smell worse," he said to the reeve.

"A man does not die of bad smells except in hell," the reeve said back.

"It makes the people fearful," Brother Harald said.

"There is none that have run away," the reeve said.

Brother Harald was reassured, but he laid down a warning. "Who would hire a villein from priory grounds?"

It was not the reeve's business to tell Brother Harald, and he did not. It is a condition of political life anywhere at any time that an underling does not give his superior bad news. That is why the leader who has spent sums of money to maintain his security with a spy network, is often caught by surprise when his edifice crumbles. Who but an oracle would tell a king he is about to lose his kingdom? Certainly not the reeve. Brother Harald was pleased. There had been seven births and no runaways. He gathered the account rolls and placed them in his leather pouch and turned his horse back home. He had gone as far as Baron Roundsleigh's Barnstaple Manor to oversee the countryside. The cattle were being driven in for the yearly slaughtering which, in advance of the plague, was being done rapidly this year. Scores of cows and sheep and bulls and pigs, and even calves, were being killed in every village, and their screams were heard day and night. The villagers, accustomed as they were to this season of slaughter, nevertheless took on a greyer look this year. Like the winter skies, they darkened daily as they slumped to this task, determined to endure what had to be endured, even if it was their own brutality. The cattle could not be kept alive during the winter, and the meat had to be salted in the cold weather. It was the only food the peasant had during the winter: meat now, and fruits and vegetables during the summer. His diet was dictated by the seasons. This being the season for meat, the land ran with blood and the air was filled with the smell of animal fright.

Brother Harald kept to his purpose of getting to Bodmin Priory as soon as he could. Rumor followed him everywhere, but he saw no evidence of the plague, and interestingly enough, it did not frighten him. One would think that a hypochondriacal man would panic. Evidently, his morbidity did not issue from anything in the world at large. Reality did not frighten him. On the contrary, it frequently relieved him, and he often viewed with confidence what confident men quivered at. Thus, he sat on his horse and gazed down on Bodmin Priory Manor, filled with stricken sheep, some already dead, others staggering on their feet, leaning against anything they could find to steady them, flinging vomit in the air. The shepherd, of course, was gone. His family had stayed its ground for three centuries, through war and famine, but this offspring fled with panic.

What had become of the shepherd? Of Aristaeus, of Hermes who saved the ram and the ram who saved Isaac, of animalkind and humankind, Noah who had saved the animals and the whale who had saved Jonah. Our debts are so intertwined, we cannot tell who owes what to whom, but here the sheep were left to die without a sympathetic eye to witness their terror. The sheep and the dog and the cow, man's company through evolution, rotted in the fields and only Brother Harald astride his dextre under a November sky, counted the loss and galloped rapidly back to Bodmin Monastery to record it.

As soon as he was gone, Prior Godfrey began to groan to himself. St. George picked up his head and squinted at him. Prior Godfrey groaned so pitifully that St. George began to hop wildly about on his perch, his nerves twittering with gloom. "My sleek bird, what shall we do?" Prior Godfrey said to him. "Such a plague has not been since the time of King David. Christ keep all usurers in hell for this plague upon the land."

He had no plans for rectification at the moment beyond such uttterances, but the matter pressed on him so heavily all night that he could not sleep. He woke once, he woke twice, he woke a third time. He put his slippers and his mantle on and walked about the room with St. George, who was vexed at losing sleep and puzzled at being woken. Each time Prior Godfrey put him on his wrist he thought the dawn had come. But, no! From under his wing he saw that it was still dark. The hours were becoming jumbled. Fever take Prior Godfrey! he thought, proof that all living things are selfish mostly about their sleep.

When Prior Godfrey woke a fourth time, St. George buried his beak beneath his wing and refused to stir. It occurred to Prior Godfrey to light a candle and to pray. It was now Prime and the bell calling the brethren to prayer came through the doorway. It reminded him of those satisfactions of Bodmin Priory that eluded the economics of the situation, for Prior Godfrey had his memories and his sentiments and no man likes to see his home destroyed. He groaned, though he did not believe that it could happen. His home, after all, was the Church.

Nevertheless, he ate his breakfast soberly that morning, mindful of the difficult times ahead and after early Mass had Brother Bernard bring him the Bodmin Rolls which he perused privately in his room for three days.

How Brother Ralph came to put two and two together is a mystery. From Brother Harald's temper, from a glance of Prior Godfrey's, from a frown of Brother Harald's, Brother Ralph deduced and told everyone else, "It seems things do not go well this year on the grange." Since Brother Walter never spoke, no one expected him to respond, and he did not. Brother Namlis could not. Brothers Stephen and Anthony would not, caring not one bit about how things went on the grange, and Brother Benedict was now brought so low with his cancer that he cared not a bit about the gossip either. It fell to Will to inquire, "What mean you?"

"In former years" Brother Ralph said, "Brother Harald has looked otherwise as he returned with his accounts. Sure as I am who I am, there must be trouble abroad and what can it be but that it pertains to matters of the plague and if it pertains to matters of the plague and Brother Harald be himself not dead of it, it must be that others be dead of it, that is Bodmin serfs and sheep and that must mean a reckoning with debt."

Will's first impulse was to laugh at Brother Ralph's ratiocination, for like everyone else he took him for a harmless gossiper who hit upon the truth by accident and not due to any quality in himself, but that going about with his constant rambling could scarcely miss the mark on occasion. Brother Ralph was not a vain man and did not care if he was accredited with acuity or not. He did not even care much about the truth. It was the work of detection that he liked. "What think you?" he whispered, "serfs or sheep shall plunge us in debt?" and he puzzled about it all morning.

It being now quite cold, they were called to the Calefactory that morning for the Chapter Reading and the sermon. Prior Godfrey requested that logs be set burning in the fireplace and gave the brethren permission to warm themselves before it. Brother Benedict was not among them. He remained in his bed in the dormitory.

The time being propitious, All Hallows, Prior Godfrey had a great deal on his mind. The tide of evil was surely risen as never before and promoters of evil, false bishops and falser preachers and even some who be among his own brethren with uncharitable thoughts whose hearts and obedience he felt to be far away from the good of all at Bodmin. The time being propitious, All Hallows, he preached a sermon on the gloom of hell and the vanity of worldliness and the punishment of plague "on those who for vanity's sake decorate pulpits to raise the sacred host, this being more sacriligious than Judas himself who afterwards hung himself while this priest for his blasphemy is warmed by the bishop's fire. Through much pride and through sin from prosperity we sail into much woe. In this way, has the plague come to England, in the same way as do devils and diverse such evils, such as fly above in the air as thick as motes in the sun, dropping unclean matter from the sky and leaving unholy droppings everywhere. Now they come in such diverse shapes, now as swine, now as dogs, now as an asp or a horse, now as a spider that crawls in your pants, now as a damsel with her skirts hitched up, now as a parish clerk with incense in his nose, now as a bad servant, now as a bad bishop that rides about all day and tramples the good work of the brethren, now as a vain Brother who sets his heart upon his abbot's chair, now comes such diverse evils as these spiders and flies and gnats that sit upon a lettuce leaf or swim about in the ale causing it to sour, or they sit in the stock and make evil divinations of things to come."

He cast so wide a net, as indeed an accounting of evil must, that each of the brethren, with the exception of Brother Benedict who was not there to hear him, and of Brother Anthony and Brother Stephen and Brother Harald who had contempt for this list of evils, felt he had something to repent. Brother Anthony and Brother Stephen accepted their sinful states and could think of nothing in particular which had made them worse this week than any other. It could not be said, by them at any rate, that they had sinned more this month than last, so as to have caused the plague to come to England. Brother Claude could think of nothing he wasn't guilty of, and more so as time went on. Brother Ralph felt that if the plague was caused by his gossiping he would sacrifice his tongue, seeing Brother Namlis might get into heaven as well as another. Brother Thomas agreed with everything Prior Godfrey said, particularly the parts about evil coming in the shapes of dogs and spiders.

Prior Godfrey concluded with the worst evil yet to be told. "Five thousand sheep lay dead and so great is this evil that for three nights and three days have I thought upon it, mourning much the death of these innocent lambs and I have asked myself what can it be that Christ means by this calamity but that it is his sign that he wishes Bodmin to free herself from the evil grip of the usurer and such as keep their banks of iniquity in London."

"He means not to pay his debts," Brother Ralph told Will later that afternoon.

How so unworldly a man as Brother Ralph who had had only the unworldly ear of Brother Walter for forty years could come to know so much about the world, we worldlings will never know. However, in this instance, Brother Ralph was not exactly correct, for Prior Godfrey, after consulting the rolls and the accounts and after coming to close figures with Brother Harald who, toss the matter anyway, he respected for his opinions in such matters, decided to send to London for further consolation, for as Brother Harald said, "Let the plague rage as it will, it must come to an end and the end will bring restoration."

This view was so salutary that Prior Godfrey delayed several weeks on the good sense that one should put off the evil day of borrowing more sums before it was necessary to borrow them, for to do so prematurely would bring notice to the fact that one did not have the wherewithal to pay back the sums one had already borrowed, and was not therefore likely to inspire trust for further credit.

How long to delay? Prior Godfrey did not need sums until the next harvest. On the other hand, such was the increasing disarray of matters everywhere, it occurred to him that to delay might put him in danger of that time when there would be no credit to be had in all of England, for rumor had it that several banking houses in London had collapsed with the inability of the borrowers to pay back what they had borrowed against the guarantees of wool. The sheep were stricken everywhere and such London firms as Peruzzi, Bardi, and de la Pole, were sheared to their skins. The sheep baaed and the bankers groaned, and no one rejoiced that so pernicious an activity as borrowing and lending would come to an end by the course of nature. On the contrary, preachers blamed the plague on greed while bishops and abbots and lords tossed in their sleep as accounts of stricken sheep were brought in, and Prior Godfrey grew waspish with waiting and cantankerous with suspicion that Brother Harald's advice to wait was a trap. He did not know what to believe. When it is difficult to make an accounting of reality, all messages bear equal weight.

Prior Godfrey sat in the choir box at Mass, pained at the sound of Brother Harald's voice intoned so meticulously through his narrow nostrils that Prior Godfrey went straight from Mass to the Scriptorium to consult with Brother Bernard about his accounts. His eyes fell upon the place where Leboren's name had been and the tax that could no longer be collected from him.

"Cursed be the towns and such new inventions," he screeched, and regarded it as a divine commentary when news reached Bodmin Priory that the plague had broken out in Newool.

The brethren prayed for the souls there, and prayed that the plague come no closer. But it was otherwise, for the plague was soon in Cornwall, it was soon in Taunton, it was also soon in Launceton, in Barnestaple, in Newool, and one morning it was in Bodmin.

The news that Adam the cook was found dead in his house with such and such marks upon him was given by Michael the gatekeeper to Will.

"So," Will said grimly to himself, letting out his breath and only conscious then that he had been holding it. And how could it be otherwise? The vanity of thinking that they would be spared! Mockery alleviated the fear he felt. He said to himself that he had known all along that they would not be spared, for why should they be spared? Were they not sinners too? The vexatious problem of evil demands a rationale for those who are spared as well as for those who are not spared. Those who were spared in the Great Death of 1349 were as confused about why they were spared as those who were dead of it and were no longer confused.

Still the brethren continued to hope. They heard news about Adam and about the alewife and the miller, and still they hoped. The mill fell into disuse. No one came to bake bread in the oven. And still they hoped. The glittering edge of possibility seduced them. They hoped. Prior Godfrey gave orders that virtually sealed off the gatehouse from visitors. They hoped it would work. Michael was given instructions to admit no one, not the pudding wives, not the ale brewers, not the carters, not pilgrims, not Edward himself if he should come to the gatehouse. Only the breviator was given permission to enter to bring news of the outside world. The brethren made calculations of what food and clothing and candles and straw and wine and ale and meats were available. Brother Namlis took over the duties of Adam and Brother Thomas took over the duties of the cook's son. No one would be permitted beyond the gatehouse except the breviator whose services would only be dispensed with at the last.

Will did not sleep that night. Nor did Brother Benedict, who never left his bed again, but lay out the remainder of his days on his thin palette with a crucifix between his fingers, while Brother Namlis and Brother Stephen took turns feeding him soup and placing hot towels on his abdomen.

It is a curious thing to have a man dying of cancer when everyone else is dying of plague. Will often relieved the others of their vigil, for he wished Brother Benedict would speak to him about death. Since he had been dying for two years, Will thought he should have some notions regarding death, something Will could use in preparation. But Brother Benedict kept silent on the issue, and a spiritual courtesy did not allow Will to ask him how he felt about dying and if he had advice to leave to the others. The dying, so eager to complain of this and that pain, of the soup being too cool, of the blanket being too heavy on their legs, have nothing to say of the heaviness or the lightness, or any quality whatever of their dying.

Brother Benedict, who had been on his slow journey

towards death for two years, kept his eyes upon his crucifix and concentrated all elucidation in it. "Death be death no matter how it come," Will thought to himself, "yet I would rather fall from a horse and die of it than die of the cancer or the plague." If there were as many ways of dying as there were ways of living, he would prefer to choose his way and let it be fast and fierce and there be an end to it.

Thus died Michael the Gatekeeper on December 12. He was found dead of the plague outside the gatehouse, by the breviator who had come to report the news of other deaths. The disease had raged in Michael from mid afternoon the day before. Since no one came anymore to the gatehouse, no one had noticed. Throughout the night he called for water through his broken teeth, and tossed his bowlegged dwarfish body into pits and ditches, clawing the ground for some coolness for his burning chest. Brother Thomas, as was his nightly custom, also tossed and turned in his sleep, calling by name the twenty-three devils that besieged him. Brother Namlis, however, snored soundly, having modestly put his mind to rest that what will be will be, seeing the wise heads of Europe say there is nothing to be done. The College of Physicians at Paris had issued a gloomy report advising flight. One would not expect a tongueless hunchback to have suggestions to the contrary.

Brother Benedict kept his vigil before his crucifix and Brother Harald awoke at matins and lit a candle and bid the others follow him into the church to say their prayers. The stone floor was cold to the touch and Will carefully fished with his big toe for his slippers, not caring to make more than one toe uncomfortable. The bell rang. Their breaths made vapor on the air. Will kept his cloak wrapped around him, careful it not swish up the cold air around his legs, and filed quietly past Brother Benedict's bed in the a.m. darkness.

The news of Michael the Gatekeeper's death was brought in by the breviator later in the afternoon. He had come to tell them that two brethren from Abbot Denis' monastery were dead with plague and "that one such lays outside the gate of Bodmin." Will was sent to investigate and to take the breviator back with him with the instruction that "seeing nought can be done in this severe calamity it would be best not to come again." The breviator thought it best too. "Madness has seized the world and I would not be abroad in it. In Bodmin Village six are dead this morning and the lepers are afraid beyond all reckoning and have taken to banging on their doors by night and by day and the people cannot bear the noise of it anymore. There is terrible talk all about."

"What kind of talk?" Will asked, for by now rumor and gossip was held to be as dangerous as the plague.

The breviator scratched his head. Will pressed him. "I cannot say for sure," the breviator said at last, and he could not, "for the talk is all of doom and the world's end and such like talk that has not been heard by me. The alewife has perished, and the alewife's husband has gone daft. He has lost the good of her work and two lads and has but one left to help him bring the winter wood in."

Will thanked him for the news as he saw him to the gate. From a distance he ascertained that Michael the gatekeeper was indeed dead. He shut the gate after the breviator left, and brought the news back to the others.

"We cannot leave his body outdoors," he said.

Prior Godfrey drummed his fingers on the arms of his chair. Unholy motives might be imputed to him for being impatient with Will, but he could not see the sense of bringing Michael the gatekeeper's's body within the walls, dead and menacing, when live it had spent its time happily enough outside the walls. Nor was there any clear ruling for these times on the question of hallowed burial ground. "It is not fit," he said, "that he be buried in the brethren's cemetery."

They sat in the Chapter Room to debate the issue, and quarrelled over it, for there was no remedy that pleased two at the same time and if a remedy such as Brother Harald's advice that they burn the body pleased him, it ceased to please Brother Claude who had originally suggested it.

"Who will go outside the gate to perform the task?" he asked sneeringly.

It was a cruel question. Philosophy came asunder. Brother Ralph whistled between his teeth. Brother Claude turned choleric.

"How now, Brother Terror," Brother Harald chided him, "methinks such a man as yourself with your fiery temper would be best."

Brother Claude who, by devious intuition, guessed at Brother Harald's hypochondria, continued to sneer, "I take it, Brother Fear, you be not the man to perform this act of piety."

"It would be an act of mercy to send Brother Thomas," Brother Harald said, but Brother Thomas was not so far gone in his wits. His night time mind might wander, but his daytime mind saw the point about death readily.

Brother Anthony hissed at them through his yellow eyes. He turned his head away and mumbled his prayers into a corner of the room, fearing that his breath might be befouled by the others. When they gathered in the refectory for the evening meal, his place was empty. Silence being imposed on them, no one inquired, or cared to, nor had to, for Brother Anthony being who he was and what he was, they realized he had gone to bury Michael the gatekeeper. But having done this, he did not return, and no one inquired about this either, though everyone more or less surmised where he had gone next. He went to Bodmin Village, to the leper houses that had been deserted by their friars, and with no word to any member of the human race, not even a word of pity, only with his holy anger, he buried those he found dead in St. Laurance and brought water to the others, the dying and the frightened, and all day and all night read his prayer book to them for three weeks until the plague took him.

Brother Stephen missed the willfulness of Brother Anthony's spiritual edge, and he missed the competition of his discipline. By his mere presence, and that without affectation, Brother Anthony had kept Brother Stephen's irascibility in check, which now expressed itself with unbridled pleasure.

"You do bite well these days," Brother Harald said to him.

"Aye, with but two teeth," Brother Stephen said. "Had I a mouth of molars you would be gone."

"I say you have nothing to resent, Brother Ireland."

"I resent mankind," Brother Stephen said.

"Some men are made into saints by their anger," Brother Harald said, "and others into donkeys and insects."

"I take it, Brother Sly, you are not fit for either destiny."

They walked in the cloister, in their customary way, their voices sibilantly harsh with the irritability that comes to those who are forced to pass their lives together.

Only Brother John and Brother Walter were as before, the one mild, the other silent. Brother Bernard appeared full of gloomier thoughts than usual, and consequently more absentminded. He retired to the scriptorium more often, where he found more and more consolation in his rolls, recording the deaths of those in Bodmin Village, the falling taxes, the falling prices and the rising wages.

Neither Brother Claude's temper nor his piety wore well under the circumstances. To Prior Godfrey's disgust, Brother Claude took to wearing sackcloth and walking the length of the nave on his knees. Prior Godfrey himself kept to his room as much as possible, where he amused himself with St. George's company, thoughts of vengeance on Leboren, and who and when and how to send a messenger to London.

On Dec. 15, he made up his mind he must send someone with all haste, and went to get the accounting books from Brother Bernard in the scriptorium, but that long-legged, harmless, faithful chronicler lay on the floor of the caracel where he had died a few hours earlier, having entered his last account into his rolls: summa omnium expensarium. His face was mottled. His thick tongue hung out of his mouth. He died with the signs of the times upon him, and with an epitaph passed by Will:

decent man, kind, loyal monk who lived so quietly that none knew you.

There were no debates about where and whether to bury him, for his body lay on the monastery floor. It was lifted up by Brother Stephen and Will and carried by them to the cemetery.

"Without and within," Brother Stephen cackled.

"What mean you?" Will said, not in a good humor.

"Without and within. It is all the same. Without and within," and within two days he left Bodmin Priory and disappeared.

"Better yet," Brother Harald said the next morning, after breakfast, "seeing he took no food with him."

Brother John pressed his lips together, but passed no spoken word of censure. Will could not forebear. "Better food in his belly than in yours."

Brother Harald was the kind of man whom sentiments of this kind filled him with contempt rather than with anger. "Speak for yourself, Brother Kind," he hissed.

The argument was about reality, and Brother Harald believed he read it right, but he did not care to be thought less charitable than another because he read the handwriting on the wall. He coveted a good reputation as much as the next man did, and could not bear to have his character impugned at the expense of another's inability to read the world. The pressure lay on Will too. The pressure lay all about, the fear of witnessing presumed charities slip away. "I met a pilgrim in Wodesbridge," Brother Harald said to Will the next day, "who says the wife you married be a brothel keeper and the cocks crow all about her."

Steady, Will said to himself. He cannot, nor any man in England, know anything. "Worse," he said, jabbing the word as if it were a spear at a bull.

"Worse!" Brother Harald exclaimed. His eyebrows pinched together at the bridge of his nose. He was intriqued.

It was wintry cold in the cloisters and they took their noonday walk in boots and fur capes. Will felt his temper snapping. He was a man who could be challenged in his soul, but who could not bear sassiness. He could not hold his tongue anymore with Brother Harald. "Hold your tongue," he said to himself, but he knew the way of the tongue and the clapper, and he betrayed himself even as he admonished himself. "Would to God she were a brothel keeper," he said to Brother Harald, "and brought some coin in for her evil ways, but she be a Jewess of which evil there is nothing to be made."

Brother Harald, for the first time that anyone knew of it, laughed out loud. "The man has wit," he thought to himself. "There be not a Jew in England from the time of the first Edward," he said to Will, with a warning look on his face that he was not the man to be fooled with a cock and bull story. "They be banished now fifty years."

Will was pleased with himself. "Canst banish water? Or the serpent. Or air or an odor that blows?"

Brother Harald thought for two days about Will's response. So much did it entertain him that his thoughts moderated his voice in the choir box, though no one sung near him now, Brother Benedict being in bed, Brother Anthony being away, Brother Namlis being tongueless and Brother Stephen being gone.

The winter light came in through the window over the Majestatis, thin and gray as their voices. The place where Brother Bernard had sat seemed emptiest of all, though no one had missed him while he lived. So regular were the places where they slept and ate and prayed, that the empty beds and the empty chairs were mordant signs that surrounded everything they did.

Brother Claude was now more frequently given the duties of hebdomadarian, reading from the gospels and the Book of Martyrs in a voice that made Brother Harald spiteful. Even Brother Walter was prevailed upon to read the psalter, and with much contrition opened his mouth. So much were the routines altered, the brethren came into the kitchen to help themselves to their meals.

In the meantime, Brother Harald, with much to occupy his mind, ruminated about his talk with Will. "It cannot be, but on the other hand," etc. By the end of the third day he made up his mind that it was, and said to Will in the cloister, "So that is your great secret. Why you have become a monk. Tell me, Brother Tricked, since you were bound thigh and hoof in the nuptial bed, what is the Jewess like?"

"Brother Curious," Will said spitefully, "I will tell you that what there is between your legs would not find peace there, or elsewhere"

Brother Harald could not get more from him than spite. He asked permission of Prior Godfrey to speak with him in his private room. Prior Godfrey was compelled to consent, though he did not care to be in close quarters with anyone these days, and particularly not with Brother Harald, whom he had suspected of harboring a secret disease all these years. He lit a roaring fire in the fireplace in his room and set himself in the path of the smoke and bid Brother Harald stay on the other side of the room. His response to the news was the same as Brother Harald's had been at first. "It cannot be!" Beads of sweat broke out on his face from the heat of the fire, while on the other side of the room Brother Harald froze with chill.

"Why would a man noise such a thing about except that it be true?"

St. George did not like the smoke at all, and he was not convinced it kept the plague away. It made his eyes blink too fast. Prior Godfrey lowered himself into a chair in the path of the smoke and waved as much of it as he could on to his face as he digested Brother Harald's arguments. Could it be? But would a man say so if it were not? Will had not the wit to make up such a thing. "Praised be to God," he finally said, and raised his arms accordingly. "He will know where to raise coin." And thus it was that Will was sent to London, and told to go immediately.

But Will was disconcerted to hear this. He did not know why he was chosen and preferred not to be, for it seemed to him, as it did to the others, that if there was safety left anywhere it was within the walls, and not without, and certainly not in London.

But even this comfort was gone by the next morning

for, without warning, at the breakfast table, without preparation, without sign or symbol, in the plain barrenness of the reality, Brother Claude's hand faltered as he brought the cereal to his mouth. The trembling was noticed immediately. "Tis nothing," he said, but he had fever and he knew it. "How now, Brother Europe," Brother Harald thought, and picked up his bowl and moved to the other end of the table.

"May the English rot," Brother Claude said aloud and tried to ignore his shaking hand. With great effort he lowered his face to his arm and licked up the gruel. Sweat broke out in his armpits. Chill wrapped itself like a snake around his neck and shoulders. "Brethren, I pray you, help," he suddenly cried. His tongue began to thicken. His chest ached and rattled with mucous. Images of hell moved very close to him, deformities that had not been imagined by the Creator and could not be found on earth, but were found in books, in art, and in the imagination of mortals. Eels that lived on land bit his toes. Birds, formerly thought benign, wrapped their wet wings about him and dug their spikey claws into a thousand places in his skin. His chest burned. His voice rasped. The claws of a thousand creatures tore at his throat. Nothing on earth, not the plague itself, was comparable to the monsters that burst from his mind, spawned by a thousand creators who had painted the soul of man. His hand swept the dishes and his psalter from the table. His fingers clutched spastically at· his forehead, at the creatures that sat there. His imagination cracked open and the shapes of hell oozed out, inchoate nightforms, protean and indecipherable, unmatched by anything on earth, and very intimate. He prayed, he pleaded, he rattled, he ached. Even malignant earth seemed worth the struggle to stay alive to this mass of Christian pain, but his tongue swelled beyond the size of his mouth and betrayed his words. Black, it became obscene as it was lascivious with its curl and tip and cruel refinements. It emerged from his mouth which could no longer hold it, furry and prickly and swollen, a common organ gone awry, demented with size and discoloration. It burst all reason to think that so common an object could become so transformed that its original design was destroyed. He could not say his terrors anymore. His restraints gave way. He fled to the church, praying to be saved, but he could not say from what, so much he feared leaving this world and feared the next one. "Brethren, I pray you, help," he wept, he crawled down the nave, he beat his forehead on the church floor.

Only Will and Brother John followed after him, and they kept a distance. "What wouldst?" Will called to him, but Brother Claude could not say anything more. He found no correspondence between his fears and anything offered him. "Wouldst water?" Will called out to him. "Nay, nay, nay," Brother Claude cried and beat the floor with his head and his hands. No form of remedy occurred to him. No image fit the affliction he felt. Still he crawled to the altar in hopes of being rescued. He was a mass of discomfort, burning and freezing at the same time. What remedy could there be in this contradiction? Here he burned, there he froze. The temperature of his body fought itself. He did not know whether he wished to live, seeing his pain was insurmountable, or if he wished to die, seeing he was eternally damned. He did not know if he wished to be saved from this world or from the next. He managed the altar steps, only to feel the weight of the judgment of the Majestatis that looked down upon him, the judgment he could no longer evade as the magnitude of what he was burst his dying eardrums with a thousand snippets of gossip about his life that no Christian piety could relieve him of the embarrassment of having lived. Man who has drunk blood cannot slake his thirst with water.

Mercifully, he died quickly of multiple causes: heart failure, plague, and fear.

The rest sat in the refectory, numb and tense as they listened to his ravings. They sat until they heard nothing anymore, and the silence brought them a specious relief. Brother Harald grasped the issue in its entirety and reminded them that it would only make matters worse if the body were not removed quickly, and suggested they draw lots immediately. The lot fell to Brother Namlis who, not having a tongue to protest his bad luck, bowed to it. But Brother John and Will volunteered to help him dig the grave. The times could not elicit much better, but these three formed a liaison of spirit and acted against the narrowing of human charity.

The day was unrelieved in its tension. Each Brother crowded into himself, no longer a member of the community. Brother Namlis, Brother John and Will dug the plot silently and wrapped Brother Claude's sadly unloved body in a blanket, dressed as he died, so that no one had to touch his skin, their faces wrapped with cloths so as not to breathe in the affects. That only they attended the burial seemed worse than the plague itself, for a man, no matter what his life has been, should be buried by his peers as a sign of the generation in which he has lived, but in this generation the social context had disappeared. They buried Brother Claude in the cemetery, in a plot next to Brother Bernard and prayed for his soul, "In the name of the Father and the Son and the Holy Ghost," and fled back to the Chapter Room as quickly as they could, for the air itself had become their enemy, causing suspicion with every breath they inhaled.

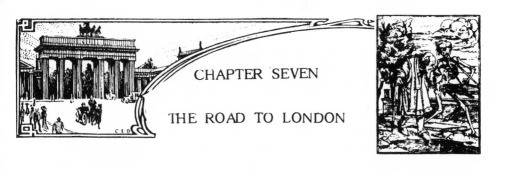

CHAPTER SEVEN

THE ROAD TO LONDON

Will avoided the moors. His memory of them was not pleasant. And because he avoided the moors, he unwittingly followed the path of the plague along the coastal towns. Not once as he rode did he see a sky not blackened by vultures nor a village not surrounded by ditches filled with dead bodies and with bonfires around it, lit to purify the air. Everywhere along the roads were streams of people, going from here to there, following rumors of safety, mostly pressing northward away from the coastal areas. Since the markets and fairs of the districts had been shut down, these were not traders or drovers or merchants, but people without wagons, pulling an ox, a sheep, a pig or whatever else was left them of their husbandry, since they could not take the fields with them. They were refugees, who had left the manors and the villages that they had lived in for hundreds of years. Some fled from villages that had not been touched at all, but fear and rumor drove them out as keenly as the plague itself. In the distance, over the fields which lay untended, Will could see the walls that circled the towns or monasteries, in every case tightly shut against the fleeing people who, in most cases, were carrying the plague with them.

Brother Namlis and Brother John had seen Will to the gate that morning to say goodbye. Will mounted Maream, and jiggled her bells diffidently, a gesture to keep up his spirits. She leaned to the right and licked the wind, for what did she know. He took several days' supply of food and instructions "to go in breeches, the times being what they are." Brother Namlis cried at his going, a sound too horrible to hear.

"For pity's sake," Will berated him. "Let me go in peace as I can."

When life becomes a matter of survival some, like Brother Harald, see it metaphysically. The meanness of the times justifies everything, including themselves. Others, like Brother Namlis, see no special message in catastrophe other than "things have gone very sour." Brother Namlis had no world view, but he wished it was Brother Harald who was leaving this morning. He had never complained about things before. He had not even complained that his mother had cut out his tongue. On the contrary, he believed he would meet her in the afterworld and that she would explain her actions to him. But he took it as a bad sign that it was Will who was being sent, and not Brother Harald. He wanted Will to stay, and he begrudged the powers that had decided otherwise.

"Christ keep you and bring you back," Brother John said, "for I know not if we can bear with the company of the others without you."

The pubescent light was gone from his face, the look of future grace. "I know not if we will meet again," he said, summoning the courage to say it. "Christ be with you always." Brother Namlis could not say anything and did not affect any courage and plainly wept, but he proved reliable nonetheless. When Brother John fell ill, he never ceased to nurse him, and when he died, he dug the pit for him and carried him to the cemetery in trembling arms.

Will rode away, his eyes on the horizon, under an unpleasant sky filled with carrion. Near the towns, the plague carts travelled the roads where there were no burial grounds left anymore. The groans of those who were not yet dead could be heard coming from the carts. Will was fearful of the gravediggers and pretended not to hear anything. He clicked noisily to Maream who bucked her head away from the noxious smelling carts. "No doubt," Will said to himself, "it be my imagination," but he knew it wasn't.

Some said the gravediggers did their job too willingly, for there never was a time when death was not profitable. Rings on the fingers, a gold piece in the hem of a dress, a brooch on a child. It's the eternal business. The dead are the safest investment. They never come back to make a claim against you. You may borrow from them forever, non-returnable goods.

This suspicion so gripped the people that the gravediggers, along with the lepers, Jews, and doctors, were accused of spreading the plague. And once aroused, European man is not known for assuaging his hostilities. Scores of gravediggers were killed from time to time, a fitting end! But more always arose to take their place, for employment was always to be had. They were drawn from the criminal and poorest classes, so they had nothing to lose but their lives and more to gain, if they survived this employment, than any other class. It was the chance of a lifetime. The grimness of it all, the tightrope of opportunity they walked on, was etched into their faces with centuries of careworn envy for little things and the dirt of burial places thick beneath their nails. Families came to bury their dead and never noticed who did the digging while they did the praying. It was clear why those who prayed prayed, but why did the others dig?

The fact was that in all of Europe there were no others to compare with the gravediggers for courage and steadfastness. They walked into houses where three lay dead, they walked into houses where a family of eight were dead, including the barnyard geese and the dog and the cat who were skinned for their fur. They walked into rooms where the priest would not come. They walked into houses where friends would not come. They walked into inns where a knight lay dead. They walked into rooms where a child in a linen cap lay with her eyes still open, with her mother dead beside her.

They were hated and needed, which is the worst social condition to be in. They were detested, and in demand. Like prostitutes, and other such, pawnbrokers and usurers, undertakers and garbage collectors, they did the dirty work of their civilization. Every family, every monastery, even peasants and reeves and knights and bishops and monks called for their service. When they came, their clients cursed them. The gravediggers knew what they were: profiteers in shadow, identified with the disease, so that even courage and sympathy, when it was found in them, could not redound to their credit, for it was counted as part of their plot to profit.

European man distrusted the doctor who perchance came to help him, he distrusted the priest who perchance came to pray him into the next world; he distrusted his relatives who waited for his death. He hid the rings on his fingers under his blankets and believed that the entire world schemed to get his little gold nugget. And this mistrust that came with the plague was both right and wrong, for sometimes it was true and sometimes it wasn't, but you couldn't tell until it was too late when many of the bodies of the plague victims were found with their ring fingers cut off.

No one would let Will in for a night's sleep, neither at the monasteries or the castles, though he carried with him safe conduct papers and other credentials. They did him no good, for no one came to answer his knock to read his credentials. He had to sleep on the ground, an unfair thing in December. He made a bed as best he could beneath Maream's body and bid her not piss or he would take measures she would not forget. Maream was sympathetic. All night, she kept watch and self control, glad to relinquish both in the morning. Will slept on his pouch of papers and covered himself with his cloak. All the same, in the morning his leather breeches cracked with the cold and chafed his legs when he rode so that he cursed Maream for her substantial hide.

"Ingrate," she thought, and like every other living beast reflected on how unjust life was, that she should carry a man around on her back when it should be the other way. Her bells jangled less jauntily that morning as they rode. Will detected the strain in their relationship and tried to soothe it away. "It be the times," he said. In all fairness to Will, he was a naturally sympathetic man to everything that lived, but conscience and cold nagged at him. Lovingkindness does best in a warm house and in breeches that do not crack with cold in the groin. In a strip of forest, out of Exmouth, to make it up to his conscience, Will offered a ride to a working man he saw on the road with a sack on his back filled with a spade and a shovel and whatever else. He offered him a ride in hopes of conversation, as well as out of charity, but the man was not the talking kind, or may have been, but was not any longer. He accepted the ride and mounted behind Will and minded his manners and thanked him, and then fell silent for the most part.

"Whereya bound for?" Will asked.

"Up ahead aways."

"Where come you from?"

"Wareham on Poole Bay."

"What brought you out seeing you ain't no carter and you have no goods to sell?"

"The plague," he said. "The plague brought me out. My family be gone in the plague, my wife, a son of ten and a set of twin gals. The lord of my manor and his wife be dead same as the reeve an' the miller. Nought left in my village but two free men as myself." Then he set his eyes on the cold air and said nothing more. So they rode in silence for two hours until Will got hungry. He took out some bread and cheese and offered them to him. The man mumbled, "thankye," and took it and said no more. So they rode in silence for two more hours, there being little to say to this history but to watch the sky and to listen to Maream's bells. Will realized that he had not seen a fire or smoke in some time, and realized too that most of the villages were deserted here. "See you a light anywhere?" he asked.

"Nane."

"They say the plague lasts not forever. It stays its time and goes."

"It is all one to me. I care not what the plague does anymore."

"Aye. It is hard to hope for shore in the middle of the ocean."

The man decided he did not need philosophy in addition to the plague and bid Will stop the horse so that he could get off. "God go with you," Will said.

"Aye. I would that He would, that I do. I wish him go with my wife and all," and he turned into the woods.

Will made his bed on the ground again that night and repeated his warning to Maream, who cared not a bit for this arrangement. Like all living things, she missed her stall, her straw, the company of other horses, natures she could understand, sounds they made that reverberated in her cells. Species comfort is not to be lightly set aside. Even Will, in cold discomfort upon the winter ground, dreamed of his home in York and smelled his old bed with his Brother Davey in it hanging on to his toe while he himself hung on to Rug's tail and the bed heaved with animal warmth as they sailed through the night in a huddle of man and beast. Will woke unwillingly, as any man would on a cold morning. Still dreaming of warmth, he clung to Rug's side while faces steamed above him in the frosty morning air and a harsh voice called to him. It was not his mother's, for it was a masculine voice, and it was not his father's, for it was a mocking voice and Will had never known his father to mock or to chide, rarely even to laugh, with little to say about most things but "yea" or "nane." He was a straightforward man and sure as Will lay on the ground in winter, this one wasn't. This one's voice curled and looped and sparkled and loved to sport with disaster, not like Brother Harald in a philosophical way but more like Walt who sucked the marrow of discord with glee as a goad to the promised land.

"Walt!" Will brawled out and jumped up from the ground. "what does you on this road in this calamity of cold?"

"Same as you," Walt said, "fleeing." Behind him pressed a crowd of fifteen like him, some villagers Will recognized, Cupper the Carrier, Simon Muleward, Hugh Alyn, Osbourne the Gardener, and Robert Leboren sporting an "F" on his forehead.

"Ah ain't fleeing," Will said. "I go to London on an errand."

"Sayest you?" Walt said, eyes already twinkling. "What may be that errand that you travel in breeches for?"

Instinct warned Will not to discuss it with Walt. "An errand," he said, and said nothing more, but climbed on Maream, flicked her bells, and bid Walt good day.

"Carest not for our company?" Walt called after him.

"I best hurry," Will said diplomatically.

"Aye," Walt called after him, "seeing how your roof covers you not anymore."

"Plague be on you," Will swore, them reminded himself it was not a thing to say these days. He whipped Maream and put as much distance as he could as quickly as possible between himself and Walt.

He passed through Melcombe Regis where some say the plague first entered England. At least, it had raged there since September. The fields were untended, but there were no plague carts on the road and Will began to hope that the worst was over in Melcombe Regis. But if the worst was over in one place, it had gone on to another. Will had no more bread left, and no food for Maream. Hunger was not much better than the plague, if it came to dying of something. "Never mind," he consoled Maream, "we shall be in Winchester on the morrow and food cannot fail us there," but Maream did not care for this form of comfort. She had been petted and kept for errands and messages and had been kept well for her duties, and she did not understand the meaning of scarcity. Food lay in the fields all about, but Will would not take it because of the ooze and rot that was on it. Maream became nervous and bucked her head. Will protested his own discomfort. "Think you I have food? I have no food. It is the same for man and beast and you best put your mind to it."

At Bournemouth, he went to the inns in search of something to eat, but they were shut. "Closed," a sign said, "because of plague," and there was a red cross on

the door which warned Will to stay away. He went to a
nearby tavern, but there was nothing to be had there but
ale, and the alewife was dead and could not pour and her
husband was sunken in spirits.

"Blast you," Maream said, "if I carry you a foot
further without food," and she sank on her knees.

"Help," Will cried to the tavernkeeper. "See you my
beast fainting?"

"There be hay on the floor of the church," the
tavernkeeper said. "The priest there is dead three days,
and none come to church anymore. For all I care, you
may eat the hay yourself along with your mare."

At the church a lad hung about and said in his
desultory way of hanging about after a great catastrophe,
"The priest is dead. There is none to hear confession."

"Has the plague been here?" Will asked.

"It's been and gone."

Will led Maream into the church where she gratefully
ate the hay from the floor. The boy followed. "Hast
food for me?" Will asked.

The boy clicked his teeth wizendly. "There was some
in my father's house, but I know not if it be gone by
now."

"I thank you," Will said, "I thank you for whatever
little." He tied Maream to a pew and walked back with
the boy to his house, who announced Will's purpose to his
father with little ceremony. "This here man wants a
piece of bread."

"The times be evil," the man said. He sat on a chair
in an empty room, like a rock that had never known
movement. "There is not food for three where twelve
must be fed." He looked Will over. "Where be you
from?"

"Bodmin Priory," dumb Will answered.

A distancing glint came into the man's eyes. "A monk
in breeches! Flee you?"

"Nay. A monk on an errand."

"A monk all the same. It be a good day when monks
come abegging for food."

Will would not let himself stand accused on behalf of

unknown factorings. "I think it be a bad day when any man begs for food."

The man was a burly, hungover sort who had been content to accept his lot until the plague had worsened it. It not only took away his family, it took away his work, for he was a carrier for the local monastery and they had shut themselves in and would allow no one to pass through their gates. The town had done the same, had posted a watchman on its walls who threatened anyone who came there, with a bow and arrow. The man now was exposed in his poverty. The plague stripped him down to belly and idle hours.

In such a mood, resentments accumulate. Hard times expose different currents. He was a poor man to whom poverty was a natural state, but he had slipped a notch below what he deemed natural and he was, in a coarsely natural way, aware of the power of a piece of bread and held it meanly in his hands.

"I never wished harm to any man," Will said.

"Nor I," the man said. "The monks wish it not, but they do it."

Will forced his eyes away from the bread. "I am a novice. I say it not for your pardon, but that I am a learner and hoped to do God's work and not evil to any man. And now though I be hungry and you have bread, I will take my leave of you."

The man relented and pushed the bread towards him, begrudging his own good instincts. "Take it, seeing an empty stomach has noght to say to any man."

"I shall surely pray for you."

"Nay, pray not. I'd sooner plant a seed in the dead earth as say a prayer."

Will took the bread and thanked the man and hurried back to the church for Maream. He mounted her and went on to Winchester, which he reached by noon the next day.

The great cathedral city was quiet. The bishop had given orders not to toll the bells anymore, for in these times they conveyed only the news of death and caused too much gloom to hear.

But everything did not come to a halt in plaguetime, and less so in England than on the continent. The persistence of life is formidable. The Hundred Years War continued, as well as other things. Some things were accelerated, like burying, while some things were postponed, like Parliament. Some things merely suffered an interruption, like the remodeling of the great cathedral, so that when Will saw it it was halfway there and halfway not, but still a landmark in every way. The height of the arcade had been doubled, and the old wooden ceiling had been replaced by a stone vault. The cathedral was being remodeled along the new architectural style of the fourteenth century, the perpendicular style famously founded by the wool merchants.

Outside of Winchester, Maream showed symptoms of sickness. Her knees buckled, whether from hunger or otherwise, and she refused to carry Will any further.

"Up," he said aggressively, but she stood her ground and would not move.

"Up," he commanded.

She flicked an ear at him.

"What say you?" a voice said, "she be of no use to you anymore."

Will wheeled around and saw six armed men standing in a circle. "Nay," he said, "you will not lay a hand on her."

"It is but a beast," one said.

"And the Scriptures say Adam was given the beast for his own."

"Nay," Will said, "I have heard that the Jews forbid the eating of an animal in the fields. So it cannot be that Adam was given the beast for such a cause."

"This be not Paradise," a fourth said, "and we follow not the Jew's law."

Will backed away. "Hear me," he said, "I am hungry too. Such be the times, man and beast are hungry together. But she is not a beast fit for a man's belly. I tell you truthfully the plague be in her, for did you not see her legs go down. See for yourself that she cannot carry herself," and he picked up a rock and flung it at her. She turned her head towards him, amazed and dismayed. He threw another rock at her, and she moved away, slowly and skittishly. Will scrambled for another rock and had only raised his arm when she sensed something unholy in this attention and loped forward, trotting on her buckling legs. The six men began to pursue her. Will threw a third rock and shouted to her to run. She loped slowly forward. Her bells jangled discordantly. Will could not bear the sound, which betrayed her wherever she went.

What to do about the beasts? If it was hard to know what to do about one's fellowman, it was harder to know what to do about the beasts. The difference between species was apparent in crisis. Will wept for her, as he would not weep for Brother Harald, but what he might have done for a fellowman under similar circumstances, he would not do for Maream, though she bore him on her back.

He turned away from the sound of her bells and the sound of the men running after her and ran off in another direction, hoping to be far away when they overtook her.

As he was now on foot, it was not long before Walt caught up with him. "How come you to be afoot?" he asked.

Will resigned himself to his presence, seeing he could not flee him without a horse. "My horse has run away and is pursued by ruffians."

Walt shook his head. "The times be evil for man and beast. Go you to London?"

"Aye. Afoot now."

"Aye, as we do. You are welcome to our company."

Will could find no ready excuse to refuse Walt's invitation. "Companionship is sweet for the traveller," he said.

Walt accepted what he wanted of this with a straight face. He could be well mannered when he cared to be, but not for long. Sooner or later his native grouch rose to the surface. He walked beside Will with an air of courteous restraint, his torn psalter swinging by the side of his torn leather pants, his hose crumpled, his teeth loosening, his hair thinning and marvellously unkempt. Cupper the Carrier and Hugh Alyn and Osbourne the gardener and some of the others thought Will strange company for this trip, but they trusted Walt, and Walt trusted himself. So they tramped altogether through the woods to London.

Walt was unusually cheerful, considering the times and Will, though he swore he would have nothing to do with the man but walk beside him, could not resist asking him the reason for his happiness.

"We be free men," Walt said.

Will told himself not to go a step further in this talk, but he did. "What mean you?" he asked.

Walt had his answer prepared. He had a sermon prepared, but before he could deliver it they heard a voice calling for help, and the taunts of a mob in pursuit of a monk who wished to bury the dead on consecrated ground within the village of Windsor. He was pursued by those who wished otherwise. So keenly did they wish it otherwise, they took strong measures to prevent it, and beat him severely on his head with their shovels, men and women alike.

"What, ho!" Walt shouted. "Let be."

"Let be yourself," they said menacingly, ready to beat Walt as well, who showed surprising strength and acumen. He dodged a shovel, raised his knee to a man's groin and threw him to the ground with a flip of his arm. So rapidly are friends and enemies made in difficult times that Walt found himself defending the monk and Will found himself defending Walt. With that, the die was cast. Cupper and Hugh grabbed branches and rocks, and teeth and eyeballs were spit out on the ground. The men of Windsor, taken aback at finding opposition where they thought the woods were empty, believed the monk had secreted sympathizers in the forest, and flung their shovels away and fled, running fast but having the time to spit out curses over their shoulders.

"God split the pants and heart of him who would defend a monk."

'Aye, brethren," Walt called after them, "I am one with you there."

"Plague take you more than ever then," they shouted back.

"Good Christian," the monk said, dazzled by the bedraggled look of his savior, "who are you?"

"Walt of Landsend, and what be the cause of this melee?"

"The cause be the plague," the monk said. "The plague be the cause of everything." He rubbed a bruise on his head and picked off the twigs from his habit. "These be unholy men who wish to bury the dead without consecration."

"The dead be consecrated by the plague," Walt said.

In difficult times, when matters are split, a sentence or two is enough to show where a man stands on an issue. His talk is a vote. The monk understood. "You are a preacher," he said.

"A man of God," Walt said.

"A man of God would lay the dead in hallowed ground."

"Where these dead lay, the ground is hallowed."

And so it went in this contest. Each man had his pithy comment, for each attitude had been bred by history and had come to its point of crystallization in this century.

The monk shook his habit free of the dirt and dung and mud that had been flung at him. "I thank you nevertheless," he said, and went his way, limping in pain, his soul hurt in the worst way a soul can be hurt: attempting to save the soul of another. His forehead bled, his shoulder was twisted, and one leg looked crippled. Even Walt felt sorry for him, Walt who hated monkhood, friars, Carthusians, Benedictines, Cistercians, or whatever kind, "who cover the land like scabs." Though they prayed for the soul of man and read the Gospel the whole day, to a man like Walt they committed the unforgiveable sin: they ate well when others ate not at all. Albeit they fasted and minced at their food for their souls' sake, they ate where others ate not at all. Still, to see a man's head crushed with a shovel was an unlovely sight, and more so if that man be almost bald.

"You deceived our cause," Hugh Alyn said.

"Damme," Walt said, "if I stick not a hand out to a man who is drowning. You all know right well my thoughts on this matter."

"He would not do so for you," Robert Leboren said.

Walt scratched his head and said aloofly, as befits a leader, "The matter is not to be debated anymore. Go we now to London or not. I say we go to London." But he felt required to redeem his position by a show of mockery, and attacked Will as they tramped on through the woods. He called him a twaddler, an idler, and a lackey.

"Let go," Will said, hanging on to his temper, still hoping to see the other side of the man. "I be not any of these things."

"Aye," Walt agreed, to Will's surprise. "But tell me, Will, what be your errand?" Will would not say, nor did Walt need Will to tell him. "I know right well your prior has sent you to London to raise coin, though he preached on Sunday last against usury and such. So do all the priors and abbots preach and do otherwise."

Will's lips were screwed shut.

"Aye," Leboren said, "we need not you to tell us how the world goes. For a man can read the times whether he can read his letters or not."

"What means that letter on your forehead?" Will asked, as much out of curiosity as to change the subject.

"Know you not?" Walt said, who could hardly forebear on such an issue. "The king has passed a law that none may leave the land to look for work and to take wages, but is to work in bondage for him who claims him."

"Aye," Leboren said, "your own reeve did capture me and brand me."

"Nay, it cannot be," Will said.

"Aye," one of the Cornish men said, "it can be and is.

Stand you now with us, Will, against prelate and monk."

Will's heart fluttered. "What mean you?" he asked ineptly, for he knew what the man meant.

"Hear me right, Will," Walt said, "I do not say the Church is not a grand thing, but her servants are fleas and maggots, swarming over the whole of it and turning soul's meat to garbage, same as the fleas and the plague does in the meadow. Christ was not a monk and he was not a priest. I tell you what, Will. I think he was like me, a rebel preacher. What church had he and what land had he? What owned he but body and soul? And any man that says I came to do him harm, or his holy mother may well be a monk, for between Christ and monk is the same enmity as between Christ and the moneychangers in the temple, for what be the monks and the prelates but moneychangers when they come through for Peter's pence and let out on lend. What did Christ say but shame on that priest that walks in long robes, intones through his nose, and burns incense. And what do the monks but such. And who be that man but yourself, Will? You came to Bodmin for peace. You cannot have peace and truth. If Christ be truth, he is not peace. You must choose between them, as Christ chose. Had Christ wished for peace, never would he have taken up the cross. He would have stayed in the desert and fasted for his soul as the monks do. But he came not for peace. This generation must enter into heaven by violence, he has told us. So it has always been. Aye, Will. The truth be in your own pocket in the letter you carry with you to London. When my brethrens' bellies are fill up like your good Prior Godfrey's whose falcon eats better than the poor then will my sword be sheathed. Peace, peace, the man of plenty cries. In plenty there is much peace. In poverty there is no peace. There is no truth, there is no love. There is not even balm of animal life. For a wolf will feed her young, but a starving man willl eat his own. A hungry man has ever the sword's edge against his throat. Sow you righteousness and justice, as the Lord says, and you shall reap mercy. Stand with me, Will, stand with me now against prelate and monk."

They were then in the manor of Friedhanman, outside of London where, if we can trust the chronicler of that priory, the abbot and sixteen monks were set upon by the people of that village in this December of 1348. A mob broke down the gate to the priory, trampled on the altar and set fire to two buildings and locked the prior into his church. The crowd was fierce looking. Many had smeared their faces with ashes, either to hide their identities or to symbolize death, while a red "F" flamed on the foreheads of others.

"What, ho!" Walt cried, who never feared an angry crowd, and caught hold of the reins of one of the horses that fled by.

"Look out, man," the rider said, intent on his mischief.

"I be with you," Walt said, who had no doubts.

"Christ redeem you," the man said, and rode on.

"You cannot fall in with these men," Will cried to him.

"Aye, I can," Walt said, "Me and my men will. You please yourself," and off he went.

Will neither fell in nor fell out, but was carried along. Hugh Alyn, Osbourne, the men from the village, the men from his own manor, went past him with torches and blackened faces. The eye of Robert Leboren went through him like an arrow. Walt said in his ear, "Hear me, Will, the devil's altar is made of gold and is covered with lace. The devil's prayer is said in Latin. I speak from bereavement. What the people need is plain speech in God's language. They need not prittle prattle dominie patria. They need God to speak to them in the language to which they were born, the language they heard in their mother's mouth before the prelate ever spoke to them. Stand with me, Will," Walt said through the forest of tramping feet.

"You be a hot tempered miscreant," Will cried back, and shuddered at this curious crisis of taking up arms against the people who had promised to save their souls. The men from his manor pressed against him with their claims and bonds. The men from Cornwall went by him with their bedraggled faces smeared with ashes to give them the look of dreadful courage. They might be doomed to hell, as they believed they were, but they would risk it for the sake of some work and this world, they would risk their eternal souls for the world, they would risk damnation for a piece of bread.

"What be the "F" on your forehead," Will asked another.

"Fugitive," the man said. "I be branded for leaving my manor."

"What be your manor?"

"Friedhanman. And now I return to take my revenge that ever I was branded as Cain was. So be it, now I ride with Cain."

"Brother," Will said, "it was an unkind thing the Church did to brand you, but you should not ride against your manor."

"Stand aside," the man said.

"Stand with us," Walt cried, as they broke down the door to the church, and shouted with one voice, "Now wait we God's visitation," and swept forward as if their grudges had burst a dam, they caught hold of the prior who was crouching within, tied him to the altar and bid him pray for his soul.

So they rode throughout the night from monastery to monastery, setting fire to fields and stones, a foretaste of Wat Tyler's ride to London a generation later when his men broke down the manor house of the Knights Hospitaller and burned Lambeth and St. John's Priory and beheaded its Grand Prior, the Treasurer of the Realm.

Those who had horses rode on to other monasteries. Those on foot could not hope to keep up with them. Walt and his men bid the horsemen goodbye "and may the spirit of almighty God and freedom ride with you," they shouted after them, and made their way to London in high spirits, except for Will, who felt uneasy about what he was doing. But the times goaded them. The times burned in their bellies with hunger and fear. The times outraged their souls, though they wished no harm to any man and prayed to be redeemed.

Walt understood their mood, but he would not have their spirits troubled by these fears, he would not have this unprecedented taste of freedom thrown up by the times diminished by their religious conscience. He could not explain to them why they should be in opposition to the Church, but his conviction that it was right overwhelmed their doubts. He jumped aboard a wagon which stood empty by the side of the road outside Smithfield. "Hear me," he said, "hear me clear. Chide not your souls for what you did this night. I promise you, heaven will be not less your reward. Confuse not Christ with prior and bishop. I say if the Church lived as the Church ought there would be no usury in the land. It is Christian avarice, love of war and land and lend that has brought this misery to us. To expel the Jewish usurer is easy, but how rid we ourselves of Christian greed. I say the dance is one of land and lend. Brethren, I say to you, this day we be free men. As the Lord God took the Hebrew out of the land of Egypt he has freed us likewise this day from the bondage of the land. Now is the earth diseased with plague as in the days of Egypt. Now is all nature sick, earth and air and water and even the animals die before your eyes. I say bless the plague as the Israelite in Egypt blessed the plague. I say bless the vermin that kills the abbot's sheep. I say hold dear its dying. We are free men today. Free to wander where our legs will take us and free to labor with our arms for wages and none can tell us nay. Justice, justice you must follow, just laws and just taxation. We need not mercy and the bread of charity, for we be hardy enough for ourselves. As the Lord God made us he made us hardy to endure. We need just laws, justice and freedom, and mercy will be abundant in the land. I say bless the plague. Good comes to man in God's time. Hold fast this faith and weep no more for your dead. We are free men this day. Brethren, march we to London now even as Moses marched and follow we the God of freedom."

So Walt and Will, willy nilly, and Simon Muleward and Hugh Alyn and Robert Leboren with the "F" on his forehead for fugitive or freedom, and Cupper the Carrier, and the others, clubfooted, crosseyed, faces blackened by the smoke of the fires they had set, went on and soon were in sight of London which they knew by the smoke in the distance and the stench and the cries of the hogs being butchered outside the walls and the increase of the plague carts on the road. The look of crisis and accomplishment was on every man's face, that they had come so far, for never had these men expected to see London or any city. Though they could see nothing more of it than the smoke around it they knew the city was the sign of history where the record of man was kept.

It being the hour of Nones, Walt took out his Bible and bid the men kneel and pray. Will was glad to kneel with Walt, glad of an act he could share with him. Walt bent his knobbly knees to the ground and prayed in the field with his followers. "It is fit we give thanks, for it is not by our might that we are here, as the Lord God has said it, but by His spirit that we have arrived."

In his hour of triumph against the world, in his hour of history, pain seized him under his ribs as he prayed and pierced him to his backbone. Sweat broke out on his forehead and in his armpits. The plague struck Walt as he knelt, and he did not rise from the field. It was the only force that had ever robbed him of his voice and his breath.

The others perceived immediately what was wrong and began to back away, except for Will. He stayed his ground and grasped Walt under his armpits and tried to raise him up.

"It will pass," Walt said.

"Nay, it will not," Simon Muleward mumbled.

"Fetch him water," Will said.

"There is but a brackish stream close by," one said.

"Aye," Will said bitterly, "now seize we the day."

"It cannot be but as God wills," one said, beginning to feel doubts again about his actions.

"This be the year of the devil and not of God, "Will cried to him.

"Nay," Walt said, "curse not this day. Though I die, it

be a fair day."

"Nay," Will cried, to his own surprise, "you will not die."

"Methinks you were always wrong in your calculations," Walt said, gasping at his old merriment, but the sobriety of death was the stronger force. "Let be," he moaned. "Surely I have done my work. Move yonder with the others. It is not grace to watch an old dog die."

To his amazement, Will seized Walt's shoulders. "Nay, I cannot, though God knows you be rotten to set me down for ignorant now."

"Will," Walt tried to laugh, "you humor me well if you curse me, but I would you moved off with the others."

"I would I do as I would and I would that I stay. Hear me, Walt, you must stay with us, it cannot be otherwise," but blood broke from Walt's nose, a fog rose over his eyes. "Bless me," he said, dizzy with fright and pain, " you were always a quarrelsome monk." He tried to get up, but he staggered back. He fell on his knees. His psalter swung out from his leather belt. His leather jacket was torn in a thousand places and had been mended a thousand times.

"Walt," Will called to him. "Hear me, Walt, you have broken my heart. I promise, you will sup with God this day."

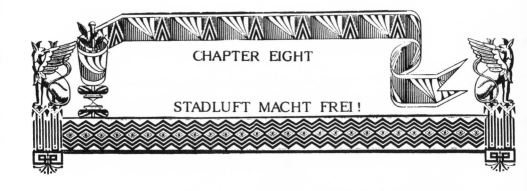

CHAPTER EIGHT

STADLUFT MACHT FREI !

It is often assumed that medieval cities not only wallowed in dirt, but wished to wallow in dirt, that they had no plumbing because they did not wish to have plumbing. We are indebted for our reassessment to the scholar, Sabine, who studied the two foremost problems of medieval London: "Butchering," and "Latrines and Cesspools." Contrary to modern judgments on medieval man, the municipal records of London for 1349, show that London citizens went to desperate lengths to rid themselves of excrement, some even suffering martyrdom. Here was Richard Raker, so keen for hygiene he built a latrine in his house, but in the course of its construction, misstepped through the rotten planks and drowned "moste monstrously in his owne ordure." Here were two men exposed at the Assize of Nuisances for piping their waters away into the cellar of a neighbor which ruse, in due time, was discovered when the water in his cellar rose unprecedently. And here was a woman who put a latrine "in her solar" and connected it by a wooden pipe with a street gutter in Queenhithl, ordered to remove "said offense." And here were good men who left bequests in their will for the repair of public latrines, unknown benefactors in the history of the city. But here were others, fined and pilloried for connecting pipes where they should not be connected: into the main street, into wells, into gardens, into rivers, into their neighbors' homes. Here was a Citizens Watch Committee set up not only to check the pipes and the flow to where and from whom, but littering of any manner, that so keenly punished a pedlar in Mary-la-Bow who in that year threw an eel skin to the ground and was immediately killed by his neighbors.

It is not true that medieval man desired his excrement. He wished it away, far away, into his neighbor's house or lawn or well. The records show that there was simply more of it than could be moved. Edward 111 registered a complaint that so clogged was the Thames that his royal barge could not make its way up that historical river.

In the economics of civilizations the two pressing problems are waste and death, both of which give rise to the problems of smell, making fumigation of the air the great need of all time, and the nose the most sensitive register of progress.

Nor is the intellect a guard against the problem. We find complaints made in Cambridge of "noxious open gutters made by the Masters of Michaelhouse and Ganville Hall, which ran from those colleges to High Street, through which many masters and scholars had access to the school of the University," having to brave "gutters which gave out so abominable a stench and so corrupted the air that many masters and scholars passing fell sick."

"Soap! For God's sake, give us a bar of soap!" That's the cry through the ages.

For what profits it if a people have a university if their pipes are clogged, or to have books if they have no pipes.

Build thy city on a mound to ensure drainage, or alongside a river or upon the shore, to ensure "watering" and "wafting" of the odors. Regard the fate of cities built on the plains. The smog cannot lift from them, and the wrath of heaven sits on them forever.

The Londoner was conscious of such matters early on. By 1307, the palace of Westminster had set the fashion in lavatories. A pipe ran from the king's room to the main sewer. The houses of lesser nobles had small platforms which jutted out over the Royal Thames where they could relieve themselves outside their rooms. In the courtyards great leaden urinals were kept at the ready. In other neighborhoods, not so fortunate to have the Thames go by, ditches were built to catch the flow. Garbage was collected, a formidable task in those days. A "raker" was appointed for each ward and there were as many as fifty carts and horses in the city for the removal of said stuff. Fines were levied: 2S in 1345 to any householder who left his "messe" outside his house. There were municipal bath houses, then as now confused with brothels, also known as stews. Many a man such as Will, got confused by the language, to his great embarrassment.

The problem was not ignorance or lack of motivation, or love of excrement. The problem was the problem.

During the plague the cemeteries were put outside the city walls, to the chagrin of the country dwellers. Two new cemeteries, one at Smithfield and one called Spittle Croft, were hastily dug to catch the overflow of death. Stowe, the London historian, claims he saw this inscription at Spittle Croft: "A great plague raging in the year of our Lord, 1349, this churchyard was consecrated wherein, and within the bounds of the present monastery were buried more than fifty thousand bodies of the dead, besides many others from then to the present time, whose souls God have mercy upon. Amen, amen, and amen."

The problem was more acute by Christmas time, and Will's spirits were low as he made his way into the city. The closer he came the more it looked and smelled like a charnel house instead of like the city it was famous for being, where the wealthy and the powerful dressed as the wealthy and the powerful should, and never was so much spent on fashions as when clothes and color were symbols of status set by the law, and everyone knew an alderman from a cardinal or a landed nobleman from a merchant by the color of his cape and the shape of his hat, by his furs and his velvets and his gold embroidered pearls, and his orient grained scarlet. Oh! age of fabric and cloth, of silks, linens and woads, worsted medley, vair, miniver, sendall and sable. London! City of foreigners, where

tradesmen of the continent, clothiers and spinners, came
to display their industriousness on the persons of your
citizens.

City of Commerce! They sailed up the Thames:
Flemish weavers, Genoese and Florentine bankers,
Venetian traders and Hansard importers. All gone in the
plague year. They lay now on top of carts like moppets
of history, dismal to Will's eyes as he came into the city
through Ludgate. A few months ago the squeals of dying
pigs drowned out the bells of St. Paul, and the smell of
their blood and their fright, as the butchers did their
work, buried the smell of the river, the air quivered with
cock fighting, bear baiting and hog killing, and the
shrieks of laughing children as they watched the animals
die, and helped to kill them with clubs and rocks.

Medieval man, famous for his heaven and hell in art
and theology, was not moved by sights such as these,
since his theology did not advise him where the animals
go after they die. They go to an animal afterworld,
where they hunt man. For surely even a cat or a bear
has its place in the great scheme of retribution which
God is said to have at His disposal, and which no doubt
consists of reversing the roles of hunter and hunted.
Seigneure Venous! You, who burned thirty horses alive for
the entertainment of your guests---surely these horses
wait for you.

Medieval Christian man did not take cognizance of
such deeds, for cruelty was not one of his seven deadly
sins.

Will made his way as best he could to Thames Street,
advised by such citizens as he found in the streets and
which he dared to speak to, where the house of Walter
Chaunton, Wool Merchant, Trader and Creditor was. He
carried with him his instructions and letter from Prior
Godfrey which Prior Godfrey had spent three days writing
and had told Will, "It is not worth your soul in heaven if
you deliver it not."

Will made his way through dreary lanes and gutters,
the gloom of that year being such it was difficult to
remember that he had arrived in London at Christmas

time, when medieval festivities were usually at their height with tournaments and jousts and ridings, with horse races in Smithfield, ice skating in Moorsefield, and boat jousts on the Thames, where the prosperity of the city was marked by the House of the Hanseatic League with its big scales in the Steelyard without which, as Daniel knew, no people can weigh their goods, bales of wool stacked in the churchyards, whose famous bells ringing at Matins, at Lauds, at Prime, Tierce, Sexts, Nones, and Vespers, at births and at deaths, shed their sounds as far as Highgate, four miles away.

For London was the "Place a l'Eglise" of Europe. On every street was a church or a monastery, with its hospital and its almonry, its college for priests and its house for priests, its charity and fraternity and endowment. The Priory of St. Bartholomew, the Priory of the Holy Trinity, the House of St. Mary Overies, the Hospital of St. Katherine, Priory of the Crutched Friars, St. Olaf's Church, the Order of St. Augustine, the Priory of St. Helen, St. Martin le Grand, the foundations of the Grey Friars, Christ Church and St. Nicholas Shambles and St. Ewin, the House of the Carmelites and the Order of the Mendicants, Tintern, and Glastonbury and Whitby.

Besant, in his history of London, gives this eulogistic description: "Every House was possessed of rich manors and broad lands; every House had its treasury filled with title-deeds as well as with heaps of gold and silver plate; every House had its church crowded with marble monuments, adorned with rich shrines and blazing altars and painted glass, such as we can no longer make....And they thought---priest and people alike---that it was all going to last forever."

The influence of St. Paul was visible in the precious relics it owned: a hand of St. John the Evangelist, a phial containing some drops of the virgin's milk, the arm of St. Mellitus, fragments from the skull of St. Thomas a Becket, a hair from St. Mary Magdalene, the entire head of St. Ethelbert, Jesus' knife, and a jewelled reliquary containing the blood of St. Paul. It was visible in the officers it employed: a bishop, a dean, four archdeacons, a treasurer, a precentor, a chancellor, thirty greater canons, twelve lesser canons, thirty vicars and fifty chantry priests; a sacristan and three vergers, a succentor, a Master of the Singing-school, a Master of the Grammar-School, an almoner and four vergers, a surveyor, twelve scribes, servitors, a book transcriber, a book-binder, the chamberlain, the rent-collector, the brewer, the baker, the singing-men, the choir boys and bedesmen, and all with their own servants. In addition: sextons, grave-diggers, gardeners, bell-ringers, makers and menders of ecclesiastical robes, cleaners and sweepers, carpenters, masons, painters, carvers and gilders. "St. Paul alone found a livelihood for thousands."

That church's opulence and industry was rivalled in its day only by the merchants who often lived in houses large enough to house six hundred guests, with courts and oriel windows and walls lined with tapestries and beds covered with skins, and walls covered with carvings of heraldic figures: unicorns, dolphins and dragons. Some merchants became legendarily powerful like Sir Henry Picard, once mayor of London, who is said to have gambled with five kings of Europe in one evening: Edward 111, John of France, King David of Scotland, the King of Cyprus, and the Black Prince. (The King of Cyprus was the loser that evening.)

"Seest thou a man diligent in his business. He shall stand before kings," went the proverb of the day, and the careers of many, like William de la Pole, proved the saying, though it sometimes cost the merchant a great deal when the king cancelled his debt to him; and it sometimes cost the merchant his life when the king cancelled the creditor; but it sometimes brought the merchant good fortune by way of a baronetcy or an earldom. Since the mayor of London, whose position was linked to his trade and guild connections, was taxed in that century the same as an earl, a mitred abbot or a bishop, he might as well be an earl.

A few random walkers were in the streets, but the usual sounds of the city were gone, the grinders and vendors and smithies, the cries of the drovers and carters and fishmongers, the clinging, the clanging, the hammering, the firing, the grinding, the screeching of animals, were silent.

Trade and work had stopped, and many who were in the streets should not have been there, being infected, though they did not know it, while others ran through the streets, driven crazy with the pain of the disease. In every parish there were daily incidents of this kind, setting everyone's nerves on edge. The dying would not die quietly but made public spectacles of themselves, though everything was done to prevent this. Every household had to report the outbreak of plague in it within two hours, and to put a large red cross in the center of its door. Watchmen were posted to keep guard over the houses where infection was known to be, so that no one could go in or out. Families were loath to report their cases, for the healthy became imprisoned with their sick, condemned to breathe their air, and were not let out even to buy food. The sick and the dying became the jailors of the healthy.

There were a few provident people who had boarded themselves and their families into their homes, and had hoarded and provided enough food to seal themselves off from the world for several months. They were those who had believed the rumors. They had some mechanism for smelling the air correctly, which the others did not have. Most others gambled with the rumors and lost, and then had to be sealed into their houses with insufficient food, and when they could, they fled through the pipes and the sewers. They bribed watchmen or tricked their way out, for boredom became as great a problem as the lack of food and the fear of death. Markets were closed and work was stopped and most people feared visiting each other. People walked abroad aimlessly, in the center of the streets, in single file, avoiding each other, carrying a garlic or a herbal ball pressed to their noses. Doctors and priests who had entered the homes of plague victims carried a red rod three feet long to warn the public of their presence. The merciful and the compassionate were shunned along with the lepers.

Midwives could not be had, and many women suffered alone in labor. The numbers of deaths from childbirth rose very high. Often an infected woman was delivered of an infected infant. Doctors' reports tell of buboes appearing in the groin of an infant not two hours old, and mother and child dead a few hours later.

Plague knows no class barrier, but famine does. The poor stand exposed in their poverty more than ever in plague time and die in incalculable numbers. But then their numbers are always greater to begin with and some, as an infamous king in eighth century Ireland, have gone so far as to see in plague a remedy for the poor.

There were others in the streets, men and women with vacant stares who had buried every member of their families and had passed the legally required forty days of quarantine. Judged to be safe, they had nothing to fear anymore. Deliverance gave them a desultory look, nothing pious, nothing triumphant. There were still others in the streets, the criers of doom who walked among the delivered and warned them of the wrath to come. They emerged from the plague fiery-eyed and filled with pronouncements of earthly corruption and judgment. The times gave birth to them as masters of it, and they rode the times like a master horseman, naked upon the animal.

Like them, quack curers and quack medicines flourished: "Sovereign Cordials Against Corruptions of the Air;" "An Universal Remedy for the Plague," adding to the skittishness, the cynicism, the desperation of the public mind, the psychotic public mind which became as injurious to itself as the plague. For when an event happens for which one explanation seems as good as another, the world loses its intellectual order. Reason and reasonableness crumble. A world in which any and every explanation will do, where everything is tried and nothing works, where every remedy is in doubt and every idea is in transit, is a protean world given over to the realm of the magician who can turn cats into rats, lepers into demons, Jews into devils, and God into Satan.

Hungry for information about its survival, the public

mind became preternaturally sharp and watched the universe for signs: clouds, wind, stars, changes in temperature. Mental processes became mercurial, too rapid for intellectual structure. Inhuman mistakes in judgment were made. Fevers, ague, tremors, chills or catarrh, running sores and rashes, were shunned as the plague. Old men with chest colds and children with scabby scales were thrown onto the plague carts. Women in childbirth were gagged and strapped to their beds lest their screams be taken for the plague and the house, with everyone in it, condemned.

Opinions about everything changed swiftly, while at the same time the actual pace of life became dull and monotonous. Individuals became isolated cells, while the public mind raged in the streets, ravenous with superstitions, its mental energies rendered inert with fear and speculations, trapped between the reality of the plague and a hypochondriacal terror of its own self.

It could be said that a flea had come to rule the world and claim the reward of the gnostic faiths. On every face that Will saw, the message was plainly written: theology had lost its accountability; religion and nature had parted ways, as religion and history have parted in our time: events were no longer consonant with the mercy and justice of God. In such times it is no mean feat to steer a boatload of terrified animals on the rising flood.

A woman made her way across a cobblestone lane, a scented ball pressed to her nose, a prostitute braving death for a few pennies, a brazen gleam of greed and need passing between her and anyone else who knew they must make good in these times or never.

The warehouses stood empty or filled with rotting goods. Their huge doors were shut tight, or swung open on a disheveled scene of unpacked goods, or goods spilled and sprawling, the signs of death and looting. In their rooms above, where it was the custom of the traders to live splendidly, they died like everyone else.

But there is a vitality to business that will carry London out of this gloom within the year, for the merchant class is singular, and from it has come the genius of Europe: St. Francis, Chaucer, Dante, Shakespeare---all born to merchant fathers.

The end of the century was marked by Sir William Sevenoake, the first known instance in England "of a lad of humble birth rising to great wealth in London," who left a portion of his wealth to found a grammar school in his native town. Hereafter, the money of the great merchants go to endow hospitals, to build roads, to supply water, to construct latrines, to sustain urban life. John Barnes, a wealthy business man "leaves a thousand marks for the use of young men to go into business." The age of endowing monasteries is over.

Prior Godfrey did not send Will in haste because he intuited the future, but because he knew from the past what his punishment would be if he failed to meet his debts. London recovered from the plague in a different manner from the countryside. Her future was no longer consonant with it. Worldliness came to Will from Prior Godfrey's nervous grumblings about his problems with debt, common to all who live beyond their means, even ecclesiastics. Love of wealth is natural to everyone, to Oriental man and to Occidental man. Who wants to be poor? Not even the poor want that.

Poor Will! He came to London at the wrong time. A year earlier or a year later would have been more suitable, but neither the future nor the past was of help now. The meaner sort of people slid by him: barefoot, brazen pilgrims, their eyes trained to look pious, slithering with holiness, lepers and leprous prostitutes, criminal looking people everywhere, except for a few of the better looking kind, women who made Will wish he had worn his novitiate's robe to ward off their warm looks, for some things go on as usual, even in plague time. Houses were shrouded and marked with the red cross where there was plague, but the taverns stood open and from the sounds inside and the swinging signs overhead, "The Cup and the Horn," or "The Plough and the Seed," and the toasts of the tipplers, "Here's to the old raker," you knew there was still life in the city, though the signs on the trade shops along the Chepway read:

CLOSED ON ACCOUNT OF PLAGUE

CLOSED DUE TO FAMINE AND WAR AND DISEASE

CLOSED BECAUSE OF HARD TIMES

Life had moved out of the markets and the churches and had gone underground into the taverns and the bawdy houses. Will was tempted, but he dismissed his temptation as much out of fear as to the oaths he had taken. Most of all, he wanted to get his errand over with. Urgency and dread of the city carried him forward. He wanted to be done and return as quickly as possible to Bodmin before temptation or plague seized him.

His path took him through the old Jewish neighborhood, whose signs and Hebrew markings on the stone walls, told him where he was: Huggin Lane, named for the Hagin family, descendants of R. Simeon of Treves, and the synagogue in Gresham, called Bakewell Hall in those times, the Domus Conversorum established in Chancery Lane by Henry 111 in 1232 as a domicile for converted Jews. There were cobblestones and whatever stones with Hebrew writings on it, which can be found in almost every city of Europe, from old tombstones now used to pave the streets or fix a breach in the city wall.

He went on to Thames Street, down near the wharves where the wool merchants kept their houses. The bales of wool lay stinking on the ground floor, and the stench from the river blew its foul air through his soul. A set of large steel scales hung from the ceiling beams, with the merchant's trademark scratched in them: a sheep's hoof and ear. The wool merchant, Chaunton, came into the hall, as if prepared to find Will there, or someone else with bad news, cancelled debts or cancelled debtors. Dressed in the silk permitted to his estate, wearing a tunic and a cap and a gold chain, he carried a letter in his hand which bore Bishop Roundsleigh's seal, and he rattled this unpleasantly.

Cancelling debts and even cancelling creditors was common business in these days. Finance, being in its nascent state, had not acquired the securities of our time. Its skeletal structure was plainly that of gambling. Risks were high and losses often drastic. This was an age when traders became very rich or very poor very quickly. When Edward 111 cancelled his debts to his creditors, great banking houses like that of Bardi and Peruzzi went bankrupt and dragged other banking houses down with them. Could the king do that? Apparently yes. He was the king. Some barons thought it was a good idea when the king cancelled his debt, hoping their taxes would be diminished. Other barons thought it was a bad idea, if they were connected with the creditors. Sometimes the barons who thought it was a good idea and the barons who thought it was a bad idea went to war with each other. The winner settled the fiscal policy. It's the winner's right to do that.

Kings were high risk investments. But if they won their wars and made a great deal of money in loot and ransom, the gamble for the creditor paid off. If the king lost his war, he cancelled his debt, or brought such charges against his creditor which might interest the Inquisition. If the Inquisition could not be interested in the charges, the king expelled or imprisoned the creditor. Could the king do that? Apparently yes. Still, there were always merchants who were eager to lend money to the king, because winning was everything, even though losing was too. The merchant might be rewarded with an earldom and his family crest established forever. The prize was immortality.

Though the risks were high, sometimes as high as death, it was the risk which justified the usury, a principle established by Thomas Aquinas: risk could justify the charging of interest rates without loss of soul or eternal life, and the investments in the Middle Ages were all very risky, so that the Christian usurer felt justified in charging as much as 83%, arguing that "he'd as lief go to hell for a sheep as for a lamb," while the Jew risked massacre and expulsion and his rates were set by the law at about 1/4 the Christian charges.

Walter Chaunton, wool merchant from Hull, had advanced monies to Bishop Roundsleigh against the collateral of the wool to be sheared from his sheep. In due time, Bishop Roundsleigh was forced to write to Chaunton: "Five thousand sheep dead due to plague. Debt cancelled. The Lord bless and keep the Church and her bishops, which has freed herself this day from the bondage of usury. In the name of the Father and the Son and the Holy Ghost, I am your gracious bishop,

Ever present with you in Spirit,
Signed this day, 30 November
in the year of our Lord, 1348
witnessed this day by my reeve and steward
to which is afixed my seal, as may be seen
by all honest men. Amen, amen, and amen.

The merchant laid the letter on the table amidst a clutter of coins he did his business with, coins of the many varieties of civilizations of his time. History need not be written in volumes and in encyclopedias. It can be written on the face of a coin and carried by ordinary people in their pockets, and they can cause revolutions. The Romans, as everyone knows, put the image of their emperor on their coins and caused a revolution in Judea. Jewish coins bore the image of the lily, a chalice of manna, a blossoming rod, the lulav and citron, a cornucopia with poppy head, and common inscriptions were, "Jerusalem the Holy," and "The Redemption of

Zion," but from the time of Constantine's conversion until the present day there are no coins minted in Europe carrying these images or inscriptions.

Like the Hebrews, the Moslems also objected to religious imagery on coins. They objected to the image of the Cross, the Virgin Mary and Christ on coins, and refused to use them in trade. Their coins bore only the date and place of minting, a quotation from the Koran and the statement in Arabic, "There is no God but Allah." In Byzantium, during the time of the Crusades, the religious iconography on Christian coins, the Chi-Rho, the Divine Hand, the Christ, was so shocking to Mohammedans it caused a crisis in trade between the east and the west. To alleviate the problem, coins were minted to accommodate the Islamic distaste for religious images. In 1124, the Crusaders in the east struck gold coins which imitated the Arab coins and proclaimed Islamic doctrine in Arabic writing. This allowed trade to continue, but Pope Innocent 111 excommunicated the minters.

There is an old saying that "money is money," but evidently it is not. Evidently, money is more than money. The Crusaders and the minters in the east sought another accommodation, one suitable to both Christian and Islamic religious sentiment. As Porteous describes it, "Thereafter the dinars of the Crusaders were distinguished by the sign of the cross and Arabic statements of Christian belief, which may have restricted their circulation farther east, but at least appeased western opinion." These Crusader coins are rare and exceptionally valuable.

The first coin in western civilization is alleged to have been minted in Lydia, in the Kingdom of Croesus. The habit of putting religious symbols or the images of one's gods on coins dates back at least to the Phoenicians who put the images of Zeus Marnas or Melkarth, the deity of Tyre, on their coins. Later, the Greeks put the head of Pallas Athene on coins, unabashedly connecting wisdom with money.

The Romans not only put the heads of their deified

emperors on their coins, but devised a monetary system designed to keep the ruling classes richer than the trading classes. They minted gold coins for tax purposes only, and used a less valuable, debased silver metal for purposes of trade.

The early Christians minted at first only for tax purposes. As Porteous points out, their mints were located "at all points where taxes might be gathered, not only royal fiefs and palaces, but also fortresses, local capitals, maritime and river ports, and toll places." But between the seventh and the thirteenth centuries, gold coinage "misteriously" ceased. During the seventh century there began an abrupt decline in the amount of available coin, which Porteous ascribes to "the persistent accumulation of treasure by the Church," causing "the withdrawal of gold from circulation." Gold disappeared, but taxes did not, and trade was on the increase, so coins were struck in other metals, less valuable metals such as silver. In the single year, 1279, 107,000 pounds of silver were used to mint coins in the Tower of London. In the following year, 1280, both Gui de Dampierre, Count of Flanders and of Mamur, and John of Brabant, minted silver coins in order to meet their wool payments to England.

During the Ages of Faith it was easy to mint coins. Almost anyone with access to the suitable metals could. No special building was required and the only requisite tools were a block, dies, hammer, and shears. A mint could be set up anywhere, in a castle or a stable. The English kings, however, always kept central control over the minting. In France, on the other hand, minting was as feudalized as the territory. Money was minted by dukes, counts, electors, lords, barons, abbots, abbesses, bishops and archbishops. Some places had several mints: archiepiscopal, municipal, and seignorial.

The Church too was prominent in minting. Coins were minted in the names of bishops and minted in abbeys, such as St. Martin of Tours and St. Martial of Limoges. Many of these coins bore the image of the patron saint of the abbey. St. Maieul appeared on the coins of the

Cluniac Priory at Souvigny, and the Virgin appeared on deniers minted by the bishops of Clermont. By the Merovingian era there were more than a thousand separate mints in Christendom, and more than 1,400 moneyers, many of whom were ecclesiastics. A stained glass window in a church in Le Mans, set in 1240, celebrates the moneychanger's trade. The irony, vis a vis Jesus, is too obvious to underscore. The relationship between money and religion was attested to by both ecclesiastics and merchants. Innocent 111 proclaimed, "Not a church in Christendom would remain standing but for usury," and the great merchant of Prato, Francesco Datini, who made his wealth in Avignon, always wrote on the first page of his ledgers: "In the name of God and Profit." Most guilds everywhere bore the names for saints and invoked their blessings and raised great funds for the churches which, in turn, celebrated their trades by devoting stained glass windows to the various guilds. In London, Florentine merchants published guides for their agents with the rates of exchange and the lists of monasteries where wool was to be had, and almost all businessmen of the day commonly opened their books with the phrase, "Messer Le Bon Dieu."

The Papacy began its own coinage in the eighth century, under Adrian 1. These first coins minted by the Papacy bore on the obverse side a full face bust of the Pope, and the Cross on the reverse side. All the Christian symbols, Christ, the Virgin, the Paschal Lamb, were put upon the coins in Europe, immediately after Constantine's conversion, and bore the Christian dies of conquest. The French Ecu, the English Noble, the Florin, the Ducat, the Byzantine Nomisma, the coins of Europe, were minted by Christians in Christian countries for the use of Christians who proclaimed the holiness of poverty and the insidiousness of finance. The Papacy ceased to mint only in the nineteenth century, when Rome became integrated with Italy.

Gold coinage was re-introduced into Europe in 1252, in Florence, when the city struck the famous Florin, the first gold coin in six centuries. It bore the head of St.

John the Baptist and rapidly became the most popular and most imitated coin in Europe. Everyone tried to copy it. It was minted at the Papal mint, under Pope John XX111 at Avignon, which had become by now an important city on the trade route between Italy and central France. Venice competitively minted the ducat d'oro which became so popular too, that hereafter all gold coins were called ducats, whether or not minted at Venice. The Venetian ducat carried the image of the Doge kneeling before St. Mark on the obverse side, and the image of Christ on the reverse side. So good were the Italians at minting gold coins Edward 111 appointed them to supervise his first issue of gold coins in England in 1344, four years before the plague arrived there.

Over the centuries the Christian designs became very elaborate. They developed from an early simple cross and monogram to representations of the Virgin and Child, the Trinity, martyrs and saints. By the fourteenth œntury, howver, religious designs began to be replaced by secular portraits, by heraldic and armorial designs. In our present age, coin designing has become so careless that, Rawlings remarked, "coins are good for nothing but spending."

In the intervening six centuries in which gold had disappeared, the coin which was most often minted to carry on the drabber work of civilization was the homely silver denarius, which became the coin of the usurer. It could not compete with gold, always valued for religious and artistic purposes, but it caused a revolution in the political and economic structure of Europe.

A peculiar snappishness afflicts merchant people. Like politicians, kings, noblemen, and newspapermen, people who have a public power, they crave and distrust expressions of regard for themselves. They know the craven center of all appeals. With one expression, the merchant sniffed through his nose and indicated to Will that he drop his letter on a grate that smoked nearby as a precaution against the plague. Then Chaunton picked up the letter with a pair of tongs and a merchant's obsessed interest to know its content. Oh! would that the good things of this world were free of taint. But worse. His caution was ineffectual, for he was dead of the plague three weeks later, to the great and short-lived delight of Prior Godfrey, who wrote a letter full of solicitous inquiry for his health:

"Master, I will call you Master, as befits a source of charity which as you well know is the sum and substance of Christian life. Did not St. Paul say it truly that of faith, hope and charity, charity be the greatest. If a man have faith, but have not charity, he is nought. If a man have but hope, but have not charity, he will not come into eternal life. If a man have both faith and hope, but has not charity he is like the Saracen and the Jew and his soul is lost forever. That man that has charity, he has a draft on heaven's treasury. Here the merits of Christ and all the saints are kept for the man of charity, and he may borrow on these merits for his earthly life here. For this reason I am instructed by my faith in Christ to set before you St. Petroke's bones as insurance for your charity. Whatsoever merit of charity the goodly saint has stored up for himself in this earthly life it will bring you interest in the Eternal World.

A man cannot assure himself of this eternal interest in any mannner better than to save the church in her hour of need. You well know what the times be that God has sent this terrible plague for a punishment on such that sin through greed and avarice so that my sheep, through God's great judgment, have died in the field and the wool that I would were yours is now the devil's. We know not whether this be God's judgment or the Jews', as it is said that they poisoned the wells.

Be it as it may we must take arms against the devil and lay up good works nevertheless. The plague cannot but pass. Christ's love is stronger than the devil and the Church's enemies, and the sheep, as I am a true believer, will frisk in the fields next year and the wool which I care not about one way or the other, I promise you will have to collect for your own. For this gift, I ask a small loan to be had at this pressing time, for coin does not die as sheep die and Christ advises us mercifully and wisely to use what we may when that which we were wont to use cannot be used since it is dead but will come again, as I may assure you of this our Saint Petroke. For such wise reason, for the sanctity of the name of Bodmin, that our monastery may continue her good works for all time, I pledge the relic of St. Bodmin if your charity is not returned with good measure.

The sum of all this is L200, for which your merit in heaven will be compounded throughout eternity in return for which Bodmin Priory pledges its haven to you in your old age so that you may pass your years of wisdom in this sacred place preparing your soul for its eternal life.

yours in Christ and the Life to Come,
Signed this day and year, 22 December, 1348.

The merchant sensed in the letter the piety that had gone rank, the sentiment that had become officious, the cynical use of it for mendacious reasons, but he took the wording of it for the manners of his day and was flattered to write in the same vein. He was originally from the town of Hull and had bought this house in London only three years ago. He was educated. He could read Latin and knew some medicine and law. He took an interest in the guilds, in mayoralty politics, in Edward's debts, in the progress of the war, the wool monopoly in Calais, and the weaving centers in Brabant. He moved the coins on his desk aside, so that he could write his response. He appreciated the images on them, whether it was the English plain cross, or the floriate cross, or the fleur-de-lis cross or the cross with lis and leopard. They all bound him to Prior Godfrey with a common expression, if not a common interest.

To the Priory of
Bodmin, and its House of Saints,
Christ keep you in Eternal Life

To the Revered and Most Reverent Prior
To Holy Grace, and Truth and Peace,

> It causes me pain not to fulfill what you have asked, but we have fallen upon evil times so that my conscience and soul sicken with misgiving that I cannot come to your aid with a full heart. Where is the sheep that does not bleat to hear her lamb call for help, where is the shepherd that does not run with alarm to see the sheep wanting. May it be Christ's will that you are fulfilled by Him.

To Will, he said more succinctly, "Here is St. Michael in Taunton offering me sanctuary in return for L3000, and here is St. Martin in Winchester assuring me prayers and safe conduct to the other world in return for the same sum. I shall come to Christ washed as a newborn lamb. The times be hard." he said, as required, "no man knows the future. There is no assurance the wool will be gathered next year. I pray you tell your prior I would for my own soul's sake I could give him this sum and let the interest be in heaven, but we have made our loans to Edward for his wars in France and this year his war is not so gainful. I cannot but give your prior coin for this amount which he may have for a period of grace for three month's time for his own, at which time seeing he cannot pay back, the wisdom of the Church does require penance for this sin of borrowing, and at such time this penance, commencing then at the conclusion of March will be 53%.

"Bless me," Will said, to his surprise, "if you be not a bitter usurer."

"Nay," Chaunton said, "this be not usury, for usury is forbidden. I have given your prior a period of grace. He knows right well that I may go to hell for usury."

Will did not argue further. He had been told not to settle for anything above 40%, but he saw no other choice, and he felt ill used that he was made to do another's dirty work. He had not come to Bodmin for this. Matters had not evolved according to the plan he had for the salvation of his soul. Moreover, Chaunton was more determined about his business than Will was about his. For the first time, the merchant realized that Will was not in clerical robes. "Be you a monk?" he asked quizzically.

"A novice," Will replied.

"Aye," the merchant said unpleasantly.

"Aye," Will said sharply, for no man likes to have others think him naive, even if he ought to be. "I will take your coins back to my prior with your terms," he said, and left, irritated for not carrying the errand through better. But he believed the fault was not his and felt pugnaciously defensive that he would be blamed for failure. The December wind crept through his vest and shirt. The few pilgrims he saw in the streets looked menacing, especially those who appeared to have just arrived from the Continent. He imagined them diseased in soul and body. The shops were shut. The sky was slate, the river was cold and choppy and smelly. Carrion sat on its surface, bobbing with the bilge. Their very insouciance gave him a sense of dread and disparity with everything about him. He wished himself out of London quickly, never to return again. A man not born to city ways should not come to the city. A man should stay where he was born. He regretted even that he had left York because, truth to tell, he was beginning to decide that it was the same everywhere, but better in York where the river ran clear, where good Rug lay in the doorway, where the church was small and made of good rude stones and where his wife, though it had come to nought with her, had warmed his bed and kept his candle lit. Truth to tell, he had not seen a man nor an animal that had gladdened his heart since he had left home, and it seemed to Will that instead of being saved, he was going sour with the merchant's talk, and Walt's quibble with the Church and his death, and his fear of the plague that prayer could not weaken the hold of, and his disappointment that for all the Latin he had learned, his thoughts came the same way into his head. He remained the same as he was when he had come earlier in the year on foot to Bodmin.

He crossed the icy, muddy lanes and made his way again through the city gate, as quickly as he could. But as quickly as he went, no man ever escaped the city without being corrupted by it. So, too, Will fell. He got as far as Southwerke, the suburb of London, famous in that day for its brothels, and he fell, laden with the triple disappointment in priory, city, and himself: a fertile condition for falling. No sooner did he enter Southwerke, with its taverns and its stores and its "Winchester geese," as the women were called after the brothels owned by the Bishop of Winchester, no sooner did he enter than Will saw what was up with him. Even while he hurried to escape his downfall, he wondered why he should hurry to escape it, it seemed all one to him in this dismal world.

It is the beguilement of depression to make things seem like this, and the call of gaiety in a dead season is hard to withstand. There was singing in the taverns and women at the windows. Old Will kicked at new Will, and new Will kicked back. "Nay," he said sternly to himself, "wouldst forfeit your vows?"

It was the plague which brought such immorality that wenches stood openly at windows with bosoms naked on the sills, so that the sight of them in this dead time throwing winks at Will pricked him with a good throb, so that before he knew it he knocked at a door under the sign of "The New Moon."

"Nay, I cannot," he thought, but he did.

However, matters turned out so that he was saved. The door opened and a voice said merrily to him, "Be you the plague cart driver? There be no dead here."

God help Will, for she was naked to the waist so that he answered her back in kind, "Nor here," and put his hand upon the knocker to steady himself.

The woman, a shrewd Betty, sized him up from top to toe. "You swing a full pouch," she said.

"Aye," he said.

HERE ENDS BOOK ONE

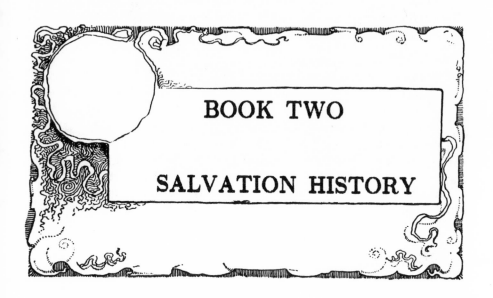

BOOK TWO

SALVATION HISTORY

CHAPTER ONE

MIRIAM'S TESTAMENT

So it was that Will came face to face with his wife in a luridly-lewdly lit room, more unlit than lit, to which he had been led to in this bathhouse in Southwerke, as he was returning to Bodmin Priory to save it from ruin.

She recognized him first, coming by what signs and in what manner as she could in the darkened room.

"What does you here?" she asked, without further ado.

Will recognized her voice immediately, so tied were they in such instant recognition, even in such a reversal of matters! His pants down to his ankles, he hitched his breeches back up as best he could.

"Whore!" he shrieked.

"Ha!" she shrieked back.

"Whore of Babylon!" he spit at her.

"Of Southwerke too!" she hissed defiantly.

He struck her.

"You be Will alright," she spat bitterly. A glint of hardness came into her voice for the unchangeableness of their lives. Will knew the mood well. A prick at his memory, and it all came back to him. "Whore!" he said again, his breeches up now, standing without a shred of the year's change in voice or manner, which was as husbandly as ever. "How come you to be in a stewhouse in Southwerke?"

"How come I? Fancy my fancy man!" She lit a better taper and held it in front of him. "How come you?"

"Be this not a bathhouse?" he blinked at her.

She registered the hypocrisy, familiar the world round,

to Will and whoever, and clicked her teeth with disgust. "So say they all. What! Ain't this a proper stewhouse? Aye, a proper stewhouse for such unclean souls as come to have their pouches cleaned of their coins."

Will checked his pouch to see that it was where he had put it. "I have been deceived," he said. "Christ knows this world has turned upside down this past season. How come you to be in England when I thought you was elsewhere?"

"How come you to have a pouchful of coins aswinging between your legs when I thought you went to become a monk?"

"So I have. I have joined myself to the priory at Bodmin. And where have you been this time?"

She stuck her taper into a holder in the wall. "I have been abroad as you well know," she said caustically, so that he would know that the trip had not been a pleasant one and he was cautious about what to ask her next, for he did not want to be liable for bad information. Still, he was ex-husbandly curious. Where had she been? Without him? What was she doing back in England? His curiosity was smoked with his past intimacy with her, which he would not acknowledge and would not forego. He felt his temper rising that she would not tell him where she had been without his having to ask her though he could tell she knew he wanted to know. He claimed her, though they had agreed to part six months ago, if "agreed" is the proper word, for each one claimed to have agreed only to what the other had coerced him to. She felt his claim, but pretended not to notice it, which he knew she noticed. Though he had been a novice for six months, with six month's training in patience and humility, he shrieked at her, "What does you in a whorehouse?"

"Same as you," she answered cooly.

God help her, Will thought, if I do not strangle her by the throat, and would any man blame him for hating her, seeing she baited him like this. "Nay, Will," she said, "we be in the stewhouse together. And you with your vows come to nought. I be here by plain bereftness to keep flesh on my bones, but what brings you here, Will?"

"You be the same as ever," he said hotly.

"Ha!" she laughed in response, "I know you right well. You want it both ways, heaven and earth, and me when the times suit you."

He practised aloofness, though his nervous system was charged. He should have known, he told himself, aye he should have known that if he fell from grace on his way back to Bodmin it would be due to her. He should have known he would meet her on the way to damnation, damned twice, once with hot desire and the second with cool aloofness. As soon as he had entered the queerly lit room with no light at all to speak of but what came luridly-lewdly from some place he could not see, but saw enough to find the spot where she lay wrapped in strange smells to becloud his mind, he should have known it was his wife come to spy on his sins. Wherever he went, no matter how he prayed and fasted she spied on him. Whether he stayed with her or left her, it never was any good though he put a river between them. She kept a record of his crimes, graven on his forehead like the sign of Cain. Even his leaving her she put down to him as a crime, though how could he take vows and become a monk and how could he save his soul if he did not leave her. She set a trap for him and he fell into it, willy nilly.

Poor Will! The near misdeed was too much for him. He could not take upon himself the blame, nor see that he was still not fallen. He felt fallen. He felt a roiling and a broiling and a good hot hatred for her because she betrayed him in everyway every time she recognized him. So he struck her on the chin again.

"You be Will alright," she said, "clapper and hand ever the same." But she stood her ground and was not shaken. Not by his threats nor by his apologies which he tended as quickly as he struck her, the whole round of which she knew well by now, as any abused wife of long standing.

"Hear me, Will," she said, "I have been abroad and have seen such things that I fear you not anymore nor your talk of hell, and I came back to tell you as much. Sit you down and let us have it out at once. Let go the look of mistrust in your eyes. I know your good side and I will not trample on it though I mean to save myself. Though you beat me sore betimes, I will not fear to have my say now. If Job could have his say to God so may I to you before this night runs out. For you know what the times be, Will. I will tell you the truth, an abbot came by here this day last week that brought the plague with him and died in this house betrayed by his own cock as it might be said, and two that were with him died soon after. So sit yourself down and hear me out. You have known me in the flesh, but I would that you know me otherwise before you kill me as Herod did the wife he loved. I came back but to tell you this. Though the past bind you to me, Will, in its strange ways, I would we go different paths now. I have set out upon a road myself and I mean to walk my road as you mean to walk yours. I saw a long while ago how it would be between us in the end as it was between my mother and father. How in the end she took her life because he said she had betrayed him as you have said it to me. I mean not to take my life, Will. I mean to walk my road.

All the time I was your wife I was a guph while you held your soul before me and told me how it will go to heaven and how you longed to sing with the angels. I knew before you how it must end between us, for eternity must fall out in a different way for you than it must for me, and I even feared the cemetery where we would lay together, for I knew that God must part us as soon as the graves were opened on judgment day. I knew not where I was bound for. I was a guph, a soul that waits around for its time to take it up while all the while you spoke to me of your soul and of the angels and how Christ will pardon your sins though you pardon me not mine, nor care I anymore for your pardon. You may keep your pardon, Will. Nay, start not. Keep your temper and hear me out seeing how the plague rages all about, and we may be dead by morning.

You know how matters ended with my mother, but you

know not the why and wherefore of it. I will tell it to you now, for how she lived and how she came to die has brought me to this pitch and place.

As you know, my mother was born to the manor at Fountainville when the Jews were put out of the land in the time of the first Edward and she was raised there by the reeve as a freeborn, seeing how she was freeborn albeit his wife from Bishop Roundsleigh's manor was not. But it mattered not between them, for the reeve had much coin which he paid to the bishop for his wife in the days before the Jews left the land and coin could be had by the reeve. He took this wife, one Alice de Brier for a true breeder, seeing how wide her hips were, but she was not. She bred not at all. He cursed her, but she cared not. She cursed him back as good and said the fault was his, she knew it for the truth but would not say how she knew. For three years she said the fault was his and that she knew it for the truth, giving the world a broad wink each time she said it so that he could not bear with it anymore, but one night brought home with him from the manorhouse a daughter scarcely born and said it is hers. 'Aye, husband,' she said, without a hitch in her voice, 'A goodly birth I had while you was gone. Lay the child by my breast that it may take some warmth.'

Neither the man nor the wife said another word on the matter, where the child came from or how, but gave it about that it was theirs and called it Belleassez, seeing the infant was fair of face, and raised it for their own. The world winked back as the world does. 'There be plenty gypsies left about,' was the say, and 'what of it? Let be, seeing it does no harm to man or wife.'

But much harm came of it later when my mother, born a freewoman as she thought, married my father who came from the manor where the reeve's wife came from. My mother, as the law would have it, came to live on my father's manor. Then the cry went up from Fountainville that my father must pay the merchet for her. Nay, he said, I pay no tax for a freeborn woman. But the steward would not have it so, saying she be not freeborn since she was born of a bonded mother from the manor of Bishop Roundsleigh. My father said the law said otherwise. There was none to ask of this matter, for the reeve and his wife Alice were now both dead, laid to rest in the cemetery at Fountainville in the village. The reeve died many years ago and Alice was brought low and died in childbirth.

My mother said she knew not that her mother was bonded, for always it was said that she was freeborn. The world winked again and some remembered this and some remembered that and told how the reeve and his wife had been childless until such time as the Jews left the land. My mother was an unbrave girl and she cared not for this disputation. She had with her one grey cat which she kept about her all the time. Sometimes in her arms, sometimes on her shoulder, for she loved this grey cat, and some began to say that this cat was a sign of the witch in her, for they remembered that she was born without Alice conceiving.

My mother feared this talk and knew not what to make of it. My father was a man of temper as you know, purple in the face with the barley and the anger, and he said full loud that he wished that he had not married my mother if he must pay the merchet for her. But the priest would not unsay the marriage as my father asked him to, but said he knew not if my mother be freeborn or not, which question was before the courts and not for him, but that he married them properly and now must be paid for the banns and his service.

My father said he would not pay the priest nor for the banns, seeing how he misliked this marriage but that he would see first how he stood in this business of the merchet, and so to court he went.

My mother declared again what she could, that she knew not but that she be freeborn to the manor of Fountainville. The abbot there lay sick at this time, but he sent his steward to declare my mother freeborn. The steward caught a cramp in his leg and came not to court that day and on the next day the abbot died and a new abbot came who would not declare for my mother one way or the other seeing, he said, he knew not of these matters but must leave it to the memory of her neighbors how things stood with her.

Up speaks the miller and tells how it was in such and such a time that she was born and in such and such a way and that she be Jewish, be she bond or free. My mother almost died of her confusion.

'Nay,' she said, 'it cannot be.'

'It cannot be otherwise,' said this miller.

'Aye,' says this and that one and the other. Then up speaks one and tells how when the Jews be in the land of York they will not eat pork and how this be a sign among them until the people came one day and said if you eat not pork we will burn you. But so fast they held with not eating pork, they marched into their church and burned themselves.

'What say you?' Bishop Roundsleigh asked my mother, well, what say you?'

My mother, in sore confusion, said she could not say one way or the other. She took communion as she had been instructed to do, and went to Mass and made the cross.

'Nought of that,' said Bishop Roundsleigh, 'the Church will not harbor false Christians.' Then asks he of my mother if she changes her linen on Friday or what day, and if she eats pork and if she can say the creed. My mother tells him the creed, but says she eats not pork because it sits not right in her, but she cannot say why except that so it has been from her childhood days.

Then my father whistles low and gives out how at night he heard the prophet Isaiah speaking in his ear, but knew not how he could hear him, seeing he knew not Hebrew.

'Well, you know,' my mother says gently to him, 'the earthfolk can speak in many languages, Latin even, or Hebrew.'

'Twas no earthfolk,' my father says.

My mother knew not what to say to any of it and the court could not declare if she be bonded because of my father, or if my father be a free man because of my mother. The new abbot declared that the merchet must be paid to him, be she Jewish or not, be she born free or not, seeing she be born of a bondswoman on his manor and now be married to a bondsman. She be thrice bonded, he said, be she bonded in birth or not and furthermore, having left the manor of Fountainville to the great cost of her working days there, her husband must pay the tax for her.

My father's face turned dark purple. In terror of it, up stands my mother and declares herself to be Jewish and not born of a bonded mother.

'How say you?' asks the bishop. My father declared it to be so. 'Aye,' he said, 'she be Jewish and speaks with Isaiah in my ear.'

Bishop Roundsleigh declared my father to be in mortal sin, 'for never,' he said, 'had he heard of a Christian man declare his wife to be Jewish to the scandal of the Church to escape the tax due for marrying her,' and he advised my father for the benefit of his soul to cease his terrible lie before he excommunicates him.

Then up speaks one and tells how he remembers how in the days of Alice's reeve the manor was in such debt to Aaron of York that none knew but that he might take the manor except that a Jew could not take the Lord's manor, but it was feared he would sell it to the Baron of Gall.

'And what became of the papers?' asked Bishop Roundsleigh.

None knew what became of the papers, but my father laughed and said it be a good day if his wife could lay her claim to the manor of Fountainville and he must still pay the merchet for marrying her.

Bishop Roundsleigh would none of this and declared Fountainville free of debt. Amen, amen and amen.

Thus ended this matter. My father must pay the merchet, be my mother what she be. In the meantime I came to a few years and not baptized yet, none knew not what to declare me to be. The parish priest came to my father and said how I must be baptized and what the cost of it will be. My father declares me born a Jew and says it boots not to baptize a Jew. Then says the priest how he will convert me and then baptize me. 'Nay,' said my father, 'it boots not to convert one born a Christian. 'What,' says the priest, 'be she born a Jew or Christian?' 'Aye,' says my father, and so it went between them while the bishop was away in Barnstaple for the while, and in his absence my father cared not what this priest said but stayed on the manor and drove his plow ever so good saying how if he must pay the merchet for my mother he had a husband's right to plow the land. Nor did my mother gainsay him, seeing she knew not where she stood in this matter and seeing he had paid the tax for her. Nor cared she one way or the other, seeing that the spirit of life had gone out from her with so much talk. Nor would she have ought to do with anyone but with her cat and me at times.

The priest came for the marrying fee and the banns and the steward came from the manor of Fountainville for the merchet. My mother and her cat and myself and our one sheep and pig be in the room when in comes the steward with his ledger and up rises my father's wrath, first a rumbling in his belly, which my mother knew well from beforetimes. Then turns his face purple which my mother knew well also from beforetimes. Then begins he to shake like an earthquake, heaving from side to side and turns his face black as the smoke from the firepit. As soon as my mother sees this blackness she runs out the house. And out jumps the cat through the window, and the pig and the sheep run away too.

The rumbling spreads itself upwards from his belly into his throat where it seizes him so that he begins to choke, and his cheeks to steam and to blow and the waters to run from his eyes. None could stop it, though all could see what was to happen. None could halt his anger, and never could, for it must run its course like a runaway horse until the strength of it be spent by itself. Alas! Alas! The rumbling now could be heard outside the house. My father's beard begins to blow in the steam of his face. His eyes fill up with mighty waters and his cheeks fill up like a cow's udders that just has calved.

Then I leap though the doorway in time to escape his hand which comes down upon the chair where I just had sat and cleaves it in two like a woodcutter's axe. The splinters fly about so one falls into the steward's eye and takes it clean away. 'I would,' my father weeps, 'I would I had been driven from this place like the Jews before this tax came to me.' The steward shook with pain and anger and put my father's words down in his ledger for a mortal sin.

This sorry business began in this way and ended in this way with my mother's demise. My father must pay the merchet and when the collector from Rome came at tithing time for Peter's Pence, my father said he had nought to pay but a daft wife with a cat. The collector cared not for such talk. My father said back to him, 'Let the pope take my wife and do what he will with her. Peter knew he had nought to give but his soul and Peter was welcome to tax that if he could.'

The collector stood by most courteously until the end of this speech and then read my father the law of the land, beginning with St. Peter himself who was the first bishop of Rome and traveling down speedily to our own day.

My father answered nought to this reading, but drank his barley and blew his beard about, then says again that he had for all his troubles one unbaptized daughter that none knew how she be and one daft wife with a cat, a cup of ale and a blight upon his land, for his livestock did not increase, nor did his fruit multiply. 'What,' says he, 'you want ten percent of my cup of ale?' and goes to give this collector a portion of it in his face.

My mother who held herself as one never to interfere in lordly matters, took it upon herself to interfere, seeing how matters were bitter with her husband and she the cause of it. 'Here is nought but ale and a few grains of barley,' she says. 'Peter cannot hold with taxing a poor man for he was but poor himself and could not but know the hard time. I hear it said Christ himself had no love for the rich and drove them from the holy temple. What would he with a tax upon a poor man's plow and ox.

Here is a good man with nought to see him through this hard winter but his daughter and his wife starving by his side.'

It was this speech that gave suspicion to the collector from Rome. So he went to the priest in the village and made inquiry and found out the whole of the scandal and threatened to excommunicate my father if he put it not to rights at once.

'And how shall I do that?' my father asked.

'You must cast her off and baptize your daughter.'

But my father said he would not pay to baptize a Jew and seeing he had paid the merchet for my mother he had a right to lay with her, be what she be.

My mother was a silly woman with nought to love but her cat and me. She laid herself down when my father bade her, caring not one way or the other seeing how matters had turned out between them. But now she saw there would be no end to this matter for it followed her about, as you know when you came to marry me and my mother declared me freeborn but the lord's court declared me born in bondage, and so again we had this matter and the scandal of it threatened us all again. My mother could not hold with it anymore and went daft from sorrow. She called me to her side one day and said, 'I raised you but I can stay no more seeing how my presence will be but a bad remembrance for you all your days. I must trust you to your own Will now, howsoever this matter ends.'

I could make nought of this peculiar speech but I laid it to her joy and sorrow at my coming marriage, seeing how mothers sometimes be at joyful seasons. For the joy was out and all about and the spring was big with birth that year in cattle and sheep and all declared that the sun had not warmed the earth so well in ten year's time. But the season would not hold, for whatever be the joy of a season the past will break out upon it.

My mother waited until the marriage was done, for she would not burden me with her deed until she could hold it back no longer, and went and took my father's coin and bought herself a winding sheet. My father thought a thief had taken the coin, but my mother wept and said it was her. And for what? 'For a winding sheet!' My father roared. 'Bless me if I make not use of it,' and began to beat her as the law gave him the right until she lay upon the floor and was near fainting but farted not from her body. Then out he went to his plow and up she jumps and takes the winding sheet and her cat and runs to the great oak tree above the river that runs by the land where the Jewears grow so bountifully upon the bank, and climbs she up this great oak tree with her grey cat in her arms. But she jumped not so fast being afraid of heights and water, and one saw her weeping there in the tree and sent for my father and the parish priest and soon all came running and shouting to her, 'Come down, come down, they call to her.

'Nay, I come not down,' she said.

'Come down, come down,' my father shouted. 'You have cost me the merchet and you might as well come down.'

'I care not anymore,' my mother said, and she clung to the branch in the tree with the cat in her hand. My father shook the tree with his mighty roar but she held fast to it though he tried to shake her loose with mickle strength, and though she was ever a frightened woman she held fast.

'Come down,' the parish priest called to her. 'You may not lay in a Christian cemetery if you do this thing.'

'What!' says my father, and lets go the tree. 'In this wise she will cost me no burial tax.'

'Aye, she will,' the priest says, and they fall to arguing.

'I care not where I lay,' my mother weeps and with the grey cat in her arms and the winding sheet upon her head she jumped into the river below her.

'Look out!' the priest yelled.

'Look out!' my father yells too, and all run to fish her out, but the sheet caught itself upon a branch and there she swings in the air like a leaf. My father shook his fist at her. 'Have I not trouble enough without to pay the cost of your death. Come down, I say.'

The tears drop from my mother's eyes. 'I cannot,' she says and down she falls holding her cat, and together they are born to the sea.

Then comes the lord's priest and the parish priest on the day next to collect the death dues.

'What!' shouts my father, 'she be no cost to you now seeing she drowned herself.' But the parish priest put down the cost of the candles to be lit for her soul, and the prayers he must say to win the mercy of Christ for a suicide, and such and such for the cost to fish her out the river and give her a Christian burial, for all which the priest claimed my father's cow and also his plow, and he wrote it out so that my father would have it legal with the lord's seal upon it.

My father's wrath was up and it shook him till he coughed up a fishbone. 'Let her rot in the river,' he shouts.

'Let be, let be,' I said to my heart, hearing this speech. 'This world cannot be set right. Let her lie with the fishes and the cat that loved her.'

Then came the lord's priest the following day and told my father how it was sinful for a Christian man to let his wife lay in the river and the cost of the great struggle he must wage for the sinning of his soul.

'Wait up,' says my father in an evil hour. 'I pay it not if she be Jewish.'

The lord's priest, hearing this, went and made inquiry about the matter but could come no way by the truth of it but declared her to be excommunicated seeing how the record gave that she be baptized though she be not a true Christian, and he wrote out the cost of it to my father: a pence to write the papal letters and a pence for letters to the lord's archbishop. L3. 4S to the nuncios to carry the letters about the realm. 2S to make the register of it in the church. 20S for sealing wax. 10S for the parchment with which the registers will be made in the Church. L2 12S for the travel money for the scribe to go from the parish of Bishop Roundsleigh about the realm to register my mother's death and her excommunication in all the churches in all the king's realm. 12S for the bellringers to ring the bells in all the churches in the see. And there it was signed and sealed, sealed and signed as legal as the lord could make it.

My father got off the cost of the candles and the prayers and had some peace at last in this matter, for he said it was as well ended as could be. Glad he was he would not have to put up with her in the next world seeing she was such a peculiar woman he could not say how matters stood with her.

That done, they began to ring the bells in all the countryside, such bells they rang they rang my mother's name and now she calls me evermore by my own name: Marymine, Marymore, Marymine, Maream, Maremare, Sarah, Sorrow, Sorrisari, Child O child, daughter, daughter, my Miriam, my Maream, you are now free of the land to wander.

That was a bell that broke my heart which tolled for me as well. I hear it evermore in all the waters of the world. With that ended my mother's life and began my wandering, as you know, Will, when we left off living together and 1 had no kin in this world and so went in search of my mother's folk.

CHAPTER TWO

THE WANDERESS

You know, then, Will, how matters ended with us. I could not but tell you the whole of it seeing how the countryside gave it out and you would not but have it your way and strike me on the chin and swear yourself for the holy life. So you have no more claim on me, and what I have done is of no account between you and me, but between me and God, for I went to find my mother's own and went where I could to see how matters stood.

I came first to Flanders with pilgrims bound for the holy land but the plague raged so among us that three that were with us died on the boat and two more upon the shore and we were driven apart by fear. Some went back to England and some to Spain, but I stayed seeing how I had nought to go back to or sidewise and knew not where to go, but that I heard God's voice for the first time and he bid me go to Rouen.

I came to this city for I had heard it said there were Jews that betimes had been in England and I looked for my mother's kin among them. I marvelled at the sights for never had I been to London, and at the great church there that never had I hoped to see anywhere but in heaven. Never did I put my foot down upon such steps, nor in a hall so vast as my mind could hold of it, but I knew not if I belonged there in a proper way, and so feared to enter within.

Two days I went about asking for the Jews but there were few in the streets for fear of the plague, and those that were about wondered at my questions until one

pointed me the way to Rue as Gyeres. As I went to find
this place a press of people gathered in the streets bound
for the market and I wondered at it, seeing that the
plague raged and all the booths were closed. Heralds and
drummers followed and men in black robes carrying big
books. It looked like a fair but none looked happy to be
there. These that came from Rue as Gyeres wore yellow
stars upon their breasts, the which I shall tell you of,
others not. Many had their children by the hand or in
their arms. All manner of people came, for what I could
see of them.

'What be the holy day?' I asked one with the star,
thinking he would speak my tongue, but he spoke it not.
Nor the next, nor the next, and I could make not a whit
of what was passing in the procession with the heralds
and the drummers and the men in black and I feared that
these be the Brethren of the Cross who are said to whip
each other.

'What be the holy day,' I asked a fourth who wore the
star. This one spoke my tongue. 'No holiday,' he said,
'but a tournament.'

'Be you from England?' I asked.

'Aforetime,' he said. 'my grandfather came of there.'

'From York, mayhap?'

'Aye. Be you of there?'

'I came by boat three days ago to find the Jews.'

He squinted at me, which I misliked. 'I wish to find
the Jews,' I said, 'that live in this city for I have heard
it said they were aforetime from England.'

'Some,' he said, and squinted at me some more. 'These
be the Jews here with the stars you see on them.'

'What? Be this the whole of them?'

'The whole of them in this city.'

I looked about and could not say if these be my
mother's people. 'Have you ever heard of Belleassiz?' I
asked.

'Belaset?' he asked.

'No, Belleassez.'

'I know not Belleassiz, but one Belaset of Lincoln that
was my grandmother was hanged for clipping the coins in

the time of the second Edward. Know you Belaset of Lincoln?'

'It cannot be the same,' I said, 'for Belleassez was my mother's name and she was not hanged but drowned.'

He shrugged his shoulders as much to say all ends are the same. 'What be your business with her?' he asked.

'Some say her people came to this city when they left England and I have come to find them.'

'Be she Jewish?' he asked. I told him I could not say, for the courts would not decide one way or the other. He squinted at me again, and seeing he wore this star, I misliked his squint, not knowing what a Jewsquint means and not remembering if ever I saw my mother squint. But I stood my ground before him, which is to say that the crowd pressed us together so that I could not see a way to leave him. I wondered at this crowd, seeing that the plague raged still, and all the time came more learned professors in cap and gown with great books and sat themselves down upon this stage, some on one side with the cross and the other on the other side with the star.

'Be this the tournament of the star and the cross?' I asked, not remembering if in England such a famous tournament had been.

'This be the tournament of the Testaments,' he said, 'and all are bidden to listen to it be the weather fair or foul.' I saw by this answer that he took this tournament not for pleasure, nor could I see any who did. None brought wine nor wore their codpieces but only sombre boks. He saw by my ignorance that I was a stranger. 'Be you Jewish?' he asked, and squinted at me full.

I would not tell him I was a guph and began to fear his squint more than the plague and resolved to move away.

More heralds came with horns, and more and more, so that the crowd must part for them and I stepped slyly away to another place where none wore stars and watched to see if these would squint. Some squinted and some did not. Some twitched and some stood idly by, sleeping on their feet, a wondrous thing to see. Some stood with babes at the breast and marketing to do and craftsmen in their leather aprons. And here one took me by the arm and said, 'Speak not with those who wear the star for they have killed the Lord.'

'What!' I said, 'he was well in York this time last month.' But I heeded this good man and kept away seeing how they had the power to kill from afar. I pray you, mother, I prayed, you had nought to do with this.

I asked one why they wore the star and I will tell you, Will, how you can keep yourself from sinning ever after and how it is I saved you this night. For you thought your wrong was that you married me, but the law has it that you must not lay with me. This man told me it was for the sake of the law which says that a Christian may not eat or lay with a Jew and that seeing how mistakes are made as you know yourself, for the Christian cannot tell if one be Jewish or otherwise except that he wear this star. Afore he wore it there was much eating and laying together in the land and much Christian sinning in this way. Glad am I that I knew this law before you sinned some more.

All this time the crowd became more and more, some with stars and some without but all with bored faces. There was no drink nor eat nor dancing nor coming together of any kind which is found in all the great tournaments. Here was only talk, and never did I see such a tournament or hope to see again. Yet none could leave, for it was the law that they must stay. Strange it was that the people abided by such a law that says you must not eat nor lay but must listen to talk. One upon the stage with a cross upon his breast spoke in Latin for an hour and the other with the star upon his breast spoke in Hebrew for an hour.

'I am dreaming,' I said out loud.

'No,' said one next to me and pinched my breast.

'Mind your fingers,' I said to him.

'I cannot,' he says, 'they go where they will. My whole life I have had this trouble.' I moved away, seeing how things were with him, but he came after me, and I moved away again, and again he came after me. 'You be a spicy lass,' he says, 'and you speak my tongue.'

'I aint for you,' I said, and fair would tell him I lost my star somewhere when the heralds raised their horns and blew a blast.

Come we now to the great debate
The Tournament of the Ages
Wits and scholars, priests and sages
Gather here to heed the call:
Mirror, mirror on the wall,
which be the fairest God of all.

So soon as they finished one with a falcon's head chirruped in a universal language. He read from a roll so long I thought he could never come to the end of it, whether Christ be messiah, shoot of Jesse, born of immaculate Mary, whether the Jews be rejected of God and have not hope of salvation, if there be a life after this one for them and what manner of life it will be, and all the time this one with the fingers follows me about. I put my mind away from him to learn what I could of this issue. It was all in a treatise called Contra Perfidiam Judaeorum, and never did I know the problems between the Jews and the Christians were so many. Heretofore, Will, I thought you may not eat or lay or marry with me, but you know not the list that was read, which as I remember it I will render it to you now so that you may have it for your own remembrance against further sinning if ever the time comes that you forsake the holy life, which I pray you will not. Seeing there be no Jews here in England anymore but myself and as I will not tempt you anymore, Will, you are surely bound for the holy life. And here is the list he read.

Testimony on the law and the Prophets,
on the Father and on the Son

Testimony of the holy ghost
Testimony of the Trinity
Reasons and authorities for faith in the
   holy trinity
Testimony of the prophets that the son
   was sent by the father
Testimony that Christ came in the flesh
Testimony that Christ was born of David
Testimony that Christ was born of the
   nations
That he did come in his one person
That he was God and seed of the man
   Abraham
Testimonies of the time and the place of
   the birth of Christ
that the desires of the prophets were
   fulfilled by Christ.

Here he finished and sat himself down to much applause.

Then came this one with the star and said no to it all. He said nay, nay, and nay, that the prophecies were not fulfilled, that it matters not that Jesus died on the cross for the kingdom of God is not yet. There was much hissing at this, but the Jew cared not about it. He said it was not anywhere in the scriptures that the Jews must believe in messiah for salvation of their souls and he said it was not written that God slays the Hebrew because he believes not in Christ but because he sins with pride and with stiffneckedness and with whoring after false Gods. So hot he waxed with his argument he cared not for the hissing. 'God,' he said, 'demandeth of the Jew faith in God and not faith in messiah for salvation. It says not in the ten commandments I am the lord your God messiah.' Then he said that for the Jew his salvation was in the law of the Lord, and so soon as he says the word law they all begin to hiss again and the one with the cross says hotly, 'Aye, it is so. You are bound by the law in your flesh and since the flesh dieth the Jew dieth. But we are bound to the spirit by faith.'

So strong did the word law work the people up they hissed so loud I could not hear the speech go forth anymore.

'Nay,' said the one with the star, 'Jesus gave a new law for the salvation of the soul and never did I meet with a Christian who obeys this new law, for he said right clear, if you would be perfect, go sell what you possess and give it to the poor, and for all I see this be harder for a Christian to do than for a Jew to follow the 613 commandments of the law.' Though I knew not what these commandments were, yet I could not but agree with him that this one law of Jesus Christ was a hard law for Christians to follow, for never do I see them follow it.

But up jumps the other and says Jesus Christ laid this not down for a new law, but gave it only in a manner of speaking.

'No, he did not,' says the one with the star, and they began to argue whether Jesus said it this way or the other way, and each one took each word and found more than a hundred meanings to each word, whether by perfect was meant perfect or only good, whether if this law made man perfect he could sell his possessions but lie and steal and copulate, whether he could sell his possessions and buy them back, whether he must sell his neighbor's possessions as it must be his duty to make his neighbor perfect, and so they spoke much that was confusion to the ear, till it began to get dark and hunger came upon us all.

The one with the star waxed wrathful and said, 'You take what you will of Scripture. Though Jesus himself upheld the law and nowhere does it say you enter the Kingdom of God if you believe in Jesus, it says it not in Scripture, you take what you will and leave the law though Jesus left it not. Did God speak with two voices in Script, one for Christians who listen but to the prophecies, and one for Jews who listen to the prophecies and to the law? God spoke with one voice to Jesus, though you hear not the voice he spoke with to Jesus. For the times were but the times and not the time.' Then he told of the many multiple signs that had not yet come to pass such as the gathering of the twelve tribes under a king from David, and seeing how ten be now lost I know not if this prophecy can ever come to pass. Another sign be the battle of Gog and Magog and the cleaving of the Mount of Olives and the drying up of the river in Egypt called Red when the dispersed shall be gathered together, and another is the running of water from the place where the temple in Jerusalem stood, and seeing how this temple stands not anymore I grieved that the prophecy could not be fulfilled. And he told of others that were fulfilled not, that must wait for the time when ten men from other nations take hold of the hem of a Jew's coat and say to him that they will go with him for they have heard that good is with him, and so it would be that in the whole world there would be the faith of Israel and the going up of all nations to Jerusalem to worship and I could not but think of the press of the people that would be there. And he said more, that the time would be fulfilled when the wild beasts of the world and the animals that we keep by our side make peace with each other, and I knew by this that the time was not yet, for you know Will that the shepherd cannot leave his sheep for fear of the wolves nor has it yet been heard that the fox will not eat a chicken if he finds him. But when he said that the time is fulfilled when sin and suffering is at an end then I knew for certain the time was not fulfilled, the time was less than what had been for confusion was more than ever and one could not be in the streets for fear of the sinning that was there and the talk one heard that Mohamet was greater than Jesus and the faith of the infidel greater than the Christian and that fulfillment was now with them. And I wondered what my ears heard, for certain it was that unless heart and soul and mind lie, the time was not fulfilled, not in these days for Jew nor Christian.

After this one finished his long speech about the signs, he said it mattered not that the Jews were in galuth and that the galuth was not a sign of their suffering for the death of Jesus, for this was already the fourth galuth and they had been in galuth before Jesus had come, for he counted the Babylonian captivity for a galuth.

He said many things such as these as plain as could be, but when I looked about in the crowd I saw that those who wore the cross and those who wore the star slept upon their feet, the men in their leather aprons, the women with the babes upon their breasts, even the babes slept, their mouths with milk from their mothers' breasts. And if it were not that the bells began to ring which signalled the end of this debate, for all I know they may have slept straight into eternity. But soon as the bells were wrung and it was known that the debate was at an end the people began to wake up and move about, and this one's fingers began to play where they could.

I moved myself back among those that wore the star, for I saw the Christian would not follow me here for fear of sinning, but I went among them with care to see what their power be and if I be of them. They saw I wore no star and wondered at me. One there told me it was not lawful for me to be among them. I wondered that I understood his tongue and asked him if he be English born.

'Nay,' he said, 'but my grandfather was.'

'Does he speak my tongue?'

'He speaks not any tongue. He is dead. But he spake not English when he lived in England. He spake then French, for his father spake French before him and I speak English though I be born here for my father spake the English tongue.' And I knew by what he told me that one speaks not the tongue of the land he is born in but the tongue of his mother and father, be they born anywhere. Seeing also that he squinted not I asked him what tongue God speaks in, French or English.

He wondered at me. 'Neither,' he said, 'you know right well He speaks in Hebrew.'

'It cannot be,' I said, 'for He spake and told me to come to this city, I heard Him and I know not the Hebrew tongue. Not the priest in the parish where I was born and married has heard the Hebrew tongue, and he gives it out that he speaks God's word.'

Then he began to squint at me and I went away in fear of him and the others that wore the star. I knew not what they would make of me that I heard God not in the Hebrew tongue and I began to fear what God it was that spoke with me and told me to come to this city.

Fearing if I heard a true voice or a false one, I left the city, though it was night and took the road to Paris, not knowing where else to go and hearing that in Paris were many more professors than be here. The plague carts came into the city to fetch the dead and carry them outside the walls. From every plague cart came the muttering voices of those that were not dead, and some with cries for help who cried that they had not the plague. But who would say? None came there to help, for such was the fear of the times that none would look among the dead bodies to find a live one. I saw piled on one cart, even babes that had their eyes open and were taken with the mother to be buried, for none wished for orphans with the famine that was everywhere. It was heard that these had no food and if there arose a fresh mouth in the house they rid themselves of it in this way. Such were the times it brooked not fulfillment, and God forbid this be the fulfillment of the prophecies.

The road grew dark and I misliked being on it, seeing I knew not the tongue of the land and mayhap not the tongue of the God so that I could not call upon him or man. Strange fears afflict one not as much as strange tongues. The sky was filled with the birds that feast on the dead and in the distance were the fires lit by the gravediggers.

Suddenly I heard this whistle behind me so that the hair on my neck stood up. This one that followed me about in the crowd followed hot after me on the road. 'Wait up,' says he. 'You should not take the road by yourself at night. It is dangerous for a woman.'

So it is, I think to myself and walk a little faster. So he too. 'Wait up,' he calls after me, 'I'll keep you company.' I hasten my step a little more, but did ever a woman outhasten a hot man. I look about for safety but there is nought but the forest on either side and the plague carts upon the road and the fires in the distance and this one whistling behind me. I heard a groan from a cart and dare not look up or down but shut my ears to it. I know not what to fear more, the dead or the living. A hand drops down through the slats of the wagon and drops a star upon the ground. Whether this be a Jewscart or not I know not, but I fetched up the star and pinned it to my breast.

'What!' says this one with the fingers, 'be you Jewish? You was not Jewish this afternoon.'

I would not say yea or nay, but hoped the star would ward him off. But he caught me by the arm and plucked it from my breast with his fingers and a laugh. 'None can say what you are now,' he says, 'and for all one can see it makes not the farthing of a difference between the legs,' and he pressed himself upon me there and then.

'You will burn,' I said to him.

'Aye,' he laughs hotly, 'if I get not my breeches down.'

I bit his neck but he took it for a sign of passion. 'Not so fast,' he says.

A plague cart came by and I called to the driver for help, but a man can make merry even on the way to bury the dead. This one jumps from the cart and says, 'Go to,' and jumps upon me as well.

Will jumped up, agitated. "What!" he cried, "the whoring devils!"

"Nay," she soothed him, "they could not take hold of me for fear of the dead of three that rose from the cart with the star upon them and made to breathe the plague upon us. So weak they were, so plague ridden, so close to death they had but strength to breathe, but it would have been enough had their breath reached us. The driver began to beat them with his horsewhip till they lay down again but my attacker ran off seized with the terror of the dead. The driver had no mind for me anymore and climbed aboard the cart and made off in fear that the dead would rise again, and went his way, carrying the living with him. It booted not to be overly nice and tell the difference. And no prelate could stop it, for when the times be bad the people govern themselves. The government governs when the times be good and the people do not care then who governs them.

I picked up the star and put it in my sack thinking it would be safer sometimes than without to warn Christian men they might not lay with me, howsobeit I saw that if the seizure took them they cared not what the law said.

I went by myself in the night, by the side of the road and hid when the carts went by, and thought all the while on the debate that was preached in the city of Rouen and how none there could resolve it. Though I cannot read the bible as you know Will, and you read it yourself and have told me that Jesus is messiah, never did I hear it said before that he was not nor can I say if my mother said one way or the other or if she knew. She went to church and crossed herself at Mass and was declared to be a Jew and was excommunicated as a Christian. Mother, my dear, I said to myself, you have reared me in darkness and I know not anything. But mayhap it was so that she knew not herself but followed the custom of the land. Now when Gabriel blows his horn she will not know where to go. I am a guph now, but my mother will be a guph forever, and I began to cry, thinking on this.

So I came with much walking and weeping and hunger to Paris and prayed that in the university they would answer my questions. But it was worse than before. Dead bodies lay in the river and the smell of it was so bad that none could stay in the city but those who wished to make mischief, like the Brethren of the Cross, who were here in many numbers and worked their evil upon the people. The times were such the bishops had no more power than the governments. I know, Will, you have not seen these brethren in England and if you had you would know how I feared the star in my sack and knew not whether to throw it away or keep it. These brethren marched in columns of two, many hundreds at a time. At the head of them marched their master and his helpers carrying banners of purple and cloth of gold but the others wore black and their faces were hidden with masks and they wore a red cross on their backs and carried their whips, and so much power had they not a priest would say nay to them though they cried down the priests themselves. The people came from everywhere to hear them. Lord, I think, in Europe the people have nought to do but to stand about in crowds and hear speeches. I kept myself to myself with care that there be none in the crowd with moving fingers, but there were many though these brethren marched right in front of them weeping for man's sins and I must think they meant such free copulation as could be had in a crowd. Men can preach against the Jews and the Jews must go away, but when they preach against sin, sin does not go away.

And these preached against sin with much gnashing of teeth that if any could drive it from the streets they could, but though the crowd agreed with every word, sin stayed. One came and stood beside me and breathed so hot into my ear I feared he blew the plague upon me. I moved away to see what I could and saw that the crowd be merrier here than in Rouen. These men in black tore off their clothes but for a cloth to cover the privy and lay themselves down in a circle around this small child newly dead and prayed for her resurrection and prayed as well for the resurrection of Frederick the emperor who they said would kill the priests and give their money to the poor. Though the priests did not like this talk and it was said the pope preached against them none would say a word out loud for fear of the times and the crowds and because these had the power of persuasion in them as could be seen by the price they paid. Their master beat them on their backs while they moaned and they groaned and the crowd moaned with them for their pain and the master beat them until they jumped to their feet and beat each other with terrible whips that made the blood fall faster so that it dropped to the ground. Then they fell themselves to the ground, then jumped they up again, all the time whipping and singing, and the crowd singing with them.

Ply the scourge for Jesus' sake
and God through Christ your sin will
   take
Woe! Usurers! woe sinners!
Except it be for our contrition
all Christendom would mete perdition
Come here for punishment good and well
In this way we will escape from hell.

And the people groaned and sang with them for they
believed these would save them. Some their bodies
swelled up so and became blue before our eyes, and some
died right there of their pain and these were held in
great esteem. So terrible were the times some drove
nails into their flesh and said it was nought to what
Christ had done for them. And this they did three times
a day, thirty-three days in each city, each day as they
said for a year in the life of Jesus Christ who died for
them. And the crowd moaned and groaned with them, for
it was near their last days in Paris and the crowd prayed
for them to stay longer and lift the evil times, for
nought else that one could see would do it.

There were some in the crowd that were Jews as I
saw by their star, but when they heard these brethren cry
up how the Jews be usurers one with the bad priests and
the bishops and how they have poisoned the wells and
spread the plague they moved away and in a little while
on the next day when these brethren came and laid
themselves down in a circle and beat and whipped
themselves I saw no more those with the stars in the
circle.

There was nought to say to any of this but to walk
with care. Food was hard to come by and I went to the
churches to find what I could. Some had now charnel
houses put by them where the dying were brought to die
and I would not go to these for I could not bear with the
crying, the weeping of the children who lay so sore, some

carried in the arms of the nuns who would not leave them to die alone, that I wondered at their courage, for hungry though I was I would not take food where there be a charnel house, though these sisters of mercy laid themselves down with the dying to pray for them. And some there were that were friars that carried the dead in their arms to bury them for they would not leave them to the ways of the gravediggers and the carrion that went everywhere, but many there were that fled in fear of the plague and the talk in the streets, and I fled in fear of it myself. For on the morrow it was said that two Jews in Chillon confessed to this poisoning and the people rose everywhere against them though the pope said against it and the doctors said against it and said it could not be. But the students rioted and the people said it could be and was, and everywhere on the morrow it was said how these Jews had by them a pouch with red and black powder hidden in a dead egg which they had thrown into the wells of Thonon and that this it was which caused the plague and any priest or bishop who said nay to this was brought before the crowd, for the crowd followed the Brethren of the Cross, and said as they said. And the power of the Church could not prevail against these Christians.

I would not stay in Paris and went my way through Christendom, caring nought to have with priests or Jews. I wandered as a wayfaress and thought to stay a guph but the times would not let me be. I came to a place where the four rivers meet where the plague and the burning of the Jews raged together. I ate as I could, finding food in the fields that the fleeing had left behind, and once some bread in a lazar house that had been emptied by the burners and sometimes in an inn where all were dead and the food was left about, for which I thanked God. For though I feared to eat it, so hungry was I, I feared more to starve. The inn was empty, only one grey cat left alive and all the food standing about. I took the grey cat as a sign from my mother and ate my fill of the food which did me no harm as you can see. Not the food, but one who lay hidden behind a door sought to take his full of me, thinking to have bread and cake together. He was hot and hungry but cowardly and before he would take anything he asks me in my own tongue if I have the plague.

'Aye,' I said, 'I have the buboes in my armpit,' and I go to show it to him. 'Hold off,' he says, and backs away.

'Be you afraid or lusty?' I ask.

'Both,' he says and laughs.

The plague gave me courage. 'You have a cruel problem,' I said, 'how come you to speak the English tongue?'

He squints at me.

'Be you Jewish?' I ask.

'What!' he says, 'better the plague. I be a pilgrim from England.' Then he squints at me again, not knowing what way to come at me, waxing and waning. 'I think you have not the plague,' he says, and steps to me again.

'If this be not the plague it must be the devil's sign,' I say and make to him again with my arm raised up.

'Hold off,' he says again, 'throw me there a piece of bread and I'll go my way.'

'What!' I said, 'don't you fancy me anymore. I may be sick but I ain't dead.'

'It would be a sin,' he says, 'copulation without the banns, it would be a sin.'

'And worse with one who be Jewish and out I take my star and show it him.' He whistled low. 'You be twice cursed to have the plague and be a Jew.'

'Aye,' I said, 'you can go to hell but once, and you might as well go because of the plague in me as the Jew.'

'I mean not to go at all,' he said, and took his leave and left me to the food which I did not waste.

I took the cat with me, for I knew her now as a sign from my mother. Whatever would be said of witches and cats never is it said of cats and Jews, so I took her with me.

I wandered as a wayfaress and enquired of all who were there and could speak my tongue, Jew or Christian,

how does the world with them and what be my mother
and I saw how this one died of the plague and another
Christian beat his wife and together they beat their
children or burn the Jews and the lepers or die alone on
the road.

I came to the wine country where the four rivers meet
and crossed over the rivers as God provided. For here
there was much plague and burning of Jews and lepers
and strangers whatever they be. Though it was almost
winter the air was hot with the burning and the ashes
were in the streets and the people had blackened faces
and walked with masks on their noses for they could not
breathe for fear of the plague and the stench and the
smoke. So fierce were the Brethren of the Cross in this
place, with many others to help them, Beghardes and
Cellites as they were called, that the power of the
church was as nothing, and I wondered at the powers that
prevail in an evil time.

I could not say what this place was called where the
rivers met for I was afraid to speak with anyone, seeing
the business the town was about. They took together the
Jews and the lepers and brought them to the river's
edge. None went willingly. Some they pulled by the
hair and some by their legs and some they tore the
children from their mothers' arms and these screamed the
worst of all, and some they tore the clothes from their
backs so hot for the coin they were that they thought to
find it on their bodies. They carried torches and made
haste through the streets and the forest to the river's
edge where they threw these into the fire that burned
there. One leper called out for pity's sake. Him they
kept in the fire with sticks until nought could be seen of
his poor flesh. My cat hissed for the heat and I went
away for I could not bear with the screams anymore.

None could prevail against the Brethren of the Cross.

The bishop came and the landgrave came and forbade
the burning, but the crowd pressed upon them and they
fled for their lives.

The bishop came and carried the cross against these
others who carried the cross, but he could not prevail.

As soon as they said he did usury with the Jews he went away.

The few who would save could not prevail against the many who would not, and all night and all day for three days and three nights they burned the Jews and the lepers. The bells of the church melted in the heat and could ring out no more and it seemed as if all Christendom was burning.

On the third night came the winegrowers with torches and winekegs through the streets and the forest, with song and with wine. They came through the forest with a heigh and a ho, with song and with carol and a ringing of bells.

> Praised be Jesus, the vine of love
> Preised be the wine that flows from the
> land

They sang and they took what was left of the living and put them afloat on the river in winekegs. With song and with praising, with prayer and with hymn they set them afloat down the river, the living. They came with torches and song, with drink and with wine from the land, for the price of the wine had fallen, and with none to buy they drank it themselves and said it was holy wine which they praised with their songs and their prayers but they spilled it into the river. Though they said it was holy wine which they praised they came with torches and song through the forest and set the winekegs into the river and put the living in with the wine and set the winekegs down the river with lights and with laughter. With song and with prayer and with mirthful tunes, with a heigh and a ho and hope on their faces for the new day when the land be rid of the Jews and the lepers. With praise of Jesus, the vine of love, they set forty winekegs down the river and they bobbed with the lights from their nailheads. With a heigh and a ho and hope on their faces though the bishop said nay and the pope forbade it they stood on the banks of the winey Rhine with their torches and songs and their heigh and their ho the winekegs bobbed on the river so gaily their nailheads gleamed in the light of the torches as they bobbed down the river that ran red in the night. For the river ran red with wine and with blood and the river glittered in the light from the torches, and the winekegs bobbed down the river like jewels down the river and out to the sea.

Soon there was nought left to be seen, the last light was gone, the last torches put out, the dawn in the sky but no bird sang. Some say they died from the smoke in the air, for all through the forest their bodies were found, the sparrows and finches and goshawks and owls. No sound was heard again of their singing, no sound was heard again of their muttering. No sound was heard in the land at all, for the bells of the church had melted, the bishop had fled for fear of his life, the animals had fled for fear of the fire, and the birds lay dead all about.

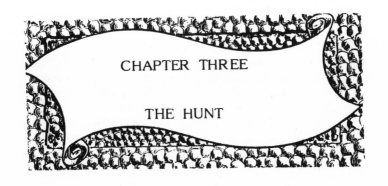

CHAPTER THREE

THE HUNT

I made my way thereafter with a fear that would not go away. I could hold with no more and never will that the time was fulfilled, and so feared to be a Christian for my soul's sake and feared to be a Jew for my life's sake. I passed my way through the mountains and the forests for I would not hold with the towns where the fires burned so hot that the animals fled, and I fled with them, I and my cat. Where there were no more fires and the plague had passed over and the animals stayed to rest, the hoof of the huntsman came back to hunt them, for things seek their past, as you know yourself, Will. And where the plague had once passed the people came back, both the high and the low, the knights with their ladies and the peasant with his plow. And peace there was not, for where the plague had been was now hunger and struggle, for the lord he wished to hunt in the land as before and many were taken for poaching and for eating the lord's birds with hunger.

I went my way in fear of it all, and in fear to be known as a stranger I would speak with no one, and kept my cat in my sack with my star if one passed me by on the road, and I went where I could find food. I came to a monastery weak with hunger and sought succor there, but the plague raged so they would not let me through and there was no abbot about to teach them better, for it was said he had gone to England and the brethren had fallen to riot without their master. So I could not hold with the towns and I could not hold with the monasteries, but wandered as I could to look for my food. I fled with the animals and went into the forests. I fled and the animals fled with me, the animals of the forest and the animals of the world, those with their young and those without, for Christendom was burning and there was no place for foot or paw.

I fled with the wolf and the deer and the hart, and found my food as ever they did. Though I could not read in a book what things mean I read the earth and found my food, for even the wind has a law. It lists not as it wills, as you have told me, but it has a law and it lists after the law. I fled with the law and the animals for I saw that in all things they did there was a law to it, but man who has a soul has no law to govern it, and it is the soul that lists as it wills.

I came into the forest when I heard the cry of the hunter and I fled with the foxes for I feared to be found a stranger with my cat and a star in my sack. The horses came hot for the hunt, bearing heralds and lords and ladies with timballs and bells and cries of Ho! Tallyho! And the horses wore cloth of gold and the women embroidered linen and tunics of silk. So bright was the sunshine upon them, their rings and their jewels, their silver horns, their pearls sewn into their dresses, their golden hawks and the falcons they carried and their hunting dogs by their side yelling with glee for the foxes which ran before them with a pounding heart, and I ran with them for I carried the mark of the stranger in my sack. I ran with the foxes through the forest and fled for my safety with the sound of the galloping horses behind me, the lords and the ladies so bright on their backs, the air so golden and green and silver and the falcons spread to the sky so blue. 'God bless the chase,' cried the lord of the hunt, 'the hunt is the fairest sport for a Christian,' and all through the forest the animals ran, the deer, the hart, the fox and the rabbit. Was only their fear and their breath was not pretty, for it was not golden nor green nor silver and it had no sound like the sound of the horn, like the singing of ladies and the ringing of bells, their merry tunes and their whistles and the tramps of the horses. 'God bless the chase,' calls the lord of the hunt, and he dashed through the forest with his thundering hoofs.

Five horses they had that were black as the night. Four, you know well from your gospel, but the fifth was called Contra Judaeos and he pulled as strong as the others. Sometimes one horse pulled ahead, sometimes the other, sometimes the horse called plague and sometimes the horse called famine, but always the fifth horse rode beside them and where they went he went with them and where they turned he turned. Sometimes he pulled ahead and seemed fair to win the race in the world, but always they stayed together, these five horses of the apocalypse, these horses of the terrible night, flank to flank and hoof to hoof, plague and war and famine and death and the one called Contra Judaeos.

The hunter rode all five at once and leaped from one to the other like a master who never missed his foot, for they stayed together, flank to flank and hoof to hoof, these horses of the terrible night, plague and war and famine and death and the fifth called Contra Judaeos.

They bore down upon me all at once with their merry ladies and lords and banners and horns and falcons and dogs. The foxes scattered beneath their hooves and I ran as fast as I could with my sack and my cat and my star when a voice came out of the universe and yelled to me, 'jump,' and I did its bidding and jumped aside into a ditch and the horses and the dogs and the ladies and the lords passed over my head. But I lay in the bottom of a hole in a faint with nothing for solace but the wind and the sky. I lay and could not move for the fear and the anger that held me so fast, I was afraid and lay like a rock. The wind and the sun and the moon passed over me and I lay like a rock with the law of the rock. Light and dark and heat and shadow passed over me in their law that went its round, and I lay like a rock at the bottom of this hole until I mastered the peace of it. I lay like a rock at the bottom of the world. The dawn came up and its noices woke me and I fed on the sounds for my stomach's sake. Fill up, fill up, I said to myself, for what your belly can't have let your eyes and your ears or you shall faint for the lack of it all. Though you starve for the lack of food, yet must your spirit be filled if only with air. And I fed on the feast of the world, for I saw there a duck upon her egg and a lamb at her mother's teats, the calf and the cow that stood together and the beasts of the field at the beck of their young. 'Lord,' I wept, 'how is it there is food for the beasts and none for mankind?'

A whimpering roused me from my hunger and weak as I was I crawled from my hole and found in the woods a mutter whelping, for she had lain herself down to do her work and had come into this ditch out of the way of the hunters. Her pups came out and she licked them clean and pushed them about with her tongue until they had life and began to move and found their way to her teats. She laid herself down with no more ado while I, cast out from the animal world, wandered with fear and with hunger. But I went now with peace for I saw there was law and governance in the world, and I cared no more for what others taught of the evil that be in nature and matter, and that the soul alone can lift this evil. I cared no more for what they teach for I saw that the mutter had a law that governed her. I saw that the sun and the moon and the birds and the beasts had a law though you have taught that they have no soul, but man who has a soul has no law that governs him. So I went my way and came back to tell you that though you left me for the holy life, I have found a better and mean not to be left but to leave.

Winter was hard now upon the land and I must go into the towns, whether I would or would not. My cat had the worst of it, for I kept her in my sack by my side, for so fierce was the hunger in the land I feared for her life. Some food we found in a church nearby where the priest shut not his door.

Many were on the road again between town and town. Many were fleeing again from hunger or plague or the law that said they must stay and serve their lord. But as many fled and as many died so there were as many left in the towns that followed the Brethren of the Cross.

And where these were I would not stay but fled from
town to town and so came to as great a church as that
which I saw first in Rouen with a cemetery for the
lepers. Here I wrote on the stones, 'What nature made
sick, man destroyed altogether.' Then I entered the
church to find some food, be the condition of my soul
what it be. Mayhap, I thought, the priest of this church
will set me right, whether I be Jew or Christian.

Great as the church was there was no one about and I
sat with the pictures in the windows and the statues and
my cat and my star until the priest came through a door
in his cassock and asks me my business there.

So faint am I, I cannot tell him. 'I have no business
but hunger,' I say, which he saw well enough for himself,
and brought me to the kitchen and fed me full up and
gave my cat milk to drink. Hungrily she sat on the
table's edge and her sweet tongue never lapped so good,
the pink end of it filled with the good of the world.
Then the priest asks me if I would make my confession
now that I have eaten somewhat, and I confess my
confusion that I know not if I be Christian or Jew.

'What!' says he. Whereupon I tell him the whole of it,
how my mother was declared a Jew in the courts and
excommunicated for being a Christian which cost my
father so many coins that he would not pay the tax to
baptize me, not knowing if I be Jew or Christian and
what boots it to baptize a Jew he said and how my
mother sick of this talk climbed the great oak tree and
drowned herself in the river with her cat which I know
not but is now the cat I have in my sack and how she
came to save herself I cannot say, nor how it was that
my talk so warmed him up that I saw how little by little
his cassock fell open. It cannot be, I said to myself, but
it was and I stood up to go.

'What!' he says again, 'never did I hear such a speech
as this,' and he stands up beside me so that his cassock
opens all the way and I saw what was up with him. I
saw that though he be a priest it mattered not that I be
Jew or Christian, the power of the moment was upon him
and I could not but strive to save him though he wished

it not. 'I have had my full and can stay no more,' I said, and though the fear of burning was upon me I took my star from my sack to save him further from sinning, but 'twas otherwise for it heated him up so that he was upon me all at once, his hand upon my dress, not so much upon as in and down and the other hand up from under.

'Let be,' I cried and pulled my skirt about my legs as best I could. But nought would stay this prepuced priest who in the twinkle of an eye took out what Adam knew well enough to hide and thrust his head where head never grew and put his hand upon my mouth to stay my screams. Nor would I for I knew if I brought the town to me I would burn faster than him. But my cat, who had had her full of milk, sprang from the table to his head before he could make his prelatical thrust, and so took him by surprise he fell out where he meant to fall in and I sprang to my feet and out the door with my cat at my heels, and we made our way into the country again, for I would no more with the towns.

There was nought to do but to steal for our food. And so sore was my hunger I went to the charnel houses close by, for some there fed the sick and though I went with fear of the plague and the dead and that one such as me would steal a piece of bread from their hands.

But so it was up and down the river Rhone and I know not whether since the time of Noah such misery was anywhere, nor can it be thought that such times will come again.

I came now to Avignon where the weather was warmer but the sky still so black with smoke I knew the plague was not gone from here. And one who lay dying upon a post I saw on the road itself. It was a little past noon and he cast his shadow upon the ground, tied to a post like a criminal so that I feared to come near him, not knowing what his crime was. But soon as my distance grew shorter I saw that a falcon sat upon his chest and ate the flesh of his breast. As he groaned for help I could not but run down the road to him to beat off this bird as well as I could with what rocks and sticks I found on the road. His wings beat on the poor man's face. Since I could not drive it away I untied the man's knots and little by little I pried him loose. Alas! poor man, so weak he was from the falcon he sank at my feet. I asked him who did this terrible thing, who tied him to this post and left him to be eaten by this bird. He told me it was his lord who did it, for he had been driven by hunger to poach on the land and he had eaten of the lord's birds and it was the lord's law that he pay in this way for this sin. He could say no more but told me to flee, for the lord's steward would be back to fetch him. But no one came to fetch him to give him water or succor, and I sorrowed with him because I saw he was dying and no one came to fetch him. I covered him with my body's shadow so that the sun smote him not so fast, seeing what his own had done to him, and when his eyes were closed I put him on the earth and made my way to Avignon.

But this city raged as bad as the others and the river stank from the burials in it. Here was no more singing, as I have heard had been, but nuns and priests hurrying in the streets with their heads bowed down and their handkerchiefs at their noses. I thought to see the pope's palace but could not come near it for the guards. I could see nought of it but the smoke that came up from the chimney over the turrets and the tapers of the Rocher des Dames, and only such as had strict business came and went, hurrying with handkerchiefs at their noses, for the pope feared the plague as well as me. Many were the palaces on the banks of the river but the river ran brown between the shores, and none but the carrion sailed on it now.

There was no more to see here than in Rouen or in Paris. There was no more to see anywhere in Christendom, and I went my way until I came to the sea and could go no further and could go nowhere else for I feared the towns, and the castles and the monasteries were all shut up.

I lay my sack on the ground and let my cat out to take her walk upon the sand and took out my star to

wonder at it. 'What boots my wandering?' I said to
myself, 'if I cannot find my mother's people and what
boots it if I find them if I must burn with them?'

With that the sea began to churn herself, to churn and
to spit and to swirl about so that I thought a mighty fish
was trapped in her waves, but it was a winekeg that
bobbed upon the waters as if it had life in it, and I
remembered the living that had been put inside them. It
cannot be, I thought, but must be the devil, but I could
not stand this thought seeing I was by myself on the
seashore. So I picked up my skirts and walked out to
fetch it to shore and see what was with it, for never
heard I such a racket of noise from wine. I took a rock
and hit the hinges to let whatever was inside out. I
knocked on the keg and the inside knocked back. I
knocked twice and it knocked twice. I knocked thrice
and it knocked thrice. I knew not what it was but that
it could count seemed certain. I learned forthwith it had
journeyed from the Moselle into the Rhine into the Rhone
and into the Gulf of Lyons and so made its way against
the tide so that it was of sturdy frame seemed without a
doubt. I took off the lid and out poured wine and
candles and books and papers and when all was finished
flowing from this barrel out steps this man and his wife.
I see he wears the star upon his breast and he be of
good birth, for the clothes he wore and the cut of his
beard and his manner and his speech which betrays not
his fear though he was old in years and came out of this
winekeg red in the face flowing with matter like a babe
with the afterbirth.

'Many thanks,' he says, 'for you have rescued us.' And
straightway began to say his prayers. The sand all about
turned red with the wine and I stood there astonished
with the sight of it all, and he as astonished as me for
he saw there my star upon the sand.

'Are you Jewish?' he asks in this English tongue I took
to be English though I knew it not, for it sounded both
right and wrong to my ears. I told him how the star fell
out from a Jew's plague cart and how I picked it up and
kept it by my side for safety's sake. Then I tell him the

whole of my wearisome story, how I left England to look
after my mother's kin and he is more astonished than
ever and begins to cry and falls upon his knees to pray
and says, Lord God who preserveth worlds, hast Thou
preserved the descendant of Belaset?'

'What!' I cried out, 'know you my mother?'

'Nay, but your grandmother, if she be the same as that
lady in Lincoln. For we be ourselves from England, many
years gone by, and though I am old my memory has not
failed me.'

'You see, Will, how his English differed from mine, so
that he spoke it different yet I understood him well.'

His wife knew not what to say to any of this but
wrung out her clothes and wept and laughed at the sight
of the sun, but her husband showed me this book he had
wrote in the winekeg and pressed it upon me to read it.
I cried out with pain that I knew not words, though all
this long travail I had been reading the world. He wept
for my failings and said he must read it to me, though I
saw his wife had no more patience to hear it, for
beseems she had heard it for twenty-eight days. She
clamoured with hunger and I took what bread I had by
me and gave them to eat. His wife was appeased not,
but he sat me down there on the sand by the sea, so
great his impatience was it was nought to his hunger. So
great was his hurry to read me his book he read it
forthwith.

CHAPTER FOUR

A TALMUDTUB

Ribbono shel olem
Baruch Melekh ho olam
Baruch Ha Shem
Baruch A'donoy
Baruch E'loheynu

That my children may set their households in order, that
they may know the Lord and that He may bless them, I
write my will for my descendants. As Jacob prayed,
'Ribbono-shel-olam, take not my soul until I have exhorted
and blessed my children,' and as my father prayed when
we brought him to the shore at Calais where he sat with
his face toward England for so long, we feared for his
mind. But he rose at last and went forward with us to
Cologne where my brother's bride and family waited to
greet us. Burdened though we were with the death of
my mother, my brother was greeted with the joy of the
bridegroom and my father with the honors due him. It
was in Andernach that he died, still grieving for my
mother, though two decades had passed since her death.
And we brought his body to Carcassonne and buried him,
as he had instructed us to do, next to the grave of his
father-in-law whom he chose for 'reasons of highest
imperative' to clasp in the Eternal Dust.
  Moses Menaheim was my father, Presbyter of the Jews
in London, physician to the Count of Hainsault,
ambassador to the courts of Henry 111 and Edward 1. He

had four sons and a daughter who lived a few weeks, and
was buried with my mother in the graves we left behind.
I, Jacobus Elias, was the eldest.   My father had been
elected presbyter, our right to elect our own rulers
having been fixed in the charter we held from the third
Henry, wheretofore our presbyters had been appointed by
the king.

Our further rights had been previously given us by the
Charter of King John:

> Know that we have granted to all the
> Jews of England and Normandy to have
> freely and honourably residence in our land
> and to hold all that from us which they held
> from King Henry, our father's grandfather,
> and all that now they reasonably hold in land
> and fees and mortgages and goods, and that
> they have all their liberties and customs just
> as they had them in the time of the
> aforesaid king Henry, our father's
> grandfather, better and more quietly and
> honourably.
>
> And if any dispute arise between a
> Christian and a Jew, he who summonses the
> other to have complaint shall have witnesses,
> viz.: a lawful Christian and a lawful Jew.
> And if a Jew has a writ about his complaint,
> the writ shall be a witness for him, and if a
> Christian have a complaint against a Jew,
> let it be judged by peers of the Jew.
>
> And when a Jew dies his body shall not
> be detained above the earth, but his heirs
> shall have his money and his debts, so that
> he shall not be disturbed therefore if he has
> an heir who may answer for him and do
> what is right about his debts and his
> forfeit.   And let it be lawful for Jews to
> receive and to buy without difficulty all
> things that may be brought to them except
> things of the church or bloodstained cloth.

And if there is a dispute between a Christian and a Jew about accommodations of some money the Jew shall prove the capital and the Christian the interest.

And let it be lawful for the Jew to sell his pledge after it is certain that he has held it for a whole year and a day.

And wherever the Jews may be, let it be lawful for them to go when they will with their chattels just as our own property, and let none stop or prevent them in this.

John, by the grace of God, etc. Know that we have conceded and by this present Charter of ours confirmed to our Jews in England that excesses which may arise among them except those which belong to our crown and justice, as homicide, mayhem, premeditated assault, burglary, rape, theft, arson, and treasuretrove, shall be brought before them according to their law and remedied, and they shall do justice thereon among themselves.

So we kept our laws and went our own way, having been here with William the Conqueror, we were assured after the events in York and sought not to go elsewhere, but governed ourselves and when events enabled us, intervened for such was were Jews in Gascony and elsewhere which, by law, belonged also to the king of England and to be taxed as he provided.

The two branches of my family came to England at different times, my mother's more recently. My father's family had been in the Moselle valley engaged in viticulture since the time of Charlemagne until the time of William the Conqueror, when the priests began to complain of the Jews who lived in the countryside because they could not collect the tax on the land from them since they did not hold this land by their allegiance to the Church, and that they were Judaizing among the peasants, for there were a few who came to us for conversion. The charter we held from Justinian, assuring us of the right to own land here, was dismissed and the law was passed that we may not own land anymore, but must now seek our livelihood in the towns. So also by the Synod of Bourges, in my mother's time, in the land where she came from, they could not live any longer in the villages and the countryside, but must live henceforth in the cities and the towns. Thus, they ceased to cultivate the vines, as our law demanded we do for the purity of our wine, but went where the new laws said we must go. My family came to England, my father's first, and settled in York where they lived from the time of the first Richard when two hundred under Reb Yomtob sanctified the Name of the Unity. My great grandfather, Reb Jehuda Menaheim, considered then to return to Normandy, but upon conditions stipulated in the charter of John, moved the family to London where we had a cemetery and a mikveh and three synagogues, and so we stayed and obeyed the king's laws.

It was here that my mother arrived from Carcassone in the year 4,627. She came with her grandmother and her father, a brother and his wife, and a servant-companion who was Clemence the Albigensian, for she would not stay behind, her family having been martyred in the Crusade. They sailed from Aigues-Mortes in the year King Louis sailed from there on his last crusade east. My mother arrived a bride and a stranger who spoke no French. Her mother had been martyred in the Crusade and sleeps in the Eternal Dust in Carcassone. My mother read Hebrew, for my grandfather held that daughters must be educated as well as sons, and as she was the grandaughter of Rabbi Simon ben Meir, no less was expected of her. But of the tongue she spoke only Occitan when she first arrived. My father spoke Hebrew, French, and Latin.

The difference between them was not only the language, but from the first, as I heard it later, commencing with the marriage ceremony, to which my father was never reconciled. My mother had been betrothed to the son of the Nasi in Toulouse, who had been struck down by the crusader's sword in their war against the Albigensis. She wished the ceremony to be held on a Thursday as for one who was widowed. My father argued that she had been betrothed, but not married, and he would not marry her as if she had been a widow. He insisted the ceremony be held on a Wednesday, as prescribed for virgins. My grandfather, who was an authority in such matters, believed she should be married on Thursday, as befitting a widow. The marriage was delayed for months with this quarrel, and then to the scandal of the community they were married on a Friday.

She stayed at my father's kinsman's house in Isenmongre Lane, Leo Cruse, whose family went with us in the Expulsion, until she was led on a Friday morning to my father's house. There was much gossip that my father had married a "widowed virgin," but none said so to his face, but blessed the union, and my mother was accompanied by our kinsmen to the altar with song and dancing.

Of our neighbors and kin came Jacob Bonami and Moscus Crispin, the armourer; Jorvin Sackerel, a silversmith, whose house passed to Benedict Shoreditch in the Expulsion; Antera vid Vines in Cateaton Street whose house passed to John de Butterleye; Leo Cresse our kinsman and musician, Gamaliel Oxon, the stonecutter. May his children leave a good memorial for him as he has left for others. Elie le Evesk, the baker from Sporier Street, Sarra Diei, tradeswoman, Muriel Cresse, precentor in our synagogue, Aaron Slemne, innkeeper in St. Olave Jewry; Abraham Matron, goldsmith, whose daughter afterwards married my son; Benedict Mayer, tanner, whose wife bore him Samson at a weight of eleven stone; Elie Braggard, the cloth merchant; Bateman Cresse from Lade Street, winemaker, afterwards settled in the city of Rashi; Sarra Oxon, cloth merchant, Benedict Muriel in Milke Street, carpenter; Mosse Bonamie, locksmith, and many others whose names I have forgotten, notables, rabbis and counsellors from Norwich and Bristol; Belaset Duelcresse and the Bishop of Lincoln

and Cok Hagin who translated Ymage de Monde of which
you have heard, and two knights of the realm. Of the
poor, for which my father set a great table, came David
Derbie the Dyer, afterwards settled in Paris during the
uprising of the shepherds; Massa ben Issac, the maker of
mousetraps; Solomon the Mule-seller, Isaac Muriel the
basketweaver and his son Eliezer ben Muriel who herded
sheep for the Bishop of Winchester. Came three hundred
and twenty-two guests withal and went to the synagogue
in Cateaton Street, afterwards called St. Lawrence in
Jewry.

Though my mother was a stranger, she walked in
procession among them in her wedding dress made of silk
and linen and a jeweled belt and a crown of pearls on
her hair. She wore also the veil, which none had seen
here before, and embroidered her star upon it. My
father's kinsmen ran beside her carrying the canopy above
her head and chanted the blessing, which I charge my
descendants to sing in her memory:

Blessed art Thou, Lord God, creator of
    the Universe
Who created joy and gladness,
the Bridegroom and the Bride,
Pleasure and delight
Peace and fellowship.
Blessed art Thou Who brings joy to the
    world,
Blessed art Thou
Who created the Bride and the
    Bridegroom.

Now is the voice of the Bridegroom
    heard in the land
And the voice of the Bride answers him.
The jubilant notes of the Bridegroom are
    heard
from the canopy and from the feast of
    song.

When she arrived at his door, she would not enter his house but sat herself on a chair and bid him read aloud the ketubah. His kinsmen murmured at this, but my father, in nice deference to her and to his father-in-law, as strangers in his home, agreed. After the reading, she gave him her ring in token of her acceptance. But it was such a ring, a box heavily wrought in gold with small bells in each corner and a sprig of myrtle inside that he laid it aside afterwards and declined to wear it because, he said, of its size but it was because of the sprig of myrtle. Then he poured ashes on his head in commemoration of Zion, whereupon my grandfather took hold of the ashes as well and, saying a prayer for his kinsmen whom they had left behind in Provence, smeared his forehead with the ash.

"It is a thing done only in commemoration of Zion," my father's kinsmen murmured. But my grandfather brooked little dispute, for he was a rabbi himself and he informed them of how matters stood with this law. My mother's grandmother hurried forward and gave my mother an egg to eat, and my father hurried to the synagogue for the morning's reading, while the kinswomen hurried to the courtyard to make ready for the feast.

My mother's grandmother fed my mother eggs from a hen we kept in the house, so that the Law could be fulfilled by us that a good master is one who feeds his animals before himself, which charge I lay upon you, be it a hen or a goat, a calf or a lamb. My mother called our hen Mellisent and ate an egg from her every day until she conceived. Afterwards, I ate the eggs and then my brothers, until the hen died. May she be gathered to the embrace of the Creator for I remember her from my youth and my infant eyes delighted in her, she fed us from her body and we fed her from our souls. My mother's brother and his wife, who took a house in Milke Street, kept a cat to fulfill the Law, but my father derided this for a cat gives neither milk nor eggs. So we had always a hen or a goat, but you may keep a cat for your soul's sake.

My mother's grandmother also lit candles for the souls

of the dead, which my father forbade. But though he forbade it, I charge you to do likewise in memory of my mother, for there is no law against it, and it was but custom which made it strange to my father and aggravated his peace of mind. It is a curious thing about the human being, though he undertake arduous travails, if his egg is not properly made his daily disposition will be soured. For this reason, look well to your homes. Be not niggardly in them. Bring to your home the largesse of your souls. He who can rule his household is a better king than he who rules an empire.

My grandfather had a fancy to wearing a sarbel to the synagogue, a handsomely embroidered mantle he had carried with him from Carcassonne, but my father had not a fancy to it at all, for he considered that it surpassed the sumptuary laws of our people. My father was strict in these matters, for he said that wealthy dress and finery in Jews not only caused envy in our Christian neighbors, but beggared our own poor. He believed that no Jew should wear on his body an article of clothing which could not be worn by the poorest Jew. He was equally strict in his diet as in his dress, while my mother and great grandmother loved to wear gold and jewelry and pearls and to carry feathered fans, so that when they appeared in the street they caused comment.

I cannot say why, and though I honor my mother, the most incurable trait in women is love of baubles, and chiefly among the Spanish women. I cannot say why it should make a woman so happy to put on fine clothes, but even our sages caution us to let them have their way in this. My grandfather, no doubt under an evil influence from Spain, would not yield his sarbel. My father was skilled in diplomacy for he was praised by the king himself for his felicitous tongue. I do not know therefore how he addressed my grandfather on this issue but I heard my mother say that never did my grandfather love that embroidered cloth so well as after that speech.

My grandfather and my mother and her grandmother and Clemence, our servant, would sing songs of winds and flowers that were not to be found in England, songs of

the troubadors, of Judah Halevi, of yearnings which made
the flesh unquiet and turned it into soul, and which
unsettled my father in his own house. Clemence, who
was almost as old as my mother's grandmother, standing
in age between my mother and her grandmother, had
been a troubador at the court of Raymond of Languedoc.
She had known the great troubadors of her time and had
many songs to sing and stories to tell, and composed
songs herself.

> In an orchard where the leaves of
>   hawthorne hide,
> The lady holds a lover to her side,
> Until the watcher in the dawning cried,
> Ah, God, ah God, the dawn, it comes
>   how soon.

I heard these songs from childhood and I found nothing
strange in them. No one in the household but my father
found anything strange in them for, until we were born,
everyone but he in the household was from the Midi. Only
when we carried him there to bury him did he come to
this land whose ways had destroyed his household peace,
this land of the sensual soul where I journeyed myself
afterwards. Here Jew and Christian had lived side by
side for a thousand years, and later Moslems and
Waldensians, Cathars and others found peace here until
the Pope preached a crusade against the Cathars and
destroyed the balance of beliefs and uprooted the habits
and loyalties of centuries. The Cathars were destroyed
and with them the Jews of this region as well as the
faithful Catholics who came to the aid of their heretic
friends when the crusaders tore out the tangled roots of
faith and daily living. 'Slay them all and God will choose
His own,' the Pope's legate had said. But the soil knew
no difference. It received alike the blood of all.
    This history I had from Clemence before I could read

the chronicles for myself, for her grandmother had been a perfecta, revered throughout the Albigensis. On her deathbed, two Dominicans came and pretending to be Cathar as she was, gave her the Consolatem which, as she received it, they had proof of her heresy and immediately took her up and delivered her to the auto da fe. Her family on her grandmother's side were martyred. She alone was saved by a Catholic neighbor who was martyred for this act. Finally, taken in by my grandfather, she fled with his family from Carcassonne and stayed with us until her death. There was no home for her in Languedoc anymore, nor could she hold with her religion in England, for there was no church for her there, and as she would not attend the one there was, the Bishop came again and again and asked for her conversion, to which she would say that she was already a Christian and needed no conversion; for which he would accuse us of Judaizing, for which my father would ask her to declare herself for what she was, for it was not lawful for us to keep a Christian servant. She would not declare herself to be a Cathar, fearing for her life, and we would not declare her to be a Christian, fearing for our own. Betwixt and between this problem, we lived with the help of God, it giving rise to argument on Monday and resolution on Thursday.

Though she did not hold with the laws of Moses, her people went unarmed in the world and pursued peace. My grandfather often held discourse with her on this matter, though never in my father's hearing. She was well versed in our Bible but, strange to my ears, regarded it as the work of a demiurge and, stranger yet, this idea did not diminish her affection for us, nor my grandfather's for her. "Come, come," he would say, "you cannot reject the Creator. You might as well reject existence." But she held that all matter was evil and that only the spirit was good and that He who created matter was evil. My grandfather never took offense. On the contrary, the idea seemed to amuse him, but we all understood that it would not have amused my father, and a conspiracy was afoot never to discuss these matters in his presence.

Clemence kept her ears and tongue sharp and since she knew our laws, 'better,' my father said 'than my mother's family did,' he could not find fault with her. She went to market every day with my mother, except on Friday when my father bought for the Sabbath.

It was not my mother's tongue and language alone that he could not understand, but all that came from this region and these people whose eyes were the color of dark olives. My mother arrived with her "languedoc air" and was set down for a stranger. She was the granddaughter of Rabbi Simon ben Meir of Narbonne, married to her present good fortune in being settled with my father. But when a woman is beautiful no one expects her to be anything else. That my mother was beautiful was perhaps too much for my father who had expected only to fulfill his responsibilities. Her customs, her songs, her "air" provided them with a spiritual rivalry that remained side by side with the bonds of their marriage. Shall one say this marriage should not have taken place? It was the wisdom of our religion to provide for my mother by her marriage to my father, that she not be left to wander in that torn land and go astray in the world.

She was the granddaughter of Rabbi Simon ben Meir, may his name be a blessing among his heirs forever. How then should she not be brought back into the house of life to raise up heirs? But she was possessed of the womanliness of Provence and was given to songs and expressions and ways and stories my father found difficult and alienating, as he was soon the only member of his own household for whom such customs were strange, for I and my brothers were born to them. She remained to the end, kin and stranger to him. Though they bore children together, she remained a foreigner to him, one who had dispossessed him from his own home and whose death brought him no relief and in the end a violent grief, contrary to his nature. The pain of his marriage was expressed in awkward verses he composed on her name, Florria-Sara, which we discovered after his death.

My grandfather accommodated himself to my father in one matter: he spoke his language, but neither Clemence nor my mother nor her mother would. If my father addressed them in French a veil would drop over their eyes as if they were dumb. My father would not or could not learn their tongue. And they would not, whether they could or could not, learn his. Hebrew my mother could read but not speak. French she would not speak, Latin was unknown to her. Yet to market she must go and speak something.

She relented and learned French after we were born, for we had to learn our lessons from her. My father forbade us to speak Occitan, and from this point he never yielded. She must yield, either her language or her place in the household as our mentor, for that we should learn our lessons in a doomed tongue could not be countenanced. What she would not yield as a wife, she yielded as a mother. For our sake, she yielded and for her sake, Clemence yielded too and thus they were permitted to prepare me for school.

I charge you, my descendants, if you wish your child to love learning, do likewise: Take him on the Feast of Pentecost, dress him in fine clothes so that he may feel like a prince, and feed him three cakes made of fine flour and honey baked by a young maiden. Thus may he learn the sweetness of learning and yearn for it as the tongue yearns for the sweet taste of a fruit that has just departed from it. You may also feed him three cooked eggs and apples or other fruit, but nothing sour or bitter must pass his lips. Likewise do as my great grandmother and Clemence did, who baked me cakes in the mold of our letters and dipped each one in honey and fed them to me as I was carried through the streets on my father's shoulders to the Beth Hamidrash where I was set on the dais. Here our kinsmen and friends greeted us with their blessings. "May the Law be sweet upon your lips." And Clemence herself blessed me in the French she now spoke. Weeping for the sound of it, she kissed me on my honeyed lips.

I charge you, my sons and daughters, grandsons and

granddaughters, for the sake of my servant, if you would live in peace with your neighbor, take not his language up as a cause of discontent, but put honey on your lips.

Afterwards, my father trusted me to their care, to take me to school or to go to the market. I went with Clemence to the wharves to see the boats from Flanders and Calais. It pleased her to see their wares laid out in the streets though there was nothing, as she would have it, to compare with the fair at Beaucaire, where the boats came from Genoa, Pisa, Venice, Egypt, and Spain, Africa, Greece and the Levant, bearing oranges and leather from Morocco, dates from Africa, cloth from France, scents and soaps and oil from elsewhere. She wondered that Englishmen were content with scarcity and coarseness. When she was like this, she spoke in Occitan, but it could not be said that she broke her word to my father, for she spoke to herself and not for my ears, and I never answered a word back.

When my brother Mose and I brought my father to Carcassonne to be buried there I listened for her tongue, but it was not heard anymore. Everything else in the city was as she described it, the paths of acacia trees and the wind called the mistral. I entered this city in which I had never been as if I had lived there in another life, passing over the bridge of my mother's past to this land of the Albigensis where she had come from, a land of crusaders and troubadors and bloodshed, a Roman land with a Roman past, which was now no more, neither by its tongue nor its laws. Until the Crusade, the Jews had lived there by the Roman privileges which had been given to them from the time of Justinian. They cultivated the land and came of vineyards and orchards under the protection of the counts of Toulouse, as did the Albigensis, until the preaching of the Crusade against them by Innocent 111, led by the ecclesiastical might of Europe, the archbishops of Rheims, Sens, and Rouen, the bishops of Autun, Clermont, Nevers, Bayeux, Lisieux, and Chartres, and the cruelest man of the century, Simon de Montfort, wherefore 20,000 Cathars fell in an afternoon at Beziers before his army.

Clemence knew bitter songs as well as gentle ones: "God confound thee, Rome! Who draggest all who trust in thee into the bottomless pit, and forgives sins only for money:

Shame to him who will not bear
In this our glorious cause his share,
Noble souls, we do not fear,
Strong in the hope that help is near

But it was not to be, and her fate became ours. Here the Inquisition was born for her people. Who knew then that what had been devised for others would catch our own in its net? Living as they did, mingled among the Albigensis in the cities of Beziers, Carcassonne and Toulouse, it was not to be expected that they would escape. I have read in the Chronicle of Shanzaler: "In 1209, the year of sorrow, outlaws came out of France to wage war, and on the 19th of Ab, there arose a great slaughter, and of the uncircumcized 20,000 were killed, and of the Jews, 200." The column of crusaders, winding its way from France into the land of the Albigensis, swollen with thousands of starved peasants as well as with knights and noblemen, led by Simon de Montfort and the Archdeacon Theodosious from the Cathedral of Notre Dame, that famed master of siegecraft and engines of assault and battery, brought terror and warning wherever it was sighted. They set fire to the land, to the castles, to the cities. At Chateau de Termes, the Archdeacon Theodosious, his cross atop his engine, set the flames himself. Fires were set in all the cities of Provence. One hundred and fifty Cathars were burned at Minerve, four hundred at Lavaur, eighty at Casses, two hundred at Montsegure. Languedoc burned for fifty years. The land was scorched to its roots, and even the animals fled from its heat.

At Beziers, Simon de Montfort gouged out the eyes and cut off the ears and noses of a hundred men, but one eye he left in the hundredth and first to lead the others across Provence as a warning to all heretics. Their tongues he also left them to tell the tale of Beziers. After that, every city flung down its gates for the crusaders. Only Carcassonne kept its closed. Here the beloved Vicomte de Beziers, hero and patriot, waited for Simon de Montfort and the crusaders. He sent his son away for safety. His uncle, the king of Aragon, pleaded with him to flee too. But he stayed, and sleeps now in the Eternal Dust. His form and his fate have passed likewise into a poem and a story. Alas! How shall we keep our history. Not in books alone. So Clemence relieved the burden of memory through her songs.

The siege for Carcassonne began on August 1, 1209, and lasted fourteen days. I have heard my grandfather tell that when the gates of the city were lowered, a stench of death from famine floated over the land. The dead were piled against the gates, clawing the earth for water, Jew and Christian, men, women, and children, whole households who died together. In the aftermath, what siege and engine could not do, the Inquisition did. The Church brought into this already burdened world a terrible new power which we have not seen the end of, and cannot reckon what it will be.

When complaint was made by Catholics, who sought to come to the aid of others, that the believer was being killed with the heretic, and when the Pope's legate responded, "Slay them all and God will choose His own," then all knew that before this force neither belief nor disbelief, neither faith nor lack of faith, mattered. Who could, fled, Jew and Christian and Cathar, seeing how the Church slew her own.

The Counts of Toulouse weakened, and the Jews lost their protector. The king's brother, Alfonse de Poitou, came to power and enforced the Synod of 1209, removing Jews from their public posts, and enforced the decree that they wear the yellow badge, though heretofore none in Languedoc, while the Counts of Toulouse ruled, would enforce this ignominious ruling. De Montfort's wife, Alice of Montmorency, ordered the imprisonment of the Jews, to be kept until such time as they were converted. Though they were in time released, the baptized children were never returned. As with my son.

My mother's family fled, but tragedy found them. My mother's cousin, Pulchellina, was martyred in Narbonne. She carried the same name as my great grandmother's grandmother who had been martyred in Blois the century before. Taken in labor she delivered her child in the flames. My grandmother had warned her sister against that name, and she groaned with heaviness of breath, "Pulchellina, Pulchellina."

But I charge you, my descendants, remember this name, for my great grandmother's sake, for her grandmother's sake martyred in Blois, she who delivered her child in the flames, for the sake of my sister to whom she gave this name and who died with my mother on the eve of our departure from England. Sons of my sons, I charge you to remember this name as you lead your wives to the altars, for the sake of the mother and the child who died in the flames. Remember your wives and your daughters who sleep in the Eternal Dust.

Began then my mother her practice of lighting candles on the anniversary of the deaths of her relatives, keeping customs that were ever more strange to us, and for which we began to ridicule her. Ribbono shel olom will have mercy for the deeds of my youth which I cannot retrieve.

She and her family left the Midi two years before the land fell and the Jews of Languedoc now belonged to the French crown, many forced by the new law to serve the treasury in Paris. When I and my brother went to Carcassonne to bury my father, we could find none who spoke their tongue anymore.

Blessed art Thou Who preserveth worlds as Thou did preserve the world of Noah, Who made and keeps faith with Thy Eternal Promise.

I keep this account for my Jewish descendants, as a will against the future, for I see that my wife and I survived the burning in the cities of Europe and that with a mighty hand Ha Shem Who created the world sustained us. As I saw that we passed our first hours in this habitat in fear but without threat to our lives, I knew that He would bring us to safety. The wine was only a fifth of the level of the barrel, and the barrel corked so well, with pitch and tar to preserve it against air and rot, that it floated on the river without hazard to us. I found a small opening above the level of the water where the staves had not been properly fastened. It was a pinhole, but I could look out on the surface of the water and see all manner of life on it and tell the hour of the day. It was night when we had first been put inside. I watched at this opening until I tired, but little by little I saw there were patterns of light on the water and that I could tell the movement of the sun by them, and could say my prayers at the appointed times. "Blessed art Thou Who has created the world wherein there is no place that is not fit for your creatures. Blessed art Thou Who multiplies berakhot."

We were immersed with our Siddurs, our candlesticks and our candles, as our oppressors meant to bury us with what to them are the hated emblems of our religion. My wife was frightened, as I was, but her fears were mixed with lamentable anger for, as the proverb says, to the sinner bring kindness, neither wrath nor upbraiding. But my wife wept and cursed and, given our confinement, I could neither blame her nor be kind. "I will only weep that my life has taken this strange turn," she cried. Her face, ruddy as her ancestors were, was also puffy with fright and from the ingestion of the wine we had almost drowned in. "What boots it to pray," she wept, "sitting in a winekeg? Can you not see, husband, what has overtaken us?"

She did not have her oppressors about her anymore and turned her anger on me. "What boots it that you say your prayers? You have not a minyan. You have only me. You are mad."

My wife's family was of Exeter and Cornwall, settled there in the time of the first Richard, and her father had owned a house and a watermill on the river Tamar. As a consequence, her complexion was ruddy to which she applied powders to no avail. She had the story from her mother how the thirty thousand dishes were served for the Earl of Cornwall's wedding to Queen Eleanor's sister, Cynthia, for which the Jews were taxed 20,000 marks, and for which reason this number never ceased to augur well or ill for her, so that she could say of a jubilant event that it was worth twenty thousand marks as well as say of a tragic event that it surely cost 20,000 marks. Such an equal expression for good and evil puzzled me, and I told her so, but my puzzlement puzzled her.

"It matters not the number," she said. "Tis but an expression meaning much, whether much joy or much tragedy," but I pointed out to her that for the sake of the Book of Life in which an accounting must be kept, that she should choose a bigger number for a joyful event, even if it be bigger only by one.

We had this argument many times, for she was a stubborn woman, coming from Cornwall, and determined to have her way. "I will not," she said flatly. "It be one expression meaning much and much and much can be the sorrow as much can be the joy. Mayhap the sum of joy in the world be not one more but one less than the sum of sorrow in the world," which thought I took to be the evil influence of her birthplace.

"Do you think I cannot add and say what be the difference between two sums as well as you?" she said.

Thereupon I remained silent for I would not broach the argument with her beyond this point. Having learned as much in so many years of marriage, I learned to live with this expression which was upon her lips twice a day, if she heard of a fire or when her cousin with the clubfoot was delivered of a normal child. From time to time I attempted to instruct her in further subtlety, that she should not use the same term of measurement for good as for evil. "Say you?" she would say and narrow her eyes to unwholesome slits, "I will say what I will say. It is nought but an expression and means nought."

"Every meaning means something," I cautioned. "One must never say a saying frivolously, for the word is a portion of the Eternal Life. Do we not say for this reason that the tongue of the slanderer brings worse death than the sword of the warrior, for it slays the soul of a people."

"Master of languages!" she then called me.

For the sake of peace in our household I shut my ears to her tongue, for what was a matter of universal knowledge she took as a personal insult if one attempted to instruct her, and as our quarters were now by so much reduced, leaving us no room to withdraw from each other, I prayed, and we quarrelled. Much thought I had to Noah as he sailed in the small ark with his wife for forty days. Certain it is that God designed the flood to test him as a householder as well as a preserver of the world.

To my father also fell that double duty when he received my mother's family after all effort to stem the tide of change in the Midi had failed. Twenty thousand liras paid to Alphonse de Poitou for the ransom of Jewish prisoners, the delegation led by Rabbi Simon ben Meir to protest the laws that sought to curb our finances, Jews now being forbidden to collect their debts from their Christian debtors though Christians could continue to collect their debts; Jews now forbidden to move from place to place, which rendered them serfs to the barons on whose lands they lived, as the Christians were.

Praised be the memory of Rabbi ben Meir, who laid down for all time and for all our descendants, the conditions, the laws, the practice and spirit of the usury by which we received our means of survival as we received our manna in the desert. We praise the everliving Master of the Universe. We praise Thee, we thank Thee, we render blessings without end to Thee Who out of the rock brought water, out of the desert brought manna, and out of this life gave us our means to live. We praise Thee, we bless Thee, we thank Thee Who preserves Thy people Israel on this soil of Christendom as Thou didst preserve her in the deserts of Egypt. We praise Thee, we thank Thee, we glorify Thee, Who out of chaos created the world as Thou sustains our world on the soil of Christendom.

So spoke Rabbi Simon ben Meir to the royal delegates. He reminded the assembly that being forbidden membership in the guilds, forbidden ownership of land except on condition of apostasy, forbidden public posts, forbidden access to the universities, forbidden to practise medicine in all of Languedoc except in Narbonne, he believed that the Living Master of the Universe had created this means for the Jewish people to survive, as a spider spins a web, spinning what it must for very survival against the calumnies of the universe. He reminded the assembly that where there is Jewish usury there is lawful usury. He reminded the assembly that profit was neither forbidden by Torah nor by the laws of Christian kings, but that like every force needed to be controlled, to be made lawful, not lawless. He reminded the assembly that where Jews were forbidden to practise usury, there sprang up Christian usury, a wild and rampant usury that knew no bounds, that escaped all effort to control it, as when Louis, the king, forbade Christian promissory notes to the Jews there began the practice of Christians to borrow on securities, and a Christian usury then flourished at extraordinary interest rates, to the dismay of this king who thirsted for sainthood. He reminded the assembly that usury is not expelled with the Jew, but that after the Jew leaves, it remains unchecked in its secret devices with the Christian, a matter of record in every province in the realm. He reminded the assembly that when the Jewish usurer departs, the people, and even the king and the barons clamor for his return, as Louis himself discovered, who so ardently wished to rid the land of usury and be a saint but knew not where else to raise his tax money from if not from the Jewish usurers, but wanting holily what he wanted urgently.

My father too had had experience in negotiating for the Jews of England for the ransom of Jewish prisoners and Jewish slaves, and told how King Henry wept: "It is no wonder that I covet money, for it is dreadful to think of the debts in which I am involved. I am a humiliated and diminished king. I am therefore under necessity of living on money obtained in all quarters, from whomsoever, in what ever manner I can acquire it." And having wept and said thus openly, levied such taxes on his Jewish subjects that in the single year of 4,605 they paid 60,000 marks in tallage, a sum equal to what all his other English subjects paid, and between 1230, and 1259 had paid more than 250,000 marks in tallage alone, sums which fell outside of the fines imposed consequent upon blood accusations, death duties often amounting to the third of the estate and multitudinous donations for royal weddings and festivals, for as the Church taxed its own for its luxuries so the kings taxed their Jewish subjects for theirs.

Did not Aquinas warn the governors that to tax the Jews beyond all just endurance must drive them further into usury.

We petitioned King Henry to let us leave England and seek our living elsewhere. Three hundred rabbis left the island and his provinces in France and went to Palestine, but he would not let the rest of us go out, as Gamaliel said afterwards at the Expulsion, when we would he would not and when we would not he would.

Rabbi Meir reminded the assembly that the Church traffics in relics and indulgences and raises revenues from the sales of the souls of its peoples. Christian coins are squeezed from Christian sin and fear, while the Jew raises coin only from coin. Did not the scholar Abelard have the Jew say, "We can possess neither fields nor vines nor any land. Our sole resort is usury by which we maintain our miserable livelihood. Yet through this we provoke your bitter hatred."

Of what use Bernard, Aquinas, and Abelard? Of what use your scholars and saints, for when you want money you ignore them all.

He reminded the assembly that if it were not for Christian love of war and pageantry, for tournaments and monuments, there would be no traffic in coins, for what was the money ever used for, for what cause? what charity? other than to pay armies of mercenaries to fight for land and loot, to celebrate the knight's prowess in war, in costly pageants and costly castles and abbots in costly churches.

Let Rabbi Meir's voice be our monument to the Jewish ages: "How shall we pay our taxes, exceeding that of all other citizens, except through usury? How shall we pay for protection against your mobs, except that you love wealth? Our nails have been torn from our fingers to raise coins for you, our hair from our heads, our teeth from our mouths.

Now you call us brother and say that we have transgressed the Law which holds that a brother should not pay interest on debt to his brother. Now you call us brother when you are called to pay back your debts. How are we brothers? Are we not your slaves, both by canon law and civil law? Are we not the servants of your treasury by your law, and by royal decree? Are brothers as slave to master, as servant to overlord? Do you not teach us that we are in perpetual servitude for the death of your God, that we may not build a synagogue but by your leave, that we may not build it high to offend the sight of the Church, that we may not sing or pray aloud to offend the ears of the Church, that we may not exchange gifts with you, or share meals with you or live among your countrymen, or have Christians in our homes, for fear of fraternizing? Are these not your laws? Stated not once or twice, but repeated in every century with renewed force, since you appeared upon the earth?

Thus does a brother to a brother? How then are we brothers? Does a brother slander his brother, his people, his book, his God? That you have slandered our books and our people, we forgive you, but God must forgive you for slandering Him. He Who brought living water out of the rock of the desert has given us the means to wring our living from this Christian rock. He Who brought us out of Egypt where we were made to furnish bricks for Pharaoh's monuments, will deliver us from this bondage to the Lord's treasury, where we are made to furnish gold instead.

And for what were your sums used? You have only to read your history books. For kings and barons who loved their wars and their castles, and for abbots and bishops who loved their costly monasteries and their monuments. And for what and from where and in what way and with what means were these sums raised? Brother Debt and Brother Debtor, we are now quits."

For this speech he was exiled and withdrew to Palestine, but his voice remains with us for a legacy. His granddaughter came to England while the fate of the others who remained behind became intertwined with the fate of the Waldensians and the Cathars, in one place for usury, in another for religion, for they were as often accused of Judaizing as of usury, so compounded was the Waldensian faith of elements of Judaism, preaching as they did the circumcision. And as the Cathars repudiated the Pope himself and all the sacraments but baptism and denied the images and the relics and came to regard themselves as the true Catholics, and in time acquired so many adherents that there were seminaries and convents throughout the land, in the whole of Bosnia, Innocent 111 took alarm and preached the Crusade against them under Simon de Montfort, after victory invested by the Pope as Count of Toulouse, and so came to rule in Languedoc. The House of Raymond went down and with him the Cathars, the Waldensians, the whole of Languedoc went down. There is none left anymore to sing their songs and few even read their chronicles.

My Jewish descendants, I would have you know this history as well as your own, the histories of vanished peoples, that you no longer believe that God has singled you out from among the nations for suffering, for many who have suffered are no longer with us. But I would have you know, again, that Moses gave it for a blessing that you were chosen for life and not for death, that your history is a history among the many who have perished and whose history has ended.

Remembering this, I passed through the gates to the city of Carcassonne with my brother, Mose.

So the first Edward too hoped to divert us from usury, for by the charter of 1275 we were granted permission to own land and houses without swearing faith in the Trinity and forswearing ourselves as Jews:

> Foreasmuch as the King hath seen that diverse Evils, and the disinheriting of the Good men of this realm have happened by the Usuries which the Jews have made in Time past, and that divers Sins have followed thereupon; albeit he and his Ancestors have received much benefit from the Jewish People in all Time past; nevertheless for the Honour of God and the common benefit of the people, the King hath ordained and established, That henceforth no Jew shall lend any Thing at Usury, either upon Land, or upon Rent, or upon other Thing.
>
> That all Jews shall dwell in the King's own Cities and Boroughs, where the chests of Chirographs of Jewry are wont to be: and that each Jew after he shall be Seven Years old, shall wear a Badge on his outer Garment; that is to say, in the form of Two Tables joined, of yellow Felt, of the Length of Six Inches, and of the Breadth of Three Inches. And that each one, after he shall be Twelve Years old, pay three pence yearly at Easter of Tax to the King, whose Bondman he is; and this shall hold as well for a Woman as a Man.
>
> And, Foreasmuch as it is the Will and Sufferance of Holy Church, that they may live and be preserved, the King taketh them under his Protection, and granteth them his

Peace; and commandeth that none shall do them harm, or damage, or wrong, in their Bodies or in their Goods, moveable or immoveable. And that none shall owe Obedience, or Service, or Rent, except to the King, or his Bailiffs in his name; unless it be for their dwellings which they now hold by paying Rent; saving the right of Holy Church.

And the king granteth unto them that they may gain their living by lawful Merchandise and their Labour; and that they may have intercourse with Christians, in order to carry on lawful Trade by selling and buying. But that no Christian, for this cause or any other, shall dwell among them. And the King willeth that they shall not by reason of their Merchandise be put to Lot or Scot, nor in taxes with the Men of the Cities or Boroughs where they abide; for they are taxable to the King as his Bondmen, and to none other but the King.

Moreover, the King granteth unto them that they may buy Houses and Curtilages, in the Cities and the Boroughs where they abide, so that they hold them in chief of the King; savings unto the Lords of the Fee their service due and accustomed. And that they may take or buy Farms and Land for the Term of Ten Years or less, without taking Homages or Realities, or such sort of obedience from Christians; and that they may be able to gain their living in the World, if they have not the means of trading, or cannot labour; and this license to take lands to Farm shall endure to them only for fifteen years from this Time forward.

Which from the time of the granting, 4,635 to the

time of our expulsion, 4,650, was fifteen years. But as we were not admitted to the guilds, neither merchant nor artisan, and as we could not go among the general population and practise a trade at large, and by law were confined to the towns and the cities where there was little farmland to be had; and as the taxes upon us remained of so formidable a nature that there was no way to raise the sums but by the way of usury that we knew, many of our kin, glad as we now were to own houses, were further impoverished by this law and many, like my uncle, who had not heretofore lent money on interest, were driven to it.

And as we saw that our heirs would not inherit from the fruit of our efforts, and we saw that what we labored for must revert to the king, we were not diverted from our usury, and there arose a great clamor among the people, for which cause we were then expelled."

"Master Menaheim," I said again, "it cannot be that this tale has aught to do with me."

"Aye, it does," he said so wonderfully that I fell silent again, and he went his way as before.

"My father laid his claim to the stone house in Huggin Lane in which we had been living, seeing he could now do so without apostasy, and furnished it grandly. My mother's brother and his wife, who took a house in Milke Street, had likewise a stone house with a chimney on the inside and a staircase within to go from one floor to the other, but since my uncle kept his debtors' notes in a chest in the house they had no window on the ground floor for fear of thieves. Our staircase was on the inside, so that we could pass from one floor to the other without exposing ourselves to the weather. We had a chimney whereby the smoke was let outside the house, and we had a window on the ground floor which looked out upon my mother's garden, to everyone's pleasure but my father's, for because my grandfather placed his lectern beside it, it caused much dispute in our household.

Our house was not as grand as our cousins in Lincoln, but there was nothing lacking for our holiday banquets.

Our festal board had three silver kiddush cups and a red wool cloth my mother had brought with her as well as an embroidered one with gold thread which my father had given her, and above the table our seven armed lamp. We had a carpet on the floor in the room where we ate, and there in a niche was an urn for handwashing where my mother hung her best cloth woven of linen and silk, which my father instructed us to use for the blowing of our noses. My great grandmother had brought with her six silver spoons, carved with lambs and lillies, but my father considered this excessive and would not let them appear on the table, to my mother's hurt.

Nor the mezzuzah which she put up on the doorpost, carved of wrought silver. He took it down at once, for he regarded the inscription in it as magician's work to ward off evil spirits. She abided by his feelings until the week before my second brother was to be born, when it went up again, and none could say how. My father returned from synagogue one day and stopping by the doorway, as if in a spell, looked at the mezzuzah hung upon the lintel. He did not move from the spot, for how long no one can say, until Clemence, coming from shopping, saw him standing thus. When she inquired, he said, "I will not pass into my house unless it be removed." The signal was given. My mother and grandmother came as quickly as they could. My grandfather was not to be found. My grandmother said she had seen it go up in a dream, and would not take it down, for she feared to do so. Neither Clemence nor my mother could say how it came to be there. The hour approached minha. My father, seeing the late time, took it down but it went up again a few days later, whereupon my uncle's wife came to the door of our house and said that she had also dreamed that the hand of God had put it there, and as my mother began to labor with my brother my aunt charged my father with her wellbeing if he took it down. My mother's screams mounted, and my aunt ran for the midwife. My great grandmother wrung her hands and implored my father to let it stay. My mother screamed and my father wavered. My great grandmother immediately grabbed his hand in gratitude.

Shortly, many visitors stopped by our door and wondered at it. My father, who felt his authority had been gainsaid, would not declare to them what it was. But my grandfather believed his authority was as good as my father's, and said he would declare its contents. Otherwise, it was an object of decoration, which God forbid it to be. An argument arose which went on at every meal, including the Sabbath, which vexed my father, for he would have us only sing at the Sabbath meal and not talk or dispute. He remarked one Friday evening, as my grandfather was heated in the defense of the inscription, "that it was a great wonder how he fell from one transgression into the next."

The next day in synagogue, in a pause between messages and declarations, my grandfather arose from his seat and said what the inscription in the mezzuzah was, and bid each Jew in London obtain one for himself.

My father never walked beside him in the street again, but walked in such a way after that, rapidly, so that it caused my grandfather to drift behind, for my father was a long man and my grandfather was not only short in his legs, but one leg was shorter than the other, so that he drifted far behind.

My mother complained at this disrespect to her father. My father said he meant no disrespect, but that my grandfather's legs being made shorter than was customarily seen in England, and of unequal length as well, he did not know how to accommodate himself to this peculiar stride without hobbling his soul. As the matter of the mezzuzah is now common custom, nothing more is to be said.

The disputes between my father and my grandfather concerned chiefly these three subjects: my grandfather's Bible, where his lectern should be placed; and the merits of the fathers; but because of these all philosophy and custom divided them.

My grandfather had brought with them from Provence an illuminated Bible. My father forbade us to look at it and was distressed that it should be in the house, though my grandfather argued that its illuminations were of such things as never had been seen on earth, objects with the faces and tails of monkeys and the bodies of lions. My father argued that they were intended for images of men. "God forbid!" my grandfather said. I learned, then, that the home requires as much diplomacy in getting about in it as the world does.

Concerning my grandfather's lectern, he loved to keep it by the window. As matters would have it, all manner of life passed his sight, birds which carried his glance away, Mellisent's feathery body, a snail on the wall. My grandfather, may he rest in peace, would say a berakhot for everything that flew or fluttered past his view. My father believed that anything which distracted from study should be removed. As he would not have us learn bad habits in such an important matter as study and prayer, he felt compelled to remove my grandfather's lectern to the side of the room that had no window. My grandfather believed that as "the Almighty had created the universe, there was no twig or flower or blade of grass that was unholy and not fit to be praised," and he moved his lectern back to the side of the room with the window. There was no rest or pause in this dispute until the coming of Solomon ibn Alfaqui, who distracted and distressed my father for three years.

Concerning the third dispute, my grandfather considered it a greater mitzva to give to the poor than to be learned in Torah. Without doubt, neither can be neglected, but neither can be fulfilled to everyone's satisfaction. The problem, though theoretical, may be crucial in a crisis and so should be thought out in advance, that events may not find us unprepared, in a spirit of surprise at the nature of the universe. The ethical imagination must imagine all possibilities, the sublime and the ridiculous, and the Jew must be prepared with his answer.

Though my grandfather neglected his studies and was content to spend each morning at his lectern and each afternoon in synagogue, he asserted that if he had a single hour left in the world he would hasten to spend it by giving charity to the poor rather than to spend it by reading Torah. He seemed or pretended to ignore my father's vexation, and put down in his will, "Next to prayer, to give to the poor is the highest mitzva." My father said it was the second highest mitzva. He was familiar with Aristotle's dictum, "mankind wishes to know," for he came abreast of the new learning from the continent in an unfortunate way, and fought to keep it holy. "To know what?" he said. "Wisdom, like the body, wants the discipline of chastity. It cannot be that curiosity for its own sake can be man's highest aim."

"Why not?" my grandfather asked.

"Why not?" my father's temper rose. "Because it cannot be. That's why not."

Nor did those who later oppose him necessarily disagree with this view. God is the God of life and not the God of learning. My father, may his soul find the peace he wished for others, rose in the Bezier Synod and said, "I abominate that learning that separates man from man, that is fit for some and not fit for others. Moses, when he delivered the Torah, spoke to all at the foot of the mountain, and they all heard with one ear. The learning which distinguishes between the fit and the unfit destroys a people. If your teaching cannot end for all with the maxim, now go forth and practise, it is not fit for the ear."

If one could have separated the issues, kept this idea from leaning upon that idea or person, finding support where it should not, we might have kept the house together. But who can contain an idea. More than the wind, it goes where it will and blows itself into shapes unforeseen so that a man who cursed Maimonides, as R. Gerondi did, died afterwards with his name on his lips, while others informed against his disciples to the Inquisition.

How much also an idea takes the color of the person who expresses it, so that it seems to be part of his manners, his behavior. For us Solomon ibn Alfaqui was the first instrument of these ideas. He it was who brought them from the continent and for my father they

carried ever afterwards the unfortunate impress of the
satirist and the courtier, though Solomon donned the
shawl twice a day and was in all ways devoted to the
Law. But said my father, "As he studies, so he is. As he
reads so is the man." Solomon read with closed lips and
with only his eyes. "He is afraid to utter his thoughts.
Can God trust a closed mouth?" Soon, because my
grandfather defended Solomon's way of reading and took
such matters differently, my father came to regard them
as allies and our visitor as a scorpion in his house.

Solomon ibn Alfaqui had been a courtier at the court
of Alphonse X, and now he was an exile. The king had
been generous and loyal to the Jews when he first came
to power, but he turned on them when his son Sancho
rebelled against him and brought civil war to Castile. He
accused the Jews of aiding his son and of giving him
money for his wars in Granada. On the second Sabbath in
January, in the year 1281 that Solomon ibn Alfaqui fled
from Castile to Toulouse and thence to England, the king
had the Jews arrested in their synagogues and would not
release them until they agreed to pay 4,380,000 gold
maravedis, for which coin was raised by the Jews
throughout the realm. Nevertheless, in Toldeo, they were
destroyed. Viziers and ministers were arrested, hanged,
burned, and dragged to death. Don Cag de la Maleha,
who had been Solomon's patron at court, fell from power
and was soon executed. Solomon's sister, who was a
mistress to Alphonse's nephew, a cousin and unfortunately
an ally to Sancho, was imprisoned with her family, and
his father was executed. Solomon himself barely
escaped.

As he stayed three years with us, his affect upon our
household history was not inconsequential. My father was
at first hospitable, as one should be to an exile and a
stranger, but he soon came to dislike our guest so
profoundly that his presence alone threw him into a
temper. Solomon carried his sword at all times. As
Jews in England were not permitted to carry weapons, my
father believed he should forego this privilege. His beard
was cut in the manner of the hidalgo, which my father

felt was immodest. He wore an amulet on his chest with Arabic writing on it, which he said his nurse had put on him when he was born, and which he wore in deference to her. Worse than this, he bore the English ill will and showed little gratitude for our hospitality. This wore my father's temper thin. For his part Solomon attributed my father's temper to the English climate. "His thinking is Spanish," my father said.

My grandfather took our guest with better humor, while my mother and great grandmother and Clemence doted on him, for Solomon had the charm of the storyteller which no one, except my father, can resist.

"Castile is my home," Solomon declared. "The tide will turn."

"Pray it will," my father said.

"We have lived in Castile for a thousand years,' Solomon said. His great grandmother, he told us, had been the paramour of Alfonso Vlll, her father, Omar Joseph ibn Shoshan had been the king's vizier. "My great uncle and his children and his children's children are Christiano viejo rancio y sin mancha." Fortunately, only my grandfather understood his language. Solomon brooked no censure against Castile or the king. He spent his exile writing a book on the art of horsemanship and a verse history of the reigns from Alphonso Vlll to Alphonso X. "His wrath will not last. We have been with his family too long. We have lived among the Moors and know their language and translate their documents for him. I assure you, my friends, he needs us and will come to his senses. His wrath will not last. He is a man of many moods."

"Kings usually are," my grandfather said.

I was eleven when Solomon entered our home. The Eternal alone knows why a gilded mortal will set the heart of a youth aflame, so that until I married and other responsibilities set my mind elsewhere, I wished only to fly from this island, to soar and to see the world Solomon ibn Alfaqui sang to us about, a world of fountains and black-eyed ladies, of speech spoken like song, I wished to be an eagle and be consumed with seeing this world.

I followed Solomon everywhere, to my father's consternation. I would not be parted from him. What my father forbade, I did secretly. Mose and I followed Solomon on all his errands, to the wharves, the warehouses, the shops, and whistled to our Gentile friends, Peter Smythfield and Tom Redd who were behind a hedge, so they could hear the tales of the wars between the Arabs and Christians, the stories of el Cid and the Three Rings. "But Castile is a peaceful land," Solomon laughed, "for the Pope has forbidden us to war on Thursday, and the Moslems will not fight on Friday, the Jews will not fight on Saturday, and the Christians will not fight on Sunday."

"I warrant they do right well the rest of the week," Tom said, "for my uncle was there once and said pray Spain does not war with England, for in Spain the knights die in their armour whilst the Englishman wears nothing but leather."

Mose and I went with Tom and Peter where we should not, to bearbaiting and cockfighting, the jousts and the markets with slaughtered animals.

One day Mose and I went with them to the King's forest where we hid and waited for the hunting party to go by. We spied a deer and chased her over a wall where she jumped and fell and broke her neck. We jumped the wall and followed after her and found her bleating on the other side. As she could not be saved, Tom took out his knife and put an end to her and divided her up. He built a fire to have a meal of her, but Mose and I fled, for we were forbidden to eat an animal in this manner.

All night, the deer's eyes haunted me, for I knew I had violated the holy mountain. Afterwards, we were found out and charged with the death of the King's deer, but Peter Smythfield stood bail for me and Mose, so that my father would not hear of this misdemeanor, and Mose swore me to silence.

Soon after I went with my father one morning to synagogue, to say our prayers. Elisha the Carter,

Gamaliel Oxon, Elie le Evesk the baker, and Mosse Bonavil the locksmith, not able to go home for their breakfast, sat in the courtyard and ate their morning meal. The sun was hardly up. They rose upon seeing my father, to say a blessing in his presence, and returned to their meals.

Peace to my father's soul. May it enter the Kingdom of God and may it plead for my sins. Though he sleeps beside my grandfather in the Eternal Dust, he put down in his will to us, "Torah is a lamp which will illuminate the world."

Whether from pride or philosophy, my grandfather would not satisfy my father on this point. The issue of the Maimunists went to the heart of our generation, and set rabbi against rabbi, brother against brother and, at last, son against father.

The flowering of these ideas was revealed to my father through Solomon ibn Alfaqui who, whether he read Maimonides or not, we never ascertained, but he read such poets who spoke of the Shekhinah as la Matronita or as a day star in heaven. Yet he himself mocked those who thought like him and once surprised us with a verse satire on such thinkers.

Jews so-called who cherish Christian lore
Who walk in darkness from Moses' Law
   estranged,
Who transgress the ages' precepts,
Too blind to esteem the Hebrew faith:
Hebrew we need not know, Castillian is
   our tongue, or Arabic,

and so on. but he himself continued in the same way, and he told us that educated people did not speak Hebrew in Castile, that Arabic was the language of civilized people, and that only Englishmen spoke French, for even in Provence anyone who wished to study philosophy must know Arabic.

"He is worse that the Gentiles," my father said, "for at least their learned men honor Hebrew."

So much wrath did Solomon cause in him, that even as he stood at his lectern one morning, wrapped in phylacteries, he burst out, "Cursed be those who speak of Abraham and Sarah as matter and form. Cursed be those who speak of God, rock and redeemer and everlasting fountain of mercy, as first cause. Cursed be the allegorist, and cursed be the astrologists who fix laws in the stars and say there is no divine will. Cursed be those who say there is no creator, no miracles, no redemption, and no resurrection of the flesh. Cursed be such Jews who pray with closed lips, who do not say grace after their meals, who do not bless the world and soon will come to say, as there is no Creator so there is no world but only cause and effect. Cursed be they who write such scabrous poetry, for what can be the practice of their ideas?"

My grandfather too stood in prayer at his lectern, at the window. "Practise!" he said. He was not himself easy with these ideas, but he considered it his duty, as he was the sole defendant in this community in England, of the scholars of Provence against whom anathemas were growing, to defend them. He was proud of the place of his birth and sometimes let slip the feeling that Solomon was not altogether wrong in his impatience with our community. He respected my father's learning but believed my father lacked a quality of refinement which he had in abundance. "Your father was," he once said to me, "bred an Englishman. This is no fault of his. No doubt the Creator is fond of him, and as we are made in the image of Ha Shem, we should be likewise."

It was not fair of my grandfather to say this, hinting at his own lineage, but not less fair than it was for my father to walk with him with a huge stride and make him lag behind.

"Can a poor uneducated man read philosophy?" my father asked, winding and unwinding his phylacteries. "Will this new teaching not divide rich from poor, for the unschooled must be left behind, and who are these philosophers and proponents but courtiers and grandees who speak Arabic and Catalan but cannot read Hebrew aloud in a bountiful voice? What can be the aim of such teaching?"

"The aim?" my grandfather said in a voice he deemed suited to the message. "The aim is contemplation."

My father left the room.

The issue was not Aristotle or Maimonides, but our civilization which we now felt threatened from within as from without. But what a man will not say in life he will say in death, for who would wish to write a lie into the Book of Eternity. Thus, my grandfather put down in his will to us, "More than the calf needs to suck, the heifer needs to suckle it. Remember always to praise the universe, though the Creator does not need your praise." And though he quarreled with my father every day that he lived, he inscribed on his tombstone, "Wisdom is acquired, but charity is from the heart."

Solomon made his home with us for three years, until Alphonso's son came to power and word went out that the new king welcomed Jews back to the realm. We heard that Solomon's cousin, Don Abraham el Barchilas, had secured a two year lease from Don Sancho and had the crown's permission to mint the coin of the realm. The new king turned over the revenues of Fronteras Toledo and Murcia to Jews, so that they could raise interest on it. We heard that friends of Solomon, the courtiers el rab don Yucaf and el rab don Samuel de Vallodolid, were called back and in time Solomon was too. He wrote a poem to commemorate the occasion.

Before I go to one of flesh and blood, I
   shall praise God
That He might turn to my will the heart
   of the king and the nobles
May my liege command his vassals.

"All is well again," my grandfather said.

The pleasure of soon returning transformed Solomon. "Castile is my home," he said. So much goodwill he now had that he complimented my great grandmother and Clemence on their cooking, who had always taken pains to please him. My great grandmother baked special breads for him and at the Sabbath meal covered his fish with special wines and herbs. Now, in turn, he gave us dainty riddles to puzzle us with at the table and sang such songs as we had never heard: "Ophra bathes her garments in the waters of my tears and dries them in the sunshine of my bright eyes," and all day long sang songs of adoration to women: to Clairette, to Adelasie, to Bausette, to Florette, to Emeline, to Beatrice, to Stephanette.

"It is well that he is returning," my father said, "he needs a wife."

Solomon confessed that he was betrothed "to a beautiful woman from Navarre," whose name, Preciosa, he uttered like a nightingale. My father expressed his surprise, seeing his years, that he was not yet married to her. With greater generosity of spirit than my father was prepared for, Solomon answered him that if he married her he would not be able to worship her, and he continued to sing his songs to Rambause and to Jeanne, to Laura and to Flora, and soon addressed my mother as Donna Florria-Sara.

My father wrote to Rabbi ibn Adret in Barcelona of his misgivings for the Jewish people in the Sepharad, and there began a correspondence between them which determined my father to enter the Maimunist controversy which, as it affected then only the communities of the Midi and Champagne, we never expected to entangle ourselves, or that this small wedge of concern would grow so wide as to cause division among our people.

In the meantime, Solomon made his preparation to depart for Castile in a spirit of gaiety which embraced us all. I followed him about in the markets, through the wharves and the Chepe. Sometimes my grandfather joined us. They would speak together in Arabic, or Solomon would recite verses from Judah Halevi and ibn Gabirol. So much he knew that I did not! Stars fell from his lips.

He accompanied my grandfather to synagogue, and as he managed to adjust his gait to my grandfather's, my grandfather announced that he "walked once more as a man among men and not as a stranger among strangers," and regretted his departure. I did not see him again until I went to Rome in the year of the Pastoreaux, where I had heard that he now made his home, and sought him out. The year in which he left our home, Castile eclipsed Zion for me as a place where Jews lived as they lived nowhere else, where they carried swords and wore jewels and where kings beckoned to them.

My father left us that year for a brief while, for our great leader and light, Rabbi Meir ben Baruch of Worms, had been imprisoned as he planned to leave for Palestine, and was kept as hostage for the Jews who had left the city, as it was charged that the taxes from them were now lost. He was imprisoned in the fortress Enisheim near Colmar. My father and my uncle went abroad to raise money to redeem him, and went with the others where they could to redeem him, but Rabbi ben Baruch refused to come out, fearing to set a pattern for extortion from our communities. Great sums were raised, but as he forbade payment to be given for him he lingered in prison for eight years where he died, whence we later paid for his body to bury it.

When my father returned home, he hastened to betroth me, seeing I was now fifteen. But troubles ensued in that year. The prophet of Avila came out and declared himself to be the Messiah and went to Rome to undertake the conversion of the Pope, causing much dissension and anger, as did the Dominican friar, Robert de Redingge, who converted to Judaism. He underwent circumcision and took the name of Haggai and married a Jewess, for which reason riots broke out in Exeter, in Lincoln and in Norwich. My uncle's house was broken into. The thieves contrived to enter through a window on the top floor, broke his box and made off with the debtors' notes. My uncle could not protest, for he did not wish it known that he continued to lend on interest. His daughters, of which he had four, having now no dowries, my grandfather and my father pledged for two of them. A year later, my uncle received back the capital from one borrower and a note which said that that was all that he was required to do by the law, and seeing that the king profited more than all, and seeing that his children were now penniless, he would not have him think all Christians poor debtors, and wished to set his soul straight and be quits with the Jew. It lifted my uncle's spirits, but no more was returned and nothing more to be done, for which cause he fell into greater trouble, and was later hanged.

At this time we travelled to Lincoln for the wedding of my father's niece, that Judith, daughter of Belaset of Duelcresse, of whom you now know. This wedding was grander than my father's wedding to which many notables in the realm came, and two illustrious knights and a great table set for the poor, so that I heard it said there were no less than five hundred guests, and my father brought my mother fine clothes for it. She carried a fan of ostrich feathers and had a bodice of pearls. The house stirred with preparation for the trip. There now were I and my brother, Mose, my brother Elie, Clemence, my mother, my grandfather, my great grandmother, my father, my aunt and my uncle. We gave Mellisent to a neighbor to care for while we were gone, and with boxes and gifts went across the frozen roads. It was my first journey from the city. Beyond the cemetery and the fields and the woods, Mose and I had not been. We sat quiet as we were bid, but alert. Elie cried most of the way and was passed from hand to hand. In Lincoln the other wedding guests stayed at the inn, but we stayed in the house of our kinswoman, Belaset Duelcresse, in High Street, which as I have told you was grander than ours in London, all in stone, with a corbelled chimney over the doorway, decorated, I have heard it said, after Bishop Alexander's work in Lincoln Cathedral, for which pride she paid dearly. The windows had a shaft between them, and gave out two lights. The wedding feast lasted seven days, and never did the food or the music stop, for her Gentile neighbors played on the Sabbath when the Jewish musicians would not, and as Judith was her only child and she was widowed and a woman of great skill in business, said to be able to cast sums and to read Latin as well as Hebrew, who had done business with knights and bishops, she stinted nothing for her daughter's wedding, not in wine or food or song so that even my great grandmother, with flesh and age, danced withal. As the proverb says, the woman of sixty runs to the sound of music as a girl of six.

Descendants, keep all your occasions for rejoicing, keep the festivals of life with joy, be not niggardly with your pleasures, for they are your guarantors against pain. The Lord God has given you these festivals for rejoicing. Remember them, for they will keep your souls sweet with memory in your time of travail. As spices are to a meal, so are festivals to the soul.

So we sang to the groom and fetched him at dawn on Friday to go to the synagogue where we greeted him with light from our torches and with music from our instruments, and then fetched his bride to meet him in the courtyard and when she entered, the congregation cast wheat to them and sang their blessings, the bride led back to her house to await her groom who went with us inside the synagogue, attired in his tallith, and we blessed him with psalm and with hymn and brought him back to his bride, and I gave them honey and milk and a white egg, and everything that was done, and the words that I was bid to bless them with, Be fruitful and multiply, because I was young, seemed done for my sake and burdened with mystery, and I looked upon everything that happened, the breaking of the glass, the wearing of special shoes, the canopy over the bridal pair, as immemorial gestures from the deep well of our being, not knowing then that custom is as mortal as the flesh, and that we may grieve for its passing as for the passing of a friend.'

"Aye, Will, so we mourn when we be taken from that home upon which our eyes first set. In truth his heart was heavy with memory for I know myself that never is that grass so green as that which grew beneath our feet when we were young. But as he saw this Belaset no more, and as he had seen her the once, what more could he say of her? And before he could say the little that he knew, his wife called Gertrude, asks me how does the world in Exeter, for she hailed from there a long time ago. I tell her I have never been to Exeter, have never been but in York until I came to go out of England.

Aye, says her husband, it is of York I wish now to tell you and of your ancestor there. And he tells me again of this Belaset to which he bids me hearken, for she was a great usurer or usuress and cast her sums so well she cast up great wealth for herself which was sent by and by to be kept in the king's chest in York. For as you have heard, Will, when the Jews were in the land the king ordered their treasure chests to be kept in each city where the Jews lived nor could the Jews live but where their chests were kept, so that the king had the record of their doings and could know whereof to lay the tax on them, and the treasure chests were kept by the king's lock and key, so no ruffian could come by it. As the Jews were the servants of the treasury in the realms of Christendom, the kings kept their treasure where they could mind it, for by his law he was the inheritor of the usurer's wealth when the usurer died. So the king laid his claim to this Belaset when, lo! the treasure was absconded with and disappeared from the king's realm. A like treasure appeared in York and the baron there laid claim to it. He said it was from that time of Aaron of York of which you have heard. All this while Belaset's treasure moved about from Lincoln to York to Fountainville Abbey and many there were who laid claim to it, the king and the baron and the bishops and the abbots, for the bishops said that inasmuch as the church disliked usury, and inasmuch as the Jew was in servitude to the church, the church had the right to the Jew's treasure, and the king said that inasmuch as he made the

laws of the realm and inasmuch as the Jew was the
servant of his treasury and the law declared that the
usurer's profit went to the crown, he had the right to the
Jew's treasure and often times, as you know, the king and
the barons went to war with each other for the Jew's
treasure as when they burned the Jews in York and the
barons broke open their box and King Richard was so
wrathful he put in down for a law that henceforth he
would keep the box himself.

And what shall I tell you, Will, that as he went on
with this tale, I saw where it would take me, for this
Belaset was charged with the clipping of the coin, which
scandal you have heard about, and she was hanged by the
neck on the scaffold for this with two hundred and
ninety-nine others, Jews and Christians. And this Judith,
as you shall hear, lived this while in York with her
husband's kin and when the news was brought her that her
mother was hanged by the neck for the clipping of the
king's coin, she sickened and could not be delivered of a
child until such time as the Expulsion came, when she
was brought down in labor and this time delivered withal,
but she died in the doing of it. Her husband was taken
as a prisoner and went from the island in the Great
Expulsion and the child was brought to Fountainville
Abbey, but what became of the treasure I know not.

My heart began to knock within, for so long I sought
my own, that I could not be but bitter to know that my
own was hung as a common criminal, withal two
illustrious knights and a bishop had come to her
daughter's wedding. And I would I had not found my
own. Nor was this all the misfortune, for it seems the
uncle too was hanged in that year for the clipping of the
coin and his grandmother died from the grief of it and is
buried in the Jew's cemetery in London. Misfortune fell
fast upon these Jews for their misdeeds for all in the
realm were put in prison as a punishment for what this
Belaset and the others did, and his own mother was put
in prison and was delivered of her fourth child there, and
this Menaheim and his betrothed and his father and his
grandfather and that servant, Clemence who said she

would go where they go for she would not be parted from her mistress, were all put into prison.

Master Menaheim could see by my face that I was not pleased with my past now that I had it. In truth, I cried out, 'What! Have I searched this long while to find that my great grandmother was hanged by the neck for crimes against the king, for usury and counterfeiting of the coin!'

His wife, who lay snoring on the sand this while, roused herself at my outcry and said, 'Have you no better word?'

I looked at my star on the sand. 'Nay,' I said, 'I have not. My soul is pinched with this past,' and I began to cry.

His wife who had little patience with her husband's tale had no patience at all with my sorrow. 'We be your kin,' she said. 'Kin come as kin come. I be of Exeter English and speak the English tongue as you do.'

I looked fully at her now to see how I would like her, seeing she was my nearest kin. In truth, she was nothing much to look at, ruddy in complexion, as her husband said she was of Exeter, with a wen upon her face, by the nose with a tuft of hair upon it, and stocky in the hips. I wondered if they all be so ruddy in that part of England, or only the Jews be that way.

And further more and moreover, rousing herself more and more, she dismissed her husband's tale and said she would tell her own, for while she could not read nor write, her tongue failed her not and telling him to hold his, she told me the sad tale of how her husband came to fetch her as a bride and she came to London with her dowry and her kin when the order went out that all the Jews in the island be put in prison again, and so she went with her wedding party and knew not her husband until the king prevailed upon the Jews to pay him 20,000 silver marks for their release. 'Aha!' she cried out and spat upon the sand.

'What!' I said, 'spent you your wedding nights in prison?'

'Aye. And that was a wicked thing to do to a young

maid. I know not if it be not more wicked to put a young maid freshly married in prison than to put an old one in a winekeg. Fair I was then, fifteen and waiting to be plucked, as fair then as am I now fermented.'

Such misfortune I did commiserate with. 'I trust you found him in the hale afterwards,' I said.

'Six children I have birthed. Each one fell ripe from me as an apple, but one was plucked by the monks of the Rhine.' And here she began to weep, so fresh the memory of it was upon her mind though it seems that it happened a score of years ago or more. Her husband went to head her off from her lament, but she would not be headed off and her ruddy face got ruddier and her sorrow bubbled forth. 'My sweet, my sweet,' she wept, 'I cannot find you anymore, for there is not even a grave to mark the place where I may come and pray for you. Our father Abraham when he pledged his son to God, God courteously returned him Isaac, but the Christian returns me not my son,' and down she laid herself upon the beach and began to wail and we began to plead with her to come to, come to. 'What boots the tears?' I said.

'It boots not,' she said, but gave not up her bubbling.

'Then give over,' I said and gave her my skirt to blow her nose in.

The waves began to dance upon the shore and she sat up again to settle her misery. 'Aye,' she said, "I know not what boots it in this world anymore, for sometimes I would I were back in England, in my mother's lap among the hills and the cows and the river I knew in my girlhood. Give over, I say to myself, you are now a grandmother. What boots it to long for the hills of your youth and the cows that be no more. I know not where it has gone, but I would I be again with my babes about me and I would I be with them in the hills of Exeter where my mother could lay her eyes upon them and say a word to them. I would I were away to the place where I was born.'

'Give over,' I said again to her, 'and I shall listen to you and Master Menaheim can rest his tongue.'

'Nay,' she said, 'he has written it down in his book and

though I cannot read it I would that it stood for us twain, for he is a learned man and I have nought but the tongue in my head. His will is for our children both.'

Such was her strange way that with one hand she put him forth and with the other took him back. She said he was a learned man and she had no learning at all, but she corrected everthing he said and would have it no way but her own. She urged him to continue, but ever he opened his mouth she had something to say. But continue he did as a man must do the best he can even in a storm of winds, and he began again.

'We soon left England, my grandfather first. For Clemence sickened with a cough and soon after died and my grandfather returned to Provence to bury her there. What more shall I say? More than any people I have known, she was a stranger in this earth, for there was not even a cemetery to bury her in. For which reason my grandfather returned with her though he gave it out as the reason that he would stay no more in England, that the English king was as bad as the French one and knew no government for the Jews but tax and tallage and ransom, and he could no longer eat food that was always moist and where the salt would not flow. He prepared her coffin from the wood of his lectern, and we went to the wharf to see them put upon the barge.

We left England ourselves in the following year, but saw my grandfather no more, learning that he was buried in Carcassonne, for his will was delivered to us in which he conjoined upon us these promises: Be not dreaded in thy own house, for this is the cause of many evils; honor your wives, withhold not honor from them, but do not permit them to rule over you. Sleep not with the light of the moon on your face, especially if the moon is new. Give of all thy food a portion to God. Let God's portion be the best, and give it to the poor. Keep faith with everyone, Jew and Gentile. Utter nothing but the truth to mankind. Sleep not overmuch, but rise with the birds. If they can, you can. Take care of your books; guard them against mice and dampness. The women of our family are used to the ways of scholars; therefore help them to prosecute their studies that they may speak with their husbands. They have no luxurious tastes and will not waste themselves with extravagant expenditures. Marry a woman who is beautiful in body, and you will want for nothing more. Be constant to her and train her character, and if she is beautiful many blessings will flow. Keep from scholiasts to whom philosophy is the handmaid of scoffing. How can I know God and that He is One unless I know what knowing means and what constitutes unity? Why should these things be left to non-Jewish philosophers? Why should Aristotle retain sole possession of treasures he stole from Solomon? No one really knows the true meaning of loving God and fearing Him unless he is acquainted with natural science and metaphysics. Why should I be ashamed of pursuing this knowledge? Can one man be skilled in everything, even a Jew in the Law? Once I had guests to dinner and the maid accidentally put a butter spoon into the meat dish. Not knowing how to correct the matter, I hastened from the table to consult a wiser rabbi. He told me the law and I returned home where my guests greeted me with commendation for my zeal. But is not the faculty of expounding the knowledge and the unity of God of as great weight as familiarity with the law concerning a butter spoon? I say nothing against those who devote themselves solely to halachic matters, but I would say that they also give ear to my plea, and I will pray for their reward in the World to Come. But if my descendants should acquire a love for philosophy, I caution them not to commence metaphysical studies until the age of twenty, and to continue in all things to read the Torah. Cast my vote thus if it should come to it among the scholars of Lunel. Remember to carry my voice there and to cast my vote without rancour.

For which reasons my father instructed us to bury him next to my grandfather's grave, and for the reason that we could not return to bury him in the Wood Street cemetery where my mother sleeps with her daughter. For this reason, too, I pray you, my descendants, raise the money to petition the king, bring him a goodly gift with your request, and return to remember the graves of your ancestors that they not be cut off from the house of Israel.

For our house escheated to the king, our synagogue to the Friars. We made our way to the wharf with our belongings, our kin and neighbors, my brothers Elie, Jehude, Mose now seventeen, for whom we had a wife chosen in Cologne. He would be settled in her father's house, who was a silversmith and so would be one too. The musician, Leo Cresse, Rosia Truyte the widow, Manser Aaron and his wife, Flora; our shoijet, Anter vid Vines, his wife and children, Gamaliel Oxon, the stone-cutter, Jorven Sackerel, Elie le Evesk the baker, Muriel Cresse, Aaron Slemne in St. Olave Jewry; Abraham Matron the goldsmith, Sarra Diei, tradeswoman; Benedict Mayer, tanner, his wife and son, Samson afterwards settled in Troyes; Jacobus Bonamie permitted by the king to settle in Paris; Elie Braggard, Bateman Cresse from Lade Street, Benedict Muriel the carpenter from Milke Street; Sarra Oxon, cloth merchant, Solomon the muleseller, Isaac Muriel the basketweaver, and Eliezer ben Muriel the sheepherder; kinsmen from Norwich and elsewhere, all who walked in procession at my mother's wedding, and their descendants.

Much talk and rue and glances from the sailors, sympathy in some and greed in others. Gertrude weeping that her mother stayed behind whether for good or ill, we could not know, for many among us believed we would return, but others spoke otherwise, and the elderly who remembered petitioning Henry to let us leave when we could no longer raise the tax, spoke bitterly: 'When we would, he would not and when we would not, he would.'

Aye, aye, aye, and aye.

So the talk went. Much rue and regrets that such and such should have been done, or such and such should not have been done, but the event being unprecedented in its scale, our talk brought us little comfort and no enlightenment. Gamaliel put it down for a memorial on my mother's tombstone: Departed, the Jews of England: 4,650.

The crowds were kept away by the king's army, which he commanded and watched from a distance. My father, as Edward's delegate, was kept in the Tower until we were all answered for. Many had departed from Hull and elsewhere and were gone by now. I stood with Gertrude, Mose, Elie and Jehude together, until my father was permitted to join us on the wharf. In the distance, Edward sat upon his horse, surrounded by his noblemen. He ventured to say goodbye, for some services my father had done him.

'Know I bear you no grudge, for you have served the realm faithfully in a faithless task, but as I can no longer protect you, I send you out for the peace of the realm, for the people will not have it otherwise. The means of your service is foul corruption and breeds corruption, and for this we cannot thank you. Nor for this alone do we banish you, but that your religion too is false to Christendom, and is a worm that eats up our roots. It is therefore in the interest of this realm to put your bodies outside our kingdom. Your souls we must leave to God.'

We stood, Gertrude and I, my brothers, kinsmen and friends, surrounded by the lords of this English realm. I write words now that harried me silently that day: 'Kings of Christendom, Lords, Masters and Prelates, for you are the masters of the earth today and we are the servants of your treasury. But not one of us here is confused by this earthly arrangement. We know who our true Master is.'

My father said only to Edward: 'May you stand at the gate to the world's treasure-house. May I hear only well of you, that you thrive. As England has been our home these many centuries, we will pray for her safety and yours.'

Mastering his grief for this and our mother's death, he

turned and gave us his blessing. 'The God of Abraham and Isaac and Jacob will be with you and keep you. Think nothing of this journey. He will surely follow you and be with you.'

So we crossed the channel and came to Calais. It being a short while to Rosh Hashanah, we stayed for the Holy Days, and as the Jews here have the custom to cast their sins into the water on the holiday, we stood with them on the shore and said with them the words from the prophet, Micah. Some of our women wept to watch the waves roll backwards to England, but my father bid them turn to their new homes and give thanks that we found Jews on this shore to receive us with honey and with apples.

Soon after, we went our separate ways. As we could not stay in Philip's realms, we went north and south, but for Bonami whom Philip sent word to that he was to settle in Paris as he had use of him there. Rosa Truyte and Abraham Matron to Rome, where we had afterwards good news of them, and I betrothed my son Ephraim to his daughter. Moscus Crispin and his family to Galicia, Isaac Muriel and his kin to Sicily, Leo Cresse and his kin to Bexier whence they Sanctified the Name in the year of the Pastoreaux, Elisha the Carter and Mosse Bonavil to Troyes withal the king said no; also Benedict Mayer and his son Samson to Blois where he too met with others who stayed secretly. Jorvin Sackerel to Venice, and Gamaliel and his kin to Troyes, and afterwards to Rome. The rest north with us to Worms and Strassbourg, our shoijet with us to Andernach, some to Regensbourg, others to Cologne.

My father, Gertrude and I to Andernach, for we heard that Archbishop Siegfried there had much sympathy for Jews and upheld their rights. May the Eternal grant him the reward of the just, for his fame was founded on truth. While he lived, we had his protection. In all matters affecting our well being he consulted us, and when our lives were threatened he brought us into his fortress for protection, nor would allow a Jew who had committed a misdemeanor be tried only by Christians.

Because he sought justice we found mercy, and while he lived we were safe and pursued judgment in our own courts and had our school and synagogue and mikveh for our women, a cemetery, a bakehouse and a dance hall for merriment. My second son, Ephraim, was born here; my first, Isaac, was born upon the sea, and we lived again in a stone house and had a garden and a goat for its milk and a hen for her eggs and for the sake of the Law; three daughters, Josette, Margit and, Henne, and two more sons, Ephraim and Jeshua, our youngest. Mose and his wife stayed in Cologne where he worked and traded in silver and his wife bore him Leo and Ali, Bikette, Ester and Jurette. Our only dismay during this time was that his wife's father, with thirteen other Jews, were pawned to the Margrave in return for debts which the king had incurred. I was confirmed by this to stay in Andernach and not move to Cologne, albeit one could practise medicine there more prosperously. I pursued my studies in Talmud, and clandestinely in philosophy, for my father lived with us. For the sake of peace in the household, I pursued these studies in silence, for I am by nature not an argumentative man.

'What!' Gertrude said. But Master Menaheim paid her no mind and went his way and I could see in truth he was not an argumentative man.

'My father grieved for my mother's death. He sent word many times to Edward, asking permission to return for a short while 'for reasons of memory.' But Edward first responded that he could not answer for my father's life and he should allow more time to pass; and then that the time was not propitious; and then 'that it was neither suitable nor seemly,' and so on. My father kept my mother's ring on his lectern and continued to wait for a favorable response.

Other affairs called him out. The clouds of discord were gathering in the communities of Provence, and many now pressed for a ban on the study of philosophy though each community governed itself and was responsible for the education of its own, and no one wished to trespass on these rights. But Jewish learning had decayed so far that many who wished to uphold the independence of our communities, also wished to lay down a uniform code of guidance. I and my father went to the Synods. We disagreed with each other here and there and there and there, but not there and here and, at last, when it came to the issue of the ban, we separated.

Rabbis and students came to our house to consult him on this and on matters closer to home. Archbishop Siegfried was a frequent visitor too, for great souls find one another. When the persecutions of Rindfleisch drove the Jews from the east into our valley, and there was fear for our own lives because of their swelling numbers, he took counsel with my father, and his word among his own people did much to calm them so that when the tide looked to break upon us as well, he turned it aside where it lost itself amid other doings.

For this reason, my descendants, you shall keep his name for a memorial in the Book of Life, for it is written that the Righteous of all the nations shall enter into the Kingdom of Heaven.

Our problems were more often of smaller moment. Here was a husband who wished to divorce his wife because hair grew upon her bosom, and though hair had grown upon her bosom when he first married her and though he had had six children by her, he could abide it no more. Here was a woman who came to our court and complained that her husband had deserted her for six years, in which time she had made a good business for herself in trading and lending money on interest, and now he claimed his place back as her husband. Here was a tanner who was brought to our court by two wives, both of whom claimed him, a small man with no prepossessing qualities, no learning, no bearing, not even height, yet both women claimed him with ardor. Here was a woman who set herself up to live apart from her husband, and when he brought her to court, could give no reason. As she remained silent under all questioning we were perplexed as to what to do. This trial continued for many months and her case became notorious. Her husband ranted and cursed, but the wife would say neither yea nor nay. My father wrote to others for an opinion. Rabbi Holtzner declared her intractable and advised that she forfeit all claims in the settlement. Rabbi Perez and Rabbi Hushiel came to Andernach to give their judgment. Rabbi Perez said that perhaps for reasons of delicacy and honor she not say what her reason was and that she should not be punished for her silence. Rabbi Hushiel said if she would not say yea or nay she must forfeit her right to the Ketubah, at least. Rabbi Perez contended that one must not confuse delicacy for intractability, or be punished for wishing to preserve the honor of the Name. 'Perhaps the husband beat her and she will not say for the sake of the Honor of God.'

'What's that!' Rabbi Hushiel said.

'What!' Gertrude said, and sat bolt upright.

'What's that?' Rabbi Hushiel said. 'That is a thing not done among our people and Rabbi Perez should not raise the suspicion of it.'

'I only wish to suggest that the woman's silence may be to her honor. Perhaps we should not coerce her to tell us.'

'But where there is silence, how can there be a decision?'

My father heard them out and then gave his judgment, which became known as the Law of the Intractable Wife, and which became a judgment for all time among our people. 'Silence for some issues may be deemed a more honorable defense than babble. Where a wife no longer can speak of her husband it may be from a surfeit of causes rather than from the absence of any. If the husband has developed such habits or infirmities which make her life intolerable, he is obliged to divorce her. They can neither deny their original relationship nor deny their present need to separate, but must affirm both and go their separate ways as distant relatives. The wife forfeits her right to the Ketubah but receives back intact the property she came with.'

'How like you this ruling?' Gertrude said to me.

'I knew not the Jews had such a ruling,' I said, which I tell it to you, Will, that you will lay upon your heart all that Master Menaheim said in the following.

'Where such cases involved our own we went our way, while Archbishop Siegfried lived and guarded our interests. When attacks were made upon our synagogues or our lives, he pursued our molesters, and in times of riot brought us into his fortress for protection. In the sixth year after we arrived, a Jew who lent money on interest was attacked and killed by his Christian debtor. Archbishop Siegfried had the man captured and tried by a jury of Christians and Jews. Though he condemned the Jew for his usury he pointed out that murder was not a remedy for it and he who would borrow knowingly from a usurer was no less guilty than he who lent knowingly, that Christians could not be quit of their debts to Jews by murdering them. For this reason, we had much cause for sorrow when he died. Afterwards, his successor transferred us to the Archbishop of Cologne who pawned our income to Constantine von Lysolfskirchen.

Even though we went our way but according to the laws lived in the towns, there were many cases of injury and assault and battery between Jew and Christian. Here a man claimed that a Jew's cart had overturned in the street and killed his pig and he claimed damage for the pig; and the Jew claimed that a stone from the man's well lay in the path of his cart and he claimed damage for the cart. Here a Christian claimed that a Jew had made the harness for his horse and that the harness was not made properly and that he fell from the horse and broke his leg and he claimed damage for his leg and the harness; and here a Jew claimed that he had hired a mason to build his house and the chimney had fallen in and the house had caught on fire. While Archbishop Siegfried lived, he consulted us on all such issues and required a Jewish witness in cases involving a Jewish defendant.

At this time, there were two cases that acquired such fame that bishops and clergymen and rabbis from the Rhine valley gathered to hear them, and the citizens of Andernach were pleased by the prosperity this brought them. One was the case of the Jewess, Matilda, who objected to her husband's occupation as an innkeeper, for she said it made a servant of her and she had nought but cooking and cleaning to do and she wished to go about the town like her neighbors. She made her complaint known to her Christian neighbor, whose house she would frequently visit and in whose company she was wont to go about in town. In time she left her husband, and her Christian neighbor took her in, but the neighbor asked a priest what to do for she knew not how to feed her. This priest, Egbert, zealous for his faith, took the Jewess to Cologne and put her in the Domus Conversos. The husband made complaint to my father that his wife had been abducted. My father learned of her whereabouts and went to Cologne to examine her, and brought back the news that the wife had left her husband's house willingly. The Christian neighbor swore that this was so, that the woman had come to her house at twilight, of her own will, but that she herself had sought the priest for she did not know how to feed her, and did not wish to offend. The priest was examined and said that he had explained all in plain terms to the Jewess, who had agreed to go with him to Cologne and undergo conversion. As she was a simple woman, his terms, though plain, were not plain enough for her. In time, she repented of her decision and as she was instructed in Latin by the nuns who cared for her, which language she could not understand, she tired and asked to be returned to her husband. As he was a Cohen by descent, he was loath to take her back, for though she swore that nought but grass and salt had passed her lips, he suspected her purity and, moreover, her chastity, for the reputation of the neighbor was known to all. She was examined by three rabbis for her chastity, and by the Archbishop and the bishop as to whether she was now a Christian. The nuns swore that as she had not yet been baptized, they served her from separate plates and neither mixed their linen nor their wine with hers. Archbishop Siegfried deferred the matter to my father. After a time, my father agreed that he was satisfied with respect to her chastity, but the priest Egbert was not satisfied on any account and caused us much trouble, for he gave out that the woman had become a Christian and that we had abducted her back, for which reason some Christians burned down her husband's inn and he, no longer being an innkeeper, his wife no longer had this complaint against him.

While Archbishop Siegfried lived, our people began to go about in fine clothes again and took to playing cards among themselves and even with their Christian neighbors. They raged for adornment, particularly the women, so that we took alarm for the harm it might cause us. Heretofore, because of the decree that all Jewish men above the age of twelve should dress in black but that our Jewish women, because of their weakness, could dress in colors, there was now a saying abroad that our Jewish men were akin to the coalburner's mule but our women to the Pope's horse. They even put off wearing the badge, for the priests in Andernach looked the other way. We passed decrees that our women must yield their jewels and their silks, but many more would not than would, my wife among them. And others who had come to our valley from Spain, said they would return to Spain where they could wear all the jewelry they wished to.

We issued stricter laws regarding the dress of our women, but so much they came under the influence of Italy and Spain where even the Christian women go about bejewelled as birds, as I saw on my journey there, wearing silks and sashes and gold chains and strings of pearls and headgear as I cannot say how they sit upon their heads, that it was no use. So much our women loved these new fashions, that they defied us openly and caused us much harm. My wife flung off her judicious clothes and went abroad with her neighbors in jewels and pearls and even to synagogue dressed ever more in stranger attire so that we knew them not from one year to the next. And worse on Purim, when the young men also threw away caution and took off their black clothes and went about in masks and even carried swords and daggers.

Rabbi Perez and Rabbi Hushiel made their views known to my father, and my father made them known to Archbishop Siegfried that he must take measures to restrain our women, for they no longer would be restrained by us, and on holidays filled the streets with their headgear and bejewelled clothes, causing many to gape at them.'

Master Menaheim was interrupted by his wife, for she would not give over that it was a sinful thing to go dressed in finery. 'I do not like green and it was all the law would allow.'

In truth, it did not suit her, for she was green in color, but whether it was from mold or nature I could not say.

'What shall I say?' Master Menaheim said, 'the time of Archbishop Siegfried was coming to an end, when we would be transferred to the imperial fief, but we knew it not and reckoned it not. Our women went abroad in any manner they wished and my father sat in judgment, and they ignored his judgment.

Came that year a clamor from our people that there was no meat to be had and none could say why. An investigation was made, and our shoijet was brought before the court, whereupon he threw himself on our mercy and asked permission to leave his work. He complained that of late his heart troubled him when he slaughtered the animals. He told the court how one afternoon when he had gone to the barn to take out a calf for slaughtering this calf's mother had let out a terrible moo. So terrible it was he heard the voice of Rachmana holding back his arm even as it had held back the arm of Abraham from slaughtering Isaac. At first, the shoijet said, he ignored the Voice and led the calf away, though its mother continued to moo so that he heard it now in his sleep all the time and could not sleep anymore. When he brought the calf into the slaughtering house she lay her head in his lap and began to cry. His arm became paralyzed. He could not do his work anymore, and begged to be retired.

There was an uproar in the court when my father

commanded him to go back. Rabbi Perez said it was unjust to demand that a man do the work of slaughtering when he would not. Rabbi Hushiel said it was work which only one of strong heart must do, and as this shoijet was no longer fit, he should be retired. My father said, 'No, he and he alone is fit, for his heart is filled with mercy and dread.' He reminded the court of Rabbi Gaon's judgment, that the animal was not created by God in order that evil should be inflicted upon it, but for the sake of good. Animals that do harm, snakes and scorpions and such, may be killed. Living creatures that do not harm us and that are not needed for food should not be killed but allowed to go their way. If suffering comes upon the shoijet for his deeds this is the chastisement of love that God sends upon His chosen. For this reason the shoijet must go back: to find the path between necessity and mercy, for another may not search for it.'

Thus, my youthful deed was judged and I was found guilty. Praised be he who judged me. May he be received with honor upon the Mountain of the Lord.

We lived in peace with our Gentile neighbors, but my father's health began to fail, being now in his seventieth year. Still, he prepared himself to journey to Montpellier, to make his voice heard in the debate. Rabbi Asher had asked for a convocation to consider means of reconciling our divisions. No one wished to see again the time when Rabbi Jonah Gerundi denounced Maimonides to the Inquisition in Montpellier, who afterwards repented of having been an informer and died with the name of the sage on his lips. Now Abba Mari pressed for a ban against the teaching of philosophy, and Rabbi ibn Adret of Barcelona, who had taken up the cause so reluctantly, fearing to impose his rule on another community, was now being censured for having done this. But Jew, Christian and Moslem alike feared this new learning. Pristine though it was at its source, in half a century it had assumed such diverse shapes that rabbis were heard to preach sermons from the pulpit how the five sons of Leah prefigured the five senses, that

Manasseh and Ephraim were to be understood as the principles of practice and theory, and that the twelve tribes were the twelve constellations, astrology having spread so far. The land was covered with prancing preachers who went about with these ideas, giving them out with a pleased air as if they alone had just received enlightenment. The Council of Vienne interdicted the writings of the Arab philosopher, Averroes and the Church even questioned Aquinas and all who spun their web from Averroes' teachings.

Cursed is the teacher who spawns such poor disciples as the niggards who appeared on the earth in three generations since Maimonides died, and under the guise of his banner unleashed their buried hatred for the teachings of Moses and went about with twinkling eyes and brazen clothes, new cut beards and whippish tongues, and mouthed these mouthings in our yeshivas.

One such had the misfortune to be a guest at our home. Learned, very learned he was, for he told us so. The Garden of Eden was another name for science and philosophy, which he preached was the true Paradise of Man, for as Aristotle said that mankind wishes to know it cannot be but that Paradise is the fulfillment of this craving. Eve was not forbidden to eat of the apple, but forbidden to overindulge!

'Aye,' said Gertrude to my father, 'I have ever forborne with her disobedience, for I took it to be a sign of intelligence and needed not the philosopher to tell me.'

My father waved her down, but showed no other sign of impatience. Indeed, he appeared to have fallen into a trance from which he emerged slowly.

'In that case,' he said, 'we must know how big a bite Eve took.' He motioned to me. 'Bring me the Bible there and let us see if the size is given, for my memory fails me. We must know if she bit to the core and swallowed the pips. 'I do hope so,' Gertrude said. 'Or whether she spit them out one by one or altogether,' my father said. 'We must know if when she gave Adam to eat he took the same size bite.'

'Not likely,' Gertrude said.

'His teaching is worse than the Gentiles for the Jews,' my father hissed after our guest left, 'for they at least believe that God created the world and that the righteous shall inherit His kingdom. But these who preach that God is a first cause cannot preach love, for what love can there be in a first cause?'

He rose from his sickbed and asked permission to journey to Montpellier. Earlier, he had said nothing against Maimonides, but now his words made me anxious. 'There is no help but to tear out the disease by its roots,' and 'Greek philosophy is a jar of honey with a dragon wrapped around it.'

We embarked from Andernach in the month of Nisan. He was tired and anxious and spent the journey walking back and forth between his seat and the ship's rail. 'How shall we hold it all together?' he asked.

On board were traders and merchants, two from Essen who were members of the Hanseatic League, lately come from London where they kept a warehouse in the Steelyard. We conversed, but forebore personal inquiries. London, they said, 'was now over-run with Lombards, Cahorsins, and Florentines and a plague of usury had descended upon the people there.'

'The king will be crushed by their interest rates alone,' one said.

'Or will crush his people,' the other said, 'for he raises such a tax on the wool that grumbling is heard everywhere.'

'Where are you from?' the other asked.

'Andernach,' I replied.

'Aye,' one said readily, 'the city is the only place for free men. The only abundant crop that can grow on land is taxes.'

We came to Koblenz where the Rhine crosses the Moselle. Everyone but the traders went to the rail to look at the landscape. 'Shtadlach machen frei,' they laughed after us. We gazed at the castles on the banks. I reflect now, from my present vantage point beneath the river, on a difference in motion. The view beneath the river is wholly strange to me, but above it took us many days to pass between Koblenz and Bingen, for we must stop and pay a toll at almost every castle. Now, I travel otherwise, according to another law.

At Wiesbaden and Speyer came on board Rabbi Hushiel and Rabbi Perez, whom we expected. They were already filled with arguments for Montpellier, and we had no more pleasure in the trip.

'There must be not only a ban,' Rabbi Hushiel said, 'but reform, for the Sepharad live as the Moors do. They no longer speak or read Hebrew, and they take more than one wife. They only do not make graven images or eat pork, for the Moslems do not let them.'

'And those who live among the Christians,' Rabbi Perez said, 'obey our laws in this respect but in no other, except that they do not eat pork. But I will say nothing about the wine that they drink.'

My father put his elbow on the ship's rail and rested his head in the palm of his hand. I thought he was tired, but he said, 'Come, let us say a berakhot for this valley.'

Came aboard at Karlsruhe two of those preachers who sit in the forests as the Franciscans do and praise poverty, but these lay tfillin and wear their prayer shawls and preach, 'In the kingdom of God there are no taxes.' They saw by our clothes that we were co-religionists and approached to preach to us or to quarrel.

'Away,' Rabbi Hushiel said, but one cannot drive them away once they have made up their minds to preach to you.

'Come with us to Palestine,' they said. 'For shame to live among the foreign dominations who suck your souls out with their taxes.'

'These are like the others,' Rabbi Perez said in a low voice, meaning the Franciscans, 'for they too worship poverty and the bees and the rabbits.'

'Nay,' one said angrily, his eyes glaring from under his shawl, 'we worship the Eternal, but practise poverty for His sake.'

'There is no sin in wealth,' my father said. 'It is no offense to God to be prosperous. Job was prosperous, and God restored him to his prosperity after his sufferings.'

'True,' one said, 'but where there is wealth without wisdom there is wickedness. Job prospered, but Job was a righteous man. Prosperity without righteousness is a great evil. With righteousness, it is the union of heaven and earth. In Christendom, none can heal the division between wealth and righteousness, for he who would be wise and just must be poor to be wise and just, and he who has wealth wishes for power and dominion over others. Go, rabbi, be poor and cure Christendom of her wickedness.'

'To be sure,' the other said, 'what is a Jew's prosperity worth in Christendom? Here if he has wealth his life is threatened. Come, what do you say, Rabbi? Can you tell me otherwise? Do you not see what your wealth builds here? Castles and fortresses and walls. You make the kings and the barons and the bishops wealthy. All your wealth of coin and spirit and learning is for the Gentile. And when they have taken everything, they will cancel the debt and drive you out.'

Such dismal talk, I thought then, and tried to cheer myself by looking at the passing landscape. 'We have been in this place a thousand years,' I said. Winds from the valley filled my nostrils. I smelled the vines of my ancestors.

They laughed coarsely.

'Aye, and steadily, steadily, steadily driven from its land so that you can no longer tend the vine. Steadily, steadily, steadily,' they chanted.

'Come, tell me,' one said, 'these castles? Whose money paid for them? And when the priest preaches against you and raises a mob, you must knock on the door of the castle like a beggar and ask for protection, and often enough pay for it again. Who owns the castle, Rabbi, you or the lord? You own nothing but your feet. If a Jew owns land, it is taken from him because the Church cannot tax the land owned by a Jew.'

'Steadily, steadily, steadily," the other one cackled, 'you will have no land to stand upon, but plenty of payments to make.'

'Come, come with us to Palestine. Leave Christendom to the Christians. Come with us to Palestine.'

'Let us keep our taxes for our own,' the other one said, 'for our brides and our poor. In Christendom, we are taxed for the king and the crown, the lords, the bishops, the cardinals and the popes.'

'Come with us and build up the vine again.'

'Come, come with us. In Palestine, 'eretz macht frei. Shtadlach machen nicht frei fer der yid.' 'Come with us, for how can the Jew drink holy wine if he cannot raise his own vines?'

'Come with us. In Palestine, in the Kingdom of God there are no coins with foreign seals.'

'No graven images.'

'No war.'

'No profanity.'

'Only the air and the sky and the spirit of God.'

'Come with us, for there we shall not only be holy, we shall be free, and we shall be holy and free together. Come with us. In the forest, in the vine, in the desert, in the mountain, in Palestine there is nothing to fear.'

Came aboard then at Strassbourg a band of knights and their squires bound for Aigues-Mortes to meet with the Crusaders there. Some were in armor, some were not. But as the noonday sun reached its height and the day grew warm, those in armor grew cross. 'S'done,' one knight said, but his cheerful squire leaped to his side to undo his master's vizier and breastplate, the metal already hot to the touch, and we moved away adroitly as the vermin and the lice came out of their secret feasting places. The squire cleaned and scratched his knight, while the other squires did likewise, and undid their knights' buckles and armors and all scratched remorselessly.

'S'done,' the first knight said again.

'Not so, m'lord,' his squire soothed him. 'We shall be at Aigues-Mortes shortly.'

'Where are you bound for?" one of the traders asked.

'The Holy Land,' the squire said.

The trader clicked his tongue, whether from courtesy or not, I could not say. His friend ventured neither a click of the tongue nor a nod of the head, but one of the preachers said, 'We go there too.'

The knights looked at him. 'Without armor or horse or banner?'

'We have our prayer shawls,' he said.

The knights were amused. 'Les juives,' they laughed. One took his sword out with a flourish and said, 'Do you not know that this can run through your prayer shawl and your heart? You'll never take the Holy Land without a sword.'

Rabbi Hushiel turned away and whispered to us, 'I know not what my sin is that I should live to hear such talk.'

'The door to the bridal chamber is without protection,' Rabbi Perez said. 'Anyone enters at will.'

'What's that?' the cross knight said.

'It is only their manner of speaking,' his squire said to him in a conciliatory voice so that we gazed at him, but he avoided our eyes.

We disembarked at Basel. Rabbi Perez and Rabbi Hushiel went with us to Montpellier. The preachers stayed on board to Kostanze with the knights. 'We go with you,' they said to them, 'right behind your swords,' and us they bid goodbye.

'What do you think?' my father asked me. Before I could answer, Rabbi Hushiel said wrathfully, 'Mockers, scavengers, mumars. They live apart in the forest and pray without a minyan.'

We were soon in the mountains and the air was cold. My father drew his cloak about him and began to lag behind. 'Do not wait for me,' he said, 'I shall never leave this place, for my gravespot is here.'

The words of the aged who know their death is near are remembered too late.

We arrived in Montpellier in the month of Elul. Came also ibn Adret from Barcelona, Abba Mari ben Moses who afterwards collected our words, the poet Jedaiah Bedersi, Rabbi Meiri from Perpignan, Menaheim ben Solomon, the great Talmudist; David Maimoni, the grandson of Maimonides, Bonifas Vidal, Rabbi Solomon de Lunel, Isaac ben Abraham of Avignon, Solomon ben Joseph of Marseilles, Todros ben Kalonymus of Narbonne, rabbis and sages from our academies in Baghdad, Damascus, Spain and Provence. Came we in that month and that year and that place to set our course for the future. While Maimonides lived no word was said against him. Now it was said that he had denied the resurrection of the flesh and had argued only for the immortality of the soul. In the heat of the argument, my father's strength returned.

'As we are so shall be be in the Eternal Kingdom. He Who created life out of nothing is not limited in any manner by His triumphs over nature.'

David Maimoni rose to defend his grandfather, afterwards his defense was written in a book called The Wars of the Lord. 'Come, Rabbi,' he said, 'you say that in The World To Come man will keep his corporeal nature and will retain his Being, for Being to be Being it must be corporeal. But we say also that God is Being, and yet we do not say He is corporeal, for we know that that which is corporeal is finite and limited. But if, in your view, God is not corporeal, then He has no Being. You would not wish to say this, for we know He has Being and is not corporeal. It is in this manner we speak of the soul in The World To Come, that it will be closer to the nature of God and further from the nature of man, for if it retains the nature of man, with all his appetites and senses what use is The World To Come? We cannot take the Bible literally. There are those who say, like Saul ben David, that God sits on a throne but is separated from our world by a curtain. Does God then sit behind a mehitzah like our wives?

'For my part,' Abba Mari said, 'I cannot see the use of The World To Come if man does not keep his corporeal nature. I have heard that in the Moslem heaven they eat delicacies and recline on silk cushions. I cannot see what the point of a soul without a body would be. It may fulfill some law of logic, but I doubt if it is useful or gives pleasure, and if The World To Come has neither pleasure nor delight, I must ask what the use of it is?'

'The use of it!' my father said wrathfully. 'The use of it is nothing more than contemplation! It is a Greek word made out of facts and figures and numbers where you may count to infinity. That is your sole delight in this World To Come.'

David Maimoni jumped to his feet. 'If you believe in the corporeality of the spirit then God too is corporeal, as the Bible says, He reached out His hand, He spoke, and He is Father, as He is called. What then is your quarrel with Christianity? If God can suspend the laws of nature, then He can have a son if He wills so.'

My father was not perturbed, for what arguments had he not heard by this time? For every yes there is a no. He rose to his feet. 'Truly,' he said, 'as the prophet has said, Thy sons, O Zion against thy sons O Greece. God may suspend and contradict the laws of nature, but He does not suspend or contradict His own nature, which is unity,' and with that he sat down with an air of triumph.

'Forebear, forebear, the charge of heresy,' David Maimoni shouted.

'Are you threatening us?' Abba Mari laughed. 'Are we to live in everlasting fear of the Inquisition. They at least know how to deal with their heretics. They put twigs in their hair and set them on fire.'

'Forebear yourself,' my father said, and pulled him down into his seat.

Rabbi ibn Adret rose. I applauded silently, for he was a man of many virtues, tactful and tolerant, though in the end he helped cause the very thing he feared and drove the Ashkenazi and Sephardi apart. 'Rabbis, sages, poets, academicians, Talmudists, Cabbalists, it is a wonder we survive our arguments. Let it not be said that what the world could not do to us, we did to ourselves, that where the sword did not slay us, our tongues did. There can be no proscription against the works of Maimonides. What have we to fear? Pope Nicholas himself defended his writings. Maimonides himself instructed us how to proceed with his learning. He warned against the instruction in philosophy and metaphysics to the young, and we shall follow his advice and his example who himself was learned in the Talmud before he was learned in Aristotle and Averroes.'

'If the study of metaphysics is dangerous,' Abba Mari said, 'an old fool may die of it as well as a young one. I tell you, Aristotle would have made a good Jew had he been present at the crossing of the Red Sea, for when he heard the chariots behind him and saw the mountains of water on either side he himself would have grasped God's Saving Hand. I would I had been beside him to say, What! Are you stretching forth your hand to grasp the Saving Hand! Stretch forth your hand and grasp the first cause and see if it can lift you over the waves.'

'We are not engaged in denials or proscriptions,' Rabbi ibn Adret said, 'but in a search for procedure, not what not to study, but how best to study what we must.'

'Nowhere are secular studies proscribed in Torah or Talmud,' the exilarch of Baghdad said.

'Only those studies which touch on medicine and healing are permitted,' my father said.

'Which must needs be the earth itself,' Bedersi said, 'for what is more in need of healing?'

Rabbi ben Solomon rose and said that for his part he had no quarrel with philosophy or secular studies, it was philosophy and science which quarrelled with him and wished to gainsay his view of matters. 'Saadia ben Joseph of Sura was an eminent rationalist who did much to further the study of science, yet he held that the flesh was resurrected, and before him and after him were others the same. There is no contradiction between science and the Divine Will. But those who say there is no Divine Will do so because they wish to make science pre-eminent. They do not like to believe that God can suspend the laws of nature because they want to believe that the laws of nature are at the will of man and not at the will of God.'

'Unjust!' Rabbi Solomon of Lunel cried out. 'We are not men of vicious temperament. We are searching for truth.'

'Aye, truth!' Rabbi ibn Adret said, 'truth is a roaring lion, but peace is a lamb.'

'Meshiach will come when peace and truth lie down together,' my father said.

'Pray Israel be free of foreign domination at that time and that the prophecies will be fulfilled,' Abba Mari said.

'Why,' my father cried out to David Maimoni, 'why do you believe that God can create the world and can create the soul for everlasting life, but that He cannot resurrect the body for The World To Come. Man wishes to know? What more does he wish to know, if he knows God?'

The poet Bedersi leaped to his feet. 'We have construed an argument here where there is none, for what man does not have need of both faith and reason? What learning can dislodge the faith of the Jew who knows that God alone created the heavens and the earth? Has the psalmist not said, The earth is the Lord's. How then am I separated from God if I study His works? Without reason and science, faith becomes a dream dreaming itself; without study of the earth, without history and knowledge of what we do and what is done theology becomes a casuistical illusion, an argument against others. We stand perilously balanced between faith which can become superstition and knowledge which can become arrogance. Yet some glory we have created here in Provence. We have been here a thousand years, in which time we have cultivated the vine, Torah and science, and reared up academies and sages, and a great philosopher. The heart of this people cannot be turned from the love of science and literature, while their body and soul are kept together. If Joshua himself were to demand it, they would not obey him. For they feel that they wage war in defense of Maimonides, and for holy teaching they will sacrifice their fortunes, their future generations, and their very lives, for as they are God-fearers so are they world lovers. I pray you, Rabbi Adret, you have kept the mountains of Seir and Kedar from falling upon us in Spain, heal our divisions, for is not our fate precarious enough in this world without further aggravation of it from ourselves.'

I would, my descendants, you take this one's voice for a legacy, for shortly the academies here were shut and his tongue was nailed to the door. Provence! What shall I say of you? Thrice you tore out my father's heart, nor would slake your desire for him until we yielded him to your grave.

We went home, weary with argument. Some good accomplished. No ban was passed against Maimonides or astronomy or medicine. The anti-Maimunist wrath was restricted to a ban on astrology and allegory. Came we then to Blois on Rosh Hashanah and greeted our kinsmen from England, Samson now grown so fearsomely he caused us to wonder. Solomon the mule-seller suffered some misfortune, for his wife ran away; Isaac Muriel and his son Eliezer and Benedict Muriel the carpenter, whose wife had borne him eleven children, to his wonderment; and we went together to pray and to usher in the New Year, and afterwards to say Kaddish at the grave of my ancestor Pulchinella who had found favor with the Count Theobald, to our great misfortune, martyred with the proselyte, Justa, and Hannah who gave her seven sons, and sleeps now with these in the Eternal Dust.

Joy and news on our arrival, and grief at our departure. But we could not tarry longer, for my father wished to return by way of the Moselle Valley, which lengthened our journey. Came we then to Troyes and fasted with Gamaliel the stonecutter, Elisha the carter, Elie le Evesk and Mosse Bonavil the locksmith, and said our prayers in the house of Elisha. Afterwards, as we broke our fast, he told us of rumors to be heard that the king would imprison his Jews. 'Gamaliel leaves for Italy, for he says it is a wise rabbit who runs when he hears the hunter's horn. What do you think, Rabbi? What have you heard in your travels?'

Prophet! Poet! It was a year later in the month of Ab our yeshivas and academies were closed down, our synagogues were closed down, our graves were torn out and the sages of Montpellier slept in the dust.

'Have I made the journey for this!' my father exploded. Heard what! What rumor! What pestilence! We have been in this valley a thousand years.'

'As we were in England from the time of William,' Elisha said.

'Do not vex him,' I said to Elisha, and motioned with my eyes that he regard my father's years.

'It is but a rumor,' Elisha said, 'all will go well.'

'Aye,' my father said as we took our leave the next morning, 'I promise you that.' Then we went together, Gamaliel, his wife and children, Elisha and his family, Mosse Bonavil, Elie le Evesk and his eldest son, to the grave of Rashi to say Kaddish. My father gathered us there, Gamaliel and his wife and children, Elisha and his family and the others, and said the prayer: 'The generation in which Rashi lived was neither orphaned nor exiled. We shall redeem our people, generation by generation.'

The women and children stayed by the gate when we departed. Gamaliel and the others accompanied us on the road for a while, until some warmth we felt from the sun. The morning was brisk, a sign of winter in the sky. The leather of my father's boots were stiff and he walked carefully. Loath to part, our friends stayed with us a little more and a little more on the road, until part we must. 'Take care. Be well,' Elisha said.

'I promise you we shall be,' my father said, and embraced him. 'You who greeted us in the dawn, we shall see God in the flesh together. I promise you, Elisha, I shall greet you in the World To Come, and we shall feast together in Eternity.

He left us three laws for a legacy, which I would have you abide: the first concerning the woman of silence, which you remember; the second which brought the shoijet honor but no joy; and the third which caused us calamity.

A case arose soon after we returned, involving a Jew and a Christian girl. As this concerned a woodcutter who had taken up with a nun, it caused us great harm and notoriety, and brought great prosperity to the citizens of Andernach. The woodcutter was a youth by the name of Jacob Sisbert, who was now more than eighteen. Had he been married by this time, as our law prescribes, harm would not have come to us. He lived in the forest with his elderly grandmother, and had no other kin. He delivered wood to the nunnery there, and in the course of things took up with a novice who had just arrived, a maid of fifteen. The infraction was very serious, involving the possibility of death for the novice and the woodcutter. Furthermore, it was against the law for a Jew to live outside the town and none could say how he and his grandmother had come to be in the forest. All he would allow, when examined by our courts and by the civil authorities, was that he had always lived in the forest and had not heard of the law which required Jews to live within the walls of the city. My father, noting the Jew's age, said it was no use attempting to keep people lawful if they were permitted to stay unmarried past the age of eighteen. An inquiry was made as to why he was still unmarried, why his presence was not known by the Jewish community, how had this happened? How had they been left to themselves?

Their Christian neighbors said likewise, that they had always lived there. His father had been killed by a crusader, his mother had died of plague, he had been an orphan almost from birth. His grandmother was old and blind and lived in this hut and as she loved this unsafe patch of ground, cared to go nowhere else. In this way, she had raised him as best she could, tilling a piece of earth and having an apple tree and a goat. The youth owned no tallith and my father forebore asking him if he had been called to the Law. He knew his letters and the Sh'ma. His grandmother knew the Torah by heart and he had had portions of it from her. Her Christian neighbors came to the door of the hut and told us it was no use to speak with her for she was not only blind, but lately deaf as well. They had told the grandson to take her to Andernach where she would be among her own, but she would not go. He could not force her, so he stayed with her because 'somebody must.' The novice said she would convert and marry him and live in the hut in the woods with them. The boy was accused of Judaizing. Riots broke out. My brother's house was set fire to. The Dominican Friar, Rudolf am Main, headed an inquiry in Cologne and the youth was brought before the Inquisition. Archbishop Siegfried contended that Friar Main had no jurisdiction, for there was no case of heresy here. The Dominican friar said he suspected Archbishop Siegfried's loyalties. The scandal of it spread throughout the valley and traders and travellers, visitors, pilgrims and pedlars of every sort came to Andernach.

Seeing no way to resolve the issue, for the novice swore that Jacob had never Judaized to her but that she freely resolved to become a Jewess, to marry him and live in his hut, and our Jewish community pleaded with my father not to convert her. The wealthy burgher, Aaron Heilman, came with a delegation. 'See here, Rabbi, you know as well as I do this is not a case of someone wishing to become a Jew, to worship the Eternal, praised be His name. The woodcutter, Jacob, is a likely looking lad. I would never urge you to shut the gates against a convert, but I tell you frankly that if you do not prevent her conversion, you will cause great harm here. I bear this message from the community.'

Came Archbishop Siegfried with the same message. 'Prevent it. You know as well as I do what the issue is here.'

My father's lips went white and dry. 'All this while they have not been dissuaded from their course to marry by threats and punishment. As I would not have him convert to marry her, I must allow her to convert to marry him. I would he remain a Jew.'

He ailed from this issue and the noise it stirred up. He feared his day was soon to end, and wrote to Edward again for permission to return to the place of his birth, 'for reasons of sentiment.' Much delay in response, causing him anxiety, and in the end his request was denied, 'for reasons touching the realm's good.'

In the end, Archbishop Siegfried excommunicated the

nun and my father prepared her for conversion and
married them. Riots broke out. Our house was torched
and my son, Isaac, taken from our home. Some boys
stoned the old woman's hut. Her neighbors drove them
off and pleaded with us to remove her as they could not
protect her any longer. The poor woman was speechless
with terror and clung to the very lintel. As she would
not go willingly, we took her by force.

Nor could Archbishop Siegfried help us in the matter
of our son, for we could find him nowhere. I went with
my father to the synagogue where he wrapped me in the
mantle of the martyr and prayed with the congregation
who came to weep with me:

Thy son is once more sold
Redeem him, Lord God,
Father of Mercies,
Redeem Thy son
In mercy we pray,
My son, my son, my son,
Thy grief is mine
Ruach Hakodesh

And he urged that we never shut the door against the
returning apostate or the convert, that we shoulder the
dangers and receive all who would come to the House of
Israel, and he went home and lay himself down and died.

Mose and I, accompanied by his son Leo, and Ephraim,
now my eldest son, took his body to Carcassonne as he
instructed us to do: Wash me clean, remove my shoes,
comb my hair as in my lifetime, that I may go cleanly
to my Eternal resting place, as I went every Sabbath to
the synagogue.

We received permission from the bishops to come this
way, albeit there were no homes to stop in, and made
our way as best we could. We entered the city by the
Porte de l'aude, his coffin in a wagon drawn by a horse,

and followed the path lined by the acacia trees. Everything was as Clemence and my mother had told us. Everything was and at the same time was not. This was our land by song and story, everything was familiar to the memory and new to the senses. In the countryside the peasants worked in the fields. The sweet odor from the earth that my mother used to walk upon so filled my nostrils, that I saw her kneeling there under a tree nearby, talking to our hen as she did in our garden when she came to feed her. Such an impression of the living from the dead I have never received again.

Mose nudged my arm and we went up the path and found my grandfather's grave. Terrible sorrow and joy again. He had written on his tombstone: I lay buried here in my embroidered sarbel, in the clothes I went to synagogue. In death as in life I go to Ha Shem so that He shall not mistake me for another. I would He know me as I was.

Mose, who was always instructing me in the ways of the world and held me for a naif, Mose wept. We spoke in low voices, though there was no one about but ourselves and the gravedigger we had arranged to meet. Leo and Ephraim looked at us with restrained faces, for we were separated by our memories. For this reason I was constrained to set down my father's will, to make clear the matter of their inheritance:

Do good to all men, evil to none, even to the non-Jew, even to an enemy who has pursued you with hate. Do not avail yourself of the opportunity of revenge; load your adversary with favors. Refuse no kind deed to anyone, even a non-Jew, even an enemy. If your foe seeks your harm, prevent it, but do not injure him beyond the point of preventing harm to yourself. If an opportunity presents itself to serve your enemy, thank God for it. Make yourselves wings like eagles to succor him, and remind him not of his injuries to you. Eat and drink only what is necessary. Be content with your lot. Give your wives and sons and daughters always to wear nice, clean clothes, but not extravagant clothes. Do not adopt non-Jewish fashions of dress and never change the fashions of your fathers. Never make a vow or swear. Let your word be your word. If your word is not your word, a vow will not make it so. Keep your homes clean and tidy, for disease can be bred indoors as well as out. Study the Torah, for all that is noble of thought is in it. Keep your fast days for yourself and your feasts for the poor. Judge every man charitably, find the favorable explanation for his actions. Avoid gossip, slander, hypocrisy and falsehood. Daughters must respect their husbands, and their husbands must honor their wives more than themselves. I earnestly entreat my children never to gamble except on the Festivals, and their wives may gamble on the New moon, but without money. Most strongly I beg that my sons' wives never be without work to do, for the work of a woman's hands is like the spider's web, a house for her family. Give no cause for resentment to the non-Jew, for there is none among them who has not his hour, and their wrath is implacable and lasts forever. Avoid listening to love songs which excite the passion. If God has bestowed on you the gift of a sweet voice, use it in praising Him and not each other. If thou aspire to authorship, revise thy works carefully, for error creeps in everywhere, even as mold. Be careful as to grammatical accuracy in conjugations and genders, for a man's mistakes are quoted against him. Endeavor to cultivate a concise and elegant style; attempt no rhymes unless your versification be perfect. Honor thyself and thy household, keep the festivals for a blessing and the Torah for the honor of God.

We buried my father as he requested, in his synagogue clothes, with my mother's ring on his finger, and we wrote on his stone as he instructed us to do: My dearest wife, it has been my greatest misfortune to have outlived you. Neither fame nor honor has taken your place. May the Eternal unite us in His kingdom through this air and this earth and His will. Moses Menaheim now lies forever with his wife, Florria Sara, in the Eternal Embrace and in the earth that was dear to her.

We tarried in Carcassonne to find the grave of Clemence but could not, and so returned in grief and to grief, for in this year Archbishop Siegfried died and his Jews were transferred to the imperial treasury in Cologne, and we too. So it was: Mose's fate and my family's became one. The Jews of Andernach passed first under the rule of Archbishop Wichold and then under the rule of Archbishop Henry. Some of our privileges were reaffirmed, but others were dismissed. The Cologne burgher, Johann Stolle, took a Jew from Archbishop Henry and held him captive and the Jew died in captivity. Though Stolle was rebuked for this, he was not punished, and some Christians were made bold because of this. Moreover, Archbishop Henry was always in debt and encouraged moneylending among us to ensure the payment of our taxes to him. Against my advice, Mose increased his trade in coin. Here a Jew was stoned in the marketplace, there a Jew's house was set on fire and his box was stolen. Rebuke from the Pope and encouragement from his bishops for such actions went hand in hand. Criminals were not apprehended, for the Archbishop feared to be kidnapped by them and wished to appease them. He wished also to ingratiate himself with the Pope's decrees against usurers and he wished also that his debts be paid. In this disorder, each man chose his own path.

Our son, Jeshua, was born to us during this time and we heard soon after that Philip recalled the Jews to his realm. As he could not read the debtors' notes which they had written in Hebrew, which he now claimed, and there was no one left in the realm to read the language, he must have his Jews back to read the notes and collect the debts, in return for which he promised them a third of their money. So they were let back in.

My son, Ephraim, soon a bridegroom, I went with him and Jeshua to Rome in the year of the Shepherd's uprising, to meet his betrothed, the daughter of Abraham Matron, and to arrange for their wedding. I also had news of Solomon ibn Alfaqui, settled in Rome since the year of the Jubilee. The Castilian Cortes had passed a decree forbidding Arabs and Jews to own land. His family had lost their estates and when King Sancho died Solomon lost his influence at the court. He went to Granada, but the wars between Seir and Kedar continuing he went to Rome and settled among poets. I heard from Abraham that he was made much of in Rome and that his reputation for verse grew. I understood he was affable and his style much improved though given, as many as others of the day, to imitating Dante and writing of journeys to heaven and hell.

We embarked from Andernach after the Passover. A good season. My son, Ephraim, a bearded groom, a reader in the congregation. I went with him to meet his bride. A good journey we had. The ship had three masts and nine sails and a fair wind. The land green on both sides, I traced the places to Ephraim and Jeshua where Judah-he-Hassid founded yeshivas in the valley, and where Rabbi Tam founded yeshivas in the forest and spread learning throughout the Rhineland as Rabbi Natroni Gaon had spread learning among the Sepharad. And pointed out the city of Rabbi Baruch ben Meir, the Immortal Light, and the Hassids who went into the Schwarzwald and practised poverty and would not pay their taxes to foreign dominations, and down the river and through the valleys of the Rhineland traced the places where we sleep in the Eternal Dust.

We stood by the boat's rail, Jeshua, Ephraim and myself, whose voice was growing old, while Jeshua's was still honeyed. I wrapped him in my cloak, but his chatter made my thoughts stray: Isaac, my son, we shall not say kaddish for you, nor take our portion in the World To Come until you can feast with us at the Eternal banquet table.

We came to a place in the Moselle Valley where Bateman Cresse was, and found there a company of Jews. As it was Shavuoth, we stayed and rejoiced with them, and the whole company walked with us afterwards upon the road with branches and song, as they said it was the journey of the bridegroom.

What shall I say of this, my descendants! Lay the

psalmist's words upon your hearts: Grief tarries for the night, but joy cometh in the morning. There is nothing the Eternal has given you that you cannot recover from. Lay this thought close to your hearts and let your thoughts leap over the burning land.

We went by foot across the mountains. Such was the glory before us I bid my sons say a berakhot for the beauty of the earth. We removed our cloaks and cut ourselves walking sticks and came soon to Rome.

Abraham had six daughters and gazed fondly at Ephraim. For my son's part, his heart was satisfied for the girl, Hinda Flora, was good to look at. Abraham had prospered and we undertook for Ephraim to stay with him for a year and learn the trade. After which we would be together in Andernach for the wedding, and they would live with us.

Gamaliel Oxon now in Rome with his family and his cousin, Sarah Oxon, who had become a lively and prosperous tradeswoman. Moscus Crispin, the armourer, came from Florence with his family, and Rosa Truyte, the widow, who also thrived at a trade with a Gentile partner. We embraced fervently. As Moscus' daughter was to be married to Gamaliel's son in a month's time, we were prevailed to stay, and having stayed thus long, we stayed through the Holy Days, dividing our attendance amongst the synagogues, so as not to give offense.

Of a great city there is no end of what to see. Our own sages travelled from Palestine to Rome in the time of Caesar to ransom the Jewish slaves and bring learning to those who stayed behind. Did not Rabbi Judah comment on the great works and monuments of the city.

'For me there is much work here,' Gamaliel said.

I walked beside him and saw that here everyone dressed alike, one could not tell Jew from Gentile, and I felt awkward in my apparel. 'But where there are many monuments, there are many taxes,' I said.

'True, Rabbi,' Gamaliel said, 'but there is little work for a stonecutter among our people elsewhere. Here there are three synagogues that need repair, one built in the time of Caesar, the floor has been worn by the floods of the river and the roof leans perilously forward. In Provence, my chisel knew only the touch of the tombstone. Here there is work for Gamaliel Oxon, for our stones here are very old.'

We passed under the shadow of a Roman arch. 'What shall happen to our presence in Europe?' I said, 'if we cannot build monuments.'

'Here am I,' Gamaliel said, 'for history is written in stone, and I shall write what I can.'

We came to the Colosseum and walked alongside it, I amazed to see such painted faces upon the women, Jew as well as Gentile, and such fashions that I wondered how they were permitted to go about in them.'

'Give over,' Gertrude said suddenly, 'I would I had gone with you.'

'To see such outlandish things!' Master Menaheim said,

'Aye,' she said sadly, ' a bit of purple, a bit of red, for my part it is lovelier than a monument. I would rather have the cloth than the stone, for all stone is gray, more gray or less gray, but gray it is, and I have had enough gray.'

'I brought her back a piece of cremona weave,' her husband said, 'which I had from Rosa Truyte who kept a bench near the river and plied a trade there with her Gentile partner, a widowed woman with a lame child.'

'It was but large enough for a shawl,' Gertrude complained.

'It was large enough for a cloak,' Master Menaheim said.

'Aye, but I cut it in twain so that Henne should have some.'

'Enough,' I said myself then, for I wished Master Menaheim to continue with his tale of Rome and seeing I was kin I silenced her, and so he continued.

'The popes now in Avignon, the city lost some splendor but I went about in the company of Solomon ibn Alfaqui to see Yehiel Academy and our other schools and the places where our forebears buried themselves in catacombs, and the illustrious society amongst which Solomon now dwelled. Many of our scholars from

Provence and the Sepharad now in Rome, one never looked far for learned company or for wine. Philosophers and physicians, translators from Arabic and Latin, tutors to King Robert of Naples, grammarians, exegetes and the poet, Immanuel ben Salomon who drew a circle about him of those who wrote like Dante. The pen of the poet, Immanuel, was dipped in many inks, albeit he knew how to write a sonnet in Hebrew.

As Rabbi Judah said: He who wishes to see the world in a single place must go to Rome. Here I met Leon Romano and Benjamin ben Judah Bozecco, the great grammarian; Judah Siciliano al-Sha'ari who had written a rhyming dictionary; the eminent physician, Benjamin Anau, Jehiel Moses, Isaac ben Mordecai, the physician to Pope Boniface; Immanuel's cousin, Judah ben Moses ben Daniel, who taught Hebrew and the Bible to King Robert of Naples, and translated the philosophers Aquinas and Magnus into Hebrew; and Kalonymus, whom King Robert of Naples had brought from Provence to be his own translator.

Such was the company here that I said with Rabbi Judah, Jerusalem for our home and Rome in our exile.

Solomon had rooms before the Porta Portese in the Trastevere. He still cut his beard in the Spanish style and carried his sword and wrapped himself in the air of Castile. But like a cloak no longer in fashion, it betrayed him.

I came often to his home and met his poet friends, Gentile and Jew, and two who had known Dante. In this circle, all were treated alike, but the bent of the writing was satirical. Everything was judged by scorn and laughter, the quarrels among scholars, the ways of our women, even the teachings in our schools. I was disturbed by this new mode, but Solomon regarded my concern as unworldly, and pronounced his judgment in a way that irritated me.

Yet Jeshua was much taken with him and Solomon, perceiving he was admired, lavished tales on him and took him about in the city, as a personal charge.

On Tashlikh we went to the river, as the Jews here

have the custom to do, and cast in our sins. Jeshua was much taken with this, though afterwards the Jews in Andernach began to do likewise, gathering on the river and reading from the prophet, Micah.

After our fast, I bid Ephraim goodbye. He, with God's help, to prosper and be well in Rome, I and Jeshua to Fiesole. Rosa Truyte and her partner came with us as far as Arezzo, for they were bound for the fair in Casalmaggiore. We went by horse and foot, the weather fair, her companion also a gossip, as all women are, and much to say about everything, the priests and the monks and the popes and the moneylenders and the Lombards and women's clothes and the new decrees and the discomforts of travel, but she was mindful of our customs and put up for the Sabbath and ate no pork in our presence.

May the blessing of Eternal Life be with them both, but the two women wearied me. I know not how they conversed with each other for neither finished a sentence or a thought. 'I had a piece of bolt from Ancona,' one would say, and the other, 'Twas no match for the goods that came from Marseilles.' And the first, 'Aye, for the weave was weak and the colors poor.' 'Aye, true,' the other would say, though neither had seen the other's cloth. It gave me much to think about the need for learning.

We bid farewell at Fiesole. They to Casalmaggiore, and Jeshua and I to stay at the home of Moscus Crispin who had preceeded us after his son's wedding, and was now at home to greet us. Twelve families here with a shoijet, and David Derbie who had come hither in search of work soon after we parted in Calais, for cloth was abundant here. Much pleasure I had in seeing him again, now a father of eight, though his wife was a small woman.

They lived in the countryside, for they could not lease houses in Florence or Fiesole, but trade was permitted to them. We prepared for the Festival of Booths. It was their custom here to go from booth to booth on the first and the seventh nights, for they kept the holiday as a remembrance of the pilgrims who went up to Jerusalem on the Succoth, and for the pilgrimage out from Egypt. As there were but twelve families, they went all together and their way was made sweet with cakes and wine in each booth.

So fair the weather, we were loath to leave, and a rumor of massacres by way of our return.

'When shall we see each other again?' they cried.

'We shall stay in Venice until the rumor has passed, for Jorvin Sackerel the silversmith is there, and Benedict Muriel and his kin. We shall not lack for a home or safety.' We embraced, and Jeshua and I went our way.

Jeshua was much taken with the ships and the traders in Venice, and the cloth merchants and crusaders in armor to be seen everywhere, going and coming from the Holy Land, and merchants from the Orient with spicers and silks and paper so thin we wondered at it, and coins from everywhere and in everyone's hands so that even women sat at benches along the canals and lent money on interest, and hollered their rates out loud.

'The whole world comes here for coins,' Jorvin said, 'the pope's collectors and the baron's stewards, who borrow on their crops. Every man in armor you see here has borrowed money for his breastplate or pawned his breastplate for a horse or put up his land as collateral.' We stopped by a bench where a moneylender weighed florins in a scale for a crusader. 'All the tributaries of Europe flow into these canals,' Jorvin said.

'And we shall be caught in their nets?' I asked.

'We shall be caught,' Jorvin said, 'for the Christian will not forgive us for his greed.'

'And you, Jorvin? How is it with you in Venice?'

'I am safe. The Jew cannot compete here, with the cardinals and crusaders, Lombards and Florentines. Our rates are fixed too low. Our violations cannot be disguised, but these go to church on Sunday and hear the story of how Jesus drove the moneychangers from the Temple and come here on Monday and in front of the church they prayed in yesterday, bellow their rates and weigh coin by the pound, for they believe the moneychangers in the Temple were the Jews, and not themselves. They weigh out one plus one and come out with a holy three. But I am a silversmith and a candlestick maker. As long as men light candles, I have my work to do.'

We stayed through the Festival of Lights, Jeshua much taken with their custom here. We went in Jorvin's boat with his wife, at night, and stopped by the homes of friends who held out lanterns for us to light, and greeted us with song and sweetmeats. And went with Benedict Muriel on the second night with his kin, with Isaac, on the third night and with Eliezer on the fourth night, until the eighth night, when every Jewish home was hung with eight lights and their boats on the canals also hung with eight lights, and so lights to be seen everywhere, in the reflection of the water.

But at last, I decided we must start back, though it was winter, for the Pastoreaux who roamed the countryside would surely put up for the winter, so it seemed best to me that Jeshua and I go now. Spring, as the proverb says, brings flowers and war, and better an icy road than a robber or a crusader.

Our way was difficult for the rivers were frozen and no passage to be had upon them. Jeshua did not mind these difficulties, for everything was an adventure to him, and he was filled with questions about the world and too many about Solomon ibn Alfaqui: Why he wore a jewel on his breast and why he carried a sword when we could not, and so on and so on. I did not want to talk against Solomon, but I did not care for Jeshua's interest in him. I thought of the many attempts one makes to master the world, and found my council in silence, like the woman who had come before my father. I buried my multitudinous arguments with the world and my worries for my son beneath my tongue, for which I was afterwards glad that I had said no word against Solomon. I learned later that he had returned to Castile. He sent me a letter in which he quoted the poet, ibn Sason: 'And the man Moses went forth with joy and all the Jews in the Kingdom of Castile rejoiced and were glad because of the goodness the Lord had shown to Israel.' I heard afterwards that he had gone to Palestine, where he perished beneath a crusader's sword. He was my friend and my enemy. He made my spirit restless with myself and restless with my son. More than any woman one may desire, more than a song that comes bursting from the past, more than the hope for wealth or fame, is this temptation to be like him. He was my friend and my enemy, a satirist, a courtier, and a Jew.

We went towards the Jura Mountains, hoping to escape the bands of shepherds we heard rumors of. Many Jews were on the road with us now, fleeing to Paris where there was safety. Uncommonly, the winter roads were filled with wanderers and, as the shepherds had stirred up hate against us, many huts were shut and food hard to come by. But the Eternal has planted His Righteousness along every road and where six huts were shut, one was open. And though there was famine in the land, which had stirred the Shepherds to revolt, the righteous stayed and came at night and brought us bread and onions.

We slept on the ground, wrapped in our cloaks, in barns when we could. One night I heard unwholesome footsteps. I woke Jeshua quietly and motioned to him to say nothing, but follow me quietly. We found a path into the mountain and took it, for we saw that the shepherds were lighting fires in the villages.

'Come, Jeshua,' I said, 'we go unarmed in the world. Let us climb into the mountain. You will mind the words I say to you, for they are your portion in this world. There is a place in the kingdom of the spirit where the righteous of all nations meet. You shall know them because they go unarmed in their spirit. You shall know them because you will have nothing to fear from them. If you feel fear, you will know you are in the presence of an unrighteous person. But take you anywhere, Jeshua, among Christians or Saracens, and you will find righteousness if they do not make you afraid, for Isaiah laid it down as a law of the righteous life that none shall make you afraid.'

As it was dawn, I bid him kneel and pray with me.

Ribbono ha-'olomin
Lord of all worlds
Not trusting in our own merits do we
    pray before you,
But trusting in Thy great mercy.
What are we,
What our life,
What our love,
What our devotion,
What our help.
What our strength,
What our might,
What should we say of Thee,
Lord our God,
Father of Mercies,
Shield and Redeemer;
Heroes are nothing before Thee
Nor men of great name,
Wise men are without knowledge;
We have no other wisdom but this,
No world but Your world,
And go as servants for Thy sake.

It was Tishubat and I bade Jeshua take a twig and plant it in the earth, though the ground was still frozen. Once my mother had planted such a twig in our garden, because her cousin had brought it from Carcassonne. We derided her for it. Dead it was for three years. Then one day a small bit of green, no bigger than an ant, appeared on it. She carried my brother out in her arms to look at it. What is death? I asked, and who can know what carries life within it.

With God's help, we came to Paris on the Feast of Esther and found there our good friend, Jacob Bonamie, prospering and in good health. He lived under the protection of the king and in a stone house, so we found refuge there. Came there also in that year Benedict Mayer, the tanner, Elie le Evesk the baker, and his family, now with seven grandchildren, and Mosse Bonavil, the locksmith, all who had fled to Paris. Lived here also Elie Braggard, the cloth merchant, a widower with three daughters, one married and with child, one a tradeswoman, and one a weaver. Went we all to the synagogue on the Feast of Esther, with candles and noisemakers, and all the Jews came into the streets with costumes and baskets of apples and chose for themselves a queen and a king and Haman and Mordecai, and though we heard rumors that the shepherds were outside the city gates, as the Bishop promised he would protect us, we continued with our celebration and all through the night the children ran through the streets in their masks and costumes, with songs and with shouts, Am Chai Israel, and Jeshua ran with them.

When the roads were clear and there were no more rumors, we bid our friends goodbye, with sadness and with promises to come to Andernach for Ephraim's wedding. So Jeshua and I made our way home and arrived before the Passover.

Soon afterwards Archbishop Henry prevailed upon us to raise eight thousand marks to help him redeem his cities of Rees, Xanten and Kempen. In return he decreed for us the Privilege of 1321, assuring us protection and safe conduct in all his domains for ten years. Against my warnings, Jehude and Leo now lent money on interest to raise the sums. But as we were permitted to stay in Andernach and none threatened our streets or our homes, we were content and thrived. My daughter Margit married and gave birth to twins and I received for our schul a great ram's horn from Jacob Bonami which Jeshua blew on the Holy Days, to the astonishment of the congregation. We must soon choose a bride for you, I thought, and began to look about. Abraham Matron will come with Ephraim and Hinda Flora, and his other daughters and will cast eyes upon you. We will see what the year has done with his daughters. And we began to watch for the river to thaw and for Ephraim and Hinda Flora and the bridal party to appear upon it.

It was Jeshua who brought us the news that they had

arrived. 'They're here,' he shouted, running up from the river. 'I see a ship and everyone we know is upon it.'

Gertrude and I ran down to the wharf. Yes, it was Ephraim and Hinda Flora and Abraham and his wife and his other five daughters. Came with him Gamaliel Oxon and his family and Sara Oxon and Rosa Truyte. Came with them Leo Cresse, our musician, and Moscus Crispin and his family, and Jorvin Sackerel who brought candlesticks as a wedding gift. And came with them Benedict Muriel the carpenter and all his kin, and Davie Derbie the dyer. As we had word from Jacob Bonamie that he would be with us, we waited for him. Mosse Bonamie and Massa ben Yssac, now settled in Paris with their families, came with Elie le Evesk and Bateman Cresse. So huge a gathering there was, some stayed at the inn of our innkeeper, Aaron Slemne. Some stayed in our house, some stayed with Jehude and Leo and Mose in Cologne. Came finally Solomon the mule-seller on the day of the wedding, and we all walked in procession alongside the bridal pair and brought them into the shul with blessing and with song. And Ephraim said the words of that time, 'I shall work for thee, Hinda Flora, honor, support and maintain thee in accordance with the custom of Jewish husbands. I shall go with thee, Hinda Flora, according to the ways of the world which the Eternal has implanted in us.'

Amen, amen, and amen.

And she sang to him the song of the bride.

She goeth out to meet thee
Look thou and listen and hear her cry,
She is calling in the fullness of her
    heart,
In her warbling throat,
In her fainting soul

And we set a crown upon them and Gertrude gave

Hinda Flora an egg to eat from our hen every day until she was with child, and Jeshua was betrothed to Abraham's second daughter, Henne married Rabbi Hushiel's son and went to live in Dusseldorf, and my daughter Jurette married a trader in cloth and went to live in Rouen.

And again, in 1342, we bought up the archbishop's debts and were able to renew the Privilege of Protection and safe conduct for another ten years. We negotiated for the release of Rabbi Peshe, who had been captured by Baron Strohnne and held for ransom. I too now lent money on interest and we raised in these years, I and my son, Jeshua, and Rabbi Hushiel's son and Rabbi Pesha himself and his congregation and the Jews of Dusseldorf and Essen and Cologne, and the whole of the Rhine Valley, we raised the remarkable sum of 20,000 marks which we sent through the banker Vivaud, to the Dauphin as a gift from his Jews of France, to remove the edict of expulsion which threatened them again.

'Aha!' Gertrude exclaimed. 'Aha! and aha! Have I not declared this number to be the sum of all evil. Are we not the Lord's treasure?' And she would not be quieted, though her husband spoke sternly to her, that her bubbling said nothing. Sank he then upon his knees and began to pray in such a way as I had not heard even in church.

'Danim-efshar mi-she-i-efsher. With memory I was enlightened. For this law which used to puzzle my father---to deduce the possible from the impossible---I was given the privilege to prove. We raised the sum from the dust, again and again. We raised the sum for cathedrals and crusades, for Jewish prisoners and Christian wars. We raised the sums for Christian territories bought and sold and bought again. We raised the sums for our people in exile, we raised the sums for our people in Palestine, we raised the sums for our prisoners and our slaves, our poor and our brides, and ransomed them one by one.

The Jews of Dusseldorf and Essen and Cologne pressed on me and chose me to advise them in the clamor that rose all about us, as the news of the plague came to us from Rome and Florence and Venice and the news of the massacres spread through the valley. We met with bishops and barons. The Council of Vienne assured us that we would be protected, Pope Clement issued decrees that our lives were not to be threatened, and we were taken from our homes and our synagogues and Jeshua, my son, Jeshua whom I had gone into the mountain with, Jeshua, my son, was martyred before my eyes and his dying body searched by perfidious hands for coins.

On the twenty-fifth day in the year 4,708, our winekeg fell below the surface of the river. The small hole that had been mine for a view of the world was now darkened completely, and we were utterly disconsolate. We descended through darkness with our Siddur and our candlesticks and candles, as our oppressors buried us with these. In darkness, we sat on the bottom of the river, rocking with the motion of the water. It was dark and we were separated from time. I could not know when to say my prayers, but did not leave off praying. Blessed art Thou Who rescued Noah. Blessed art Thou Who saved a gourd, and would Thou do less for man? Saw I then a piece of light as small as the head of a pin where the staves were not fastened properly, and laid my eye against it, and saw with amazement a whole world of life beneath the life I had known. Fish and plants of every size and shape drifting in the universal water, some with eyes that searched my own and bumped against the winekeg. Others with lights in their heads, swimming busily, and I saw that these fish swam all about us and feared nothing. A shaft of light fell beneath the water, to the very depths where we sat, and I surmised that this was the shaft of sunlight from the dawn. My heart was lifted. Blessed art Thou Who rescues and restores worlds. Blessed art Thou Who rescued Noah and through Noah the whole of creation.

Soon I knew when night was upon the earth, for the light disappeared. As it reappeared and disappeared with regularity, I could tell day from night. The fish themselves drifted in this light as the birds move with the air and come with the dawn. And I blessed the

Creator, for I saw that there was no place in the universe, neither among the stars nor the shells, that He had not created with orderliness, and I bid Gertrude light the candles, for by my calculation it was the Sabbath night. 'What boots tears,' I said. 'Come, light the candles.'

'You are mad,' she said. 'Rebono shel 'olam, rescue me from my husband, at least. He likes it here, but I do not. He has gone mad.'

Since our space was so small and we could not escape each other, we had no choice but to master ourselves. 'What boots it not to light the candles?' I asked. 'Either way, we must sit here.'

'Aye,' she said bitterly, 'our space grows ever smaller and smaller.' And as she saw that there were few choices in calamity, she lit the candles as much as to hope she still had the power to do so.

So we remained on the floor of the river with the other creatures the Eternal had put into our world, and came to know them as they came to know us, and I came to see that each had its appointed way. 'One and Eternal,' I prayed, 'with what love you have created every corner of the world that I, living in my small part of it, could not know until now. Blessed art Thou Who has created the world wherein there is no place that is not fit for Your creatures and for blessing. Blessed art Thou Who multiplies berakhot and has brought me here. I see how difficult it is to encompass you in the human world where your Unity is torn apart. I see now that however natural our life appeared among humankind, it was unnatural, and however unnatural I had first thought this existence beneath the river to be, that it abides by the laws of Your universe. One and Eternal, may it be Your will to give us what You have given these fish, for how can it be that You would deny us the order and the light and the reasonableness which You have given Your lowest creatures.'

"With that, my own dear Will, his tale came to an end. He said he had no more to say to me, and as his wife was hungry and he had kept her long enough, they must be gone. So they went their way, he in his tunic as he had it still about him and she, my kinswoman, in a moldy skirt and cap, hobbled beside him. And there was nothing left more on the beach but my star and my cat. A fearful emptiness seized me for the sudden loneliness. For though he left me his book, I could not read it and could only wonder at its letters.

The tide came and took up the winekeg. I went after to retrieve it and was caught by a wave, as my own hunger had weakened me, and I was dragged beneath the waters. But I saw not the glory he spoke of, but dark and mold and fish with sharp teeth in their heads and no kindly lights, but sharks of which you have heard and other creatures that I found not reasonable at all. Much parchment and papers and documents went by, swirling papers and books wherein the ink was purple from fungus and glad I was then that I could not read, for I would never have come to the end of it. And so many caverns and caves and chambers of archives and catacombs of wills and registers and rolles and letters and cartes and declarations, so many sums that I knew not whether I was beneath water or paper, for I saw no fish anymore, for fish could not live in so shameful a matter as I saw with my own eyes, such copulation that for shame I cannot tell it to you, not alone one book atop another but at times three books atop one, or four books altogether jostling and copulating such as would strain the spine of a human. So there were halls and halls of them, and in every hall such shameful acts took place and scribes sat there behind their desks and recked not what was happening but looked boldly upon it all and wrote their own news sheets that were carried everywhere by the falcons, and the news sheets and the books said the same message, for they could not come to the end of it: That the Jews had killed the Lord Jesus and trafficked in usury.

I was afraid for my kinswoman, Belaset, and fled with my cat and my star, I fled and it seems I fled as I fled before, for the animals of the world fled with me: the hare and the rabbit, the fox and the fieldmouse, for the land beneath us was burning again. I fled and the animals fled with me, for wherever we put down the foot the land sprang into flames. There was no place for foot or hoof, but galloping, galloping, roar and rumble and fleeing. Everything with the breath of life in it was hunted and harried and fled. There was nought but a thread to guide me through the mountains of Seir and Kedar. So narrow the passage there was no room for an ant to pass through, and I passed as a worm through the passageway, I passed through the passageway through the mountains, as Moses through the Red Sea.

And came then with the fear upon me and my cat on my shoulder, to this door with one word upon it: EUROPE.

'I cannot go back,' I cried, and banged on the door to open. 'I cannot go back for the land is burning. Let me pass through to safety.'

The door opened, but there was my mother as she was in life, not drowned in the river as I thought, but in the flesh in the sea, and still in the court as ever it was her custom to be when she was in the land.

'Mother,' I cried and ran forward to meet her, but she was ever the same, confused and daft and knew not her own, or what to say, for if she said one thing they said another and if she said the other they said the first. There was no end to their eternal wrath, but she must stand trial forever. And her jury was ever betwixt and between and first said one thing and then another and if the people said this, the scholars said that, and if the scholars went one way, the people went another, for they said and unsaid and said and unsaid that their God was the prince of peace and judge not and love your neighbor, and with the other tongue they called this God the prince of death and slew the saracen for his disbelief and forgave not but sent the sinner to eternal hell where, as the poet said, was no hope at all.

The pain of the place was too much for me, a God that would punish eternally. 'Come away, come away,' I called to my mother, but she could not hear me for the murmuring tongues which did such shameful things that I cannot tell you. Each tongue had a say what the other tongue unsaid, and so they said and unsaid and said and unsaid and ever and again the tongues twisted and flicked, so that many of their sayings fell out together and went hand in hand though they said opposite things and opposite sayings copulated and gave birth to sayings the sayings knew not. And with it all there was nought to say to any of it, for the sayings were nought in themselves, but the power was all, though these would that their sayings mattered, but I saw that they carried their swords in secret places and would that the judge believed their sayings so that their tongues licked his ears in a shameful manner. And this judge was none but her own husband who himself could not move for the tongues that gave him such pleasure.

'Come away, come away,' I wept, but she could not, for she wished her husband to love her. 'He cannot love you,' I cried, 'Mother, my dear, he cannot love you, for you have taxed him with the tax of life.'

Then the waters of the world flowed into my lungs so that I struggled and clutched my cat, for neither of us could live in this sea any longer. Froth and churning, the waters roared upwards and spit me back upon the shore. I was not gone but a minute, though it seemed like a lifetime, for it passed before me as before one who is drowning. I wept for my mother, for I could not save her, I wept for my mother beneath the sea, I wept for my mother who was but a simple woman, and however she said her say she remained in the stranger's land. I wept for my mother and I wept for my kinswomen, Hannah and Gertrude and Pulchinella, for the one lost seven and the other lost two and the third brought forth her child in flames.

I wept till I could hold no more with my weeping when a voice called me by my name, 'Miriam my own,' in my own tongue. And this voice came not from the mountain, Will, as you once taught me, but out from the midst of the sea in which I floundered.

'Why quake you?' the voice asked me, and I could not but guess that this was the voice of God, or I was daft, for there was nought but air about me. 'What!' I said, 'can you speak my tongue?'

'Surely,' He said, "and why do you weep?'

'If you can speak my tongue, you know why I weep.'

The voice laughed and said back to me, 'Aye, but do you know why you weep, for you have wept for many things in my book.'

'Aye,' I said, "but I weep now because I cannot save my mother. She is damned eternally by your judgment.'

'Not by mine,' He said.

'What!' I said. 'Is it not by your hand that my mother died and did you not say that death is the wages of sin, and my mother could not help but sin seeing she knew not the way to light.'

'Nay, not by my Hand,' He said, "for I gave no such law that death is the wages of sin. For all my creatures die in their time, the fox and the hare and the rabbit and they know not sin. Though man sins, he shares with my creatures the universal of birth and death. As I gave not birth for a wage of goodness, so I gave not death as a wage for sin. Man pays for his sins but not by my laws of birth and death.'

'What!' I said, 'what then of eternal hell?' I asked with wonder, for it seemed I had just been there.

'There is none with me.'

'My mother then is not doomed forever?'

'Not in my domain. You have written it down yourself in your book and you have forgotten it. My judgment is for four generations, but my mercy is forever. Did I not make a covenant with you, and will I destroy what is mine? Man destroys what is his. Self destruction is with man, not with Me. Did I not create, and will I then uncreate? Will I unravel the world I ravelled up? I made my covenant with man, but man makes not his covenant with earth. I made my covenant with the beasts of the field and with the fowls of the heavens, even with the creeping things of the ground, but man keeps not his habitation and unlike my other creatures, fouls his own nest. I made my covenant with creation, but man makes his covenant with destruction. I make my covenant with all the living. Did I not save the gourd because it was mine when Jonah would destroy the whole of Ninevah for its sins. He judged, but I saved.'

'But see how the plague rages,' I wept, and 'you stay not your Hand.'

'The plague will pass, but man will not. I will stay my hand for the sake of my covenant, but man stays not his hand ever. You have forgotten the lesson I gave to the psalmist. There is but one remedy for adversity, which Moses gave you when he showed you the two paths and bid you choose the path of life. And this path the psalmist chose when he went through the valley of death. Feared he not death? He feared it much, but he said, to honor Me, that he feared it not and in this way he overcame his fear. This is the hard law, Miriam, that man must walk through the valley of death, let them say what they will and debate until doomsday. There is no passage for man but through the mountains, there is no passage but through the night, there is no passage but through the wilderness of thought and world and deed, and man has no choice but to go, whether he take the passage for blessing or curse. All this Aristotle knew, but he knew not the blessing. If life heal you not, Miriam, will death or philosophy? Though I have numbered your sins and have judged you, I am the God of life and my mercy is forever. Man's contrition is but a gift of the moment, and not an everlasting remedy. Only my mercy is an everlasting remedy. All this you have written down yourself in your book, but you have forgotten the names by which you were wont to call me.

God and restorer of worlds
God of nature and of creation
God of justice
God of righteousness
God of mercy,
Without beginning and without end
Who was not created and cannot be

destroyed
God of time and of eternity
Who binds and keeps the centuries.

Now call you me god, and I like not this name. For
as the name is little you have made me little, and you
reck not this evil. Moses was wise, for he asked me
first, what shall I call you? And I would that you show
me this courtesy. I speak with you in your own tongue,
call me my name in mine: Rachman, Ha Shem, Adonoi,
and Eloheynu. These names I like and not god nor senor
nor mister nor what. Memory is mine forever and I
remember my names. I remember and wait to be
called. I am the God of life and all creatures, the hare
and the fox and the rabbit, the wolf and the mutter and
her whelps. Fear not the prince of death, Miriam, for I
am the God of life. My judgment is for the hour, but
my mercy is forever. I am the source of life and all its
keeping. All this you have written yourself, and I abide
by your word, but you have forgotten it. I alone
remember. It is an ancient wisdom. Therefore I say it
in an old tongue. There is no more.'
Fell I then upon the beach where I stood and wept,
'Your servant, Lord!'
'Nay,' He said, 'my handmaiden, Miriam,' and raised me
up, and departed.
There was no more, as He said, and I took up my cat
and my star and went my way, for I saw I must now go
back to you to give you my get. For this reason, Will, I
have returned, for I mean to leave and not be left. For
I may now be judged in the Jew's court, even as
Archbishop Siegfried said, and there is no law in their
court that my mother must be punished forever.
"Nay, Miriam," Will said, "have you told me this long
tale for this end that we are now to part?"
"Aye, husband, I have, for I would that you understand
my heart for its rancor and its love, for I would live
with you in amity, though apart. I want not your guilt
nor your sorrow, but I would that I walk my path alone

and bid you do the same. Ever and again you would not let me go, but would have me as you wanted me, in your image, whether I would or no, and I had no will of my own anymore. I would judge myself now and judge my God with my own wisdom, for though you say your God is the God of love yet is punishment with him eternally, and though judgment and righteousness be with my God, mercy is with Him forever. This perplexity which held me captive I have unravelled from the confusion of sayings and tongues, for by my book His judgment is but for four generations, for the keeping of man's memory, and not for eternity, and by this law is my mother free, for it is four generations and more from Belaset."

"What!" Will said, "would add to your sins such heresy?"

"Nay, husband, I cannot be an heretic and I cannot be an apostate, for you sent me away and declared me unredeemable."

"Nay, Miriam, I meant you no harm, but that your ways have always angered me."

"Aye, husband, I do believe you, but you hit me on the side of my head and raised a bump there, and I would end my mutterings, but go my way, for as Jesus was crucified in the flesh so I have been crucified in my spirit and comes now my season of resurrection. I will go my way and we must part, but I would that we harvest what goodness there has been between us. I would we go in memory of what love there has been and not in memory of the enmity we must lay to rest, for we cannot with it anymore. Oh! love, even to the charnel house comes spring and green memories of good times when you came knocking at my door with the glint in your eyes and called to me, Mistress Maree, your goat strays yonder in the fields, and I walked with you in the grass for company's sake."

Here ended Miriam's testimony. She left Southwerke

within a fortnight, seized with longing to return to her birthplace. The plague struck her down on the road between Peterborough and Lincoln, near a small town called Crantham, not far from the Witham River. She was seized with violent pains in her chest, fever and dizziness. There was no one close by and the ground was still hard, but she lay herself down upon it as she had lain in the forests of Europe, and went to sleep in the Eternal Dust.

CHAPTER FIVE

THE COIN OF SALVATION

Will returned to Bodmin by the beginning of February. The gates were shut and no one came to open them for him. He had seen enough on his return trip to feel forboding for Bodmin demesne. Though it was Lenten season, the fields were abandoned, a sure sign of coming famine. There were other signs as well. The cattle in the fields, domesticated for a millennium, were now left to stray by themselves and had become skeletal, niggardly in flesh, wandering haphazardly, mooing weakly to be milked. But the keepers were gone. The villages were deserted. The mills and the baking houses were idle. There were not enough people left to grind, to bake, to plow. In plaguetime, the balance between population and land is reversed. The problem is one of underpopulation, not enough hands to do the work of sustenance. Sometimes Will saw a peasant in the field, salvaging what he could, but most often he saw the plow standing idle, a dismal sight to a rural man.

One disease breeds another. Man becomes infected and cannot tend to his fields. The fields go to waste and cannot support the cattle. The cattle sicken and become unfit for consumption. Where there is not enough to eat, suspicion and hostility thrive. Morality and personality are unstable and human nature undergoes a change.

The plague by now had spread north and inland, to Malvern, Leicester, Coventry and Stratford, most often carried there by those who fled the coastal areas, and by the flocks of sheep they took with them. The infected rats which carried the fleas stayed in the coastal areas.

The penetration into the interior was made by those who fled the plague. The advice from the University of Paris to flee was only temporarily useful, or useful for those who could escape everyone else. Abbot Roland, who was in York by the middle of February, heard of deaths in Coventry, and by the time Will returned to Cornwall the whole of Exeter had become infected. Taunton and Launceston were deserted. The holidays were not celebrated this year, neither St. Distaff's Day nor Plow Monday nor Candlemas.

Will stopped at the Launceston Inn. There was no one about but the innkeeper's wife who had survived everyone else, and faced the future with a wholesome wrath. She screeched at Will, "Christ be dead if I beat not the devil in this game. I will give him no more breath, for I have buried seven from this plague and there be none to bury me. I'd as lief curse God and go to hell and be done with it than not be buried properly and rot upon this earth with the sheep."

Will asked for Claryce.

"Ha!" the innkeeper's wife said, "I warrant she has pulled the devil's tale by now." She gave Will a piece of bread and bid him be gone, "for there be nothing left to eat here," she said and sat down in front of her fireplace and stared gloomily into the fire, now and then poking it harshly with a piece of iron.

Common clay endured the plague as well as uncommon clay; acts of charity and kindness were found as often among the illiterate and the vulgar as anywhere else, and the Black Death is the story of the endurance of these.

Will arrived at Bodmin gate at Vespers, but no bells rang. No bells had rung in the countryside for weeks. The Bishops of Winchester had given orders to cease all bellringing because "it attracted unnecessary attention, pilgrims and others, rabblerousers about the countryside, who were tempted in loose times to come against the monks." For Medieval man, for whom the passing of every hour had been a communal and audible experience, the silence told him that his connection with religious time was broken.

Abbot Denis' monastery had been attacked again, the larder broken into, every scrap and morsel of food, its chief relics, the gold on its altars, the enamel crucifix, and moveables of every kind taken, and his monks fled in panic for fear of starvation or murder at the hands of others. They had come battering at the gate of Bodmin itself for help.

"Christ help them," Prior Godfrey said, and gave orders to barricade the gates and silence the bells. For three days and nights they were besieged by Abbot Denis' monks who sat outside the gate and said incantations against those inside. Sons of Belial! God help them, if he would open the gate to such as these.

Brother Ralph and Brother Walter kept watch from the Calefactory and sent Brother Namlis out every hour to make sure the barricade was holding. The howling and the cursing were nerve smashing, but eventually the voices grew fainter, though no one knew if they had gone away or had perished outside the gate, and no one cared or was brave enough to go outside to see.

There was such thievery abroad these days, of relics from churches and monasteries, lootings of altars and sacred vessels, no stranger could be trusted past the monastery gate.

Thus, Will halloed and halloed, but no one answered him. What! he thought, will he not be let back into his own monastery? Who sent him out? Had he not risked his life and walked to London and back through plaguey villages, and not a drop of cheer this Christmas, only to be shut out now! Hallo! Hallo! Bang! Shut! Closed! And night coming on. Cold Cornwall night full of freezing rain. The first drop already hit him on his collarbone. Ping! A drop of slithering cold that found its way down his neck. Ping!

"Damnye," he called out.

Human discomfort struggled with the speculation that everyone inside was dead. He looked about for something he could use as a battering ram, but everything that could be burned or made to serve in some way had long ago been taken by whoever had passed this way before him.

"Damnye! Open!" Will cried again. Did they mean to betray him? Had they sent him out, not to let him back in for fear that he was contaminated? Dark thoughts crossed his mind, too dismal to think. "Damnye, let me in. It is nought but Will back from London. Have you not a heart for your own brother?"

At last, a shuffle of footsteps, though no voice accompanied it. Then a pause, then nothing more. "Christ rot your bones. Open up, I say. This be Will, and I be freezing. Have you lost your heart as well as your tongue?"

The gate was opened, half a crack at first, hardly enough for an eyeball. The man carried no candle. There was no moon in the sky, no light to see by, no voice from this brother, nothing to trust a man by. Maybe it wasn't his own on the other side? Well, what of it, he cannot freeze outside. He put his shoulder to the gate and pushed, but the barricade would not yield. "I am Will," he cried, "mean you to leave me out here?"

The barricade was pulled back at once. There in the cold darkness, as Will could make out by his hump, was Brother Namlis. And was ever a man more desperate for speech than he was, cautious of what dead bodies might have come to rest against the gate, judging that it was only Will and Will alone, yet fearing to embrace him. Conflicting emotions seized him with the misery of speechlessness. He could not tell him: Brother John was gone, Prior Godfrey was gone, Brother Walter was gone, and Brother Ralph could not cease his grieving. He growled and cried in huge gulping sounds, so that Will surmised many things.

"Curse a world where a man cannot embrace his friend. Curse a world where he cannot say hello." Vexation overcame him, and he began to cry too. As soon as Brother Namlis saw this, he stopped crying, for he would not have Will suffer on his account, and joy overcame him as he realized it was Will indeed who stood before him.

"Christ strike me if I will not love the man that

opened this gate for me," Will said, and embraced Brother Namlis. "Enough weeping, for I must have warmth and food or my parts will cease forthwith." He ran for the refectory, leaving Brother Namlis to barricade the gate again, after him.

Will saw at a glance how matters stood. Brother Harald sat in Prior Godfrey's place. Brother Walter's place was empty. Brother John's place empty too.

"Welcome," Brother Harald said, without much change in his accustomed tone. "I will not ask you how does the world, for you can see by our state that we know ourselves how it does."

The death of Brother Walter had stricken Brother Ralph's tongue. He who in former times would have been the first to come forward with, "What news? How does it in the outer world?" was silent. He greeted Will for formality's sake, though the kiss of peace had been dispensed with, and he did not care what news Will brought from London or anywhere else. Brother Benedict, Will learned, was still alive. Whether the cancer kept the plague from him could not be said, but "his hold on life is wonderful," Brother Harald reported. Brother Harald was now Prior Harald, as Bishop Grandisson had decreed when word was sent to him that Prior Godfrey was dead. It had been feared, but only by Brother Harald, that Bishop Grandisson would appoint a prior from somewhere else. Bishop Grandisson had considered this, but there were no priors or abbots to spare. In one monastery, a boy of fifteen had assumed the office, for lack of anyone else. Brother Harald suffered from a want of charity, but nothing else. Bishop Grandisson, after a night of counsel with himself, taking everything into consideration---the man, the emergency, the times, the plague, the political disquiet, the lack of other capable men, sent word of his sorrow for Prior Godfrey's death, and his commendation that Brother Harald be elevated to the position of prior.

Bodmin Priory might not have survived the time of the dissolution but for this fortunate change. Prior Harald took immediate steps to provide against the imminent collapse of the monastery. He it was who gave the order that the bells not be rung. He it was who laid down the rule against the opening of the gate. He set in motion an inventory of every possession in Bodmin, what was left of food, mead, tallow, fish, wood, clothes, fur, and meted out accordingly.

The plague increased his efficiency. It whetted his appetite for administrative action. He was not a brooder, and he did not bother with inquiries into God's motives, or the causes of the plague, or its relationship to the sinful nature of man. He did not feel curiosity about any of these matters. Plague was plague, like cancer was cancer, or a chill was a chill. No one asked God's motives when a chill struck him, or a fit of sneezing. Why should anyone see more meaning in one disease than another. He had no patience with speculations, only with measures.

The plague distracted him from his own internal disease, his hypochondria. From the moment he had become prior and took matters into his own hands, he had ceased to have these fits. In fact, he almost forgot them by now. After his first hectic week of undoing Prior Godfrey's mismanagement he remembered that he had not had an attack in days. As he could not account for why he had suffered from them all his life, he could not account for their sudden disappearance, and he felt only momentary alarm that they might return. He could not "resolve" to combat them as he could resolve to combat inefficiency. This he knew from the past. They had always outwitted and defeated every resolution he had made. They were wholly mysterious, for him the one true mystery in life. But he had lived long enough to outlive them, and soon even this last fear that they might return was not remembered. For him the plague was a godsend. Prior Harald's personality concluded itself, and when his time came he died in peace.

His plan had been to outlive the plague, to conserve the energies of Bodmin, to shut themselves into the priory and stay until the plague was gone. If they remained inside the walls and husbanded carefully, they might pass safely through the winter. He gave orders for the brethren to say their prayers in their own cells to save the cost of candlelight in the cathedral. They kept to their schedule of praying at Matins, Prime and Tierce; and scrupulous care was given to every detail of food, clothing, hay, wood, and wax.

Prior Harald told Will to have his supper and sleep, and that he would hear his report on how matters stood in the morning.

Will learned before the night was out that they did not stand well with Bodmin Priory, for St. Petroke's bones, the precious relic of Bodmin's founding saint and its primary source of wealth and collateral for emergencies, had been stolen from its resting place, from the very vault that had been dug for it in front of the cathedral altar.

Brother Ralph relented from his silence bit by bit and by nightfall, somewhere between Compline and Matins, told Will how it had happened: The alarm had been given by Brother Thomas who, in a fitful nightmare, had wandered from his bed into the church and had startled the masked thieves in the act of it. One went at him with a sword, but fortunately for Brother Thomas' early training in the Scots army, he sidestepped quickly. His assailant was caught off balance, giving Brother Thomas time to flee to the dormitory and give the alarm.

The relic could have been saved had he been believed, or had he believed himself. But so accustomed were they to his nightly fits that, though he wept and cursed and swore that it was so, that his very life had been attacked, no one believed him. Prior Godfrey was still alive and heard the tumult and feeling a want of courage if he did not go to curb it, put on his cape and slippers and made his way to the dormitory. First, he lectured Brother Thomas on breaking his vow of silence. "It matters not that you say your tongue wags by itself in your sleep. The spirit of Christ cannot go from you when your eyes be shut."

Brother Thomas wept from vexation. Brother Harald, as he still was then, perceived that it was Prior Godfrey's tongue that wagged unnecessarily, and advised that they go quickly and see how matters stood.

It was frosty and no one cared to cross from the dorter to the church on a fool's errand, so that Brother Thomas' life stood in danger should he be proven wrong. For a moment he surmised the gamble, and the thought that he had been carried away by a dream made him hesitate. He had been carried away before. It was his nature to be carried away by dreams of violence. Once he had fled from his bed, claiming it was on fire. Yet, he had been so certain only a moment before! And now he was not certain at all. Why was he always tormented thus in the middle of the night!

They then surmised how matters stood with him. "Get you to bed," Prior Godfrey screeched at him. "Christ keep you in purgatory for a millennium if you break your vow again this night.

So they knew nothing of the matter until early Mass. Where the slab of neatly fitting stone had been was a black hole. Brother Harald was the first to enter the cathedral that morning, the first to notice that the stone was missing from its place. He struck his forehead and rushed forward. But for what? He knew that no one would remove the stone except to remove the relic, for stone qua stone had not a shilling's worth to it. But man's intelligence has little control over his instincts. Momentum carried Brother Harald forward, though he knew St. Petroke's bones were gone. But before he could stare into the dismally empty hole, something else arrested his attention. "Christ slice Brother Thomas' tongue for once and all." The rubies, the jewels of blood, were missing from the stigmata of the Majestatis.

Brother Thomas fled. He took to his bed and claimed he had the plague. For three days no one came near him for fear it might be true, and by the time they decided it wasn't true the shock of their losses had diminished, and Brother Thomas felt at liberty to come into the refectory to get some food.

"He looks never the worst for fasting three days," Brother Ralph said.

Now that Will was back, his spirits lifted a little. "God help you if you go again from us," he said.

"There is no place to go," Will said. "But who is it that did this thieving?"

Brother Ralph's tongue became salubrious as the night wore on. There were many suspects, but after a little debate it was decided it was either Bishop Roundsleigh, Abbot Denis' monks, or that Walt of Landsend.

"It is not Walt," Will said, "for I fell in with him and he died of the plague along the way to London."

Brother Ralph was now recovered enough to be impressed by this piece of news. "Some good there is in the plague," he said.

Will forebore and did not answer him.

In the morning, after their meager breakfast, he came to Prior Harald's room as he was bid. The fire was roaring in the fireplace and billows of smoke curled from it. The tapestries of the hunting scenes were now hung over the window to keep out the winter air and the chills. The heat inside the room was remarkable. St. George was overcome by it.

Prior Harald had the accounting books open before him on the lectern. "I trust your trip to London was rewarding," he said.

"If you mean met I with the usurers, I did as I was told."

Prior Harald had none of Prior Godfrey's rhetorical flourish, but so bald a statement of the matter took even him aback. He snivelled his disapproval through smoke clogged nostrils and said through severely dry lips, "I know not what usurers you speak of, seeing I had it from Prior Godfrey that he sent you to the wool merchant."

"Oh, aye," Will said edgily, forgetting his vow of obedience, and not minding an argument, "he may be a woolman as he shears the wool from the sheep's back but he be a lenderer as I could see plainly by the coins on his table."

"Usury is forbidden churchmen and Christian alike," Prior Harald said, in the tone proper to his new status, "and if you call this usury you lend yourself to the devil's tongue and you may be sure the devil will pay back this loan with interest."

Prior Harald did not care about the ethics involved in the problem, for he knew what it must take to keep Bodmin Priory from sinking into irreparable condition, but he did care about a peasant's come-uppance and a novice's impudence. If he did not call it usury, it was not for Will to wax sardonic and call it what Prior Harald said it was not. Prior Harald represented the church now, and the church represented the truth, and Prior Harald always hewed to form.

"Read you the letter Prior Godfrey sent?" he asked. Will said he had not. "Then you know not the terms on which the request was made."

Will had nothing to respond to this, but said, reluctantly working his way into apology, "it but seemed to me that he usured by his manner."

"Oh, aye," Prior Harald said, "and this is the whole of your judgment?" He waved his hand, dismissing the issue with a generous gesture. "Let us see the answer the woolman gave you and be done with it."

Will took off the pouch and emptied its contents on the table.

Prior Harald looked at the coins for only a moment, and he said, "Plague take him that he has no mercy on the Church." He took each coin, bit it, held it in his hands to test its weight, then separated three counterfeit coins and marked their identification in his book. He put all the coins together on the table again, and swirled them about to see how similar or dissimilar they looked. "Can mark the clipped coin?" he asked.

"I cannot," Will said.

Prior Harald dexterously drew them out from the others, and held one up for Will between his thumb and forefinger. "Mark how the cross is clipped. Thought you not to watch closely what he put in the pouch?"

"I have no skill with coins and never did I see one such as this."

Prior Harald mixed them up again on the table. "See now if you can mark it and improve your skill."

Will looked closely and saw little. He had seen but a few dozen coins in all his life. "That one with the long cross upon it," he said, without confidence. But he was right, and Prior Harald was pleased, for there was in him the instinct of the teacher as well as the administrator, and ignorance offended him as much as inefficiency. "Aye," he said, "that one," pleased too at his own skills in detecting fraud, a necessary virtue in high places and for a man of the world. "We cannot let the matter rest. They must go back."

"No," Will said quickly and to his amazement, "I will not return to London this season."

"You will not disobey your prior."

"Let the plague abate a little and I will think upon it."

"Know you not what treasures have been stolen from Bodmin? We cannot pledge collateral now less we pledge the grounds themselves."

Will felt something harden in him. The feeling oppressed him. He had not given up the world, as others had, because he feared it or disliked it or had belittled its value. He had given up something which he had a great longing for. It seemed to him he had changed his mode of living, but little else, for everything else went on as before except for the pleasure of living. The conditions which had seemed so cogent to make him go in search of spiritual salvation had dissolved like mist, and what remained were problems of plague and debt and how to keep Bodmin Priory from falling into ruin.

Prior Harald had an intuition that if he sent Will out again, he might not return. "We will think upon the matter," he said, and shuffled the coins together.

Will left and went to the Calefactory room to warm himself. Brother Thomas, Brother Ralph and Brother Namlis were already there, waiting for the Chapter reading to begin.

"Well?" Brother Ralph whispered.

"It seems I knew not that I brought back three coins that were clipped," Will said.

"Trust that one to know," Brother Ralph said.

"Devil take him," Brother Thomas said, "you be not the man for such mean work."

"Aye, but I care not to be a fool," Will said bitterly.

"It matters not," Brother Ralph said, "whether the woolman fleeced the prior or the prior fleeced the woolman, for they milk the same sheep."

"How come you to be so worldly wise?" Will said.

Brother Ralph accepted the compliment without embarrassment. "I have been in monastery all my life. Now tell us, Will, how does the world in London, for I must confess to you I have had it on my mind the whole night to ask you, met you with whores?"

Brother Namlis bent forward.

"No," Brother Thomas said hastily, "you will not talk on such a matter!"

"I know he met not with dice," Brother Ralph said, "for never did I see him dice, but I only meant that seeing how he was married aforetime, mayhap a fit seized him for his former life, for they say that a man who has once been married cannot cease his burning."

Brother Ralph was a wonder in what he knew of the human race, and Will expressed his admiration. "How come you to know so much?"

"I have ever kept my ears open," Brother Ralph said with pride. "If a man hears nothing but prayers and pater nosters all day, though it may do his soul much good and bring him into heaven, it will bring him no account of the world."

Brother Namlis longed to say something here, but could not. It seemed to him that Brother Ralph did not know as much about the world as he thought if he thought that only married men could not cease their burning. Brother Ralph was a braggart and an ignorant tattler. All his tales had to do with gaming and dicing and what the bishop said to the prior, and never at all about whores. Brother Namlis did not care what the bishop said to the prior. He wanted to hear what Moll said to Mae, for the talk of women struck him as more wonderful than the talk of prelates. He tapped Will on the shoulder and gesticulated and grimaced.

"What would you?" Will said.

"He would hear of the whores," Brother Ralph said.

"Nay," Will said, feigning astonishment, but Brother Namlis nodded his head vigorously.

"What!" Will said, "it cannot be," but Brother Namlis nodded his head still more vigorously.

"Forebear," Will said, "to speak of fornication is a sin." Then he burst out laughing. "But God help me if it be not a worse sin not to regale a friend in such times as these and as I live the brothels and the taverns be all that is left in London where a man may meet a fellowman. I must confess the fit seized me. Aye, it seized me fore and aft, going and coming, for something there is about a road that brings such loneliness to the traveller that makes the bed beckon him."

Was there ever such a storyteller full of self justification. The plague raged outside, but here in the Calefactory the fire crackled and Will told of his adventures, or misadventures, as the case might be, in Southwerke.

"Heigh ho, she says to me at the door. What! Is this not a stewehouse? I asked.

'Aye, yea, and many be the hens and the cocks that be stewed here,' she said. 'I see you swing a full pouch ready for the pecking.'

'Aye,' I said, 'double full,' and with that she lowers the bar to the door and what was naked up above I see is but the anteroom to what lay below. Full bosomed was she everywhere and her pouch jingled merrily, so keen she was for the coin she unties my pouch swiftly and whistles at the wealth. 'I have a harlot here what waits for you,' she says, and takes me by the hand and leads me to a room dark and full of wondrous smells with a couch and one such as Samson had his full of was lying naked there upon it, so that I laughed, 'Be you Delilah,' for I felt my strength go from me at this wondrous sight.

'Aye,' she said in such a voice that my hair and other parts stood straight up.

Brother Thomas put his fingers in ears to hear no

more. "This is the devil's tale," he said.

"Aye, it is," Will said dolefully, "for she betrayed me, not once, not twice, but ever and again, so that my strength went from me with her dalliance."

"What!" Brother Ralph exploded, "did you not enter her?"

"No," Will said, caught in a cross of emotions, embarrassment and relief.

"What!" Brother Ralph exploded again.

"Aye," Will laughed sheepishly, "I could not, for as she was a Jewess she would not have me sin with her but would save me."

Brother Namlis fell off the bench and somersaulted on the floor, rolling over his hump, but Brother Thomas took this grimly and made the sign of the cross on his chest.

"Nay, it cannot be," Brother Ralph exploded yet again. "It cannot be, there be no Jews left in England."

"Aye, there be," Will said, "one or two, I believe. Like fleas upon a dog, you cannot get them all out."

"And she would not have you enter her?" Brother Ralph asked.

"Nay, she would save me," Will said, "and ever as I made to go in she took out her star and pinned it where it stopped me."

Brother Namlis somersaulted again. This was better than outright fornication. Hey, diddle diddle. Brother Ralph, more sober, said, "Dice be a better vice for all I can see, for any man who has a will may have a throw at it."

Will felt better and better about his mishaps. "Bless me," he roared with laughter, "if it weren't the woolman that clipped the coins but the whore that dallied with my pouch."

"As for that," Brother Ralph said, "you will never know, for there be many who know how to clip the coin and practise counterfeit."

"Aye," Will said, "aye, for I was with such more outside Southwerke, the next night, on hallowed ground itself, that never in my life saw I such things as happened there."

Brother Thomas put his fingers in his ears again.

"You did not see fornication on hallowed ground?" Brother Ralph said.

"As ever I live. Between two bears that they caught there, one a female and one a male which they set upon each other, and set them up in a tug of war to pull them apart with screaming and laughing to see which was the stronger and would hold on the longer, the male or the female bear in heat, and they would not let these beasts do their coupling but beat them with rocks and sticks in the act of it until the beasts fell dead upon the ground with roaring and vexation."

It was enough. Brother Namlis did not wish to hear anymore and moved away to the other side of the fireplace.

"Aye," Will said, the cheer gone from him too, "I am right sorry my feet took me in this path that my eyes did see such Christian manners. Came this evil priest with a cross hung with a vulture upon it and set his candle down upon a tombstone there. 'Death and doom and plague and rot,' he sings, and strikes a stone and loosens it from the earth like a rotting tooth. 'Strike, strike,' the others shout and pull at the stone till it gives way and they rush forward to lift out the buried treasure.

Bless me, I think, if I be not fallen in with graverobbers, and fear to open my mouth. This priest walked about with his crucifix in his hands and raises up the vulture. The air is filled with a terrible smell and the dead come out of their graves, and the stones are overthrown and the dead lifted out for their rings and their things of baubles and jewels. They roll from their winding sheets, bones and sinews and buried treasures that so foul an odor flew from their graves that one there cried out in alarm, 'Enough! Stop the dead from coming back, stop the miracles afore we die of suffocation!'

Then came this preacher again and led us all in procession and I could not but fall in with them, round and round the open graves, round and round the messy dead, ever faster totentanz, past the booths of miracles and relics and amulets and salves. 'God rescue us,' we cried, 'God rescue us from plague and famine.'

'Life, life,' the dead cried back, 'give us some wind, some sun, a bit of green that grows in the spring.' Then one jumped upon this platform. Newly dead he was, as we could see. 'Give us back our lives,' he wept, 'give us back the earth or we shall come and take it back.'

'Revolt, revolt,' the others shouted, 'give us back our lives.'

'Who is more oppressed than us?' their leader shouted.

'None,' they answered back. 'Give us back our lives,' and the hallowed ground became a battlefield, a tournament. Came the knights and friars, preachers, bishops, swordsmen, teachers, trumpeters and hunting dogs.

'The wonder tournament of the world,' the preacher said, and cracked his whip. Came the Knight of Utmost Reflection galloping across the hallowed ground, his banner unfurled for all to see his motto:

Mirror, mirror on the wall
Which God be the fairest
Of them all,
The Father, the Son, or the Saracen's Allah,
Lord Jesu Christ or the Jew's Jaweh

'Well, what say you,' the preacher said, and all began to preach their sermons, but the priests carried swords where their tongues should be and cut as they spoke so that their very words drew blood. Then they put all their good deeds in a scale they had with them, the deeds of the saints and the martyrs, the hermits and paupers, and a few bad deeds they reckoned they had, like false modesty. The scale tilted first to the good and a cheer went up, then it tilted to the bad, and the priests cut the scales in fear of the judgment and the mess ran out over the earth, and we fled in fear of drowning.

'The weights have been tampered with,' someone cried.

'The scale has been tipped,' someone said.

'Gamblers, false weighers, deceivers of weights and measures are among us.'

This priest jumped up again, with a bull pizzle in his hand. 'This way to the carnival,' he said, 'there are scales a plenty to be judged and to be weighed.'

And all about the hallowed ground, in the twinkling of an eye, were carnival booths and arks and merry games, all tended by the dead. Jugglers, actors, mimers, masques, booths where miracles were sold, relics of cloth and blood and skin, the teeth of saints and the hairs of martyrs, for the things of the dead have great power. And we went about and about from booth to booth until the early dawn, for every relic was fairer than the other, set in jewelled cases with gold and enamel, ivory and pearls I did not see upon the living, wondrous containers for a drop of blood. In each booth was a treasure box guarded by a dead who collected the payments, coin upon coin upon coin upon coin, so that the treasure boxes overflowed with the longing of the living to be saved.

'Where go the coins?' I whispered to one there. 'Our souls go to heaven, but where go the coins?'

'They go also to heaven,' he said, 'to buy the pearly gates. Lay up, lay up thy treasure. Canst not see who is the Eternal Banker?'

We looked up and saw no less than Christ behind the pearly gates and an endless stream of the living come to deposit their merits into The Bank of Souls.

'Iron rusts, but not the soul,' the preacher said. 'Lay up, lay up thy treasure in heaven,' and cracked his whip again, and before our eyes transformed himself from preacher to knight, to merchant and woolman, for he was whatever he wished to be and could play two parts at once, Judas or Jesus.

'Behold the nature of the universe,' he said, 'and behold the universe of nature. Who has slain more, God or man?'

And we beheld the afterworld in more terror than we thought, for the animals here sat in judgment upon us, the slain and the hunted, the tortured and the maimed judged us and rode in chariots and hunted man.

'Forever,' the preacher said, and at once came forth that notorious Seigneur de Venous and the thirty horses he burned to entertain his guests. These sat in judgment upon him and passed this sentence: the worst crime done for the sake of amusement, Seigneur de Venous, who sleeps in the hallowed ground of the Christian, we resurrect you now in your color of cruelty. What punishment in the afterworld can mark your cruel passage in the above world, cruel to us who were burned to amuse you.'

And the horses began to weep in memory of this deed. So fearful the sound was of their crying through the halls of the afterworld, the living could not bear it. The horses wept from the grave of man's doing. What punishment will give us back our lives, our glossy coats, the wind in our mane? Oh! life! That we were burned to make your company laugh. Eternity is impotent, wretched, bankrupt. There is nothing it can draw upon to match your passage upon the earth. You did what no God would do, Seigneur de Venous, and we are dead forever. Not mercy or memory can give us back the wind in our mane. God gave us life and you gave us death, Seigneur de Venous. We died while your company laughed.

'Gone!' the preacher shrieked, and drew the curtain across this sight. 'Gone!' The law has perished from the priest and vision has perished from the prophet. Comes now the plague of covetousness, and the plague of greed, the plague of simony, the plague of ignorance and the plague of confusion, bearing false witness and making false judgments, slandering with eye and tongue and hint and rumor. Would that the Roman had nailed the slandering tongue to the cross and not the man called Jesus!'

'Open the graves and let the dead back in,' someone

cried, 'have we not enough of our own plagues?'

"Ha! It is too soon, the preacher said, 'for the sermon has but begun.' And he blew upon a horn so loud that even the dead quaked and almost trampled us beneath them.

'Make way,' someone cried.

'Give us room,' someone said.

'Put the dead back in their graves.'

'Aye, back, for they are trampling us beneath them.'

'We will not go back,' the dead said, and their bones flew at us. 'There is nought left in the graves but earth and dirt,' they cried. 'You have stolen our rings, you have stolen our treasure. Gravediggers, graverobbers, you have buried the living with the dead. They moan beside us in the Eternal Dust and will not let us rest. Their flesh smells of life, their hair of grass, their mouths of milk. Our graves are empty but for their cries.'

'Son of man,' the preacher howled, 'son of Man and son of God, the dead are restless and cannot sleep. Their bones migrate through the earth like birds and their souls travel with the worm. Son of man,' he said and kicked the ground with his boot, 'I call this earth our heaven and hell, for our judgment is here.'

"Forebear, Will," Brother Ralph said, "methinks this preacher is a heretic."

"Aye," Will said, somber again. His mouth was dry, without spittle. Panic seized him for a moment, but it passed. Prior Harald stood on the threshhold to the room. "I see you had more cheer on this trip than was thought," he said. But he did not wait for an answer, or even to lecture further. Other things were on his mind. He cancelled the reading for the morning and beckoned Will to follow him. "It matters not the clipped coins," he said, deciding to be diplomatic and resigned to the problem. "We will bury what we have in the treasure box. The plague will pass, let it rage as it will. All evil comes to a halt sooner or later, and we will lay up for the days ahead." He bid Will fetch a spade and a shovel and follow him into the rose garden. "In a dark time be like the mole. We will bury these coins with the treasure we have kept these many years, and with Christ's help may yet help ourselves."

They went into the rose garden and he showed Will the place where Bodmin Priory's treasure box was kept. Though the ground was frozen, it did not take Will long to dig the hole which Prior Harald requested, but the hole was empty.

"Mayhap it is the wrong place," Will said.

'It is not the wrong place," Prior Harald said with unaccustomed shrillness, sounding more like Prior Godfrey than like himself, for their old enemy had made a laughing stock of them. "It is the very place this treasure has been kept for centuries."

Will's bitterness came from another source, his curiosity, and he asked, "What treasure be that, for methought the whole of Bodmin's treasure was with St. Petrokes bones."

Prior Harald gazed at Will with the impatient contempt of one forced to deal with fools in times of crisis. His suspicion of Will's lack of perspicacity deepened. The plague be cursed that he must do with novices! "What treasure!" he said with undisguised contempt, and answered rashly, "The treasure we had from the Jews when they were in England which we buried here for the bitter day."

Will did not feel so much enlightened as confirmed in his disappointment. Prior Harald's voice was demeaning, wrapping him in the guilt of the problem, when Will felt befuddled and called upon to do something about the missing treasure, though Christ knows if he had ever laid eyes upon it!

"What can be done?" he asked ineptly.

"Put back the earth. It is of no use to bury these coins here, for what the thief has taken once he can take again."

Will filled up the hole. Prior Harald returned to his room with the coins from the woolman and Will went to the Calefactory room, feeling improperly blamed for Bodmin's troubles, and blaming Bodmin for his own.

Brother Ralph as usual surmised what had happened,

but he did not come right out and say so but let Will warm his hands first while he sat there with a knowing look on his face. Finally, he said, "I warrant it was Bishop Roundsleigh who has been busy these many days." Will shrugged his shoulders disconsolately, and Brother Ralph wagged his head. "It matters not, for if it be not one knave then it be two. Gone is gone, whether it be by one or by a thousand."

"His son be gone now too," Will said, with a spice of vindictiveness to his voice. "Much good it may do him to have St. Petroke's bones and the prior's treasure." Such a despondency hung over all of them that Will added, "Let be, seeing memory bears grief in an evil time."

Brother Ralph accepted the advice, but had one last word. "Without doubt to that, but I trust the message of his son's death has been brought to him by now, for we posted a breviator after Abbot Roland's party who must have come to York by now."

Unknown to Brother Ralph, however, no messenger had been sent. Prior Godfrey had considered sending one, but delayed until it was too late. By the time Abbot Roland and his party arrived in York, the plague had spread as far as the Scottish border. Dorset, Somerset, all of Exeter, Southhampton, Hampshire, Bristol, up and down both sides of the coast, on the English Channel and on the Bristol Channel, the plague had broken out in such numbers that England began to look and sound and smell like Europe.

Abbot Roland had left Fountainville for the end of the journey, for sentimental rather than for diplomatic reasons. They went first to Baron Roundsleigh's manor who, he felt, welcomed them with an alarming gusto in the panoply of his bishop's dress. Baron Roundsleigh had seen fit to remove himself from his manor in Cornwall to his manor on the river Swale in York, where he was Bishop of the Church. Blessed with long legs and a large frame, a healthy constitution exercised in the hunt, a joyful appetite, the exuberance of the warrior, the horseman and the huntsman, he filled the altar space at the end of the nave with an energy that is the envy of religion. More devoted priests might turn wan in the pursuit of the hereafter. Bishop Roundsleigh grew ruddier and stouter in pursuit of this world. Whether he went to battle with a mace or to the hunt with hounds, as long as he was astride a horse, the world for him was faultless. He might have said the same for being astride a woman, except that she breathed in his face and occasionally spoke, while his horse never did.

Bishop Roundsleigh was famous for his appetites. All of them. Foxes, boars, rabbits and village wives scattered at the sound of his horse. He had two score of illegitimate children whom he had given to the Church. Except that his legitimate heir, John, had become a cockless monk and that he had arthritis in his thumb, the world was as complete a place as he could wish for. He was the bane of clergymen and priests, a thoroughly sinful, happy man, a lecher, a glutton, a wencher, a dicer. Some might regard the death of his son, still unknown to him, as providential. Baron Roundsleigh would be apt to regard his death as less grievous than the desertion of the family line.

Abbot Roland perceived that in his host he had met the climax of his experiences in this undertaking. Bishop Roundsleigh saw fit to dine him in the great hall of Leigh Castle on boar and venison and badly skinned rabbit while he rehearsed the details of how he had hunted down each animal on his table. "Now, this fellow," he said, jabbing the poorly skinned rabbit, "got himself trampled upon before I put my sword to his ribs. Nary a hole in him. But this one," he jabbed the boar who, though thoroughly dead and resting in deserved peace, grinned at the tale of his own dying, "this one was a cool and cunning fellow, running never in one straight line but in such a path that the dogs got dizzy and the horses confused. Christ love a clever boar for a good hunt," he said piously, for he never set out on the hunt without sprinkling his horse and hounds with holy water, and a prayer to Hubert of Liege.

His wife and mischievous other ladies kept silent at

the table while he spoke, but spoke plenty when he was silent, making up with a voluble chatter what they lacked for in leisurely conversation. Their voices added cackle to the fire, in front of which stood two small boys, turning the spit and going blind from the smoke.

The table was set with wonderful plate, pewter and silver and carved cups, each with an endearing name and credited with its worth as collateral. On the wall hung two famous tapestries of The Hunt, with spaniels and peregrines and falcons abounding.

"Eat," Bishop Roundsleigh said, "ye might as well or the dogs will get it."

Abbot Roland hesitated before the forlorn dimensions of his stomach. "Your generosity is wondrous," he said.

Monks, villeins, Jews and prelates, Christ pickle them in their own wine, Bishop Roundsleigh thought, for he sniffed a flavor to the phrase which pricked his spirits. "Trust me," he said to Abbot Roland later in the warming room, in spite of the fact that he disliked his guest's runty look and elegant language. He bid Abbot Roland lift his robes high and let the heat have its way. "'Twill do your bones good to say nothing of your cock."

Abbot Roland was content to rub his hands in front of the fireplace, but the bishop lowered his breeches and warmed himself into heaven.

"The winds of Scotland blow late this year," he said. "Trust me, I shall abide by Clement's wishes as behooves his bishop."

Abbot Roland was duly grateful and did not forget the requirements of courtesy. "I trust you will bear no hardship for this decision," he said.

Bishop Roundsleigh roared with laughter and hitched up his breeches. "What! No, no! I will bear no hardship. The future is with weaving. Devil take Edward for taking wool out of England. And if I can skin that cockless prior who has yet to see the backside of a woman, trust me I shall do my duty to the pope."

"Yes," Abbot Roland said and remarked to himself how political wisdom is expressed in unexpected formulas. He had surmised Bishop Roundsleigh's sympathies while crossing his demesne. Fulling mills had been erected along the river. Peasants could be seen weaving in the doorways of their cottages. Abbot Roland had learned that independent sheep owners were on the manor grounds, diverting sacks of wool for the weavers. Wonderful indeed, Abbot Roland thought, that it should be Bishop Roundsleigh who could see that the future of English wool lay with manufacture.

"No," Bishop Roundsleigh said to him again in the morning as he saw the party to their carriage. Edward should be left to manage his own affairs. If he wished to wage war, let him pay for it out of his private purse.

"No," he shouted after them, "L2 on the sack is as good in my pocket as the king's. Joy and peace be with the pope and Christ keep you on this journey and may the cockless lechers who have fleeced the wool from my good sheep lust for weavers which they cannot have."

Only Abbot Roland did not flinch before this speech, but waved his thanks and blessing, and bid his servant drive as fast as he could.

"We are succeeding," his secretary said, his face pale.

"In a manner of speaking," Abbot Roland said.

They travelled east, crossing the valley between the Swale and the Ur. It was a short journey and they came to Fountainville by Vespers. Abbot Roland asked the servant to stop the horse. He wished to look at the building before approaching it. "I'd best enjoy now what I can of it," he said. They caught the rueful note, for there are few things an old ecclesiastical scholar, who has spent years in church administration, can return to without feeling that he has betrayed himself.

Fountainville looked as he remembered it: reverential against the twilight sky. The spaciousness of the architecture, the stones built in their symbolic style, conveyed the solemnity of their purpose, to house the guardians of mankind. He leaned across and touched Philip's knee to draw his attention to the belfries in the distance, from whose perch a crowd of birds flew up, as they had done every evening when he had lived there and had watched them ascend from the ground without warning, their impulses secret to mankind.

They were outside the gatehouse. The servant presented papers to the gatekeeper which were written in Latin and which the gatekeeper could not read, but which he studied carefully. After descending from the carriage, Abbot Roland paused at the fountain, then made his way to the Chapter Room where Abbot Benedict, who had succeeded Abbot Thomas, waited for him.

Abbot Roland would not offend his spirit with personal regrets that a new abbot sat in Abbot Thomas' chair, but he could not avail himself of kind feelings for him, and he was not sure whether the fault was his or Abbot Benedict's supercilious manner. Abbot Roland suddenly found it difficult for him to master his anger, and made a mental note that he should retire from missions after this one. Aging was not having the mellowing effect upon him reported of others.

Abbot Benedict had his steward bring warm wine and bread, which they took in the Calefactory, for the weather was still cold and winter clouds in the sky.

"We are quite far north," Abbot Benedict said.

"This is my native land," Abbot Roland reminded him.

"Indeed?" Abbot Benedict said.

"I spent my novitiate here with Abbot Thomas."

"Indeed, I should welcome you then as an old member."

"You were not here when I left."

"No, I came from Rievaulx. When Abbot Thomas died, matters were in such disorder it was thought unwise to choose his successor from his monastery."

"Disorder!"

"His accounts had fallen into arrears. His tax collectors were unstable." Abbot Benedict did not expect Abbot Roland, who had been away for thirty-five years, to know what a disorganized state Fountainville was in when Abbot Thomas died. He had been sick for two years, during which time his reeve cheated him mercilessly, the fees for the use of the mill found their way into the miller's pocket, the rents found their way into the collector's pocket, and the bailiff pocketed the money on every third sack of wool. "Typical behavior," Abbot Benedict said, "when the lord of the manor cannot perform his functions. Mankind needs watching."

"He must have been very ill," Abbot Roland said.

"He was no longer an able administrator."

Abbot Roland looked away. Abbot Benedict surmised that he had piqued him. "Forgive me," he said, "I should not like to tamper with your memory of him."

"My memory," Abbot Roland said, "is undisturbed." He bid Abbot Benedict goodnight and went to his room, but found it difficult to sleep. A thousand pieces of argument assailed him. In the end, he decided that Abbot Thomas must have been sicker than he had admitted to being. He had lost his grasp on his world and he, his disciple, should have returned to help him. Better a life spent here than anywhere else.

He was not fit to converse with Abbot Benedict in the morning. He prepared his arguments for the evening and spent the day in a personal indulgence he rarely permitted himself. For all his debilities, he was a great lover of the world, of air and sky and clouds, and walked through the fields, filling his eyes and breath with these and with the flocks of birds ascending with their hidden motives for the air. Even the habits of the worm entranced him. He paused before everything living and enquired after its motion: the charge of the animal mother and her lightning reversals of cruelty and protection, a fly, a wasp, a spider. Where others swatted at an insect, he stopped and watched it. Where others hurried with messages and pronouncements, each one of which was believed capable of changing the world, he amused himself with letters written to the dead. Mankind fretted that he wasted his great intellect. Requests were made of him constantly to write a summa on this and a summa on that. "Leave us more," they shouted, "more widsom, more thoughts, more ideas on the nature of sin." He left very little, and who knows what Abbot Thomas did with the letters that came to him. Nor do we know how Abbot Roland came to be, fighting bodily aches daily, content if he spent a day without a headache, patient with bureaucratic blunder, gross error and violence. How did he avoid cynicism where others ate it?

Perhaps it was only by a hair's turn in his constitution that he responded to the immanently living with greater attentiveness than he did to the ideological and the theological. Certainly, this was one of the secrets of his constitution: his vigilant balance between "sympatico" and intellectual formulations, and the reason he left so little behind. It was not given to Abbot Roland to solve anything or to be remembered by later centuries for his philosophy, but only before his night fell to trace the origins of his soul to a loving servant, a wise teacher, and a close friend, which he now acknowledged with the brief and piercing amplitude of the dying, had been God's special gifts to him, and to leave in return for these the memory of his presence.

His feet got damp from the fields and he returned to the monastery by way of the fountain and the cemetery. He wandered through the Scriptorium and found his former carracel, his place, even his old quill. All day he haunted spiritual trails which, in the evening, led to Abbot Benedict.

"We have two thousand sheep," he told Abbot Roland. "When I arrived here, Fountainville was in debt. From the revenue on the wool, I was able to cancel these debts, restore the cloister floor, the ceiling in the refectory. So many repairs must always be made. You cherish the glory of Fountainville. Wisdom suggests that I not change the means of maintaining it."

Afterwards, Abbot Roland went to visit the grave of Abbot Thomas again. He did not feel, in this cemetery which housed the remains of centuries, that he was in a place of death, but of the living where the margin between the visible and the invisible was erased. "Advise," he said conversationally to Brother Thomas, "you who sent me away from this place we both loved." That he had gone and had now come back, that he had lived for thirty-five years among strangers, away from the friend and place he loved, struck him as most strange. For unknown reasons, one's life always does: how it was that we started from here, how we became involved with affairs that always take a surprising turn, how we evolved for better or worse than we expected to, how certain people died whom we thought would outlive us and how all this changed the landscape we thought would never change; how we thought our generation was the summit of time and history, and how aging taught us humility and reversed the order of the importance of things.

The February sky was too dark and too cold. His chest hurt. His knees stiffened, suddenly and completely. He was so familiar with his infirmities, he was struck by the strangeness of these new pains, afflictions around the heart and the tongue and the loins. "You do see," he said to Brother Thomas, "that my entire body bids me stay. My knees will not unhinge, my legs will not move." The symptoms were perplexing, an array of aches he had not yet experienced. He took his psalter out and tried to pray, but his tongue thickened in his mouth and his mouth became like a small cage into which this animal, his tongue, could not find room for itself. An organ he had lived with all his life, the size and shape of which he took for granted, became an enemy in his mouth. It swelled ludicrously and drained him of moisture. He thought of the arguments he must present to Abbot Benedict, the arguments he must present to the world. Europe was dying! and he could not master his tongue. Thirst conquered his mind. He could think of nothing but water, but he could not form the word for it. His body formed it. It cried for water. His tongue would not let him shout for help. He panted, he raved, he screamed for water. His psalter dropped from his hands. He crouched to the ground to look for it. His chest burned with the movement. Yes, he understood. Yes, yes, yes. It had come. The universal disease. Europe could not be saved. He crouched, looking for his psalter. His mind groped for an image of faith, to beat back the nihilism that sprang from the ground.

A servant came running with Philip. They had become alarmed by his long absence. The servant grasped Philip's arm. With a feeble gesture, Abbot Roland waved them away. Blood and water ran from his mouth and eyes.

Philip freed his arm, but the servant grasped it again. "Do as he bids," he said. "It is the plague and he knows it."

"Go for water," Philip said. He pushed the servant to hurry. "Do as I say, instantly." The servant turned and ran, but he did not come back.

"Human charity is dead," Guy de Chauliac had written from Paris that summer. In the chronicles that deal with the plague, there are records of a few acts of mercy: a group of friars who jumped into the pits with the dying to bring them water, priests who administered the last rites at risk to themselves; but on the whole, the chronicles record few of these acts. In 1349, Christian Europe suffered an irreparable affliction in its soul, one among several in its history: It is told that when St. Roche, patron saint of the plague-stricken, lay dying of the plague, he crawled beneath a tree and the only living thing that would approach him was his dog, Gothard, who licked the fever from his face.

Abbot Roland could not solicit this much help from his servant. Philip cursed the man and ran himself to the kitchen for water, but when he returned with it, Abbot Roland was on his back, his eyes were already glazed and his chest rattled. Philip put drops of water on his lips. Abbot Roland tried to speak, to grasp his crucifix where it had fallen on the ground. Philip found it and put it in his hands. Abbot Roland wished to thank him, but his tongue pressed on his larynx and his vocal cords. A frivolous worry assailed him. What would happen to Philip? He knocked on Philip's chest and tried to say something, but it was difficult, difficult. Philip bent his ear to hear. Oh, it was dangerous, dangerous to do this. Better for Philip to go away, but he did not. Imperial messages locked themselves into Abbot Roland's eyes, inarticulate messages from servant and teacher to friend, which broke his dying brain into fragments of affection.

Some men, being very good, are nevertheless of their generation, like Noah and Bishop Grandisson. We cannot ask more of them than that they "save their times." But some men, being very good, go beyond their generation. They have an insight about the universe which becomes a spiritual legacy. No one can explain how they come by it. "Innate holiness" will do for an explanation. It is said that when St. Hugh, Bishop of Lincoln, died in 1200, the Jews of England put ashes on their heads and ran alongside his casket.

Some compared Abbot Roland to St. Bernard, others to Bishop Hugh of Lincoln. The latter comparison is the right one for, like Bishop Hugh, it is not known where Abbot Roland's bones are, since his body was removed immediately after his death and buried outside the monastery walls, most likely in a common grave with other victims of the plague. Everything disappeared except his spirit.

Little more can be said of Philip. Numbed from the cold, he returned and told Abbot Roland's servant and secretary what had happened. He himself looked dazed and feverish, and the others moved discretely away from him. But Philip was not yet sick, only overcome with grief, and he went to his room to be alone.

Abbot Benedict came soon after and told Philip that though it grieved him to do it, he had arranged for a carter to remove the body. He scarcely crossed the threshhold into the room, and kept his hands folded at his waist. He regarded Philip from this distance, with as much consideration as the times and the crisis and the manifold difficulties of the moment, could allow for. "We must bow to God's will. I shall give orders to mark the place of burial so that his bones may be removed hereafter when the times have improved," and he left, the sound of his footstep and the swish of his habit on the stone floor growing fainter down the hallway.

The thought had crossed Philip's mind often, that Abbot Roland must die one day. The thought would occur to him walking alone in the cloister or coming into the cathedral at Primes, that one day a new abbot must take Abbot Roland's place, and he would be among strangers again. He lay on his bed, convulsed with the image of Abbot Roland's death. Once or twice he heard a footstep outside his door, but it only paused and soon went away. Others were sent to check on him in the same way. No one opened the door and made inquiry. His absence at breakfast and throughout the day was noted and put down to the disease of the times. No one knew what to do about it. Someone knocked again, later in the day and asked if he was all right. Philip said that he was, and that he would say his prayers in his room. The enquirer went away and told Abbot Benedict, "He is grieving." Abbot Benedict had nothing to say to this. He did not know either what to do about Philip, for his history followed him about, and the times suggested nothing better than caution. The enquirer was sent again, from time to time. Philip heard him pause outside his door.

The pattern continued for two days: remote courtesy on one side and a stubborn resistance on the other. There was not enough in the poise and caution of those around him, to deflect the inner motion of his soul which now broke through the wall he had built around it. He succumbed to it like a fateful infatuation, experiencing the destruction of his resistance with cunning and delirium. Its voices came back to speak to him, fearfully low at first, indistinguishable, but then louder, humming and singing, whispering in languages which he was astonished and delighted to recognize. At first, he responded with sardonic silence, as if punishing the lost voices, and testing his discipline to resist them, but no one at Fountainville offered him a better alternative, and little by little, a jerk of his head, a nod of his chin, a small parting of his lips to frame a vowel, a gesture of his hands in response no longer seemed unnatural, and the voices, in turn, broke through with a consuming reality. He had held them at bay for so long, had held the little pieces of himself together with one thing and another, it was a relief to let go and let the invasion have its way.

When he left Fountainville, he looked out through the windows of his eyes on a world which could no longer displace his inner one, and he knew that he should not tell anyone about it. He went back and forth between the two worlds with facility and if he became momentarily lost between them, no one took notice. It was not unusual to see people wandering about, dazed. The effects of the plague broke down the personality structure of many. Some were thrown into an antipathy that took years to wear away, others became violent persecutors and joined in massacres, some became religious fanatics, and others deserted their religion altogether and became atheists. Reversals of habits and traits and character were not uncommon.

Philip left Fountainville on the third day and took the road from York to London. Still in monk's habit, nothing about him suggested that the outer world had become obsolete to him. He met others along the roads and made the proper responses. A sharp-eyed person would have observed that his lips were too dry, that the spittle on them looked old and yellow as if he hadn't wiped it away for days, that there were signs of plague on him except that he did not seem to be in pain, and that his smile was too wily, as if he had a secret, and his air disembodied, when within was a turbulence that drove him miles and miles each day, sounds and voices and smells, grimaces, sighs, yawns and sneezes, gestures of daily existence which wrought a human design compelling and natural to him so that he felt nothing morbid about it. On the contrary, its ordinary commonplaceness was surprising and amusing, and overwhelmed his immediate past, the one he had occupied spatially and monastically, the one which had declared this ordinary world strange and had found it sinister when it was merely commonplace.

He found food as others did and in a week's time had passed through Lincoln and was in Peterborogh. He then knew where he was going.

It was near the end of February. Though the air was still cold, the songs of the birds were different. Sky and light and sounds were re-assembling themselves. Only he looked up to take note of this phenomenon, for unlike the others on this road, he had never seen the seasons change here, though he followed the route his father had told him about when he had journeyed from London for the first time to attend a wedding in Lincoln.

Philip recalled his early readings about converts and apostates, Jews who had converted to Christianity and had converted back to Judaism, Jews who had converted to Christianity and had become hostile to Judaism, Jews who had converted to Christianity and were afterwards suspected of Judaizing, Jews who had converted to Christianity and then had lapsed into strange heresies that fit no pattern. Who could account for the variations, and if one were looking for truth, how could one find it in any one person's actions? He himself was not sure what his journey would prove. Whatever he proved about himself, what would he prove about the world?

It was not Abbot Roland's death which had made the journey imperative. His death had made it possible. Almost from the time they had come ashore, Philip sensed that he would do this. Nor would he have said it had anything to do with religious truths as he had been taught to regard them.

No one enquired into the purpose of his wandering. Where so many wandered, no one enquired into anyone's wandering. If he wandered in the past, he wore monk's clothes and a large silver cross and carried a psalter, and seemed to wander in the present. They could only tell by his clothes to what station or time he belonged. Had he changed his clothes, had he put on the required star, they would have perceived that he wandered in a different time, though he occupied the same space with other Europeans. And because they would have perceived him to be in a different time, they would have thought of him as someone who was not European, because Europe was Christendom. Though he occupied European space, as a Jew he did not occupy European time, for the Jew kept his own calendar, his own history, his own eschatology, his own prophecies, his own portents and signs of God's way. Be reverent and wary of calendars. They are the root cause of wars.

Philip came to the outside of London and entered the city through the North Gate. It was three weeks since he had left York. The crisis in London had passed. That is, the chronicles register the peak of the plague in the city to have been about Christmastime, but few there noticed that the crisis had passed. Famine and grief and disorientation were still paramount.

He passed through Isenmongre Lane and St. Olave Jewry and passed by the synagogue in Cateton Street, now called St. Laurence in Jewry, and came to the stone house in Huggin Lane, long since escheated to the realm. There was a red cross on the door, but he ignored it. What was important was that he had found the house on the spot where he had expected to find it, where prophecy and dream and household anecdote said it would be, and he did not know which of these forces had propelled him to this place. What was important was that he had found the house, exactly where he had expected to find it, and its existence was not an arbitrary matter of his memory, of half dream or half legend. Its existence was fact and history, and his memory of it was not eccentric, but belonged to the nature of the world. He swooned with joy. He remembered through what others had told him, and they now remembered through him: how they had waited on the wharf for his grandfather to be released from the Tower, how his father had stood with his brothers and his wife, how the king had addressed them, mounted on his horse and surrounded by his noblemen; how his mother had spent her wedding night in prison, how he had been born on the passage to the continent, how one Gamaliel Oxon had carved a memorial on his grandmother's tombstone; how his grandmother had walked in procession with his grandfather's kin through these streets, under the canopy, to be his bride.

Sweat broke out on his forehead and almost immediately his back and chest were pierced with pain.

Loneliness, as painful as the disease, afflicted him. The neighborhood was, after all, unfamiliar to him. What was he doing here? He stumbled about, as if the land were a heaving ocean, following a curious gleam, a marker in his brain. He left Huggin Lane and found his way to the Wood St. Cemetery. Two centuries of Jewish dead lay there. He himself was in acute physical pain and near death by the time he found the graves he was looking for:

Hinda Jurette
Born in Carcassonne, 4,560
Died in London, 4,647

Florria-Sara
granddaughter of Rabbi Simon ben Meir of
    Narbonne
wife of Rabbi Moses Menaheim, Presbyter
    of London

Pulchellina, her daughter,
age 3 weeks, died 4,650, together with her
    mother

Chill and fever gripped him. A fog rose before his eyes. He brushed the unholy dizziness away and traced with satisfaction Gamaliel's inscription on his grandmother's tombstone: Departed, the Jews of England: 4,650.

He bore no seed. The honor of his kin had ravaged him. Afterwards, he disappeared. Neither the chronicles of St. Bernard nor of any other monastery mention him again, nor is it known who buried him or where. He took no part in European affairs of any kind, nor is there mention of his remarkable voice anywhere.

The news of Abbot Roland's death was brought to Bodmin Priory by the breviator of Fountainville, who was sent by Abbot Benedict who deemed this information important enough to risk the journey. Abbot Benedict knew that Harald of York was now prior of Bodmin, and he felt he ought not to withhold this news.

There are times when the death of a great name evokes a communal ceremony of response. Heads of states attend the burial, and an atmosphere of reflectiveness settles over civilization. There are times when an era appears to end with the passing of a particular person, who seems to take with him the whole of his generation into the grave. This was not one of these times. There is no one death that was singled out to signify the era. Petrarch's Laura died in the plague, but it is not for this that she is remembered, but because the death of a poet's mistress is romantic, and the atrocious pain, the ugly disfigurement of vomiting and shrieking, is forgotten in her name. For the rest, the subject matter is repellant. Where death was the communal experience of everyone no one's death could symbolize it. Death itself symbolized the age. And death itself, the manner of its dying, whether by war or disease, or famine or the attrition of withering energies, is as much a part of a civilization as its way of life.

No one came to the gate at Bodmin Priory to open it for the breviator from Fountainville. No one heard him knock, for since Will's arrival, no one kept watch at the gate at all, there being no reasons, as Prior Harald said, to let anyone in or anyone out. These measures were not harsh under the circumstances where contagious villages were torched, inhabitants and all. Will and Brother Namlis and Brother Thomas and Brother Ralph felt, huddled together in the Calefactory through the long winter months, like the family of Noah adrift in a world where everyone else had died. This monastery, this room with sufficient logs in it to burn for several months, God willing spring come early this year, and just sufficient food and tallow to last a few more weeks, was their ark of safety.

The breviator tired of knocking on the gate and went away. Abbot Benedict waited for a response from Bodmin Priory as to what arrangements should be made for Abbot Roland's final burial. Abbot Roland's servant and secretary waited too, several weeks for the breviator to return, but he did not, and soon after a monk in the monastery of Fountainville was stricken with plague.

Night came, and Will and Brother Thomas and Brother Ralph and Brother Namlis ate a meager supper. Prior Harald read to them from the Psalter, but they were not called to prayers at Matins for it was too costly to burn a candle during the night. Prior Harald bade them say their prayers in the dorter. They covered themselves with fur blankets and kept their fur slippers on, for the fire would not be lit in the Calefactory room tomorrow until past midday.

Brother Ralph was relieved that Will had returned, for neither Brother Namlis nor Brother Thomas nor Brother Benedict were fit company in such a time, so empty was Brother Walter's cot next to his, so empty was the dorter now, and the places in the refectory. None could dismiss the thoughts from their minds that they might wake in the morning and find another brethren stricken, or two, or even all, and himself alone. The thought terrified Brother Thomas so that he prayed to fall asleep quickly, for his nightmares seemed preferable to such thoughts. Every five minutes, it seemed to him he could not breathe and he wanted to cry out that he had the plague, but then it would seem to him that it was Brother Ralph's breath which labored unnaturally, and he felt as if the air with all the contaminants known to man was settling in the room and crawling through his nostrils.

He was warm and could not sleep and threw off his fur blanket. Brother Ralph perceived this immediately and sat upright. "You be sick," he said.

'Nay," Brother Thomas said, "I be but warm. I tell you truthfully, fear will give a man a fever sooner than the plague," and he laughed spritely.

Brother Ralph lay down again, uneasily. Devil take Brother Thomas, he thought, for the man was so constituted one could never tell what part was rational and what part was not. But he could no longer sleep himself. He himself felt unnaturally warm. His ears were burning. There were unwholesome noises in the room, coughs and rattles and whatnots. Finally, he threw his blanket off and got out of his cot. He wrapped a cloak around his shoulders and went to Brother Benedict's bed. A hissing sound issued from his mouth, though his eyes were still open and stared into the dark room, passing over Brother Ralph's face as he bent to listen to his chest. Brother Ralph wished to flee, but he did not. Brother Benedict was dying of cancer, not of plague. This was a reassuring thought.

Will got up from his bed too and hastened to Brother Benedict's cot. Brother Benedict's eyes moved again, passing with an intense gaze over Will's face. Will divined what it meant, and groped in the darkness until he found Brother Benedict's crucifix and put it in his hands. Brother Benedict's eyes closed, and the thread of his life was cut.

Will wrapped himself in his cape and went to inform Prior Harald, who gave orders that Brother Benedict could be buried in the cemetery on the grounds, since he had not died of plague. Will sat with the body throughout the night and said prayers for Brother Benedict's soul. No one else slept either, tormented by a sense of guilty relief. Husbanding resources, it was reckoned a blessing that Brother Benedict had not died of plague, a sign of God's recognition for his piety. Only Brother Thomas felt there was no distinction. Death was death and it was all terrible, massive and irrevocable. Faith in eternity might extend the boundary of life, but still a finished life seemed to undergo a transformation. Christian man mourned the death of his fellowmen, as elephants mourn and sea porpoises and whales mourn, sensing that, in spite of philosophy and theology, their kind has gone from them, and that an irreversible act has occured. Underneath the layers of faith, Brother Thomas confronted this truth head on every night and was convinced of the power of death.

Of the remaining brethren, only his death came as a release from his nightly terrors. He had not known a single dreamless night in twenty-five years, he had fought with devils and winged things and all manner of imaginary beasts, with mournful and devilish determination to live another day and fight another night. At last, he was freed into a dreamless sleep.

He died a week after Brother Benedict was buried in the cemetery where the stone statue of Gabriel keeps watch over the community of the dead. Harried dreams had tormented him all night long after Brother Benedict's burial. He dreamed that Brother Benedict's hands were re-emerging from his coffin, unlocking the lid and fluttering in the night. He moaned and tossed and called out for five nights, keeping the others awake. Brother Ralph grimly pulled his fur blanket over his ears.

"I dareye, I dareye," Brother Thomas cried out with indignation, and jumped from his cot to fight. "I dareye. Come, now. What! Wouldst harm a Scotsman! What!"

On the sixth night, his bed was quiet.

Will was the first to wake about three a.m. and realize that Brother Thomas' dialogue with the devil had come to an end. He felt no fear that someone in the cot next to his had just died of the plague, only depression at the uncustomary quiet. No one had woken on this night to curse Brother Thomas. Every night he had waken them with his fits and his muttering. Now he slept through his last dream.

Will heard Brother Namlis sobbing.

"Nay," Will said, for want of something to say, "I warrant he went peacefully and shall not be haunted anymore. I will tell Prior Harald," and he wrapped his cloak about him.

The floors were chilly and unpleasantly damp, but Will was beyond sorrow or reaction. Like others, he followed the reflex to bury the dead unreflectively and brought the message of Brother Thomas' death to Prior Harald, only to inquire where to bury him and returned with the message that they must carry the body out immediately and bury it in the field outside the priory, and take Brother Thomas' clothes and his cot and all his belongings, even his psalter, on the wagon and transport it outside the gate to the field and bury the body there and burn everything else.

That Prior Harald knew how to go about such matters was a blessing. Will relayed these orders to Brother Ralph and Brother Namlis, but Brother Namlis would not stop crying, and Brother Ralph lost his temper and became quarrelsome.

"Let be," he said, "we need not your sorrow to make matters worse."

They carried Brother Thomas' body out on his cot, so that they would not have to touch the body. Will brought the wagon round to the door of the dorter and fetched spades and shovels and candles. He opened the gate and they made their way out down the dark road to a field, halfway distant to the village, which was being used as a burying ground. Others were there as well, digging graves by candlelight, some because they did not want it known there was plague in their house, others because they wanted the body out of the house as quickly as possible and would not wait until the morning. Fires were set all about the field where the clothes and effects of the plague victims were being burned. In some places, they were forced to burn the bodies themselves where there was no more burial ground left.

Billows of smoke rose from the air in the cold night. Only the sounds of shovels and spades were heard. Sometimes a hasty prayer. There was no weeping except for that of a young girl recently married. Mainly hushed statements of hurried directions, as if those who were there were engaged in a disrespectable business.

Brother Namlis and Brother Ralph and Will returned by mid morning, chilled and hungry. A cold dew was on the ground. A cold March rain fell. No one looked at their wagon as it went by. Other wagons passed, carrying other dead, and the work of burying went on for weeks.

They went to the lavatory and scrubbed carefully. Brother Namlis did not cry anymore, and was desultory and depressed. He could not speak, but a grim acknowledgement that more was to come was in his eyes, plainly to be read. Brother Namlis did not require much to be happy, often enough a modicum of warm friendship; and the thought that Brother Ralph and Will might be stricken and leave him alone with Prior Harald seemed the worst of fates for him.

They went to the refectory and each fetched his own food, bread and bear and cheese. It was not the proper hour for their meal, but since they had missed their breakfast, Prior Harald gave them permission to eat now. He joined them in the refectory and told them to set their thoughts in the best spirit they could, "for it will not pass better if we are overtaken by our fears." He told them he would increase their rations so that hunger would not weaken them and bade them prepare the fields for the spring planting.

All week he kept them at this work and imposed the routine of prayer and study and labor as much as he could, so that they began to feel almost grateful for his presence, and escaped the anarchy of desperation that seized so many other monasteries. Prior Harald had fought the fear of death so long, his inexplicable own self-born terror, that the plague seemed, by comparison, a small evil to him. It only marshalled his resolve not to be done in by an evil that came from somewhere else when he had not been done in by an evil which came from within himself. He made Brother Ralph and Brother Namlis and Will clean and scrub the dorter. They tossed out the old hay and found new hay still in stock and laid it on the floors. Though their supply of wood was low, Prior Harald was generous in keeping the fire going.

These little comforts were valuable in building into them the expectancy of life and that they would endure, and only Prior Harald, who took the trouble to count what was left in the larder or the stockroom, knew that they were racing with time. But he felt that each day by itself had to claim its victory over the powers of defeat. He would let the future account for itself; he would account for the present. The others were content to let him make these decisions, and perceived him now in a different light. If they still felt little affection for him, affection itself seemed an unnecessary emotion. He held them together, and this sufficed.

His death traversed the manner of his living. He was a man of little sympathy for others, little tolerance for frailty, but his loyalty for Bodmin Priory was certain. Two weeks after Brother Thomas' death, he woke one morning in the early dawn, and knew he had been stricken. The fire in the fireplace had gone out. An unbearable chill afflicted him, with sweat and shivering and pains in his chest. He rose, almost immediately, and went to his lectern and worked on the accounting books for as long as he could stand on his feet.

When the others missed him by midday, Will went to his door and enquired timidly. Prior Harald answered the knock in a firm voice, and said he "was busy with much work this day. The brethren take their meals and prayers without him," and asked Will to come back at Vespers.

They speculated the whole day about the meaning of this, but Will did as he was told and came back in the evening. He found Prior Harald in bed, sweating profusely, his tongue already so swollen he could barely speak, but he acknowledged that he was grateful Will had come back. Struggling over the gross size of his tongue, he told him where the coins were and that he must now take charge, novice though he be. He bid him inform Bishop Grandisson of the plight of the priory, then he bid him leave.

"I cannot," Will said, to his surprise. Some law took charge over him, which bound him to this man. He sat down abruptly on a chair and stayed throughout the night and the next day, and wet Prior Harald's lips when he could, and went to tell the others when there was no more to do.

They buried Prior Harald in the cemetery on the priory grounds, for it seemed not to matter anymore where the dead were buried, and no one cared to make the trip to the burying field again. Within and without was all the same. They burned his clothes and his personal things, his bed sheets and covers, but left the room intact, except that they let St. George fly free.

Will and Brother Namlis walked with Brother Ralph to the gate, who would make the journey to Exeter and deliver the message of Prior Harald's death to Bishop Grandisson.

'It is my grievous duty," Will had written, "to tell you that our new prior has been taken away as well as the others, and all but three from Bodmin Priory are now gone. We beg you to appoint us someone to guide our lives, for we have been left as orphans in a dark night."

"And did you not tell him that St. Petroke's bones and the treasure has been stolen?" Brother Ralph asked. "I know not if the coins we have from the woolman will pay our debts now that the treasure that was buried is gone."

Will had not thought about this problem. There was no doubt that the money they had borrowed would not cover the cost of putting Bodmin back on a secure foundation. The priory would only go into further debt. Like a sinking boat, the water was filling up faster than the sailors could bail it out. For Will, in his present state of mind, the problem seemed insurmountable, not merely an administrative one as Prior Harald might have considered it but, as one might say, in the very nature of things of how men acted and behaved.

They walked across the hard, rutty ground to the gate, Will thinking of what else to say to Brother Ralph. It was a curious consolation he finally offered, making do with things as they now were. "It matters not," he said, "for we but wasted the Jew's treasure."

It was unpleasant for Brother Namlis and Will to part from Brother Ralph, but it was necessary for him to go. The extremity of their condition had to be made known to the proper authority. "We have been left as orphans in a dark night."

The message is recorded in the register of Bishop Grandisson for the date of March 17, 1349. On March 19, Bishop Grandisson wrote to the Prior of Launceston to appoint a member of that house to the office of prior at Bodmin, and on March 22 the mandate for the induction of the new prior was issued. On this date, it was known that there were two surviving brethren still at Bodmin Priory.

Brother Namlis and Will walked back from the gate. The cold March rain fell again. It fell all that week and softened the ground. They spent almost the whole of this time in the Calefactory. Will wished Brother Namlis very well, but it was hard, in such circumstances, to put up with a man who could not speak, and little by little he too lapsed into silence. They sat, desperately, in front of the fire and tried to keep the routine of prayer and mealtimes. Brother Namlis was unhappy with the idea of new monks coming to stay at Bodmin. He did not want a new prior. He would even settle for Prior Harald. He would settle too for Brother Thomas and Brother Claude. He wanted the world back as it was. He stayed close to the fire and fell to dreaming over his life spent here, the sights and sounds of all the monks who had passed through the halls, the visitors, the pilgrims, the gossip, the wicked rumors, the tricks and small betrayals and trips to the market. How had it all passed away?

On the fifth day, he was stricken and suffered frightfully for three and a half days. Not terror or fear or regret or sorrow at the passing of life, but wicked pain wrapped his body, and fever dragged him into a delirium where he heard the voices of everyone he had ever known, the laundresses and the pudding wives and his mother, and with his tongueless mouth struggled to answer them.

Will sat by his side and kept moist towels on his lips and forehead and packed his chilled body in fur blankets and chafed his hands and his toes, and believed his heart would break irremediably. "Could you not have left him, at least?" he argued with the dark powers. Deep, terrible sounds of distorted cries came from Brother Namlis, until Will finally prayed for him to die quickly. "Devil take you and be done with it," he said. Brother Namlis' parched lips curled back over his yellow teeth.

He had never had a harsh thought against any living thing, and fought desperately for his life, minute by minute, and hour by hour, groaning on his cot. In his last hour, whatever there was of charity and goodness in the world, Will gave to him as he closed his eyes. He wrapped his body in his blanket and carried it in his arms to the cemetery. The rain had stopped and the ground was ready. He lay Brother Namlis down on it and began to dig the grave. He dug it with love and with fury, and bade Brother Namlis mind how well he dug it, and when it was finished he lay him in it. "Sleep, good monk," he wept, "thou didst fulfill all thy vows."

"Who?" Petrarch had written, "who in future generations will believe what we have endured?" Only the chronicles remain as a memorial to the time.

> "This plague laid low equally Jew, Christian and Saracen, together it carried off confessor and penitent. In many places it did not leave even a fifth part of the people. It struck the whole world with terror. Such a plague has not been seen, or heard of, or recorded, before this time, for it is thought so great a multitude of people were not overwhelmed by the waters of the deluge, which happened in the days of Noah."
>
> "And the multitude of the people who died in the years 1348 and 1349 was so large that nothing like it was ever heard of, read of, or witnessed in past ages."

"What more?" Boccaccio asked, "what more can be said save that such and so great the cruelty of heaven and, in part, peradventure, that of men."

Cornwall was stricken with the force of the plague between November 1348 and February, 1349, but it continued to rage in Cornwall until May of that year, while Will waited for Brother Ralph to return. He kept himself busy and distracted by reading Brother Bernard's accounts in the Scriptorium, and entered his own record of those who had died, where they had been buried, what he knew of Bodmin's financial condition, the value of its relic and treasures, and kept a record of the weather and the progress of the plague.

"This pestilence," he wrote, "has deprived our villages and cities, our castles and towns of human inhabitants, so that there is scarcely found a man to dwell therein, and I only am alive here, having lately buried our last brethren. This pestilence is so contagious that whosoever touches the skin of the dead is immediately infected. Many have died of boils and abscesses and postules on their skin and under the armpits, as I have seen myself. Others have been driven frantic with pain in their head and could be seen wandering on the roads, and others to be spitting blood. I, waiting for death, have written these things lest the writing perish with the writer and the work with the workman. I leave parchment for continuing this work, if haply any of the race of Adam escape this pestilence and return here and continue this work which I have commenced."

Will died shortly after this, for his chronicle was found years later with a notation in Latin, in another hand: "Here it seems the writer died."

We, the descendants of this generation, know what Will could not have known: that life continued. Its continuance was commented upon in a statement in a chronicle from Limburg, which no historian or theologian can improve upon:

> After this, when the plague, the flagellant pilgrimages, the pilgrimages to Rome, and the slaughtering of the Jews, were over, the world once more began to live and joy returned to it, and people began to make new clothes.

Amen, and amen.